THE FA

DAU

MW00846876

WITH

DANGERS OF COQUETRY

THE FATHER AND DAUGHTER

WITH

DANGERS OF COQUETRY

Amelia Opie

edited by Shelley King and John B. Pierce

broadview literary texts

National Library of Canada Cataloguing in Publication Data

Opie, Amelia Alderson, 1769-1853
    The Father and daughter with Dangers of coquetry / Amelia Opie; edited by Shelley
King, John B. Pierce

(Broadview literary texts)
ISBN 1-55111-187-X

1. King, M. Shelley (Marilyn Shelley), 1954-
II. Pierce, John Benjamin, 1957- III. Title. IV. Series. V. Title: Dangers of coquetry.

PR5115.O65F38 2002   823'.7   C2002-901570-7

Broadview Press Ltd. is an independent, international publishing house, incorporated in
1985. Broadview believes in shared ownership, both with its employees and with the general
public; since the year 2000 Broadview shares have traded publicly on the Toronto Venture
Exchange under the symbol BDP.

We welcome comments and suggestions regarding any aspect of our publications—please feel
free to contact us at the addresses below or at broadview@broadviewpress.com.

North America
PO Box 1243, Peterborough, Ontario, Canada K9J 7H5
3576 California Road, Orchard Park, NY, USA 14127
Tel: (705) 743-8990; Fax: (705) 743-8353
email: customerservice@broadviewpress.com

UK, Ireland, and continental Europe
Thomas Lyster Ltd., Units 3 & 4a, Old Boundary Way
Burscough Road, Ormskirk
Lancashire, L39 2YW
Tel: (01695) 575112; Fax: (01695) 570120
email: books@tlyster.co.uk

Australia and New Zealand
UNIREPS, University of New South Wales
Sydney, NSW, 2052
Tel: 61 2 9664 0999; Fax: 61 2 9664 5420
email: info.press@unsw.edu.au

www.broadviewpress.com

Broadview Press gratefully acknowledges the financial support of the Book
Publishing Industry Development Program, Ministry of Canadian Heritage,
Government of Canada.
This book is printed on acid-free paper containing 30% post-consumer fibre.
Series editor: Professor L.W. Conolly
Advisory editor for this volume: Professor Eugene Benson

Text design and composition by George Kirkpatrick
PRINTED IN CANADA

EcoLogo Certified, 30% Post.

Pub. March 1.1801. by Vernor & Hood. Poultry.

Figure 1: Portrait of Amelia Opie, designed by John Opie, engraved by
Mackenzie, published March 1801 *Lady's Monthly Museum*

Contents

Acknowledgements

We would like to thank the Advisory Research Committee of Queen's University, Canada, for travel grants that allowed us to carry out the research necessary for this edition. We are grateful to a number of archives and libraries for their generous assistance: the Norfolk Reference Library provided the first edition of *The Father and Daughter*, on which our text is based, as well as the 1843 edition, the last in Opie's lifetime; the British Library holds the first edition of *Dangers of Coquetry*, which was used to check the text of this edition; the Norfolk Record Office provided access to their extensive collection of Opie's correspondence, and permission to quote from her letters concerning the publication of the final edition of the novel in her lifetime; Dr. Williams's Library, London, granted permission to quote from letters by and about Opie in the Crabb-Robinson manuscripts; the Friends' Library in London also allowed access to their substantial collection of correspondence, and permission to quote from Opie's letter to J. J. Gurney; Opie's letter to Hayley quoted by permission of the Syndics of the Fitzwilliam Museum to whom rights in this publication are assigned. The British Library, the Wellcome Institute, the Thomas Fisher Rare Book Library of the University of Toronto, and the Stauffer Library of Queen's University provided access to primary materials for the appendices.

For help with footnotes, we thank Lisa Berglund, Vivian Folkenflik, David Richter, and Lars Troide; special thanks to Leslie Ritchie for sharing her expertise in Opie's songs, and to Ursula Rempel for help with sources for both music in this period and tracking down the location of the earliest published portrait of Amelia Opie. All of the foregoing were contacted through C18-L, the on-line discussion group for eighteenth-century studies where help with specific research questions is offered generously and quickly: we are grateful for the opportunity to share in this community of scholarship. Closer to home, thanks to Karen Bourrier, Heather Evans, Joan Robicheau and Yaël Schlick. Finally, thanks to Peter Sabor and Claire Grogan for their energy and enthusiasm for women writers.

Introduction

The Father and Daughter and the Literature of Sensibility

In its own time *The Father and Daughter* was as much a cultural phenomenon as a simple work of literature. Passing through at least nine editions of between 750 to 1,500 copies per printing in the first three decades of the nineteenth century, it became a familiar contour on the literary landscape. Like many culturally significant texts, *The Father and Daughter* was soon exported to other cultures and other literary forms: it was translated into a number of different languages, including French, German and Spanish;[1] it also became the subject of an opera, two plays, and verses written to extol the virtues of the book and its author.[2] Nearly 30 years after its first appearance W. T. Moncrieff remarked in the second edition of *The Lear of Private Life*, his loose adaptation of Opie's tale, "WHO has not wept over MRS. OPIE's popular and pathetic story 'Father and Daughter,' upon which this piece is founded? It has been translated into almost every modern language, and dramatized at various Foreign Theatres, and has ever proved a fruitful source of interest and tears" (Appendix F.1). Moncrieff's puff to Opie attests to the rapid, wide-ranging and sustained dissemination of this short tale and hints at the reasons for its success.

Repeatedly, commentators on *The Father and Daughter*, whether they are creative writers, professional critics or private correspondents, praise the tale and Opie's artistry for the use of the "pathetic." Defined by Samuel Johnson as "affecting the passions; passionate; moving," the pathetic was the essential element of the literature of sensibility or sentiment, a literary form popular in the second half of the eighteenth century and still in vogue at the turn of the century. The term "sensibility" is itself difficult to define, but tends "to suggest delicate emotional and

---

1   *Le père et la fille; traduit de l'Anglais de madame Opie, sur la second édition par Mademoiselle *** (1802); Fadren och dattren (1803); Cecilia; ó sea, El padre y la hija, sur novela, tr. del inglés al francés y de este al español por J. M. Barcelona Brasi (1822).*

2   For excerpts and reviews of the opera, see Appendix D; for the plays see Appendices E and F; and for verses written in commendation of Opie see Appendix C.4.

physical susceptibility" and "to denote the faculty of feeling, the capacity for extremely refined emotion and a quickness to display compassion for suffering" (Todd 7). The "sentimental," although often difficult to distinguish from sensibility,[1] frequently indicates a development or further refinement of sensibility towards "a moral reflection, a rational opinion usually about the rights and wrongs of human conduct" (Todd 7). Quickness of emotion, innate virtue, delicacy of feeling and acuity in perception are the hallmarks of the heroine of sensibility; the "arousal of pathos" (Todd 2) in the audience creates the dramatic tension in the structure of the work and thematic core of the sentimental message. Heightening the emotional turmoil of the central character heightens the pathos of the work and, as its numerous critics suggested, may tip the sentimental into the excesses of melodrama. Opie herself reports that Walter Scott "told me [the] father & daughter made him cry more than any thing he ever read,"[2] a response typical of the kind expected from a sentimental work.[3] Reviewers of *The Father and Daughter*, however, found Opie's use of the pathetic a balanced model for sentimental expression. *The Critical Review*, for instance, states flatly, "Seldom have we met with any combination of incidents, real or imaginary, which possessed more of the deeply pathetic" (Appendix B.2.i), and *The Monthly Review*

---

1 Ellis argues that "The terms 'sensibility' and 'sentimental' denote a complex field of meanings and connotations in the late eighteenth century, overlapping and coinciding to such an extent as to offer no obvious distinction" (7), but goes on to add, "However, though sensibility and sentimental may not be separated, that is not because they share a single unitary meaning, but rather, they amalgamate and mix freely a large number of varied discourses" (8).

2 Opie goes on to say, "I *likes* to make people cry, indeed, if I do not do it, all my readers are disappointed—I *wish* they would let me make people happy my own way—but even *my Co.* say *indeed* Madam, you must be horrid pathetic" (To William Hayley, 27 November 1815). Her comment suggests that market demand and publisher's interests as well as authorial inclination may have contributed to Opie's continued use of the pathetic.

3 A reviewer for *The Monthly Review* describes a similar reaction when writing about Opie's *Tales of the Heart*: "The tale of 'The Father and Daughter' was so tender and affecting that it drew tears, and those not of iron, down our cheeks" (376). Prince Hoare affords a more extreme sentimental response to the tale. Opie reports that "The Hoares ... expressed themselves much pleased and affected by it [*The Father and Daughter*], Mr H. could not sleep all night after it; it made him so wretched" (Brightwell 86).

goes further in isolating the affective power of Opie's use of the pathetic: "For ourselves, we own that we have been truly affected by the perusal of it, since it is replete with interest, and possesses pathos enough to affect the heart of the most callous of *critical* readers" (Appendix B.2.ii). As *The Monthly Review* indicates, the affective power of pathos or the pathetic is transformative, opening a *"critical"* (or what a modern reader might think of as slightly cynical) mind to some excellence beyond self-interest. Indeed, the power of pathos lies in its ability to stimulate sympathy among fellow beings, to articulate the notion, as Moncrieff describes it, "that nature has an echo in the human heart to which she never speaks unanswered" (Appendix F.1). Other critics of the time similarly argued that the experience of representations of the pathetic was ultimately ameliorative, correcting literary, psychological and philosophical error. The anonymous writer of an early biographical sketch of Opie sees *The Father and Daughter* as standing

in opposition to the fantastic fictions which have disgraced the regions of romance, ... —a tale, founded in simple nature; as such, perhaps, there never was a composition so admirably calculated to rouse the passions in the cause of virtue, and to correct that false sensibility, that degenerating excess of sentiment, which have been proved to be incompatible with the real interests of humanity. The concluding sentences of this pathetic and deeply-affecting story cannot be too often impressed upon young minds: they breathe the purest spirit of philanthropy and good sense. (Appendix C.3)

Virtue, the correction of excess, and the inspiration of the individual with "the purest spirit of philanthropy and good sense" are the ethical effects arising from the emotional affects of the pathetic. These effects were widely recognized as part of the literature of sensibility generally, but Opie's fiction in particular seemed to exemplify the full potentialities of the sentimental.[1]

---

1 Todd argues that "the cult of sensibility was largely defined by fiction from the 1740s to the 1770s" (4) and contends that "From the 1780s onwards, sentimental lit-

The power of Opie's pathos resides in the writing of tales whose "structure of feeling" is, in the words of Gary Kelly, based on "overpayment of suffering for real or imagined transgressions" (Kelly, *English Fiction* 86). Agnes Fitzhenry, Opie's heroine in *The Father and Daughter*, is described as a model of sensibility; she unites "to extreme beauty of face and person every accomplishment that belongs to her own sex, and a great degree of that strength of mind and capacity for acquiring knowledge supposed to belong exclusively to the other" (65). She is admired "for her sweetness of temper, her willingness to oblige, her seeming unconsciousness of her own merits, and her readiness to commend the merits of others" (65). Indeed, her innocence matched with intelligence is only compromised by a "vanity and self-love" (72) which prevent her from discerning the complex machinations of her suitor, George Clifford. Clifford is an Officer of the Guards, an expert in the "knowledge of the human heart" (66) and a "consummate deceiver" (77). A formidable opponent, with the ability "to betray the unwary of both sexes," his "knowledge of the human heart" allows him to turn the virtues of sensibility against their owner; he has the "power of discovering the prevailing foible in those on whom he has designs, and of converting their imagined security into their real danger" (66). Clifford rapidly turns Agnes against her widowed father, a man who joins "the steady, manly affection of a father ... [to] the fond anxieties and endearing attentions of a mother" (65). Torn between filial duty and erotic attraction, Agnes chooses the latter, eloping with Clifford. Not surprisingly, Clifford, "the slave of sordid selfishness" (66), never legitimates the relationship through marriage, and Agnes becomes a mother before she is a wife. Not until overhearing discussion of his plan to marry another while maintaining herself as his mistress does Agnes fully comprehend Clifford's duplicity, and she then makes her way to her father's home, only to discover on the way there that he has

---

erature and the principles behind it were bombarded with criticism and ridicule" (141). Markman Ellis, however, challenges the idea of a decline of sensibility by the 1780s and 90s in *The Politics of Sensibility* (190–220).

been driven mad by her act of disobedience against his explicit injunction that she not continue the courtship with Clifford. Opie is careful to emphasize Agnes's virtues and to qualify her fall as emanating in part from her own overconfidence in her ability to judge character; still, Opie makes clear that Agnes is more victimized than vicious, the prey of more hardened vice and the unequal advantages the unprincipled Clifford possesses. As a result, the calamities that befall her seem punishment in excess of her true moral worth, and in excess of her transgression against her father. Opie's heightened pathos therefore develops in proportion to the "overpayment of suffering" experienced by her heroine, and Agnes's conduct within this state of suffering resides at the core of *The Father and Daughter*.

A passing comment by Moncrieff hints at the artistry of Opie's tale in its choice of "domestic heroism" (Kelly, *English Fiction* 84) as a central subject instead of a conventional story of courtship. Stories based in "passions" and designed to "affect the heart" might be construed as emerging from erotic desire and the lure of the amorous; Opie's tale, however, turns away from the embrace of the amorous to engage with the activities of the domestic, the filial and the companionate. Moncrieff argues that Opie

> did not act unwisely in discarding the adventitious and artificial woes of love, in all her stories, for the more genuine and stronger emotions, produced by the kindred feelings of relationship, and the sacred sympathies of nature's dearest ties.... (Appendix F.1)

While the tale begins by setting up a conflict between the filial duty of Agnes Fitzhenry to her father and her erotic desire for Clifford, "the adventitious and artificial woes of love" are quickly relegated to the background of the tale, as Opie warns the reader at the outset: "I have been thus minute in detailing the various and seducing powers which Clifford possessed, not because he will be a principal figure in my narrative, for, on the contrary, the chief characters in it are the father and daughter"

(67).[1] Agnes's conflict between the choice of marrying Clifford or remaining with her father is completed within the first few pages of the tale; the bulk of the work explores her regret, not over the disastrous courtship with Clifford, which leaves her alone and with a child, but instead over the catastrophic consequences of her abandonment of her father. Emotional agony supplants the conventional interests of "strong character, comic situation, bustle, and variety of incident, which constitute a NOVEL" ("To the Reader" 63). The "SIMPLE, MORAL TALE," on the other hand, redirects the reader's attention to the moral interests of a story, particularly as individuals suffer under the consequences of personal action.

One might expect clarity and certainty in the condemnation of immoral behavior and the commendation of correct moral action to emerge from a "MORAL TALE"; however, *The Father and Daughter* does not offer a simplified moral lesson. In Opie's tale transgression is not punished in proportion to the nature of the offence. Agnes's moment of choice itself is steeped in ambiguity:

> This was the moment for Clifford to urge more strongly than ever that the elopement was the most effectual means of securing her father's happiness, as well as her own; till at last her judgement became the dupe of her wishes; and, fancying she was following the dictates of filial affection, when she was in reality the helpless victim of passion, she yielded to the persuasions of a villain, and set off with him to Scotland. (71-2)

While it is clear her choice is made in error, her intentions emerge from the well-meaning desire to resolve the conflict between father and lover. Further, isolated and outmatched by Clifford's cunning, her position as "helpless victim of passion"

---

1   Ty notes that in shifting "the focus of the tale from a struggle between two lovers to larger, more classic conflicts between a father and daughter, between social norms and individual convictions, ... Opie expands the subjectivity of her heroine, and, implicitly, that of woman not just to include the customary roles of maiden, mistress or wife, but to highlight and encompass roles of daughter, caregiver and provider, mother worker, and nurse" (134).

would seem to explain, at least in part, her actions and possibly relieve the degree of her punishment. Such is not the case, and the extent of her suffering is virtually unrelenting. Yet this suffering does not always carry a clear mark of moral judgment. While certain characters like Mrs. Macfiendy dismiss Agnes as a seduced and therefore wholly corrupt individual, such extreme positions become the object of authorial ridicule and satire. Indeed, Agnes is regularly surrounded by figures aware of her moral transgression but supportive in their care of her. The cottagers, the servant Fanny and, above all, Caroline Seymour find differing ways of reincorporating Agnes within a social context despite her previous moral transgression.

Caroline's letter written to Agnes, ostensibly in support of her attempt to take over the care of the mad Fitzhenry, complicates the moral message of the novel while advocating a radical politics in dealing with seduced maidens. Though overtly critical of those who, like Wollstonecraft and Godwin, "inveigh bitterly against society for excluding from its circle, with unrelenting rigour, the woman who has once transgressed the salutary laws of chastity" (139), the letter nevertheless seeks to reclaim the once fallen. "Mistaken writers, of both sexes," Caroline goes on to note, "have endeavoured to prove that many an amiable woman has been for ever lost to virtue and the world, and become the victim of prostitution, merely because her first fault was treated with ill-judging and criminal severity" (139). Such assertions are, according to Caroline, "fraught with mischief," "dangerous," and "calculated to deter the victim of seduction from penitence and amendment" (140); she observes that there are many cases "of women restored by perseverance in a life of expiatory amendment, to that rank in society which they had forfeited by one false step, while their fault has been forgotten in their exemplary conduct, as wives and mothers" (140). Caroline's sentiments, although praising "the virtues of self-denial, patience, fortitude, and industry" (140) as part of a program of "long and painful probation" after an act of transgression, seem to accord with the overall tenor of the tale. Agnes is not fully excused for her actions but neither is she expected to live a life condemned to exile and humiliation.

The ambivalence in Opie's presentation of Agnes's ruin and the responses of the world to it seems designed to turn the "MORAL TALE" away from designating proper behaviour and towards an investigation of the struggle for moral identity. Formed from the choices she makes, Agnes's moral identity evolves and changes as she lives with the consequences of her actions within a society which sometimes accepts and sometimes rejects her.

This depiction of Agnes situates Opie in a peculiar political position with respect to female chastity. After reading *The Father and Daughter,* Thomas Robinson reports to his brother, Henry Crabb Robinson, first on the power of sentiment and sympathy in the work and then immediately on its sexual politics:

> It is quite enough for me to say of it, that it interested me, and I was pleased to find that I have a few strings about my heart, which are capable of receiving a vibration of sympathy.... The story is very simple, and the distress of it arises from seduction. Many modern Novels seem to be written with a view to inculcate or censure some fashionable moral or political opinion. And I have imagined that Mrs. O. in her production intended to support a middle opinion betwixt the free notion of Godwin, on female chastity on the one hand, and the puritanical prudish doctrine of Miss Hannah More on the other. (Appendix C.1)

In naming Godwin and Hannah More, Robinson identifies the two extreme poles occupied by contemporary writers. William Godwin's *Political Justice* (1793) was controversial for a number of reasons not the least of which was its open opposition to marriage. Describing it as "evil," "a system of fraud," and "the worst of all monopolies,"[1] Godwin argues that the institution of marriage inhibits individual development and perpetuates prejudice, selfishness, and despotism. Although he and Wollstonecraft ultimately did marry, Godwin remained unapolo-

---

1 See Godwin's Appendix to Book VIII, entitled "Of Co-operation, Cohabitation and Marriage," in *Enquiry Concerning Political Justice*, esp. p. 762.

getic concerning their prenuptial relations. In his *Memoirs of The Author of a Vindication of the Rights of Woman* (1798), he offers up himself and Mary Wollstonecraft as living examples of the "free notion" of conjugal relationships outside of marriage. In defending his co-habitation with Wollstonecraft, he states, "certainly nothing can be so ridiculous upon the face of it, or so contrary to the genuine march of sentiment, as to require the overflowing of the soul to wait upon a ceremony, and that which, wherever delicacy and imagination exist, is of all things most sacredly private, to blow a trumpet before it, and to record the moment when it has arrived at its climax" (Appendix H.3). Hannah More's *Strictures on the Modern System of Female Education* (1799) stands in direct opposition to Godwin's position, even going so far as to attack Wollstonecraft's writings on the grounds that they justified adultery.[1] She also depicts Rousseau as a seducer not unlike Opie's Clifford:

> The rare mischief of this author [Rousseau] consists in his power of seducing by falsehood those who love truth, but whose minds are still wavering, and whose principles are not yet formed. He allures the warm-hearted to embrace vice, not because they prefer vice, but because he gives to vice so natural an air of virtue: and ardent and enthusiastic youth, too confidently trusting in their integrity and in their teacher, will be undone, while they fancy they are indulging in the noblest feelings of their nature.... (Appendix H.4)

The "puritanical prudish doctrine" Robinson speaks of appears in statements affirming a ruthless and unforgiving religious law supporting the imperative for women to remain chaste:

---

1   More writes, "About the same time that this first attempt at representing an adultress in an exemplary light was made by a German dramatist, which forms an æra in manners; a direct vindication of adultery was for the first time attempted by a *woman*, a professed admirer and imitator of the German suicide Werter. *The female Werter*, as she is styled by her biographer, asserts, in a work intitled 'The Wrongs of Women,' that adultery is justifiable, and that the restrictions placed on it by the laws of England constitute one of the *Wrongs of Women*...'" (Appendix H.4).

thanks to the surviving efficacy of a holy religion, to the operation of virtuous laws, and the energy and unshaken integrity with which these laws are *now* administered; and still more perhaps to a standard of morals which continues in force, when the principles which sanctioned it are no more; this crime, in the female sex at least, is still held in just abhorrence: if it be practiced, it is not honourable; if it be committed, it is not justified; we do not yet affect to palliate its turpitude; as yet it hides its abhorred head in lurking privacy; and reprobation *hitherto* follows its publicity. (Appendix H.4)

More is uncompromising in her argument that female transgressors of the law of chastity should be exiled from society: "be not anxious to restore the forlorn penitent to that society against whose laws she has so grievously offended" since "her soliciting such a restoration, furnishes but too plain a proof that she is not the penitent your partiality would believe" (Appendix H.4). Endorsing neither position, Opie tends, in *The Father and Daughter*, to investigate and critique both radical and conservative claims with equal intensity. Caroline Seymour offers the argument that Agnes should not be permanently stigmatized for losing her chastity, but still maintains the importance of marriage; Mrs. Macfiendy would render Agnes a social pariah, but her position is not treated with sympathy by Opie.

In commenting on the eighteenth-century interest in tales of seduced maidens, Susan Staves has noted that what is at stake in literary representations of chastity, or more precisely, the loss of chastity, is the fate of the family. She notes that in many instances (including that of *The Father and Daughter*) "Scenes of fathers weeping over the loss of their daughters, of fathers pining away with grief, and tearful scenes of final reconciliations when the errant daughter comes home repentant are more common and much more fully rendered than seductions themselves" (Staves 120). Moreover, "The emotional core of many of the stories," argues Staves, "does not lie in the seduction itself; in fact, in most novels the climax of the seduction is not even rendered but simply alluded to in a perfunctory way. Instead, attention is devoted to rendering the grief of the girl's parents, especially of her father" (Staves 120). *The Father and Daughter* stands as a model of this tendency: although Opie's focus throughout is on the daughter, Fitzhenry's madness stands as an index to an emotional distress that itself seems in excess of Agnes's disobedience and ruin. In the historical moment in which novels like *The Father and Daughter* were popular, Staves suggests that ruined daughters signify ruined families and register a subtle shift in the nature and definition of the family itself. She concludes that the stories of seduced maidens "acknowledge the ruin and its irreversibility and lament the loss of an idealized older family undisturbed by the free exercise of the wills of its inferior members" (Staves 122). Agnes, despite the enormous forces of coercion around her, attempts to define herself in individualistic terms first through the error of choosing to elope with Clifford, and later in her attempt to control and shape the treatment of her father's madness.

Madness and The Father and Daughter

The phenomenon and treatment of madness held a special interest for Opie in particular and for her age in general. As a young woman of sixteen, Opie paid a visit to the bedlam near her home in Norwich. Her reminiscence of this event shows an early sense of the tension between the desire to idealize the insane as persons of heightened sentiment[1] and the disappointing reality of their condition:

> I consented to accompany two gentlemen, dear friends of mine, on a visit to the *interior* of the bedlam. One of my

---

1   The sentimental finds two poles of interest in the insane. First, the sufferer, given his or her loss of rational powers, illustrates (and experiences) an uncontrolled sensibility, becoming a creature of excess feeling unmoderated by reason. Second, sentimental observers of the insane witness and perhaps learn from such displays of feeling and are offered the chance to respond with sympathy and charity. Augustus Harley, the sentimental hero of Henry Mackenzie's *The Man of Feeling* (1777), visits a Bedlam where he witnesses a series of scenes that leave him "fixed in astonishment and pity!" (35), and cause him to make a charitable donation of "a couple of guineas" (35) to the keeper of the Bedlam.

companions was a man of warm feelings and lively fancy, and he had pictured to himself the unfortunate beings, whom we were going to visit, as victims of their sensibility, and as likely to express by their countenances and words the fatal sorrows of their hearts.... but our romance was sadly disappointed, for we beheld no "eye in a fine phrensy rolling," no interesting expression of sentimental woe.... (Appendix J.1)

This visit, though not productive of empirical evidence of a connection between sensibility and madness, nevertheless was central to Opie's later literary representation of the condition. On leaving the building, she observed closely one of the residents, and the memory remained vividly present to her years later:

I ... lingered behind still, to gaze upon a man whom I had observed from the open door at which I stood, pacing up and down the wintry walk, but who at length saw me earnestly beholding him! He started, fixed his eyes on me with a look full of mournful expression, and never removed them till I, reluctantly I own, had followed my companions. What a world of woe was, as I fancied, in that look! Perhaps I resembled some one dear to him! Perhaps — but it were idle to give all the perhapses of romantic sixteen — resolved to find in bedlam what she thought *ought* to be there of the sentimental, if it were not. However, that poor man and his expression never left my memory; and I thought of him when, at a later period, I attempted to paint the feelings I imputed to him in the "Father and Daughter." (Appendix J.1)

Indeed, this recollection underwrites the portrait of Agnes's reunion with her father after he is "driven to madness by his daughter's desertion and disgrace!!" (92). Often taken as the scene of greatest pathos in the tale,[1] the reunion of father and

---

1 In a review of Paër's adaptation of *The Father and Daughter* to the opera, *L'Agnese*, *The London Times* mentions the dramatic force of the reunion between father and daughter: "We shall not soon forget the fixed look with which, at his first appear-

daughter is marked by her "mute and tearful despair" (93), arising from the fact that Fitzhenry no longer recognizes her—his
mania tells him that his real daughter is in the grave. To complete the pathos of the scene, Opie has Fitzhenry emerge from
his "phrensy" to comfort the distraught Agnes with the utterance, "Poor thing!"; he "then gazed on her with such inquiring
and mournful looks, that tears once more found their way and
relieved her bursting brain—while seizing her father's hand
she pressed it with frantic emotion to her lips" (94).

But the portrait of Fitzhenry is of interest for more than its
record of one writer's youthful fascination with lunatics and an
imaginative sentimental engagement with the idea of madness.
Indeed, insanity was a topic of immediate interest to all of
Britain in the latter part of the eighteenth century, in the wake
of the very public mania of King George III. From October
1788 to March 1789 the King suffered marked symptoms of
insanity, and his condition was a matter of public record and
discussion: it was debated in Parliament and reported in the
newspapers; it gave rise to Parliamentary committees of inquiry
and the publication of pamphlets concerning the diagnosis,
prognosis, and treatment of the disorder. In 1801 the king
suffered a relapse, and Opie's tale must have seemed even more
topical: if the paternalist political analogy of the king as the
father of his country is extended, all of England, like Agnes, was
dealing with a deranged parent. A second relapse in 1804 was
followed by the King's final bout of madness in 1810 at the age
of 72, which ended only with his death in 1820. During the
King's lifetime, as Roy Porter has pointed out, "he was easily
the most closely observed mad person in English history, his
condition being recorded in official bulletins and fiercely disputed across the floor of the House, as well as featuring at
length in the diaries of courtiers such as Robert Fulke Greville
and Fanny Burney. We know how long he slept, down to the
last quarter of an hour; when he was strait jacketed or blistered;
and so forth" (235). King George's condition put madness and
its treatment at the forefront of the public consciousness, and

---

ance, he advanced to the front of the stage—his eye intensely marked the brooding
of a distempered mind" (Appendix D.2.ii). The scene is reproduced in the dramatic
adaptations by Kemble (see Appendix E.1.ii) and by Moncrieff (see Appendix F.2).

this awareness was framed amidst debates about insanity ongoing since the middle of the eighteenth century.

Although the history of the treatment of madness is exceedingly complex, the second half of the eighteenth century saw two main views emerge. More traditional, established approaches defined insanity in physiological terms and held out little hope for ameliorating the patient's condition. They emphasized medical treatment including *"rough catharticks"* (Appendix J.4.iii), such as vomits, purges, and venesection or bleeding (a process by which the doctor opened a patient's vein to draw off the "excess" blood believed to contribute to the disorder), as well as other procedures designed to shock the system such as sudden unexpected immersion in cold baths and confinement to a chair that could be spun quickly to disorient the patient. In opposition to arguments for the treatment of madness by "medicine" came those based on "management" of the condition. Advocates for improved treatments saw forms of madness as psychological in origin and therefore potentially treatable. Their remedies for mental "disease" became more concerned with the establishment of stable routines and a consistent regimen of management; *"rough catharticks"* were to be used only when absolutely necessary.

A central figure in this debate was William Battie, a one-time governor of Bedlam who turned against traditional methods of treatment in a short publication entitled *"A Treatise on Madness,"* published in 1758. He became a powerful proponent of the view *"that management did much more than medicine"* (Appendix J.3.ii) and described the use of bleeding, blisters, caustics, sharp purges, opium and especially vomits as "shocking operations" (Appendix J.3.iv) limited in their effectiveness and potentially damaging to the patient.[1] He also made the important argument

---

1   It should be noted, however, that his objections are usually a matter of degree rather than kind: in cases of *"unwearied attention to any one object"* — the type of pronounced mania exhibited by Fitzhenry in *The Father and Daughter*—Battie recommends that "bodily pain may be excited to as good a purpose and without any the least danger. It being a known observation … that no two different perceptions can subsist at the same time… Therefore vesicatories, caustics, vomits, rough cathartics and errhines,

That, altho' Madness is frequently taken for one species of disorder, nevertheless, when thoroughly examined, it discovers as much variety with respect to its causes and circumstances as any distemper whatever: Madness therefore, like most other morbid cases, rejects all general methods, *v.g.* bleeding, blisters, caustics, rough cathartics, the gumms and fætid antihysterics, opium, mineral waters, cold bathing, and vomits. (Appendix J.3.iv)

According to Battie, madness is specific to the individual, arises from a specific event in the individual life and therefore requires individualized methods of treatment. Finally, Battie's treatise distinguished between two sorts of mental disorder: "Original" and "Consequential." Original madness arises from an "internal disorder" or defect at birth and was felt, even by Battie, to be largely untreatable (Battie 43); consequential madness, however, was caused by "external and accidental causes" (Battie 44) ranging from physical shocks affecting the nervous system to emotional trauma experienced over a lifetime. Of particular interest are Battie's assertions that "*tumultuous and spasmodic passions, such as joy and anger*" and "*unwearied attention to any one object, as also love, grief, and despair*" (Appendix J.3.iii) are potential causes of madness. Fitzhenry's condition is clearly of the second or consequential type, arising from his single-minded obsession with the grief arising from the loss of his daughter. Moreover, Agnes's concern for her father and her attempts to find different treatments for him, treatments shaped to her knowledge of his past, speak to a sense of the concern for Fitzhenry's madness as psychological in its origins and unique to his circumstance and surroundings, and owe some debt to Battie's contributions to the dialogue on madness.

While Opie's tale primarily advocates the more progressive argument "*that management did much more than medicine,*" moments in *The Father and Daughter* hint at the continued

---

may be and in fact often are as serviceable in this case of fixed nervous Sensation ... inasmuch as they all relieve and divert the mind from its delirious attention, or from the bewitching passions of love, grief, and despair ..." (see Appendix J.3.iii).

existence of more inhumane treatments. When Agnes first encounters her father, she meets with some of the most distressing symbols of asylum treatment. She is distraught concerning the sound of the fetters which render so vividly the physical restraint exacted on mental patients. The narrator reflects, "The clanking of a fetter, when one knows it is fastened round the limbs of a fellow-creature, always calls forth in the soul of sensibility a sensation of horror" (90), echoing Opie's own response on her visit to the Norwich bedlam: "never can I forget the terror and trembling which seized my whole frame, when, as I stood listening for my mad friend at the door, I heard the clanking of his chain!" (Appendix J.1). Even more distressing are the blows of the keepers who use physical violence to subdue her father. Filial tenderness and concern are no match for accepted wisdom concerning the treatment of the deranged.

John Monro, in his *Remarks on Dr. Battie's Treatise on Madness* written in 1758, articulates the basis of such conventional approaches. Himself part of a family dynasty that oversaw the running of London's Bedlam hospital for the insane for four generations, Monro challenged Battie's definition of madness as "deluded imagination" directly "by contending that most madmen showed no signs of false *ideas*; their insanity lay in perversion of moral will—not in hallucination, but in 'vitiated judgment'" (Porter 192).[1] He emphasized the use of extreme medicines, stating "that the most adequate and constant cure of it [madness] is by evacuation" and that "The evacuation by *vomiting* is infinitely preferable to any other" (Appendix J.4.iii). In addition, "*Bleeding* and *purging* are both requisite," according to Monro, "in the cure of madness" (Appendix J.4.iii). Monro's talk of a "cure" sounds hollow given his opening statement that "MADNESS is a distemper of such a nature, that very little of real use can be said concerning it; the immediate causes will for ever disappoint our search ..." (Appendix J.4.i). Monro was not alone in his advocacy of these extreme medicines, and even as Opie was writing *The Father and Daughter* contemporary physi-

---

1 For Monro's definition of madness, see *Remarks on Dr. Battie's Treatise on Madness* (Appendix J.4.ii).

cians like William Cullen (1710-90) persisted in promoting physical restraint and "*rough catharticks.*" While Cullen notes that "The restraining madmen by the force of other men, as occasioning a constant struggle and violent agitation, is often hurtful," he nevertheless goes on to assert that, "Fear, being a passion that diminishes excitement, may therefore be opposed to the excess of it.... In most cases it has appeared to be necessary to employ a very constant impression of fear; and therefore to inspire them with the awe and dread of some particular persons, especially of those who are to be constantly near them ... sometimes it may be necessary to acquire it even by stripes and blows" (Appendix J.5.ii). Despite the vivid representation of the physical violence enacted against Fitzhenry, however, Opie's realism stops short of depicting the purges that were equally associated in the public mind with the treatment of insanity: though chains and blows might be polite family reading, vomit and excrement were not. Similarly, while she represents the vocal ravings and erratic mood swings associated with mania, she is silent on the sexual excesses physicians saw as commonly symptomatic of the condition.

In many ways, however, the asylum founded by Fitzhenry in earlier times was enlightened and reflected advances in treatment of the insane pioneered with the founding of the York Retreat by the Quaker William Tuke in 1796.[1] Based on a more humane "moral therapy," the York Retreat "was designed to be dwelt in as a large private house. Its atmosphere was domestic, and it was run along paternal lines. The superintendent and his assistants were the 'family', and a spiritual bond was sought between staff and patients" (Porter 223). This "moral therapy" or "moral treatment" differed from previous approaches to the treatment of insanity in that it promoted the treatment of patients as rational beings. As Hunter and Macalpine point out, "The pioneer work of Tukes opened a new chapter in the history of the insane because of the avowed aim to accord them the dignity and status of sick human beings, and to substitute self-restraint based on self-esteem

---

1 William Tuke's son, Samuel, offers the first full description of the theory and method of the York retreat in his *Description of the Retreat, An Institution Near York for Insane Persons of the Society of Friends* (1813).

induced by a mild system of management for the debasing and brutalizing coercion and restrain of 'the terrific system'" (687). Given Opie's close ties to the prominent Quaker Gurney family of Norwich and her abiding interest in bedlams, it is possible that she was acquainted with this new approach devised by the Society of Friends. She was certainly aware of the plan to construct a similar institution in the south of England, to be called the Southern Retreat, a number of years later in 1839, when she solicited Joseph John Gurney's support for this charitable institution (Appendix J.2).

Agnes's appeal to have her father removed from a formal institutional confinement and the governors' sympathetic response signal the beginning of Opie's exploration of alternative and more radical treatments of the insane. The governors' concession allowing Agnes to visit her father is one strictly advised against by many specialists of the period. According to Battie, for instance, "Madness ... requires the patient's being removed from all objects that act forcibly upon the nerves, and excite too lively a perception of things, more especially from such objects as are the known causes of his disorder.... The visits therefore of affecting friends ... ought strictly to be forbidden" (Appendix J.3.ii). Cullen, too, asserts, "It also is for the most part proper, that maniacs should be without the company of any of their former acquaintance; the appearance of whom commonly excites emotions that increase the disease" (Appendix J.5.ii). Still, as an institution, it is clearly less committed to strategies of moral treatment than the private doctor to whom Agnes takes her father on his release. Although Dr. W—— is unable to restore Fitzhenry's reason during his six month's stay, it is clear that at least he thrives physically. Agnes notes that "the air of the place agreed so well with her father that he became fat and healthy in his appearance" (144), perhaps a veiled suggestion that purges did not form part of his regimen. The precepts articulated by the private doctor on the release of his patient suggest that his treatment is modeled on prevailing notions of moral management. Like the directors of the York Retreat, the doctor is interested in placing the patient in a domestic rather than an incarcerating situation: "Let him resume his usual habits, his usual walks, live as near your former habitation as you possibly can; let him hear his favourite songs, and be as much with him as you can contrive to be; and if you should not succeed in making him rational again, you will at least make him happy" (145). As Andrew Harper advises, "When the disease has been of some duration, it is then requisite that every notion, whether whimsical or rational, should meet with some degree of indulgence.... If the mind should adopt some particular amusement, be partial to any favourite study or employment, or imbibe some new fancy, it would be very improper to restrain these sallies, or to force the mind suddenly from its choice" (Appendix J.6.iv). The practitioners of the moral treatment took as their goal the humane treatment of the patient, and re-establishment of self-restraint in the sufferer through the desire to retain the esteem of those around him. The mild management advocated by Dr. W—— seems precisely designed to restore Fitzhenry to self-esteem and thus self-restraint through returning him to a rational domestic setting.

The Father and Daughter and Theatrical Adaptations

Though the way in which Opie's tale incorporates medical discourses concerning treatment of insanity in the period marks it as a significant fictional portrayal of a critical moment in the history of psychiatry, her contemporaries were far more concerned with her representation of the disorder itself, and specifically in the powerful effect of madness on the sensibilities of both Agnes and the reader. It appears to have been this quality which attained central importance in adaptations of the tale for the stage, where emphasis is given to the portrayal of Fitzhenry's madness. The earliest adaptation was an opera, *Agnese di Fitz-Henry*, by Paër, first produced in Italy in 1809 with a libretto by Luigi Buonavoglia based on the Italian translation of the tale by Filippo Casari. *L'Agnese* premiered in London 15 May 1817, with the role of Agnes's father played by the celebrated Ambrogetti. The first of two reviews of the performance in *The Times* highlights the popular currency of Opie's work: "Mrs. Opie's interesting tale of *The Father and Daughter*, from which the drama is taken, was translated ... into most of the European languages; and it is a proof of the fidelity to general nature with which her portraits are drawn, that her writings have become almost universally popular" (Appendix D.2.i). The second turns its attention to performance, and it is Ambrogetti's portrayal of the mad father that excites interest: "Ambrogetti seemed to have abandoned for the occasion all idea of fine singing; it was throughout a voice choked with emotion, distorted with frenzy, or sinking under insupportable anguish. We shall not soon forget the fixed look with which, at his first appearance, he advanced to the front of the stage ..." (Appendix D.2.ii). More than a decade later the author of "Chronicles of the Italian Opera in England" recollected,

> the *vraisemblance* was too harrowing; Ambrogetti had studied the last degrading woe of humanity in the hospitals, where all its afflicting varieties were exemplified, and had studied it too well. Females turned their backs to the stage to avoid the sight; but a change of posture could not shut their ears to the dreadful scream of partial recognition with which the first entrance of his daughter was marked (Appendix D.2.iii).

While there is some recognition of the performance of Agnes, the emphasis is decidedly on the powerful effect of the portrayal of paternal madness.

While the opera exploits the pathos of Fitzhenry's madness and Agnes's penitence, some of the effects Opie insists on in her tale—the deaths of both father and daughter, and the absence of reconciliation with the vaguely repentant but ultimately unregenerate Clifford—are significantly altered. While Agnes's meeting with her mad father follows Opie's fiction closely, the opera introduces a happy ending, with Hubert restored to sanity and Agnes restored to the arms of both a loving father and a repentant seducer, now ostensibly her husband. Thus Paër's opera retains the powerful pathos of Agnes's guilt and contrition and of paternal madness, but ameliorates the tragic conclusion by superimposing a comic structure in which seducer and victim are transformed into stock young lovers and the father who initially blocks their happiness, through his resistance to Ernesto/Clifford's suit, ultimately embraces both. These tendencies are also evident in the British stage adaptations. The first to appear was *Smiles and Tears; or, The Widow's Stratagem*, written by Marie Therese Kemble, wife of Charles Kemble of the famous theatrical family which included the tragic actor John Kemble and his sister Sarah Siddons.[1] *Smiles and Tears*, first acted at Covent-Garden Theatre on 12 December, 1815, offers a pastiche of source material. As Kemble notes in her advertisement to the first edition of the play, "I should be wanting in candour as well as gratitude, were I not fairly to acknowledge the sources from which that applause has chiefly been derived. To Mrs. Opie's beautiful Tale of *Father and Daughter*, I am indebted for the serious interest of the Play; upon a French Piece in one Act, entitled *La Suite d'un Bal Masqué, some* of the lighter scenes were founded" (Appendix E.1.i).[2] If this combination of sentimental domestic tragedy and French farce seems at first glance unlikely, the play itself does little to challenge expectations. As the reviewer for the *Theatrical Inquisitor* notes, "This production is what they term *Comèdie larmoyante*; it has been rendered such by the union of one of Mrs. Opie's most affecting tales, with a frivolous little piece called *La suite d'un bal masqué*; the latter is the very epitome of French manners" (Appendix E.2.ii). Kemble follows Opie's original quite closely in its portrayal of the key scene where Cecil, the character based on Agnes, encounters her father, mad, for the first time, repeating key phrases of the original dialogue, but elevating other portions for dramatic — or rather melodramatic — effect.[3] As in *L'Agnese*, however, the play offers a radical departure in its conclusion, ending with the restoration of the father's sanity and the daughter's forgiveness of her seducer, Delaval.[4]

---

1 Opie was well acquainted with the family, reporting to her friend Mrs. Taylor in 1794, "I found Mrs. Siddons in the very act of suckling her little baby, and as handsome and charming as ever" (Brightwell 43), and writing to Godwin in the following year that she plans to send a play she has been working on to Mr. Kemble for his comments.

2 Indeed, it seems possible that Kemble's title, too, owes something to Opie: "Lullaby Song," one of her lyrics from *A Second Sett of Welch Airs*, offers the line "Tears and smiles, greet thee Boy! thou'rt my shame, thou'rt my joy."

3 See Appendix E.1.ii for Act III, scene ii of the play.

4 See Appendix E.1.iii for Act V, scene iii in which Cecil confronts her repentant seducer, and Appendix E.1.iv for Act V, scene v in which the father and daughter are restored to each other.

Later in the century Opie's novel was adapted for the stage once again, this time as *The Lear of Private Life* by William Moncrieff (1794-1857), manager of the Royal Coburg Theatre (later renamed the Royal Victoria Theatre or "Old Vic"). The play featured Junius Brutus Booth in the role of Agnes's father. He "played the hero with brilliant success for fifty-three nights,"[1] though perhaps his most lasting fame came off-stage, as the father of Abraham Lincoln's assassin, John Wilkes Booth. The play itself illustrates the popularity of two features of drama at this time: the revision of contemporary literary texts for the stage and the adaptation of Shakespeare's works to contemporary tastes. Allardyce Nicholl, in *A History of Early Nineteenth-Century Drama*, notes "the interest in Shakespeare taken by the people of this period" and observes "a tendency to translate, as it were, the Shakespearian characters into terms of everyday existence. Moncrieff's *Lear of Private Life* (Cob. 1820) and *The Othello of Private Life* (C.L. 1849) may serve as examples" (1:91). Thus Fitzhenry's encounter with Agnes in the woods evokes Lear's madness in a similar setting, and the defiant but enduring love shown by his daughter is reminiscent of Cordelia's devotion to her own father in Shakespeare's play.[2]

Interest in *King Lear* was marked at this point in time. In deference to the insanity of England's current monarch, the play was banished from the London stage between 1810 and 1820; however, on King George's death, theatres were once more willing to produce the drama of majesty, madness, and father-daughter relationships, and the tragic actor Edmund Kean played the lead role.[3] Yet the *Lear* Kean performed was neither Shakespeare's nor our own; rather, as the English theatre had

---

1 *Dictionary of National Biography*, 13: 619.

2 Ty notes that the analogies between Agnes and Cordelia "transform Agnes from a pathetic seduced maiden to a heroine of heroic or tragic stature" (138).

3 As biographer Raymund Fitzsimons notes, "The news that Kean was to play the part caused great interest. It was widely reported that he was studying the character with great care, even visiting lunatic asylums to observe the effects of madness. Everyone knew of his boast that he would make the audience as mad as himself" (138). It was a memorable performance: "One of Kean's most brilliant triumphs attended him on 24 April 1820 ... His Lear was received with rapture" (*Dictionary of National Biography*, 10:1150).

done since 1681, he used Nahum Tate's *History of King Lear* — an adaptation of Shakespeare's text "improved" according to classical principles. In Tate's version Lear is restored to sanity and his kingdom, and Cordelia lives to be reconciled with her father and betrothed to Edgar. Even so important a critic as Samuel Johnson endorsed these changes. He "expressed what oft was thought when he described the blinding of Gloucester as 'an act too horrid to be endured in dramatick exhibition,' and confessed he was 'so shocked by Cordelia's death, that I know not whether I ever endured to read again the last scenes of the play till I undertook to revise them as an editor'" (Ogden 16). Given this approach to *Lear*, it is small wonder that the emotional trauma of the ending of *The Father and Daughter* was likewise revised to include the restoration of sanity and the reconciliation between parent and child in stage adaptations of Opie's text.

Moncrieff's specialty, however, lay in the lucrative business of translating popular contemporary works to the London stage. At this time popular fictional works were quickly rewritten to meet the demand for new stage plays, in much the same way as current best-sellers soon find a second life as movies or mini-series.[1] In selecting *The Father and Daughter*, Moncrieff was attempting to capitalize, not only on current fashionability, but on enduring interest: an eighth edition of the tale had appeared only the year before. Subtitling his play "or, Father and Daughter," he evoked the familiarity and popularity of Opie's narrative; yet, like the earlier stage adaptations, the play itself attests to the theatrical tastes of the day. Moncrieff retains all the pathos of the original — the daughter torn between love and duty to her father and her passion for her lover, the father fallen into madness and grief — but he adds other elements.

---

1   In 1820, for example, less than a year after its publication as a novel, Sir Walter Scott's *Ivanhoe* appeared in no less than seven different versions for the stage (Nicholl 1:43). On February 19 alone the *Times* lists a five-act drama "from Ivanhoe called The Hebrew" at Drury Lane, a "musical drama, called Ivanhoe, or the Knight Templar" at Covent Garden, and "the splendid burletta of Ivanhoe, or the Jew's Daughter" at the Surrey Theatre. Moncrieff himself later aroused the wrath of Charles Dickens by adapting *The Pickwick Papers* for the stage almost before the last installment of the serial had been published (Hartnoll 557).

The play includes a comic sub-plot involving the marriage of a rustic buffoon, as its author notes, to "sufficiently relieve, without breaking in upon the sacred sorrow of the story" (Appendix F.1). And like both *L'Agnese* and *Smiles and Tears, The Lear of Private Life* alters the tragic conclusion so central to both Shakespeare's play and Opie's novel. In the final scenes of Moncrieff's drama, Agnes's lover returns repentant and is accepted by all as her husband to be, and her father is restored to sanity.[1] The curtain falls on a tableau of reconciliation and happiness.[2]

Sentiment, Poetry and Songs

In considering the success of *The Father and Daughter*, modern readers should keep in mind that the first edition of the tale included a miscellany of poetical pieces which in themselves proved to be extremely popular. The immediate success of the volume led to a second edition of *The Father and Daughter* in the same year of first publication (1801) in which the poems did not appear, but whose final page promised "A Volume of Poems, by Mrs. Opie, Is in the Press, and will speedily be published." As projected, the poems from *The Father and Daughter* were reprinted in a separate volume entitled *Poems* in 1802, along with an additional 26 poetical works.[3] In reviewing the *Poems*, the *Edinburgh Review* noted, "we are ready to admit, that her volume of poems has afforded us much pleasure, and that it would have obtained for its author a very considerable reputa-

---

1 See Appendix F.2.

2 Finally, it should be pointed out that *The Father and Daughter* was not the only one of Opie's works to be adapted for the stage. In 1818 Thomas Dibden produced "The Reprobate," based on Opie's story, and the following year he adapted *The Ruffian Boy* from *Tales*. This story seems also to have been produced in Norwich that same year in a version by Edward Fitzball, and also in 1821 as *Geraldi Duval, The Banditt of Bohemia* at Drury Lane Theatre in London. Although we have discovered no involvement by Opie in these adaptations, we do know that she was enthusiastic about the theatre from her youth to her conversion to the Quaker faith. She hoped that her friend Prince Hoare might adapt her first published novel, *Dangers of Coquetry*, as a play, and she did write songs used in an 1815 stage production by Henry Rowley Bishop, entitled *The Noble Outlaw*.

3 The Song, "A youth for Jane with ardour sigh'd," is the only poem from *The Father and Daughter* not included in *Poems*.

tion, though her former work [*The Father and Daughter*] had been wholly unknown" (Appendix B.2.iv). And just as *The Father and Daughter* passed through numerous editions, so too the *Poems* went through several editions in the first decade of the nineteenth century (six in all between 1802 and 1811). The success of the *Poems* indicates that the phenomenon of Opie's success emerged as much from her skill in writing poetry as from the pathos of her tale. The poems included with the first edition of *The Father and Daughter* include a combination of new and previously published work. The poetry section is dominated by a lengthy narrative entitled "Epistle of Eudora, Maid of Corinth" which is followed by a miscellaneous collection of shorter "Songs and Poetical Pieces."

In the "Epistle of Eudora, Maid of Corinth," Opie takes a classical subject and imagines a Romantic sensibility underlying the narrative. The details given by Pliny are sketchy enough, as the headnote indicates: a girl in love traces the outline of her soon to depart lover's shadow on the wall, and from this silhouette her potter father forms a bust of clay, and so terra-cotta sculpture was invented. From this slight basis Opie imagines the girl's experience to create a narrative poem of more than three hundred lines. She complicates the protagonist's character by considering the event in terms of a woman's confrontation with her own physical desire in the face of socially enacted decorums, of artistic creativity, and of the rewards and costs of fame to a young woman.

One of the most interesting aspects of Opie's works for modern readers is the frankness with which she articulates female desire: in Opie the lover's gaze is no masculine prerogative, but rather a woman's pleasure in the male as a physical object of desire. This theme is present in *The Father and Daughter* in the lingering gaze Agnes directs at Clifford in the theatre: "those who know what it is to love, will not be surprised to hear that Agnes had more pleasure in looking at her lover, and drawing favourable comparisons between him and the gentlemen who surrounded him, than in attending to the farce" (80). We see it too in her later *Adeline Mowbray*: "'So then he is young and handsome too!' said she mentally: 'it is a pity he looks so *ill*,' added she *sighing*: but the sigh was caused rather by his looking so *well*—though Adeline was not conscious of it" (23). In "The Maid of Corinth" Eudora overcomes her schooling in modesty to return to gaze upon her sleeping lover: although "at first, by cold decorum taught" (l. 19), Eudora withdraws from the room, when Affection prompts her to "View that winning form once more" (l. 22) because of Philemon's imminent departure, "frigid caution" is overcome and the girl resigns her soul "To passion's sway" (l. 26); she returns to "Gaz[e] uncheck'd ... a new unwonted bliss" (l. 30).

Indeed, it is this desire to gaze upon the physical form of the beloved object that impels Eudora's creativity: "And must that form delight my eyes no more?" (l. 33). The desire to retain a physical image of Philemon after his departure prompts her first to trace his shadow on the wall, and then to seek her father's aid in turning the mere outline of desire into a three-dimensional image. Opie takes a potentially transgressive act—the eschewing of modest behaviour in the female protagonist—and makes it the example, not of correction and punishment, but of a creativity that holds a recognized social value. Granted, Opie is careful to designate this as "the art that sprang from chaste desire" (l.128), but it is nonetheless an erotically infused chastity. Eudora, referring to her art, comments, "Ah! not with pride, but tenderness / I glow, When I this offspring of my love behold" (ll. 137-138), mingling in this image the creative and the procreative.

The Corinthian community hails her achievement, because representational sculpture will transcend not just the limits imposed by space implicit in Philemon's departure, but those posed by time as well: "But, dearest boast! I've circumscrib'd the sway / Of stern-brow'd Death" (ll. 145-146). Her new-found art will preserve the image of the beloved, and of the heroes of Corinth, whose "noble features" will inspire new generations of heroes. Eudora even speculates upon the ways in which her gift might be extended: "Lo there! the maid by love like mine inspir'd, / Not only colour to my lines imparts, / See her bold hand to greater deeds is fir'd, / See the whole form to mimic being starts" (ll.197-200). Celebrity, however, is not without its price. Her companions "with coldness praise [her], or with malice blame, / And on [her] heart impress this mournful truth, / They forfeit friendship, who are dear to fame" (ll. 242-244). Yet such hardship only reaffirms the superiority of domestic ties: comfort resides in her relationships with Philemon, and with her father.

Like *The Father and Daughter*, "The Maid of Corinth" foregrounds the power of filial affection, and like Opie herself, whose introductory note suggests that the central reward her own fame could offer is the pleasure it might afford her father, Eudora relishes the benefits her art confers upon Dibutades: "Now, sight most pleasing to his daughter's eyes, / Coarse robes no more obscure my father's mien; / His ample tunic glows with Tyrian dyes, / And all his native dignity is seen" (ll. 325-328). Father and daughter combine their creative skills to develop a new artistic form, and are proud of each other's accomplishments. In this atmosphere of mutual respect and affection, Eudora flourishes, and her "pride in the object" of her affection, combined with creativity fostered by love, allows her to emerge as a heroine who both acknowledges and controls desire.

If "The Maid of Corinth" contrasts *The Father and Daughter* in its affirmation of passion and its coherent representation of filial affection, other poems in the collection duplicate the pathos and abjection associated with Agnes and her father. Of the twelve poems published with the novel, two are longer narratives, two are brief quatrains, and eight might best be described as "songs" or short lyrics. Of the latter, four originally published as songs are of particular interest: "Song of an Indostan Girl," "A Mad-Song," "Fatherless Fanny," and "The Orphan Boy's Tale." All have in common one thing: they ventriloquize in some way the emotions and identity of a figure socially marginalized and in an abject condition. "Song of an Indostan Girl" — or "Song of a Hindustàni Girl" or "The Poor Hindoo" as it was also commonly known — gives voice to the suffering of a banished "Indian favourite" displaced by an English bride; "A Mad-Song" articulates the condition of a woman whose fiancé has died, and whose reason is lost in consequence; "Fatherless Fanny" and "The Orphan Boy's Tale" express the pains of familial loss which transcend class and economic circumstances. All but one express the voice of female abjection: only the orphan boy offers a masculine persona.

"Song of an Indostan Girl" was perhaps Opie's most popular song. It was reprinted a number of times throughout the first two decades of the nineteenth century, both as part of the *Second Set of Hindoo Airs* and independently, and exists in two distinct versions, the earlier with music composed by Edward Smith Biggs in Britain and the later with music by Frances Alsop published in America. An 1807 biographical sketch attributed to her Norwich friend, Mrs. Taylor, comments of Opie:

> she may be said to have been unrivalled in that kind of singing in which she more particularly delighted. Those only who have heard her, can conceive the effect which produced, in the performance of her own ballads. Of these, "*The Poor Hindu*," was one of her chief favourites, and the expression of plaintive misery, and affectionate supplication, which she threw into it, we may safely affirm, has never been surpassed, and very seldom equaled. Mrs. Opie may fairly be said to have created a style of singing of her own, which though polished and improved by art and cultivation, was founded on that power which she appears so pre-eminently to possess, of awakening the tender sympathies, and pathetic feelings of the mind (Taylor 218).

The lyrics are designed to evoke sympathy for the disempowered, and seemingly rely in part on the performance of a sympathetically imagined identity different from one's own. Thus these songs are the essence of sensibility in their dependence on sympathy and identification.

The loss of a lover (whether through racial bias or death) is balanced against the loss of familial support. "Fatherless Fanny" (who is also motherless, but that figures less large in Opie's vision of loss) looks back with nostalgia on her former life which, if impoverished in economic terms, was rich with love and approval: labour itself was "endear'd" by the thought that her parents were fed by her efforts. Her current woes result not from poverty, but from the absence of friends and family: "That, that is the pang;–want and toil would impart / No pang to my breast, if kind friends I could see; / For the wealth I require is that of the heart, / The smiles of affection are riches to me" (ll. 25-28).

For the protagonists of most of Opie's songs, the pathos arises in part from the unresolved nature of their suffering: Fanny's parents cannot return from the grave, nor will Henry leave his "lonely tomb," and the Indostan girl, after tormenting herself with thoughts of the "British fair" warming her beloved "to rapture," can only hope that "death will endear [her]" to him, and that he will "mourn [HIS] POOR HINDOO." Only the Orphan Boy is offered hope for a brighter future. It is perhaps telling that only for the masculine voice are the imagined sorrows compensated: his tale of paternal patriotic heroism and loss, and of maternal death, meets a sympathetic ear. The Lady weeps, offering tears as the tribute of sensibility, as well as a material compensation in the form of "clothing, food, employ." The familial circle is completed once more by the parents looking down from heaven to see their son's restoration to social place.

The additional "Songs and Other Poetical Pieces" that complete the volume emerge from the same sentimental tradition that gives rise to *The Father and Daughter*. The pathos of these songs, however, lies more in the emotional self-reflection of the speakers than in the outward representation of the kind of personal fortitude sustained under immense persecution and suffering depicted in *The Father and Daughter*. The sentimental poet, according to Schiller, "*reflects* upon the impression that objects make upon him, and only in that reflection is the emotion grounded which he himself experiences and which he excites in us" (116). Opie filters the impressions of objects through a variety of poetical personae who reflect on states of separation, failure, and loss. Often the situations that bring speakers to their current state is only sketchily rendered; their immediate reflection on emotion is the source of interest and identification for the reader.

The Song "I ONCE rejoic'd, sweet Evening gale" affords a good example of Opie's practice of sentimental poetry. It portrays a speaker lamenting over the death of Henry and wishing to join him in the grave, but unlike the typical elegy the poem offers little in the way of consolation for the speaker. Moreover, the narrative details that might distract from the rendering of an emotional state are sketchy at best: we are not told how or when Henry died; while it is likely there is some erotic attachment between Henry and the speaker, the nature of the connection is not explicitly stated. Given Opie's interests in domestic affections, Henry could be a brother, son, or father to the speaker. Instead of focusing on Henry, the poem turns inward to the reflective state of the speaker. The emotional state awakened by the loss of Henry acts to define the natural setting—the "sweet Evening gale" and the "setting sun"—as alien to the speaker. Indeed, the poem becomes a study in the way impressions are grounded in emotional reflection rather than empirical accuracy. Impressions from the world and the perceptions they create are not inaccurate in this case but they are insufficient—they are not "grounded," to use Schiller's word—because they are mismatched to the emotional state of the speaker. The only stable ground or truth for the speaker resides in the desire for and grief over Henry. Facing the impossibility of fulfilling desire for Henry in an indifferent natural world transforms the powers of affection into the desire for self-destruction. Yet the ultimate pathos of the poem is compounded by the inability of the speaker to enact the desire for death. The speaker would "wish" for the Evening gale "o'er my soul to waive" and for the setting sun "soon" to "beam / On mine, as well as Henry's grave," but there is a sense of the speaker locked in inactive reflection, perpetually suffering from a loss of the object of desire yet never able to terminate this state of emotional turmoil. Drawing out the state of suffering is a mark of these poems, as it is essential to the pathetic power of *The Father and Daughter*.

Other poems in the collection ring interesting changes on

the longing that engulfs the individual and defines the power of emotional reflection. Death and the response to it is the preoccupation of "The Mourner" and the "Mad-Song." In the first of these poems, the speaker turns inward to a state of perpetual mourning, refusing to exhibit "The sacred pomp of grief." Instead the speaker "in secret state, / Shall live the reverend form of woe." "A Mad-Song" stretches suffering toward madness as the speaker fixates on her "bridal hour" even after her fiancé has died. The refusal to acknowledge the source of suffering—the death of the betrothed—leaves the speaker victim to a felt but unrecognized weight of grief "that on my brow / Presses with such o'erwhelming power." Unrequited love consumes the speakers in "Song," "Yes Mary Anne," and "Song—To Laura," with a witty reversal present in the Song, "A youth for Jane with ardour sigh'd." In that Song, a youth pines for Jane who "to his vows ... replied / I'll hear you by and by." After repeatedly deflecting the speaker's desire, Jane eventually loses his attentions when the speaker turns to a new object, Emma. The conclusion leaves Jane isolated after her own change of heart causes the speaker to say, "I'm busy now ... —but Jane! / I'll hear you by and by." The speaker's escape from suffering is overshadowed by the grim irony that transfers this suffering to Jane. The poem seems to suggest that suffering is perpetual and attaches itself freely and regularly to human experience.

"The Despairing Wanderer" stands slightly apart from the other poems in the "Songs and Poetical Pieces" not by virtue of its mood but rather by its representation of emotional misery experienced apart from any distinct cause or object. The poem portrays the indulgences of melancholy with its speaker enclosed within "an hour to misery dear" and registering only a natural environment in which "midnight reigns with horrors crown'd." Indeed, any sense of an objective context quickly dissolves as the power of fancy intervenes and transforms the "dashing waves," the "hollow blasts," the "clouds" and "tall rocks" into living "gigantic figures" led by the figure of "Pale Terror" that has its only true life within the melancholy turmoil of the speaker's mind. Reason and understanding are nowhere to be found in the speaker's consciousness or in the landscape. Ultimately therefore, the "gloomy pleasure" gives way to "phrensy" and "Madness." Unable to escape the state of melancholy and its attendant gloom, terror and horror, the speaker invokes — indeed, seems almost to pray to — Madness:

> Come, Madness, come! tho' pale with fear
> Be joy's flush'd cheek when thou art near,
> On thee I eager glances bend;
> Despair, O Madness! calls thee friend!
> Come, with thy visions cheer my gloom.

Madness seems to act as an anaesthetic that allows the speaker to remain in the state of melancholy but without an affecting sense of the surrounding horrors and terrors. "Let me all ills, all fears deride!" and "Horrors with dauntless eye behold" become statements of ironic defiance, a defiance paid for with the loss of sanity but without any sense that melancholy has defeated indulgence in the world of "gloomy pleasure."

Preliminary Pathos: *Dangers of Coquetry*

Although *The Father and Daughter* was Opie's first wide-ranging success and the first work of fiction to appear under her own name, it was not Opie's first published novel. That distinction is held by *Dangers of Coquetry*, a brief narrative published anonymously in 1790 under the imprint of W. Lane, Leadenhall-street.[1] Response was mixed in the three reviews that mention

---

1   Lane's was a name already familiar to novel-readers of the late eighteenth century. From small beginnings in 1773, he had gradually expanded his publishing operation, and by 1784 "was advertising for 'several Novels in Manuscript for publishing the ensuing Season'"; in the year *Dangers of Coquetry* was published, Lane "adopted the name which afterwards became notorious, and his activities were henceforth conducted 'at the Minerva, Leadenhall Street'." As the Minerva Press, Lane's printing house became a by-word in some circles for less than stellar literary products. In 1805 Opie's friend Sir James Mackintosh wrote to her from Bombay, lamenting the literary taste of the colony which did not distinguish between serious novels and "all the common trash of the Minerva Press" (Brightwell 90). One suspects that Mackintosh was unaware of Opie's earlier venture with the press fifteen years before.

the novel. The *Critical Review* extends both praise and biting criticism: "The moral to be drawn from this work is so good, that we are blind to the dulness, the insipidity, and improbability of the narrative" (Appendix B.1.ii). The *English Review* is more enthusiastic, referring to it as a "sensible and moral novel" and commenting that "The characters are well drawn; the incidents arising naturally from each other exhibit in their fatal catastrophe a solemn warning to the fair sex to avoid the dangers of coquetry" (Appendix B.1.iii). These reviewers are united in their endorsement of the moral injunctions offered to women by the novel, and recent literary critics concur, Gary Kelly referring to it as "a conventional novel of manners, sentiment, and emulation" (*English Fiction* 29). Only the reviewer for *The European Magazine* finds a slightly different moral: "The Tale however by which these lessons are inculcated possesses a double aspect; for while it attributes the most mischievous and dreadful consequences to a little innocent coquetry in the character of a *wife*, it shews them to have proceeded from an idle, ridiculous, and unfounded jealousy on the part of her husband" (Appendix B.1.i). Although perhaps rooted in part in a misreading of the tale's conclusion (the reviewer believes Mortimer engages Ormington in the duel, rather than Lord Bertie), this recognition of a "double aspect" in Opie's work is curiously apt, for the novel both condemns and excuses its heroine's coquetry. Opie herself remained positive concerning its merits. In 1801 she wrote to Mrs. Taylor, "I am glad on reperusing 'The Dangers of Coquetry,' that you think so highly of it. I read it at Seething soon after I married, and felt a great respect for it; and if I ever write a collection of tales, I shall correct and republish that, as *I originally wrote it*, not as it now is, in the shape of a novel in chapters. I believe I told you that Mr. Hoare was so struck with it, as to intend writing a play from it. I wish he would" (Brightwell 85). But though Opie did indeed write several collections of tales, *Dangers of Coquetry* does not reappear, nor does Mr. Hoare appear to have followed through on his plans for the drama.

Despite its modest success, *Dangers of Coquetry* is in many ways an intriguing text, in some ways running counter to the traditional critique of the coquette in the late eighteenth century. Works such as the anonymous *Memoirs of a Coquet: or the History of Miss Harriot Airy* (1765) present the coquette as a stock figure beyond social redemption and largely outside the reader's sympathy. It offers a satirical account of a young girl's absorption in the arts of coquetry: "She had several intrigues before she was out of her hanging-sleeves, and was thoroughly versed in all the mysteries of *jiltism* ... before she entered into her teens" (Appendix I.3.i). The bulk of the narrative offers social satire of a type familiar earlier in the century, recounting Harriot's encounters with characters owning names such as Miss Meanwell and Mr. Vainlove, Boozewell and Hairbrain. Harriot herself stands as a negative model throughout the work, designed to be amusing but still the object of the reader's scorn. Only at the conclusion does the narrator adopt a high serious tone designed to reinforce the moral lesson: turning to Harriot's old age, he comments,

> In this miserable state *Harriot* languishes out the winter of life in obscurity, for she cannot bear those scenes in which she can no longer excite the least attention; and the recollection of the ill use she made of her vernal years, is a perpetual torment. — By indulging the most mortifying ideas, and dwelling on the most gloomy reflections, her mind and her body are both impaired: and she who was only the object of ridicule and contempt, now deserves the highest compassion;—for, with a good heart, and a cultivated understanding, superior to thousands of her sex, she, though guilty of a thousand follies, committed no crimes; and tho' she was often indiscreet, abhorred vice. — She lost her character, but she preserved her virtue. (Appendix I.3.ii)

The reason for her loneliness is made explicit: "who would think of *settling* with her who behaved with equal freedom to every man she met with, and discovered, by every turn of her eyes, and every movement she made, that the love of admiration was her ruling passion?" (Appendix I.3.ii). For this narrator, the ideal of all right-thinking individuals is the monogamous companionate marriage, guaranteed by female discretion and devotion. In many ways, *Dangers of Coquetry* imitates the moral message of *Memoirs of a Coquet*: it concludes: "for the perusal of the thoughtless and the young, is this tale given to the world—it teaches that *indiscretions* may produce as fatal effects as ACTUAL GUILT, and that even the appearance of *impropriety* cannot be too carefully avoided" (256). In the tragic consequences of Louisa Connolly's transgression, the tale seems to endorse the standard cautionary morality of earlier eighteenth-century condemnation of the coquette. But in its power to evoke sympathy for Louisa's fate, where the punishment seems incommensurate with the woman's intent, Opie's novel looks forward to the emphasis on the pathos attendant upon the fate of the transgressive but well-intentioned heroine of sentimental fiction, and distinguishes *Dangers of Coquetry* from earlier portraits of the coquette. Louisa Connolly is no mere *type* like Harriot Airy—she is a complex mixture of virtues and flaws. Her first introduction establishes the contradictory elements of her character: "Vanity and the love of admiration had possession of her heart, and tho' in her moments of reflection Louisa, listening to the dictates of self-reproach, resolved on suppressing her indiscretion, and discarding the train of admirers whom she alternately encouraged, she still remained eager for admiration, even from those whose understandings she despised: and though shrinking with anguish from the thought of being regarded as such, was at eighteen a finished coquette" (187). Thus when Louisa falls in love with Mortimer, who asserts that "a finished coquette ... will ever deserve and ever meet my abhorrence!" (198), she faces a daunting inner conflict in which her desire for the domestic companionate marriage offered by romantic love must contest with a culturally fostered desire for social standing based on the power of coquetry.

Moreover, Opie throws the flaws and virtues of Louisa into relief by situating her between the developed virtue of Caroline Seymour and the hardened manipulations of Mrs. Belmour. Caroline, Louisa's childhood friend, has "all those perfections which Louisa wanted" (189). Although she herself lacks the beauty, accomplishments and vivid sensibility that Louisa naturally embodies, Caroline "had an exquisite sense of propriety, which led her instantly to condemn and avoid every action which her reason disapproved. She was charitable more from principle than impulse; her temper was good from effort rather than nature; it had been tried in the school of unkindness, and resolution had made it equal to the trial" (189). In Caroline there is a schooled sensibility, a conscious development of charity and temper that is refined by suffering and always directed towards virtue. The friendship between Louisa and Caroline is part of a secondary plot that speaks to the ennobling power of sympathy, particularly for a character like Louisa who is driven by coquettish ambitions, but is still capable of fellow feeling not guided by envy or design. Her friendship with Caroline exists "in spite of her [Louisa's] beauty, in spite of her errors" (188), and renders Louisa more sympathetic to the reader.

Despite her failure to imitate Caroline's example, Louisa's early unselfconscious connection to her starkly contrasts her later, more socially driven, connection with the hardened coquette, Mrs. Belmour. Soon after arriving in London, Louisa hears that Mrs. Belmour is among those "who were most frequently mentioned by the fashionable of both sexes" (218) as "a leader of the ton" (218). Her surprise at discovering Belmour's social superiority attests to her ignorance "of the world, and its caprices" (219), and sets her apart from the empty artifice that comprises Belmour's character. In contrast to Louisa, Belmour is the truly hardened coquette: "she had the happy art of adapting her manners and sentiments to the manners and sentiments of those she conversed with. With the open and ingenuous, she was blunt and apparently unthinking; with the reserved, she was timid; with the young and volatile, lively and affectionate; with the vain, flattering; in short, she, Proteus like, assumed all characters, while she kept her own concealed from every one" (220-21). As in Addison's portrait of the coquette's heart, Belmour's character is marked by its convolutions, indirectness and changeableness: Addison writes that "The Fibres [of the coquette's heart] were turned and twisted in a more intricate and perplexed Manner than they are usually found in other Hearts; insomuch, that the whole Heart was wound up together like a Gordian Knot, and must have had very irregular and unequal Motions, whilst it was employed in its Vital Function" (Appendix I.1). Her coquettish arts reach their apogee when she plots the downfall of Lord Ormington, who has previously rejected her. Belmour hatches a plot to produce "disappointed passion" (228) in Lord Ormington and "pangs of jealousy" (228) in his fiancée, Lady Jane. She directs Lord Ormington's attention away from her rival, Lady Jane, to a new object of desire, Louisa, secure in the knowledge that Louisa will never return his interest; the effect of this action is designed to humiliate Lady Jane, the woman who has replaced her in Lord Ormington's regard. Through this act of conscious manipulation, Belmour reveals herself as the archetype of the finished coquette. She turns Louisa into a version of herself, the manipulative coquette, thus jeopardizing Louisa's domestic happiness with Mortimer. Belmour's actions promote dissatisfaction and unhappiness to gratify her own vanity and precipitate the tragic conclusion to Louisa's narrative. It is Belmour rather than Louisa who merits the kind of criticism formulated by writers like Catharine Macaulay: "every love intrigue ...," writes Macaulay, "must naturally tend to debase the female mind" and as a result "the mind becomes corrupted, and lies open to every solicitation which appetite or passion presents" (Appendix I.4).

In establishing this marked moral contrast between Louisa and Mrs. Belmour, Opie's novel epitomizes the radical changes in attitudes towards women's character in the latter part of the eighteenth century. If writers earlier in the century criticized the coquette for her anti-social behaviour, writers like Catharine Macaulay at the end criticized society itself for fostering the conditions which produced coquettes. From being a victimizer of others, the coquette herself is drawn as the victim of the culture which created her. Although Macaulay acknowledges that "By the intrigues of women, and their rage for personal power and importance, the whole world has been filled with violence and injury," she is equally adamant that women in a society in which "power is only acquired by personal charms" can hardly be expected to become anything other than coquettes. By creating Louisa as a coquette and victim of a coquette, Opie opens the possibility of regarding coquetry not as an innate characteristic or personality flaw but as a learned social behaviour fostered by the rewards bestowed upon beauty and sexual power.

After *The Father and Daughter*

In the years that followed the immediate success of *The Father and Daughter*, Opie continued a prolific writing career. Over the next 20 years, Opie produced at a steady pace in a variety of genres. Before 1825, she produced four novels—*Adeline Mowbray* (1805), *Temper* (1812), *Valentine's Eve* (1816), and *Madeline* (1822); four collections of tales—*Simple Tales* (1806), *New Tales* (1818), *Tales of Real Life* (1813), and *Tales of the Heart* (1820); and a collection of poems called *The Warrior's Return and Other Poems* (1808). The direction of her career was to change significantly in 1825, however, after her conversion to the Quaker faith. Opie had long been closely associated with the Gurney family of Norwich, one of the most prominent Quaker families in early nineteenth-century Britain: one of her young friends while growing up was Betsy Gurney, now better know to the world as Elizabeth Fry, the staunch advocate of prison reform; her brother, Joseph John Gurney, was a life-long friend and, indeed, life-long critic of Amelia Opie's engagement with the worldly values of London society. But after her father's prolonged illness and subsequent embracing of the Christian faith, Opie followed suit and prepared to abide by the simple values and plain faith of the Quakers. Among her most difficult challenges was conforming to the Quaker belief that the writing of fiction was morally suspect, directing the mind and heart away from truth by indulging in what might be termed untruths or lies. So Opie abandoned a completed manuscript for a novel entitled *The Painter and His Wife*, and turned her attention instead to writing more fact-based didactic works, including *Illustrations of Lying in all its Branches* (1825) and *Detraction Displayed* (1828). She published one volume of poetry, *Lays for the*

Dead (1834), a collection of elegies as fully sentimental as her earlier work in tone, but devoted to the lament for actual living rather than fictional figures.

Although she now composed within more circumscribed bounds, Opie continued to see herself as a writer, and to value the fictional works of her youth, and in 1843, at the age of seventy-three, she returned to *The Father and Daughter* one final time. She had been approached by a London printer, William Grove, who was interested in re-issuing some of her tales.[1] By now living in straitened circumstances, Opie hoped for some financial reward from this transaction, but above all she was eager to correct some details in her early work—primarily to remove any profanity from the dialogue. Her participation in the project aroused harsh criticism from her old friend Joseph John Gurney, but her response to his comments has left one of the clearest records of Opie's commitment to the moral value of her work and to herself as a writer. She begins by apologizing for "hav[ing] given pain to thee by permitting to be done what I felt was an act of *justice to myself*," but soon launches into an impassioned defence not only of her own work but of fiction in general:

> I never thought, nor do I *now think* that in doing this I have *at all* violated my engagements as a Friend—I promised never to write things of the same sort again, nor have I done so—but though I freely admit that *novel-reading* ... has a tendency to make young persons disinclined to serious, & more instructive reading ... I never said, because I never *thought*[,] that *works of fiction* were *never to be read*—on the contrary, I believe simple moral tales the very best means of instructing the young & the *poor*—else *why* do the pious of all sects & beliefs, spread *tracts* in stories over the world. And why did the blessed Saviour teach in parables? (Amelia Opie to Joseph Gurney, 23 February 1844, Appendix A).

---

1 Around the same time she playfully wrote to her friend Simon Wilkin, a Norwich publisher, "*All* my *egregiously sublime & delightful* works for such they *undoubtedly* are, are quite out of print in England" (Amelia Opie to Simon Wilkin, 18 January 1843, Appendix A), and she seeks his aid in arranging the details of this new edition.

Yet she prizes her works for something beyond their moral value—she acknowledges the enormous degree to which her own identity is connected to them: "These books, however full of errors, will survive me, and in many languages, (some of them at least) and when a few weeks (now months) ago, I thought my days were numbered, I remembered with comfort that I had nearly executed the task I had undertaken—& felt no remorse of conscience for having assisted the printer nor did I think myself responsible to any human being for having undertaken the task. I considered myself responsible to my God & my conscience" (Amelia Opie to Joseph Gurney, 23 February 1844, Appendix A).

When Amelia Opie died in December 1853, periodicals across Britain remembered her as one of the most celebrated writers of the century, and the work they remembered her for was *The Father and Daughter*. *The Leisure Hour* wrote: "In 1801, Mrs. Opie published her celebrated tale of 'The Father and Daughter,' and it is considered on the whole to have been her best work; indeed, there are one or two touching scenes in the book, which would of themselves have immortalised the author had she never written another line" ("Mrs. Opie" 634). *The Athenaeum* stated: "She was sought and prized as one of the women of genius of her time,—and the list then included HARRIET LEE, CHARLOTTE SMITH, Madame D'ARBLAY, Mrs. INCHBALD, the PORTERS, Lady MORGAN, Miss EDGEWORTH, and ANNE RADCLIFFE: —most of these pioneers if not positive inventors in fiction,—who opened in Romance, in historical and supernatural, in Domestic fiction, and in the National tale,—paths that the proudest men (as Sir WALTER SCOTT bears witness for us) were only too glad to follow further...." It went on to say of her works: "They won for their authoress a Continental reputation, and one of them, *The Father and Daughter*, in its translated and dramatized form as the opera 'Agnese' with PAER's expressive music ... and AMBROGETTI's harrowing personation of the principal character, will connect AMELIA OPIE's name with opera so long as the chronicles of music shall be written" ("Amelia Opie" 1483).

Yet by the time of her death in mid-century, literary tastes had already shifted dramatically, and Opie was remembered as an index to past notions of excellence, not present standards. The same *Athenaeum* obituary that asserted her importance offered explanations to a generation unable to understand Opie's popularity as a writer: "Were they published now, Mrs. Opie's 'Simple Tales,' her 'Tales of the Heart,' her 'Father and Daughter' (the most popular, perhaps, of her novels) would be thought to want both body and soul;—to be poor as regards invention, slight in manner—unreal in sentiment,—and so they are, if they be tried against the best writings by the Authors of 'The Admiral's Daughter,' and 'Mary Barton,' and 'Jane Eyre.' In their day, however, they were cherished, and wept over, as moving and truthful." As literary tastes moved away from the literature of sensibility and prized instead the social realism of writers such as George Eliot, Elizabeth Gaskell, and Charlotte Brontë, the works of Amelia Opie became the subject of nostalgic remembrance sustained by the memory of a literary celebrity. However, growing recent interest in the literature of sensibility calls for renewed examination of works such as *The Father and Daughter*, works which captured and represented for their age the culture of sensibility.

Amelia Alderson Opie: A Brief Chronology

1769   Birth of Amelia Alderson (12 November), only child of James and Amelia (Briggs) Alderson, in Norwich, England.

1784   Death of her mother (31 December); at fifteen Amelia enters society and assumes control of her father's household.

1786   Writes *Adelaide*, a five-act play; wide social circle includes the radical Mrs. John Taylor, as well as literary figures Dr. Aiken and his sister, Anna Letitia Barbauld, and the Quaker Gurney family, including John Joseph, who was to become an important figure later in the nineteenth century, and Elizabeth, who after her marriage to Joseph Fry became a leading advocate for prison reform; meets Sarah Siddons, the actress, in Norwich (September).

1789   French Revolution begins (14 July), greeted enthusiastically by Norwich circle.

1790   Anonymous publication of *Dangers of Coquetry*, her first novel, by W. Lane (Minerva Press).

1791   Production of *Adelaide* (Jan 4 and 6) at private theatre in Norwich, with Amelia Alderson playing the lead role.

1793   Introduction to Godwin at a dinner given in his honour by her father in Norwich.

1794   Visit to London where she spends time with Godwin and attends treason trial of Horne Tooke, Thomas Holcroft, Thomas Hardy, and John Thelwall; she and her father consider emigrating to America should the trial end in conviction.

1795   Publication of 15 poems in the Norwich *Cabinet* (Vols I-III), a radical periodical; publication of song "My Love to War is Going," music by Edward Smith Biggs and words by Amelia Alderson (an early example of a collaboration that was to continue for many years).

1796   Introduction to Mary Wollstonecraft; close friendship ensues in spite of rumours of Godwin's attachment to Amelia; energetically engaged in the writing of two comedies for the stage for which she seeks criticism from both Godwin and Wollstonecraft (neither apparently was produced).

1797   Death of Wollstonecraft, cooling of connection with Godwin.

1798   Marriage to painter John Opie (8 May); social circle includes women of fashion such as Lady Cork and Lady Caroline Lamb, artists such as Northcote, and writers such as Elizabeth Inchbald.

1799   Publication of 4 poems in first *Annual Anthology*, favourably reviewed.

1800   About this time AAO emerges as skilled amateur singer and author of a number of songs published for Robert Birchall's Musical Circulating Library.

1801   Publication of *The Father and Daughter, a Tale, in Prose: with an Epistle from The Maid of Corinth to her Lover; and Other Poetical Pieces* by Longman and Rees; 2nd edition (of the prose tale only, but advertising a volume of poems soon to be published); engraved portrait (Mackenzie after John Opie) with "Memoirs of Mrs. Opie" published in *The Lady's Monthly Museum* (March).

1802   Publication of *Poems* and *An Elegy to the Memory of the Late Duke of Bedford*; songs solicited by Thompson for his collection of Welsh airs.

1803   Engraved portrait (Ridley after John Opie) with biographical notice published in *European Magazine* (May).

1805   Publication of *Adeline Mowbray: or, The Mother and Daughter* (Jan.), a novel based in part on the relationship between Godwin and Wollstonecraft.

1806   Publication of *Simple Tales*, a collection of stories.

1807   Death of John Opie (9 April), buried in St. Paul's (20 April); AAO returns to Norwich where she edits her husband's lectures delivered to the Royal Academy just prior to his death; publication of *The Warrior's Return and Other Poems*; engraved portrait (Hopwood after John Opie) with "Memoir" attributed to Mrs. Taylor published in *The Cabinet* (June).

1809　Publication of John Opie's *Lectures on Painting*, with a Memoir by AAO; Paër creates opera *Agnese*, libretto by Luigi Buonovoglia based on Filippo Casari's Italian adaptation of *The Father and Daughter*, *Agnese di Fizendry*.

1810　Production of *Twenty Years Ago! a new melodramatic entertainment in two acts*, based on "Love and Duty" from *Simple Tales*; music by Pocock, libretto by Welsh.

1812　Publication of *Temper; or, Domestic Scenes: A Tale*; quotes four lines from William Hayley's *The Triumph of Temper* (1781) leading to sustained correspondence.

1813　Publication of *Tales of Real Life*.

1814　Leaves Unitarian church and begins attending Quaker services.

1815　Production of *Smiles and Tears*, a play by Mrs. Kemble based on *The Father and Daughter* (15 December); production of *The Noble Outlaw*, a comic opera by Henry Rowley Bishop with songs by Opie: one lyric, "The Pilgrim of Love," republished many times throughout the century; engraved portrait (Heath after John Opie) published in *Lady's Magazine* (October); introduced to Sir Walter Scott, who tells her he wept on reading *The Father and Daughter*.

1816　Publication of *Valentine's Eve*.

1817　*L'Agnese* first produced in London; engraved portrait (Hopwood after John Opie) published in *The Ladies' Monthly Museum* (February).

1818　Publication of *New Tales*, including "The Ruffian Boy," which is later adapted for the stage by Edward Fitzball and by Thomas Dibden.

1820　Publication of *Tales of the Heart*; production of *The Lear of Private Life; or, The Father and Daughter*, a play adapted from AAO's novel by William Moncrieff.

1821 Engraved portrait (Cooper after John Opie) with "Biographical Sketches of Illustrious and Distinguished Characters: Mrs. Opie" published in *La Belle Assemblée* (January).

1822 Publication of *Madeline: A Tale* (her last novel).

1825 Application accepted for admission to The Society of Friends (11 August), cementing a long friendship with the Gurney family; because of Quaker prohibitions concerning the worldliness of fiction, AAO shifts to more didactic works; publishes *Lying in All its Branches*, as well as *Tales of the Pemberton Family* (for children); death of her father, James Alderson (20 October).

1826 Publication of *The Black Man's Lament* (anti-slavery poem for children).

1828 Publication of *Detraction Displayed*.

1829 Visit to Paris: profile medal sculpted by Pierre Jean David (David d'Angers), entertained in social circle of Lafayette; AAO records that she was "courted for … [her] *past*, not … [her] *recent* writings"; she returned again the following year.

1831 Production of "The Ruffian Boy: a melodrama in two acts" by Thomas Dibden, based on the story from *New Tales*.

1834 Publication of *Lays for the Dead*.

1835 Visit to the Continent.

1839 "The Novice: A True Story" solicited for *Finden's Tableaux*, ed. M.R. Mitford.

1840 Attends Anti-Slavery Convention in London, sits for Benjamin Haydon for his group portrait of the convention; publication of "Recollections of Days in Belgium" in *Tait's Edinburgh Magazine*.

1841 Publication of "Reminiscences of an Authoress" in *Chambers's Edinburgh Journal*.

1842 Approached by printers Grove and Sons for permission to reprint her works, which she grants despite Quaker prohibitions on involvement with fiction.

1843 Publication of revised edition of *The Father and*

Daughter (Longman and Grove).

1844   Publication of revised edition of *Adeline Mowbray* (Longman and Grove).

1853   Death of AAO (2 December) in Norwich; subsequent burial in her father's grave in the Friends' Cemetery.

A Note on the Texts

The Father and Daughter

The present text is based on the first edition of *The Father and Daughter* as published by Longman and Rees in 1801 in one volume. The first edition also contained a collection of poems included here. Further editions of the work appeared regularly over the next two decades, with a second appearing in 1801, a third in 1802, a fourth in 1804, a fifth in 1806, a sixth in 1809, a seventh in 1813, an eighth in 1819, and a ninth in 1825 (although we have been unable to locate a copy of this edition). Starting with the second edition, Longman included a frontispiece for the tale designed by John Opie, and the poems were removed to be included in a separate volume, entitled *Poems.* Opie's poems were nearly as popular as *The Father and Daughter*, appearing in at least six editions (1802, 1803, 1804, 1806, 1808, and 1811). The text of *The Father and Daughter* varies little from edition to edition with only minor corrections and variations in spelling, punctuation, or wording (see Appendix K).

In 1843, "A New and Illustrated Edition" of *The Father and Daughter* appeared with Longman's name on the title page, but Opie's correspondence (included in Appendix A) indicates that its appearance was part of a scheme by the publishers Grove and Sons to reprint all of her works (which had by this time gone out of print in England). A complete reprint of Opie's works appears never to have been completed, but *The Father and Daughter, Adeline Mowbray,* and a group of small volumes of Opie's tales were produced by Grove and Sons throughout the mid-1840s.

This edition of the 1801 text is based on a copy in the Norwich Public Library. In reproducing the text we have modernized the use of the long "s" and have normalized the positioning and use of quotation marks. Original spellings have been retained.

Dangers of Coquetry

Dangers of Coquetry was produced by W. Lane in two volumes in 1790. No other editions of the novel were produced, and it is among the rarest of Opie's works. The present edition is based on the copy in the British Library. Spelling has been preserved and the use of quotation marks has been regularized; the long "s" has been modernized throughout.

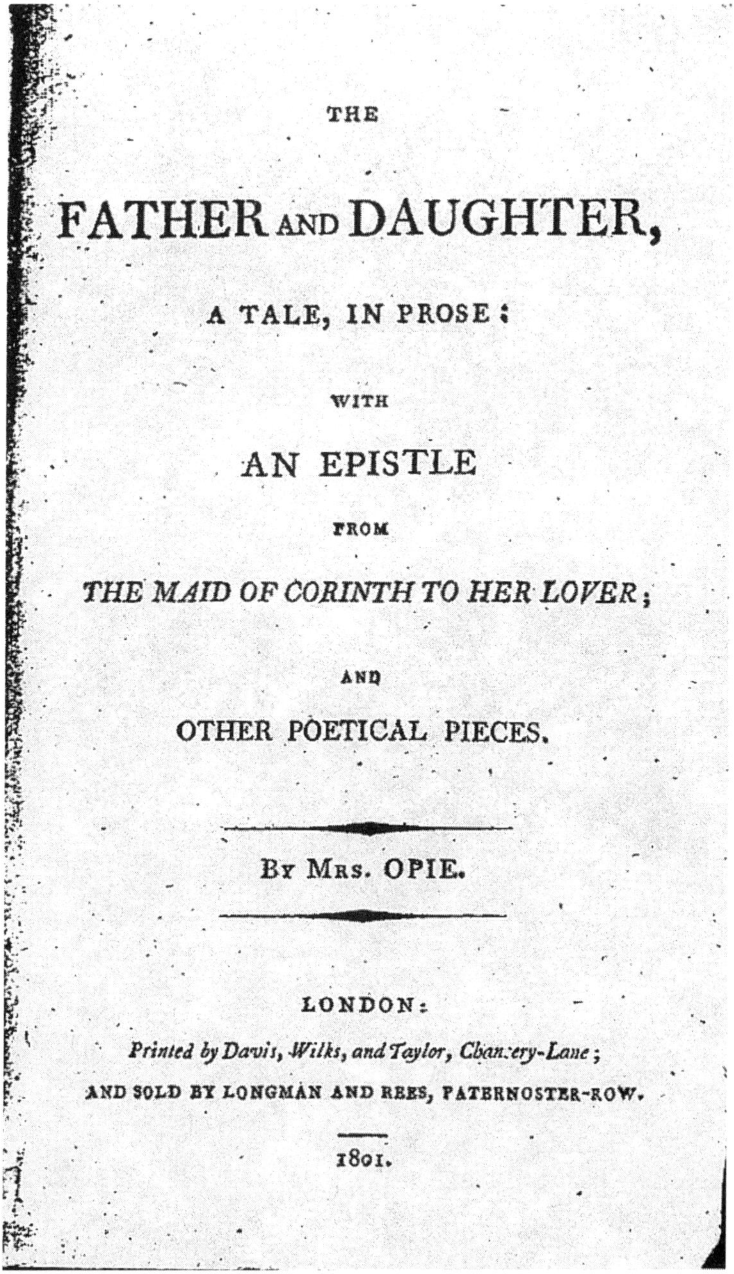

THE

FATHER AND DAUGHTER,

A TALE, IN PROSE:

WITH

AN EPISTLE

FROM

THE MAID OF CORINTH TO HER LOVER;

AND

OTHER POETICAL PIECES.

By Mrs. OPIE.

LONDON:

Printed by Davis, Wilks, and Taylor, Chancery-Lane;
AND SOLD BY LONGMAN AND REES, PATERNOSTER-ROW.

1801.

Figure 2: Title page, first edition of *The Father and Daughter* (1801).
Reproduced by permission of the British Library.

Page 105.

Designed by Opie R.A.   Engraved by Reynolds.

—————— she saw that he had drawn the shape of a coffin and was then writing on the lid the name of Agnes. ——————

Published May 1803, by Longman, Hurst, Rees, Orme, & Brown.

Figure 3: Frontispiece to the second edition of *The Father and Daughter* (1801); designed by John Opie and engraved by Frederick Reynolds. Reproduced by permission of the British Library.

THE

FATHER AND DAUGHTER,

A TALE, IN PROSE.

"Thy sweet reviving smiles might cheer despair,
On the pale lips detain the parting breath,
And bid hope blossom in the shades of death."[1]
Mrs. Barbauld.

1801

---

1   Anna Letitia Barbauld, "To Miss R[igby], on her Attendance upon her Mother at Buxton," ll. 20-22.

DEDICATION.

To
Dr ALDERSON, of NORWICH.

DEAR SIR,

In dedicating this Publication to you, I follow in some measure the example of those nations who devoted to their gods the first fruits of the genial seasons which they derived from their bounty.

To you I owe whatever of cultivation my mind has received; and the first fruits of that mind to you I dedicate.

Besides, having endeavoured in "THE FATHER AND DAUGHTER" to exhibit a picture of the most perfect parental affection, to whom could I dedicate it with so much propriety as to you, since, in describing a good father, I had only to delineate my own?

Allow me to add, full of gratitude for years of tenderness and indulgence on your part, but feebly repaid even by every possible sentiment of filial regard on mine, that the satisfaction I shall experience if my Publication be favourably received by the world, will not proceed from the mere gratification of my self-love, but from the conviction I shall feel that my success as an Author is productive of pleasure to you.

AMELIA OPIE.

BERNERS STREET,

1800.

TO THE READER.

It is not without considerable apprehension that I offer myself as an avowed Author at the bar of public opinion, ... and that apprehension is heightened by its being the general custom to give indiscriminately the name of NOVEL to every thing in Prose that comes in the shape of a Story, however simple it be in its construction, and humble in its pretensions.

By this means, the following Publication is in danger of being tried by a standard according to which it was never intended to be made, and to be criticized for wanting those merits which it was never meant to possess.

I therefore beg leave to say, in justice to myself, that I know "THE FATHER AND DAUGHTER" is wholly devoid of those attempts at strong character, comic situation, bustle, and variety of incident, which constitute a NOVEL, and that its highest pretensions are, to be a SIMPLE, MORAL TALE.

THE FATHER AND DAUGHTER. A TALE.

THE night was dark — the wind blew keenly over the frozen and rugged heath, when Agnes, pressing her moaning child to her bosom, was travelling on foot to her father's habitation.

"Would to God[1] I had never left it!" she exclaimed, as home and all its enjoyments rose in fancy to her view: — and I think my readers will be ready to join in the exclamation, when they hear the poor wanderer's history.

Agnes Fitzhenry was the only child of a respectable merchant in a country town, who, having lost his wife when his daughter was very young, resolved for her sake to form no second connection. To the steady, manly affection of a father, Fitzhenry joined the fond anxieties and endearing attentions of a mother; and his parental care was amply repaid by the love and amiable qualities of Agnes. He was not rich, yet the profits of his trade were such as to enable him to bestow every possible expense on his daughter's education, and to lay up a considerable sum yearly for her future support: whatever else he could spare from his own absolute wants, he expended in procuring comforts and pleasures for her. — "What an excellent father that man is!" was the frequent exclamation among his acquaintance — "And what an excellent child he has! well may he be proud of her," was as commonly the answer to it. Nor was this to be wondered at: — Agnes united to extreme beauty of face and person every accomplishment that belongs to her own sex, and a great degree of that strength of mind and capacity for acquiring knowledge supposed to belong exclusively to the other.

For this combination of rare qualities Agnes was admired; — for her sweetness of temper, her willingness to oblige, her seeming unconsciousness of her own merits, and her readiness to commend the merits of others, — for these still rarer quali-

---

1 The phrase "to God" was omitted in 1843. In this last edition in her lifetime, Opie authorized specific changes, writing to her friend Joseph Gurney that she had "the pleasure of knowing that all mention of the great Name, & other blemishes are to be expunged in the new edition" (23 February 1844, Appendix A). For similar changes see Appendix K.

ties, Agnes was beloved: and she seldom formed an acquaintance without at the same time securing a friend.

But short was thy triumph, sweet Agnes, and long was thy affliction![1]

Her father thought he loved her (and perhaps he was right) as never father loved a child before; and Agnes thought she loved him as child never before loved father. — "I will not marry, but live single for my father's sake," she often said;—but she altered her determination when her heart, hitherto unmoved by the addresses of the other sex, was assailed by an officer in the Guards who came to recruit in the town in which she resided.

Clifford, as I shall call him, had not only a fine figure and graceful address, but talents rare and various, and powers of conversation so fascinating, that the woman he had betrayed forgot her wrongs in his presence; and the creditor, who came to dun him for the payment of debts already incurred, went away eager to oblige him by letting him incur still more. — Fatal perversion of uncommon abilities! This man, who might have taught a nation to look up to him as its best pride and prosperity, and its best hope in adversity, made no other use of his talents than to betray the unwary of both sexes, the one to shame, the other to pecuniary difficulties; and he whose mind was capacious enough to have imagined schemes to aggrandize his native country, the slave of sordid selfishness, never looked beyond his own temporary and petty benefit, and sat down contented with the achievements of the day, if he had over-reached a credulous tradesman, or beguiled an unsuspecting woman.

But to accomplish even these paltry triumphs, great knowledge of the human heart was necessary — a power of discovering the prevailing foible in those on whom he had designs, and of converting their imagined security into their real danger. He soon discovered that Agnes, who was rather inclined to doubt her possessing in an uncommon degree the good qualities which she really had, valued herself, with not unusual blindness,

---

1 This sentence was omitted in the second and subsequent editions.

on those which she had not. She thought herself endowed with great power to read the characters of those with whom she associated, when she had even not discrimination enough to understand her own: and, while she imagined that it was not in the power of others to deceive her, she was constantly in the habit of deceiving herself.

Clifford was not slow to avail himself of this weakness in his intended victim; and, while he taught her to believe none of his faults had escaped her observation, with hers he had made himself thoroughly acquainted. — But not content with making her faults subservient to his views, he pressed her virtues also into his service; and her affection for her father, that strong hold, secure in which, Agnes would have defied the most violent assaults of temptation, he contrived should be the means of her defeat.[1]

I have been thus minute in detailing the various and seducing powers which Clifford possessed, not because he will be a principal figure in my narrative, for, on the contrary, the chief characters in it are the father and daughter, but in order to excuse as much as possible the strong attachment which he excited in Agnes.

"Love," says Mrs. Inchbald,[2] whose accurate acquaintance with human nature can be equalled only by the humour with which she describes its follies, and the unrivalled pathos with which she exhibits its distresses — "Love, however rated by many as the chief passion of the heart, is but a poor dependant, a retainer on the other passions — admiration, gratitude, respect, esteem, pride in the object;—divest the boasted sensation of these, and it is no more than the impression of a twelvemonth, by courtesy, or vulgar error, called love."[3] — And of all these ingredients was the passion of Agnes composed. For the graceful person and manner of Clifford she felt admiration, and her gratitude was excited by her observing that, while he was

---

1 See Hannah More's description of the "Danger of Sentimental or Romantic Connexions" and the wiles of the seducing lover (Appendix H.1).
2 Elizabeth Inchbald (1753-1821): actress, dramatist, novelist. She was introduced to Opie by William Godwin.
3 Elizabeth Inchbald, *Nature and Art* 1:142.

an object of attention to every one wherever he appeared, his attentions were exclusively directed to herself; and that he who, from his rank and accomplishments, might have laid claim to the hearts even of the brightest daughters of fashion, in the gayest scenes of the metropolis, seemed to have no higher ambition than to appear amiable in the eyes of Agnes, the humble toast of an obscure country town; while his superiority of understanding, and brilliancy of talents, called forth her respect, and his apparent virtues her esteem; and when to this high idea of the qualities of the man, was added a knowledge of his high birth and great expectations, it is no wonder that she also felt the last mentioned, and often perhaps the greatest, excitement to love, "pride in the object."

When Clifford began to pay those marked attentions to Agnes, which ought always on due encouragement from the woman to whom they are addressed to be followed by an offer of marriage, he contrived to make himself as much disliked by the father, as admired by the daughter; yet his management was so artful, that Fitzhenry could not give a sufficient reason for his dislike; he could only declare its existence; and for the first time in her life, Agnes learned to think her father unjust, and capricious. Thus, while Clifford ensured an acceptance of his addresses from Agnes, he at the same time secured a rejection of them from Fitzhenry; and this was the object of his wishes, as he had a decided aversion to marriage, and knew besides that marrying Agnes would disappoint all his ambitious prospects in life, and bring on him the eternal displeasure of his father.

At length, after playing for some time with her hopes and fears, Clifford requested Fitzhenry to sanction with his approbation his addresses to his daughter; and Fitzhenry, as he expected, coldly and firmly declined the honour of his alliance. But when Clifford mentioned, as if unguardedly, that he hoped to prevail on his father to approve the marriage after it had taken place, if not before, Fitzhenry proudly told him he thought his daughter much too good to be smuggled into the family of any one; while Clifford, piqued in his turn at the warmth of Fitzhenry's expressions, and the dignity of his manner, left him, exulting secretly in the consciousness that he had his revenge—for he knew the heart of Agnes was irrecoverably his.

Agnes heard from her lover that his suit was rejected, with agonies as violent as he appeared to feel. — "What!" exclaimed she, "can that affectionate father, who has till now anticipated my wishes, disappoint me in the wish dearest to my heart?"[1] In the midst of her first agitation her father entered the room, and, with "a countenance more in sorrow than in anger,"[2] began to expostulate with her on the impropriety of the connection which she was desirous of forming. — He represented to her the very slender income Clifford possessed—the inconvenience to which an officer's wife is exposed, and the little chance there is for a man's making a constant and domestic husband who has been brought up in an idle profession, and accustomed to habits of intemperance, expense, and irregularity: —

"But above all," said he, "how is it possible that you could ever condescend to accept the addresses of a man whose father, he himself owns, will never sanction them with his approbation?" — Alas! Agnes could plead no excuse but that she was in love, and she had too much sense to urge such a plea to her father — "Believe me," he continued, "I speak thus from the most disinterested consideration of your interest; for, painful as the idea of parting with you must be to me, I am certain I should not shrink from the bitter trial, whenever my misery would be your happiness (here his voice faltered); but in this case I am certain, that by refusing my consent to your wishes I ensure your future comfort; and in a cooler moment you will be of the same opinion." Agnes shook her head, and turned away in tears. "Nay, hear me, my child," resumed Fitzhenry, "you know I am no tyrant; and if, after time and absence have been tried in order to conquer your unhappy passion, it remain unchanged, then, in defiance of my judgement, I will consent to your marriage with Mr. Clifford, provided his father consent likewise; for, unless he does, I never will: — and if you have not pride and resolution enough to be the guardian of your own

---

1 Familial conflict over marriage is a recurring theme. Hannah More notes, "Fathers *have flinty hearts*, is an expression worth an empire"; see Appendix H.1.
2 Shakespeare, *Hamlet*, Act 1, sc.2, l.232.

dignity, I must guard it for you; but I am sure there will be no need of my interference; and Agnes Fitzhenry would scorn to be clandestinely the wife of any man."

Agnes thought so too—and Fitzhenry spoke this in so mild and affectionate a manner, and in a tone so expressive of suppressed wretchedness, which the bare idea of parting with her had occasioned him, that, for the moment, she forgot every thing but her father, and the vast debt of love and gratitude she owed him, and throwing herself into his arms she protested her entire, nay cheerful, acquiescence in his determination.— "Promise me, then," replied Fitzhenry, "that you will never see Mr. Clifford more, if you can avoid it—he has the tongue of Belial,[1] and if—" Here Agnes indignantly interrupted him with reproaches for supposing her so weak as to be in danger of being seduced into a violation of her duty; and so strong were the terms in which she expressed herself, that her father entreated her pardon for having thought such a promise necessary.

The next day Clifford did not venture to call at the house, but he watched the door till he saw Agnes come out alone, and then having joined her, he obtained from her a full account of the conversation she had had with Fitzhenry; when, to her great surprise, he drew conclusions from it, which she had never imagined possible. He saw, or pretended to see, in Fitzhenry's rejection of his offers, not merely a dislike of her marrying him, but a design to prevent her marrying at all; and as a design like this was selfish in the last degree, and ought not to be complied with, he thought it would be kinder in her to disobey her father, and marry the man of her heart, than, by

---

1   In Milton's *Paradise Lost,* Book II, ll.108-118, Belial is the most plausible of Satan's followers:

> On the other side uprose
> Belial, in act more graceful and humane;
> A fairer person lost not heaven: he seemed
> For dignity composed and high exploit:
> But all was false and hollow; though his tongue
> Dropt manna, and could make the worse appear
> The better reason, to perplex and dash
> Maturest counsels....

indulging him once, flatter him with the hope she would do it again, till by this means the day of her marrying, when it came at last, would burst on him with tenfold horrors. — The result of this specious reasoning, enforced by tears, caresses, and protestations, was, that she had better go off to Scotland immediately with him, and trust to time, necessity, and their parents' affection, to secure their forgiveness.[1]

Agnes the first time heard these arguments, and this proposal, with the disdain they merited; but, alas! she did not resolve to avoid all opportunity of hearing them a second time: but, vain of the resolution she had shown on this first trial, she was not averse to stand another, delighted to find that she had not overrated her strength, when she reproached Fitzhenry for his want of confidence in it. The consequence is obvious: — again and again she heard Clifford argue in favour of an elopement; and, though she still retained virtue sufficient to withhold her consent, she every day saw fresh reason to believe he argued on good grounds, and to think that parent whose whole study had been, till now, her gratification, was, in this instance at least, the slave of unwarrantable selfishness. —

At last, finding neither time, reflection, nor even a temporary absence, had the slightest effect on her attachment, but that it gained new force every day, she owned that nothing but the dread of making her father unhappy, withheld her from listening to Clifford's proposal: —'twas true, she said, pride forbade it, but the woman who could listen to the dictates of pride, knew nothing of love but the name. — This was the moment for Clifford to urge more strongly than ever that the elopement was the most effectual means of securing her father's happiness, as well as her own; till at last her judgement became the dupe of her wishes; and, fancying she was following the dictates of filial affection, when she was in reality the helpless victim of

---

1 Clifford is suggesting an elopement to Scotland. Lord Hardwicke's Marriage Act of 1753 set more rigorous conditions for legal marriage in England, in part to put an end to the practice of clandestine marriage. As Lawrence Stone notes, "From now on, the only recourse for runaway couples defying their parents was the long and expensive flight to Scotland, especially to Gretna Green, where the new Marriage Act did not apply, and where there sprang up a new trade in commercialized marriages on the spot" (55).

passion, she yielded to the persuasions of a villain, and set off with him to Scotland.

When Fitzhenry first heard of her flight, he sat for hours absorbed in a sort of dumb anguish, far more eloquent than words. At length he burst into exclamations against her ingratitude for all the love and care he had bestowed on her; and the next moment he exclaimed, with tears of tenderness, "Poor girl! she is not used to commit faults; how miserable she will be when she comes to reflect! and how she will long for my forgiveness! and, O yes! I am sure I shall long as ardently to forgive her!" — Then his arms were folded in fancy round his child, whom he pictured to himself confessing her marriage to him, and upon her knees imploring his pardon. — But day after day came, and no letter from the fugitives, acknowledging their error, and begging his blessing on their union — for no union had taken place. When Clifford and Agnes had been conveyed as fast as four horses could carry them one hundred miles towards Gretna-green, and had ordered fresh horses, Clifford started, as he looked at his pocket-book, and, with well-dissembled consternation, exclaimed "What can we do? I have brought the wrong pocket-book, and have not money enough to carry us above a hundred and odd miles further on the North road!" — Agnes was overwhelmed with grief and apprehension at that information, but did not for an instant suspect the fact was otherwise than as Clifford stated it to be.

As I before observed, Agnes piqued herself on her knowledge of characters, and she judged of them frequently by the rules of physiognomy — she had studied voices too, as well as countenances; — was it possible, then, that Agnes, who had from Clifford's voice and countenance pronounced him all that was ingenuous, honourable, and manly, could suspect him capable of artifice? could she, retracting her pretensions to penetration, believe she had put herself in the power of a designing libertine? No — vanity and self-love forbade this salutary suspicion to enter her imagination; and, without one scruple, or one reproach, she acceded to the plan Clifford proposed, as the only one likely to obviate their difficulties, and procure them most speedily an opportunity of solemnizing their marriage.[1]

Deluded Agnes! you might have known that the honourable lover is as fearful to commit the honour of his mistress even in appearance, as she herself can be; that his care and anxiety to screen her even from the breath of suspicion are ever on the watch; and that therefore, had Clifford's designs been such as virtue would approve, he would have put it out of the power of accident to prevent your immediate marriage, and expose your fair fame to the whisper of calumny.[2]

To London they set forward, and were driven to a hotel in the Adelphi,[3] whence Clifford went out in search of lodgings; and, having met with convenient apartments at the west end of the town, he conducted to them the pensive, and already repentant Agnes. — "Under what name and title," said Agnes, "am I to be introduced to the woman of the house?" — "As my intended wife," cried her lover, pressing her to his bosom, — "and in a few days — though to me they will appear ages — you will give me a right to call you by that tender name." — "In a few days!" exclaimed Agnes, withdrawing from his embrace, "cannot the marriage take place tomorrow?" — "Impossible!" replied Clifford, "you are not of age — I can't procure a license — but I have taken these lodgings for a month — we will have the banns published, and be married at the parish church."[4]

To this arrangement, against which her delicacy and every feeling revolted, Agnes would fain have objected in the strongest manner; but, unable to urge any reasons for her objec-

---

1 Clifford's seductive qualities mirror those in Hannah More's account of Rousseau's literary persuasive powers; see Appendix H.4.

2 Such care is needed because the reputation of an unmarried woman is "very precarious": see Macaulay, Appendix H.2.

3 A development of 24 terraced houses designed and built by the Adam brothers in 1772, between the Strand and the Thames.

4 Hardwicke's Marriage Act established the legal age of consent as twenty-one: no private marriage of people under that age was legal without the consent of their parents or guardians. Agnes and Clifford can marry in England only by making public their intent before the community by having it announced in the local church; this is called "reading the banns."

tion, except such as seemed to imply distrust of her own virtue, she submitted, in mournful silence, to the plan; and, with a heart then for the first time tortured with a sense of degradation, she took possession of her apartment, and Clifford returned to his hotel, meditating with savage delight on the success of his plans, and on the triumph which, he fancied, awaited him.

Agnes passed the night in sleepless agitation, now forming and now rejecting schemes to obviate the danger which must accrue to her character, if not to her honour, by remaining for a whole month exposed to the seductions of a man, whom she had but too fatally convinced of his power over her heart; and the result of her reflections was, that she should insist on his leaving town, and not returning till he came to lead her to the altar. Happy would it have been for Agnes, had she adhered to this resolution, but vanity and self-confidence again interfered: — "What have I to fear?" said Agnes to herself— "am I so fallen in my own esteem that I dare not expose myself even to a shadow of temptation? — No — I will not think so meanly of my virtue;— the woman that is afraid of being dishonoured is half overcome already; and I will meet with boldness the trials I cannot avoid."

O vanity! thou hast much to answer for! — I am convinced that, were we to trace up to their source all the most painful and degrading events of our lives, we should find most of them to have their origin in the gratified suggestions of vanity.

It is not my intention to follow Agnes through the succession of mortifications, embarrassments, temptations, and struggles, which preceded her undoing (for, secure as she thought herself in her own strength, and the honour of her lover, she became at last a prey to her seducer); it is sufficient that I explain the circumstances which led to her being in a cold winter's night houseless, and unprotected, a melancholy wanderer towards the house of her father.

Before the expiration of the month, Clifford had triumphed over the virtue of Agnes, and soon after he received orders to join his regiment, as it was going to be sent on immediate service. — "But you will return to me before you embark, in order to make me your wife?" said the half distracted Agnes; "you will not leave me to shame as well as misery?" Clifford promised every thing she wished; and Agnes tried to lose the pangs of parting, in anticipation of the joy of his return. But on the very day that Agnes expected him, she received a letter from him, saying that he was under sailing orders, and to see her again before the embarkation was impossible.

To do Clifford justice, he in this instance told truth; and, as he really loved Agnes as well as a libertine can love, he felt the agitation and distress which his letter expressed; though, had he returned to her, he had an excuse ready prepared for delaying the marriage.

Words can but ill describe the situation of Agnes on the receipt of this letter — The return of Clifford was not to be expected of months at least; and perhaps he might never return! — The thought of his danger was madness: — but when she reflected that she should in all probability be a mother before she became a wife, she rolled herself on the floor[1] in a transport of frantic anguish, and implored Heaven in mercy to put an end to her existence. — "O! my dear, injured father!" she exclaimed, "I who was once your pride, am now your disgrace! — and that child whose first delight it was to look up in your face, and see your eyes beaming with fondness on her, can now never dare to meet their glance again."

But, though Agnes dared not presume to write to her father till she could sign herself the wife of Clifford, she could not exist without making some secret inquiries concerning his health and spirits; and, before he left her, Clifford recommended a trusty messenger to her for the purpose. — The first account she received was, that Fitzhenry was well; the next, that he was dejected; the three following, that his spirits were growing better — and the last account was, that he was married —

"Married!" cried Agnes, rushing into her chamber, and shutting the door after her, in a manner sufficiently indicative to the messenger of the anguish she hastened from him to conceal — "Married! — Clifford abroad; perhaps at this moment a

---

1 The phrase "she rolled herself on the floor" is omitted in the second and subsequent editions. For a list of similar textual variants see Appendix K.

corpse—and my father married!—What, then, am I? A wretch forlorn, an outcast from society!—no one to love, no one to protect and cherish me! Great God! wilt thou not pardon me if I seek a refuge from my sufferings in the grave?"

Here nature suddenly and powerfully impressed on her recollection that she was about to become a parent; and, falling on her knees, she sobbed out, "What am I? did I ask? I am a mother, and earth still holds me by a tie too sacred to be broken!"—

Then, by degrees, she became calmer, and rejoiced, fervently rejoiced, in her father's second marriage, though she felt it as too convincing a proof how completely he had thrown her from his affections. She knew that his reason for not marrying again was, the fear of a second family's diminishing the strong affection he bore to her—and now it was plain that he married in hopes of losing his affection for her. Still this information removed a load from her mind, by showing her Fitzhenry felt himself capable of receiving happiness from other hands than hers; and she resolved, if she heard he was happy in his change of situation, never to recall to his memory the daughter whom it was so much his interest to forget.

The time of Agnes's confinement now drew near—a time which fills with apprehension even the wife who is soothed and supported by the tender attentions of an anxious husband, and the assiduities of affectionate relations and friends, and who knows that the child she is about to present them with will at once gratify their affections and their pride—What then must have been the sensations of Agnes at a moment so awful and dangerous as this!—Agnes, who had no husband to soothe her by his anxious inquiries, no relations or friends to cheer her drooping soul by the expressions of sympathy, and whose child, instead of being welcomed by an exulting family, must be, as well as its mother, a stranger even to its nearest relation!

But, in proportion to her trials, seemed to be Agnes's power of rising superior to them; and, after enduring her sufferings with a degree of fortitude and calmness that astonished the mistress of the house, whom compassion had induced to attend on her, she gave birth to a lovely boy—and from that moment, though she rarely smiled, and never saw any one but her kind landlady, her mind was no longer oppressed by the deep gloom she had before laboured under; and when she had heard from Clifford, or of her father's being happy, and clasped her babe to her bosom, Agnes might almost be pronounced cheerful.

After she had been six months a mother, Clifford returned, and in the transport of seeing him safe, Agnes almost forgot she had been anxious and unhappy. Now again was the subject of the marriage resumed; but just as the wedding-day was fixed, Clifford was summoned away to attend his expiring father, and again was Agnes doomed to the tortures of suspense.

After a month's absence Clifford returned, but appeared to labour under a dejection of spirits, which he seemed studious to conceal from her. Alarmed and terrified at an appearance so unusual, she demanded an explanation, which the consummate deceiver gave at length, after many entreaties on her part, and feigned reluctance on his. He told her his father's illness was occasioned by his having been informed that he was privately married to her, and that he had sent for him to inquire into the truth of the report; and being convinced by his solemn assurance that no marriage had taken place, he had commanded him, unless he wished to kill him, to take a solemn oath never to marry Agnes Fitzhenry without his consent.

"And did you take the oath?" cried Agnes, her whole frame trembling with agitation. — "What could I do?" replied he; "my father's life in evident danger if I refused; besides the dreadful certainty that he would put his threats in execution of cursing me with his dying breath;—and, cruel as he is, Agnes, I could not help feeling he was my father." — "Barbarian!" exclaimed she, "I sacrificed my father to you! — An oath! O God! have you then taken an oath never to be mine?" and, saying this, she fell into a long and deep swoon.

When she recovered, but before she was able to speak, she found Clifford kneeling by her; and, while she was too weak to interrupt him, he convinced her that he did not at all despair of his father's consent to his making her his wife, else, he should have been less willing to give so ready a consent to take the oath imposed on him, even although his father's life depended on it. "Oh! no," replied Agnes, with a bitter smile, "you wrong yourself;— you are too good a son to have been capable of hesitating a moment;— there are few children so bad, so very bad as I am:"—and, bursting into an agony of grief, it was long before the affectionate language and tender caresses of Clifford could restore her to tranquillity.

Another six months elapsed, during which time Clifford kept her hopes alive, by telling her he every day saw fresh signs of his father's relenting in her favour: —"At these times, lead me to him," she would say, "let him hear the tale of my wretchedness; let me say to him, For your son's sake I have left the best of fathers, the happiest of homes, and have become an outcast from society; then would I bid him look at this pale cheek, this emaciated form, proofs of the anguish that is undermining my constitution; and tell him to beware how, by forcing you to withhold from me my right, he made you guilty of murdering the poor deluded wretch, who, till she knew you, never lay down without a father's blessing, or rose but to be welcomed by his smile!"

Clifford had feeling, but it was of that transient sort which never outlived the disappearance of the object that occasioned it. To these pathetic entreaties he always returned affectionate answers, and was often forced to leave the room in order to avoid being too much softened by them; but, by the time he had reached the end of the street, always alive to the impressions of the present moment, the sight of some new beauty, or some old companion, dried up the starting tear, and restored to him the power of coolly considering how he should continue to deceive his miserable victim.

But the time at length arrived when the mask that hid his villainy from her eyes fell off, never to be replaced. As Agnes fully expected to be the wife of Clifford, she was particularly careful to lead a retired life, and not to seem unmindful of her shame, by exhibiting herself at places of public amusement. In vain did Clifford paint to her the charms of the play, the opera, and other places of fashionable resort. "Retirement, with books, music, work, and your society," she used to reply, "are better suited to my taste and situation; and never, but as your wife, will I presume to meet the public eye."

Clifford, though he wished to exhibit his lovely conquest to the world, was obliged to submit to her will in this instance. Sometimes, indeed, Agnes was prevailed on to admit to her table those young men of Clifford's acquaintance who were the most distinguished for their talents and decorum of manners; but this was the only departure he had ever yet prevailed on her to make, from the plan of retirement she had adopted.

One evening, however, Clifford was so unusually urgent with her to accompany him to Drury-lane[1] to see a favourite tragedy, (urging, as an additional motive for her obliging him, that he was going to leave her on the following Monday, in order to attend his father into the country, where he should be forced to remain some time,) that Agnes, unwilling to refuse what he called his parting request, at length complied; Clifford having prevailed on Mrs. Askew, the kind landlady, to accompany them, and having assured Agnes, that, as they should sit in the upper boxes, she might, if she chose it, wear her veil down. — Agnes, in spite of herself, was delighted with the representation — but, as

— "hearts refin'd the sadden'd tint retain,
The sigh is pleasure, and the jest is pain,"[2]

she was desirous of leaving the house before the farce began; yet, as Clifford saw a gentleman in the lower boxes with whom he had business, she consented to stay till he had spoken to him.[3] Soon after she saw Clifford enter the lower box opposite

---

1 The first Theatre Royal Drury Lane was built in 1667, but Opie probably refers to a theatre designed by Henry Holland built there 1791-94.

2 Richard Brinsley Sheridan, "Epilogue" to George Ayscough's play *Semiramis* (1776): "Still hearts refin'd the sadden'd tint retain, / The sigh is pleasure! and the jest is pain!"

3 An evening at the theatre in the eighteenth century usually offered more than one play. The bill might include a tragedy, a farce, and a spectacle of some type. When *The Father and Daughter* was adapted for the stage as *The Lear of Private Life*, the play was offered as part of a full evening of entertainment. Billed as the lead serious

to her; and those who know what it is to love, will not be surprised to hear that Agnes had more pleasure in looking at her lover, and drawing favourable comparisons between him and the gentlemen who surrounded him, than in attending to the farce; and she had been some moments absorbed in this pleasing employment when two gentlemen entered the box where she was, and seated themselves behind her.

"Who is that elegant, fashionable-looking man, my lord, in the lower box just opposite to us?" said one of the gentlemen to the other — "I mean he who is speaking to Captain Mowbray." — "It is George Clifford, of the Guards," replied his lordship, "and one of the cleverest fellows in England, colonel."

Agnes, who had not missed one word of this conversation, now became still more attentive.

"O! I have heard a great deal of him," returned the colonel, "and as much against him as for him." — "Most likely," said his lordship; "For it is a common remark, that if his heart were not as bad as his head is good, he would be an honour to human nature; but I dare say that fellow has ruined more young men, and seduced more young women, than any man of his age (which is only four-and-thirty) in the kingdom."[1]

Agnes sighed deeply, and felt herself attacked by a sort of faint sickness.

"But it is to be hoped he will reform now," observed the colonel: "I hear he is going to be married to miss Sandford, the great city heiress." — "So he is — and Monday is the day fixed for the wedding."

---

drama, the play debuted 27 April 1820: the *Times* announced "This evening, *The Lear of Private Life*, or Father and Daughter, Fitzarden Mr. Booth. After which, 9th time *What are you at, What are you after?*, or, THERE NEVER WAS SUCH TIMES; to conclude with, WINNING A WIFE." By the 8th of May, the comedy supporting bill had shifted to spectacle: the *Times* advertised "the whole to conclude with (1st time) an entirely new melodramatic Pantomime called Fortunio and the Seven Gifted Men, or Harlequin and the Horse" (equestrian entertainments held extraordinary attraction for early nineteenth-century theatre-goers). Four days later the featured concluding piece was "the CRUSADERS, or, Jerusalem Delivered. In the piece will be represented an immense ship 40 feet long, fully manned, struck by a thunderbolt, and sunk completely from the view of the audience."

1   The phrase "For it is a common remark … to human nature, but" is omitted in the second and subsequent editions.

Agnes started;—Clifford himself had told her he must leave her on Monday for some weeks;—and, in breathless expectation, she listened to what followed.

—"But what then?" continued his lordship; "he marries for money merely. The truth is, his father is lately come to a long disputed barony, and with scarcely an acre of land to support the dignity of it—so his son has consented to marry an heiress, in order to make the family rich, as well as noble. You must know, I have my information from the fountain head—Clifford's mother is my relation, and the good woman thought proper to acquaint me in form with the *advantageous* alliance her hopeful son was about to make."

This *confirmation* of the truth of a story, which she till now hoped might be mere report, was more than Agnes could well support; but, made courageous by desperation, she resolved to listen while they continued to talk on this subject. Mrs. Askew, in the mean while, was leaning over the box, too much engrossed by the farce to attend to what was passing behind her. —Just as his lordship concluded the last sentence, Agnes saw Clifford go out with his friend; and she who had but the minute before gazed on him with looks of admiring fondness, now wished, in the bitterness of her soul, that she might never behold him again!

"I never wish," said the colonel, "a match of interest to be a happy one." — "Nor will this be so, depend on it," answered his lordship; "for, besides that miss Sandford is ugly and disagreeable, she has a formidable rival." — "Indeed!" cried the other;— "a favourite mistress, I suppose."

Here the breath of Agnes grew shorter and shorter; she suspected they were going to talk of her; and, under other circumstances, her nice sense of honour would have prevented her attending to a conversation which she was certain was not meant for her ear: but so great was the importance of the present discourse to her future peace and well-being, that it annihilated all sense of impropriety in listening to it.

"Yes, he has a favourite mistress," answered his lordship — "a girl who was worthy a better fate." — "You know her, then?" asked the colonel. — "No," replied he, "by name only; but when I was in the neighbourhood of the town where she lived, I heard continually of her beauty and accomplishments: her name is Agnes Fitz— Fitz—"—"Fitzhenry, I suppose," said the other.—"Yes, that is the name," said his lordship; "how came you to guess it?"—"Because Agnes Fitzhenry is a name I have often heard toasted: she sings well, does she not?"—"She does every thing well," rejoined the other; "and was once the pride of her father, and the town she lived in."

Agnes could scarcely forbear groaning aloud at this faithful picture of what she once was.

"Poor thing!" resumed his lordship—"that ever she should be the victim of a villain! It seems he seduced her from her father's house, under pretence of carrying her to Gretna-green; but, on some infernal plea or another, he took her to London."

Here the agitation of Agnes became so visible as to attract Mrs. Askew's notice; but as she assured her she should be well presently, Mrs. Askew again gave herself up to the illusion of the scene. Little did his lordship think how severely he was wounding the peace of one for whom he felt such compassion.

"You seem much interested about this unhappy girl," said the colonel.—"I am so," replied he, "and full of the subject too; for Clifford's factotum,[1] Wilson, has been with me this morning, and I learnt from him some of his master's tricks, which made me still more anxious about his victim.—It seems she is very fond of her father, though she was prevailed on to desert him, and has never known a happy moment since her elopement, nor could she be easy without making frequent but secret inquiries concerning his health."—"Strange inconsistency!" muttered the colonel.—"This anxiety gave Clifford room to fear that she might at some future moment, if discontented with him, return to her afflicted parent before he was tired of her—so what do you think he did?"—

At this moment Agnes, far more eager to hear what followed than the colonel, turned round, and, fixing her eyes on his lordship with wild anxiety, could scarcely help saying, What did Clifford do, my lord?

—"He got his factotum, the man I mentioned, to personate

___

1 A kind of general servant, responsible for a variety of tasks.

a messenger, and to pretend to have been to her native town, and then he gave her such accounts as were best calculated to calm her anxiety; but the master stroke which secured her remaining with him was, his telling the pretended messenger to inform her that her father was *married again*—though it is more likely, poor unhappy man, that he is dead, than that he is married."

At the mention of this horrible probability, Agnes lost all self-command, and, screaming aloud, fell back on the knees of his astonished lordship, reiterating her cries with all the alarming helplessness of phrensy.

"Turn her out! turn her out!" echoed through the house—for the audience supposed the noise proceeded from some intoxicated and abandoned woman; and a man in the next box struck Agnes a blow on the shoulder, and, calling her by a name too gross to repeat, desired her to leave the house, and act her drunken freaks elsewhere.[1]

Agnes, whom the gentlemen behind were supporting with great kindness and compassion, heard nothing of this speech, save the injurious epithet applied to herself; and alive only to what she thought the justice of it, "Did you hear that?" she exclaimed, starting from his lordship's supporting hand, who with the other was collaring the intoxicated brute that had insulted her—"Did you hear that?—O! God! my brain is on fire!"—Then, springing over the seat, she rushed out of the box, followed by the trembling and astonished Mrs. Askew, who in vain tried to keep pace with the desperate speed of Agnes.

Before Agnes, with all her haste, could reach the bottom of the stairs, the farce ended, and the lobbies began to fill. Agnes pressed forward, when, amongst the crowd, she saw a tradesman who lived near her father's house. — No longer sensible of

---

1 Conduct in early nineteenth-century theatres could be tumultuous, to say the least. The actor Colman commented: "Whence arise the deafening vociferations, when there is a full house, of 'turn him out!' and 'throw him over'? ... Why, during the intervals, is the stage strewed with apples, and orange-peels, accompanied in their descent thither, by the shouts, groans, whistles, catcalls, yells, and screeches of the turbulent assemblage which has so elegantly impelled its vegetable projectiles from the upper regions? ... Why are disturbances in the upper boxes, and lobbies, among blackguards and women of the town, by no means rare?" Nicholl, 1: 9.

shame, for anguish had annihilated it, she rushed towards him, and, seizing his arm, exclaimed, "For the love of God, tell me how my father is!" The tradesman, terrified and astonished at the pallid wildness of her look, so unlike the countenance of successful and contented vice he would have expected to see her wear, replied,— "He is well, poor soul! but—"— "But unhappy, I suppose?" interrupted Agnes: — "Thank God he is well—but is he married?"— "Married!—dear me, no; he is —"— "Do you think he would forgive me?" eagerly rejoined Agnes. — "Forgive you!" answered the man— "How you talk! Belike he might forgive you, if—"— "I know what you would say," interrupted Agnes again, "if I would return. — Enough—enough—God bless you! you have saved me from distraction." —So saying, she ran out of the house; Mrs. Askew having overtaken her, followed by the nobleman and the colonel, who with the greatest consternation had found, from an exclamation of Mrs. Askew's, that the object of their compassion was miss Fitzhenry herself!

What the consequence of his lordship's addressing Agnes might have been, cannot be known: whether he would have offered her the protection of a friend, if she wished to leave Clifford, or whether she would have accepted it, must remain uncertain; but before he could overtake her, Clifford met her, on his return from a neighbouring coffee-house with his companion; and, spite of her struggles and reproaches, which astonished and alarmed him, he, with Mrs. Askew's assistance, forced her into a hackney-coach, and ordered the man to drive home. — No explanation took place during the ride. To all the caresses and questions of Clifford, she returned nothing but passionate exclamations against his perfidy and cruelty. Mrs. Askew thought her insane; Clifford wished to think her so; but his conscience told him that, if by accident his conduct had been discovered to her, there was reason enough for the frantic sorrow he witnessed.

At length they reached their lodgings, which were in Suffolk-street, Charing-cross; and Agnes, having at length obtained some composure, in as few words as possible related the conversation she had overheard. Clifford, as might be expected, denied the truth of what his lordship had advanced;

but it was no longer in his power to deceive the at last awakened penetration of Agnes. — Under his assumed unconcern, she clearly saw the confusion of detected guilt: and, giving utterance in very strong language to the contempt and indignation such complete depravity occasioned her to feel, she provoked Clifford, who was more than half intoxicated, boldly to avow what he was at first eager to deny; and Agnes, who before shuddered at his hypocrisy, was now shocked at his unprincipled daring.

"But what right have you to complain?" added he: "the cheat I put upon you relative to your father, was certainly meant in kindness; and though miss Sandford will have my hand, you alone will ever possess my heart; therefore it was my design to keep you in ignorance of my marriage, and retain you as the greatest of all my worldly treasures. — Plague on his prating lordship! he has destroyed the prettiest arrangement ever made. However, I hope we shall part as good friends as ever."

"Great God!" cried Agnes, raising her tearless eyes to heaven — "is it for a wretch like *this* I have forsaken the best of parents! — But think not, sir," she added, turning with a commanding air towards Clifford, whose temper, naturally warm, the term 'wretch' had not soothed, "think not, fallen as I am, that I will ever condescend to receive protection and support, either for myself or child, from a man whom I know to be a consummate villain. You have made me criminal, but you have not obliterated my horror for crime, and my veneration for virtue — and, in the fulness of my contempt, I inform you, sir, that we shall meet no more."

"Not till to-morrow," said Clifford: — "this is our first quarrel, Agnes; and the quarrels of lovers are only the renewal of love, you know: therefore, leaving this 'bitter, piercing air'[1] to guard my treasure for me till to-morrow, I take my leave, and hope in the morning to find you in better humour."

So saying, he departed, secure, from the inclemency of the weather and darkness of the night, that Agnes would not ven-

---

1   John Furtado, "It was a Winter's Evening" (1798): "Hush, hush my lovely Baby, and warm thee in my breast. / Ah! little thinks thy Father how sadly we're distrest / For cruel as he is, did he know but how we fare, / He'd shield us in his Arms from this bitter, piercing Air" second verse.

ture to go away before the morning, and resolved to return very early in order to prevent her departure, if her threatened resolution were any thing more than the frantic expressions of a disappointed woman. Besides, he knew that at that time she was scantily supplied with money, and that Mrs. Askew dared not furnish her with any for the purpose of leaving him.

But he left not Agnes, as he supposed, to vent her sense of injury in idle grief and inactive lamentation, but to think, to decide, and to act. — And they, indeed, met no more. — What was the rigour of the night to a woman whose heart was torn by all the pangs which convictions, such as those she had lately received, could give? And hastily wrapping up her sleeping boy in a pélisse,[1] which in a calmer moment she would have felt the want of herself, she took him in her arms: then, throwing a shawl over her shoulders, softly unbarred the hall door, and before the noise could have summoned any of the family she was already out of sight. So severe was the weather, that even those accustomed to brave in ragged garments the pelting of the pitiless storm, shuddered as the freezing wind whistled around them, and crept with trembling knees to the wretched hovel that awaited them. But the winter's wind blew unfelt by Agnes: she was alive to nothing but the joy of having escaped from a villain, and the faint hope that she was hastening to obtain, perhaps, a father's forgiveness.

"Thank Heaven!" she exclaimed, as she found herself at the rails along the Green Park — "the air which I breathe here is uncontaminated by his breath!" when, as the watchman called past eleven o'clock, the recollection that she had no place of shelter for the night occurred to her, and at the same instant she remembered that a coach set off at twelve from the White Horse in Piccadilly, that went within twelve miles of her native place. She immediately resolved to hasten thither, and, either in the inside or the outside, to proceed on her journey as far as her finances would admit of, intending to walk the rest of the way. She arrived at the inn just as the coach was setting off, and found, to her great satisfaction, one inside place vacant.[2]

---

1   A woman's long cloak, often with a wide collar and trimmed with fur.
2   Coaches for Oxford and the Western Counties set out from an inn named the White Horse Cellars in Piccadilly. Because passengers also rode outside on the top of the coach, Agnes is justly relieved.

Nothing worth mentioning occurred on the journey. Agnes with her veil drawn over her face, and holding her slumbering boy in her arms, while the incessant shaking of her knee and the piteous manner in which she sighed gave evident marks of the agitation of her mind, might excite in some degree the curiosity of her fellow-travellers, but gave no promise of that curiosity being satisfied, and she was suffered to remain unquestioned and unnoticed. At noon the next day the coach stopped, for the travellers to dine, and stay a few hours to recruit themselves after their labours past, and fortify themselves against those yet to come. Here Agnes, who as she approached nearer home became afraid of meeting some acquaintance, resolved to change her dress, and to equip herself in such a manner as should, while it skreened her from the inclemency of the weather, at the same time prevent her being recognised by any one. Accordingly she exchanged her pélisse, shawl, and a few other things, for a man's great coat, a red cloth cloak with a hood to it, a pair of thick shoes, and some yards of flannel in which she wrapped up her little Edward; and, having tied her straw bonnet under her chin with her veil, she would have looked like a country woman dressed for market, could she have divested herself of a certain delicacy of appearance and gracefulness of manner, the yet uninjured beauties of former days. But when they set off again she became an outside passenger, as she could not afford to continue an inside one; and covering her child up in the red cloak which she wore over her coat, she took her station on the top of the coach with seeming firmness, but a breaking heart.

Agnes expected to arrive within twelve miles of her native place long before it was dark, and reach the place of her destination before bed-time, unknown and unseen: but she was mistaken in her expectations, for the roads had been rendered so rugged by the frost, that it was late in the evening when the coach reached the spot whence Agnes was to commence her walk; and by the time she had eaten her slight repast, and furnished herself with some necessaries to enable her to resist the severity of the weather, she found it was impossible for her to reach her long-forsaken home before day-break.

Still she was resolved to go on: — to pass another day in suspense concerning her father, and her future hopes of his pardon, was more formidable to her than the terrors of undertaking a lonely and painful walk. Perhaps, too, Agnes was not sorry to have a tale of hardship to narrate on her arrival at the house of her nurse, whom she meant to employ as mediator between her and her offended parent.

His child, his penitent child, whom he had brought up with the utmost tenderness, and skreened with unremitting care from the ills of life, returning, to implore his pity and forgiveness, on foot, and unprotected, through all the dangers of trackless paths, and through the horrors of a winter's night, must, she flattered herself, be a picture too affecting for Fitzhenry to think upon without some commiseration; and she hoped he would in time bestow on her his *forgiveness*: — to be admitted to his presence was a favour which she dared not presume either to ask or expect.

But, in spite of the soothing expectation which she tried to encourage, a dread of she knew not what took possession of her mind. — Every moment she looked fearfully around her, and, as she beheld the wintery waste spreading on every side, she felt awe-struck at the desolateness of her situation. The sound of a human voice would, she thought, have been rapture to her ear, but the next minute she believed it would have made her sink in terror to the ground. — "Alas!" she mournfully exclaimed, "I was not always timid and irritable as I now feel—but then I was not always guilty: — O! my child! would I were once more innocent, like thee!" then, in a paroxysm of grief, she bounded forward on her way, as if hoping to escape by speed from the misery of recollection.

Agnes was now arrived at the beginning of a forest, about two miles in length, and within three of her native place. Even in her happiest days she never entered its solemn shade without feeling a sensation of fearful awe; but now that she entered it, leafless as it was, a wandering wretched outcast, a mother without the sacred name of wife, and bearing in her arms the pledge of her infamy, her knees smote each other, and, shuddering as if danger were before her, she audibly implored the protection of Heaven.

At this instant she heard a noise, and casting a startled glance into the obscurity before her, she thought she saw something like a human form running across the road. For a few moments she was motionless with terror; but, judging from the swiftness with which the object disappeared that she had inspired as much terror as she felt, she ventured to pursue her course. She had not gone far when she again beheld the cause of her fear; but, hearing as it moved a noise like the clanking of a chain, she concluded it was some poor animal that had been turned out to graze.

Still, as she gained on the object before her, she was convinced it was a man she beheld; and as she heard the noise no longer, she concluded it had been the result of fancy only; but that, with every other idea, was wholly absorbed in terror when she saw the figure standing still, as if waiting for her approach. — "Yet why should I fear?" she inwardly observed: "it may be a poor wanderer like myself, who is desirous of a companion — if so, I shall rejoice in such a rencontre."

As this reflection passed her mind, she hastened towards the stranger, when she saw him look hastily round him, start, as if he beheld at a distance some object that alarmed him, and then, without taking any notice of her, run on as fast as before. But what can express the horror of Agnes when she again heard the clanking of the chain, and discovered that it hung to the ankle of the stranger! — "Sure he must be a felon," murmured Agnes: — "O! my poor boy! perhaps we shall both be murdered! — This suspense is not to be borne; I will follow him, and meet my fate at once." — Then, summoning all her remaining strength, she followed the alarming fugitive.

After she had walked nearly a mile further, and, as she did not overtake him, had flattered herself he had gone in a contrary direction, she saw him seated on the ground, and, as before, turning his head back with a sort of convulsive quickness; but as it was turned from her, she was convinced she was not the object he was seeking. Of her he took no notice; and her resolution of accosting him failing when she approached, she walked hastily past, in hopes she might escape him entirely.

As she passed she heard him talking and laughing to himself, and thence concluded he was not a felon, but a *lunatic* escaped from confinement. Horrible as this idea was, her fear was so far overcome by pity, that she had a wish to return, and offer him some of the refreshment which she had procured for herself and child, when she heard him following her very fast, and was convinced by the sound, the dreadful sound of his chain, that he was coming up to her.

The clanking of a fetter, when one knows it is fastened round the limbs of a fellow-creature, always calls forth in the soul of sensibility a sensation of horror;[1] what then, at this moment, must have been its effect on Agnes, who was trembling for her life, for that of her child, and looking in vain for a protector round the still, solemn waste! Breathless with apprehension Agnes stopped as the maniac gained upon her, and, motionless and speechless, awaited the consequence of his approach.

"Woman!" said he, in a hoarse, hollow tone — "Woman! do you see them? do you see them?" — "Sir! pray what did you say, sir?" cried Agnes, in a tone of respect, and curtsying as she spoke — for what is so respectful as fear? — "I can't see them," resumed he, not attending to her, "I have escaped them! Rascals! cowards! I have escaped them!" and then he jumped and clapped his hands for joy.

Agnes, relieved in some measure from her fears, and eager to gain the poor wretch's favour, told him she rejoiced at his escape from the rascals, and hoped they would not overtake him: but while she spoke he seemed wholly inattentive, and, jumping as he walked, made his fetter clank in horrid exultation. — The noise at length awoke the child, who, seeing a strange object before him, and hearing a sound so unusual, screamed violently, and hid his face in his mother's bosom.

"Take it away! take it away!" exclaimed the maniac — "I do not like children." — and Agnes, terrified at the thought of what might happen, tried to soothe the trembling boy to rest,

---

1 For Opie's own experience of the sensation produced by clanking fetters see Appendix J.1. The dramatic power of this scene was such that it was adapted with very little change in stage versions: see Appendix E.1.ii and Appendix F.2.

but in vain; the child still screamed, and the angry agitation of the maniac increased. — "Strangle it! strangle it!" he cried, — "do it this moment, or —" Agnes, almost frantic with terror, conjured the unconscious boy, if he valued his life, to cease his cries; and then the next moment she conjured the wretched man to spare her child: but, alas! she spoke to those incapable of understanding her — a child and a madman! — The terrified boy still shrieked, the lunatic still threatened, and, clenching his fist, seized the left arm of Agnes, who with the other attempted to defend her infant from his fury; when, at the very moment that his fate seemed inevitable, a sudden gale of wind shook the leafless branches of the surrounding trees, and the madman, fancying the noise proceeded from his pursuers, ran off with the rapidity of lightning.

Immediately, the child, relieved from the sight and the sound which alarmed it, and exhausted by the violence of its cries, sunk into a sound sleep on the throbbing bosom of its mother. — But, alas! Agnes knew this was but a temporary escape — the maniac might return, and again the child might wake in terrors; and scarcely had the thought passed her mind, when she saw him returning; but, as he walked slowly, the noise was not so great as before.

"I hate to hear children cry," said he as he approached. — "Mine is quiet now," replied Agnes; then, recollecting she had some food in her pocket, she offered some to the stranger in order to divert his attention from the child. He snatched it from her hand instantly, and devoured it with terrible vora-ciousness: but again he exclaimed, "I do not like children; if you trust them they will betray you:" and Agnes offered him food again, as if to bribe him to spare her helpless boy. — "I had a child once — but she is dead, poor soul!" continued he, taking Agnes by the arm, and leading her gently forward. — "And you loved her very tenderly, I suppose?" said Agnes, thinking the loss of his child had occasioned his malady; but, instead of answering her, he went on: — "They said she ran away from me with a lover — but I knew they lied — she was good, and would not have deserted the father who doted on her — Besides, I saw her funeral myself — Liars, rascals, as they are! —

Do not tell any one, I got away from them last night, and am now going to visit her grave."

A death-like sickness, an apprehension so horrible as to deprive her almost of sense, took possession of the soul of Agnes. She eagerly endeavoured to obtain a sight of the stranger's face, but in vain, as his hat was pulled over his forehead, and his chin rested on his bosom. They had now nearly gained the end of the forest, and day was just breaking: Agnes, as soon as they entered the open plain, seized the arm of the madman to force him to look towards her—for speak to him she could not. He felt, and perhaps resented the importunate pressure of her hand—for he turned hastily round—when, dreadful confirmation of her fears, Agnes beheld her father!!!

It was indeed Fitzhenry, driven to madness by his daughter's desertion and disgrace!!

After the elopement of Agnes, Fitzhenry entirely neglected his business, and thought and talked of nothing but the misery he experienced. In vain did his friends represent to him the necessity of his making amends, by increased diligence, for some alarming losses in trade which he had lately sustained. She, for whom alone he toiled, had deserted him—and ruin had no terrors for him. — "I was too proud of her," he used mournfully to repeat—"and Heaven has humbled me even in her by whom I offended."

Month after month elapsed, and no intelligence of Agnes. — Fitzhenry's dejection increased, and his affairs became more and more involved: at length, absolute and irretrievable bankruptcy was become his portion, when he learnt from authority not to be doubted, that Agnes was living with Clifford as his acknowledged mistress. — This was the death-stroke to his reason: and the only way in which his friends (relations he had none, or only distant ones) could be of any further service to him was, by procuring him admission into a private mad house in the neighbourhood.[1]

---

1   Care of the insane in eighteenth-century England took place in two main types of institution: the public asylum and the private madhouse. The former were funded through subscriptions and were dependent upon personal charity; the latter were run as businesses by physicians and could be highly profitable. Subsequent details

Of his recovery little hope was entertained. — The constant theme of his ravings was his daughter; — sometimes he bewailed her as dead; at other times he complained of her as ungrateful: — but so complete was the overthrow his reason had received, that he knew no one, and took no notice of those whom friendship or curiosity led to his cell: yet he was always meditating his escape; and though ironed in consequence of it, the night he met Agnes he had, after incredible difficulty and danger, effected his purpose.

But to return to Agnes — who, when she beheld in her insane companion her injured father, the victim probably of her guilt, let fall her sleeping child, and, sinking on the ground, extended her arms towards Fitzhenry, articulating in a faint voice, "O God! my father!" then prostrating herself at his feet, she clasped his knees in an agony too great for utterance.

At the name of "father," the poor maniac started, and gazed on her earnestly, with savage wildness, while his whole frame became convulsed; and rudely disengaging himself from her embrace, he ran from her a few paces, and then dashed himself on the ground in all the violence of phrensy. He raved, he tore his hair; he screamed, and uttered the most dreadful execrations; and with his teeth shut and his hands clenched, he repeated the word father, and said the name was mockery to him.

Agnes, in mute and tearful despair, beheld the dreadful scene; in vain did her affrighted child cling to her gown, and in its half formed accents entreat to be taken to her arms again; she saw, she heeded nothing but her father; she was alive to nothing but her own guilt and its consequences; and she awaited with horrid composure the cessation of Fitzhenry's phrensy, or the direction of its fury towards her child.

At last, she saw him fall down exhausted and motionless, and tried to hasten to him; but she was unable to move, and reason and life seemed at once forsaking her, when Fitzhenry suddenly started up, and approached her. — Uncertain as to his purpose,

suggest that Fitzhenry is in fact incarcerated in a public asylum funded by his own charity, so either we understand that he was moved from his first asylum or that Opie described it as private in error.

Agnes caught her child to her bosom, and, falling again on her knees, turned on him her almost closing eyes; but his countenance was mild—and gently patting her forehead, on which hung the damps of approaching insensibility, "Poor thing!" he cried, in a tone of the utmost tenderness and compassion, "Poor thing!" and then gazed on her with such inquiring and mournful looks, that tears once more found their way and relieved her bursting brain—while seizing her father's hand she pressed it with frantic emotion to her lips.

Fitzhenry looked at her with great kindness, and suffered her to hold his hand;—then exclaimed, "Poor thing!—don't cry—don't cry—I can't cry—I have not cried for many years; not since my child died—for she is dead, is she not?" looking earnestly at Agnes, who could only answer by her tears.— "Come," said he, "come," taking hold of her arm, then laughing wildly, "Poor thing! you will not leave me, will you?"—"Leave you!" she replied: "never,—I will live with you—die with you."—"True, true," cried he, "she is dead, and we will go visit her grave."—So saying, he dragged Agnes forward with great velocity; but as it was along the path leading to the town, she made no resistance.

Indeed it was such a pleasure to her to see that though he knew her not, the sight of her was welcome to her unhappy parent, that she sought to avoid thinking of the future, and to be alive only to the present: she tried also to forget that it was to his not knowing her she owed the looks of tenderness and pity he bestowed on her, and that the hand which now kindly held hers, would, if recollection returned, throw her from him with just indignation.

But she was soon awakened to redoubled anguish, by hearing Fitzhenry, as he looked behind him, exclaim, "They are coming, they are coming:" and as he said this, he ran with frantic haste across the common. Agnes immediately looking behind her, saw three men pursuing her father at full speed, and concluded that they were the keepers of the bedlam whence he had escaped. Soon after she saw the poor lunatic coming towards her, and had scarcely time to lay her child gently on the ground, before Fitzhenry threw himself in her arms, and implored her to save him from his pursuers.

In an agony that mocks description, Agnes clasped him to her heart, and awaited in trembling agitation the approach of the keepers. — "Hear me, hear me," she cried, "I conjure you to leave him to my care: — He is my father, and you may safely trust him with me." — "Your father!" replied one of the men; "and what then, child? You could do nothing for him, and you should be thankful to us, young woman, for taking him off your hands. — So come along, master, come along," he continued, seizing Fitzhenry, who could with difficulty be separated from Agnes — while another of the keepers, laughing as he beheld her wild anguish, said, "We shall have the daughter as well as the father soon, I see, for I do not believe there is a pin to choose between them."[1]

But, severe as the sufferings of Agnes were already, a still greater pang awaited her. The keepers finding it a very difficult task to confine Fitzhenry, threw him down, and tried by blows to terrify him into acquiescence.[2] At this outrage Agnes became frantic indeed, and followed them with shrieks, entreaties, and reproaches; while the struggling victim called on her to protect him, as they bore him by violence along, till, exhausted with anguish and fatigue, she fell insensible on the ground, and lost in a deep swoon the consciousness of her misery.

How long she remained so is uncertain; but when she recovered her senses all was still around her, and she missed her child. — Starting up, and looking round with renewed phrensy, she saw it lying at some distance from her, and on taking it up she found it in a deep sleep. The horrid apprehension immediately rushed on her mind, that such a sleep in the midst of cold so severe was the sure forerunner of death.

---

1   Proverbially a pin is a thing of little worth, so there is little or nothing to differentiate them.
2   The use of fetters and beatings was considered therapeutic by many eighteenth-century specialists in madness. See Battie (Appendix J.3.iii) and Cullen (Appendix J.5.ii) for the role of physical violence in treatment.

"Monster!" she exclaimed, "destroyer of thy child, as well as father! — But perhaps it is not yet too late, and my curse is not completed." — So saying, she ran, or rather flew, along the road; and seeing a house at a distance she made towards it, and, bursting open the door, beheld a cottager and his family at breakfast — then, sinking on her knees, and holding out to the woman of the house her sleeping boy, "For the love of God," she cried, "look here! look here! Save him! O! save him!" A mother appealing to the heart of a mother is rarely unsuccessful in her appeal. — The cottager's wife was as eager to begin the recovery of the child of Agnes as Agnes herself, and in a moment the whole family was employed in its service; nor was it long before they were rewarded for their humanity by its complete restoration.

The joy of Agnes was frantic as her grief had been. — She embraced them all by turns, in a loud voice invoked blessings on their heads, and promised, if she was ever rich, to make their fortune: — lastly, she caught the still languid boy to her heart, and almost drowned it in her tears.

In the cottager and his family a scene like this excited wonder as well as emotion. He and his wife were good parents — they loved their children — would have been anxious during their illness, and would have sorrowed for their loss: but to these violent expressions and actions, the result of cultivated sensibility, they were wholly unaccustomed, and could scarcely help imputing them to insanity — an idea which the pale cheek and wild look of Agnes strongly confirmed; nor did it lose strength when Agnes, who in terror at her child's danger and joy for his safety had forgotten even her father and his situation, suddenly recollecting herself, exclaimed, "Have I dared to rejoice? — Wretch that I am! Oh! no — there is no joy for me!" The cottager and his wife, on hearing these words, looked significantly at each other.

Agnes soon after started up, and, clasping her hands, cried out, "O! my father, my dear, dear father! thou art past cure; and despair must be my portion."

"O! you are unhappy because your father is ill," observed the cottager's wife; "but do not be so sorrowful on that account, he may get better perhaps." — "Never, never," replied Agnes; "yet, who knows?" — "Aye — who knows indeed," resumed the good woman. "But if not, you nurse him yourself, I suppose, and it will be a comfort to you to know he has every thing done for him that can be done." — Agnes sighed deeply. — "I lost my own father," continued she, "last winter, and a hard trial it was, to be sure; but then it consoled me to think I made his end comfortable. Besides, my conscience told me, that, except here and there, I had always done my duty by him, to the best of my knowledge." Agnes started from her seat, and walked rapidly round the room. "He smiled on me," resumed her kind hostess, wiping her eyes, "to the last moment; and just before the breath left him, he said, 'Good child, good child.'—O! it must be a terrible thing to lose one's parents when one has not done one's duty to them."

At these words Agnes, contrasting her conduct and feelings with those of this artless and innocent woman, was overcome with despair, and, seizing a knife that lay by her, endeavoured to put an end to her existence; but the cottager caught her hand in time to prevent the blow, and his wife easily disarmed her, as her violence instantly changed into a sort of stupor; then throwing herself back on the bed on which she was sitting, she lay with her eyes fixed, and incapable of moving.

The cottager and his wife now broke forth into expressions of wonder and horror at the crime she was going to commit, and the latter, taking little Edward from the lap of her daughter, held it towards Agnes — "See," cried she, as the child stretched forth its little arms to embrace her — "unnatural mother! would you forsake your child?"

These words, assisted by the caresses of the child himself, roused Agnes from her stupor. — "Forsake him! Never, never!" she faltered out, and, snatching him to her bosom, threw herself back on a pillow the good woman had placed under her head; and soon, to the great joy of the compassionate family, both mother and child fell into a sound sleep. The cottager then repaired to his daily labour, and his wife and children began their household tasks; but ever and anon they cast a watchful glance on their unhappy guest, dreading lest she should make a second attempt on her life.

The sleep of both Agnes and her child was so long and heavy, that night was closing in when the little boy awoke, and by his cries for food, broke the rest of his unhappy mother.

But consciousness returned not with returning sense — Agnes looked around her, astonished at her situation. At length, by slow degrees, the dreadful scenes of the preceding night, and her own rash attempt, burst on her recollection; she shuddered at the retrospect, and, clasping her hands together, remained for some moments in speechless prayer: — then she arose; and smiling mournfully at sight of her little Edward eating voraciously the milk and bread that was set before him, she seated herself at the table, and tried to partake of the coarse but wholesome food provided for her. As she approached, she saw the cottager's wife remove the knives, and leave a fork and spoon only for her to eat with. This circumstance forcibly recalled her rash action, and drove away her returning appetite. — "You may trust me now," she said; "I shrink with horror from my wicked attempt on my life, and swear, in the face of Heaven, never to repeat it: no — my only wish now is, to live and to suffer."

Soon after, the cottager's wife made an excuse for bringing back a knife to the table, to prove to Agnes her confidence in her word; but this well-meant attention was lost on her — she sat leaning on her elbow, and wholly absorbed in her own meditations.

When it was completely night, Agnes arose to depart. — "My kind friends," said she, "who have so hospitably received and entertained a wretched wanderer, believe me I shall never forget the obligations I owe you, though I can never hope to repay them; but accept this (taking her last half-guinea from her pocket) as a pledge of my inclination to reward your kindness. If I am ever rich again—" Here her voice failed her, and she burst into tears.

This hesitation gave the virtuous people she addressed an

opportunity of rejecting her offers. — "What we did, we did because we could not help it," said the cottager — "You would not have had me see a fellow-creature going to kill soul and body too, and not prevent it, would you?" — "And as to saving the child," cried the wife, "am I not a mother myself, and can I help feeling for a mother? Poor little thing! it looked so piteous too, and felt so cold!"

Agnes could not speak; but still, by signs, she tendered the money to their acceptance. — "No, no," resumed the cottager, "keep it for those who may not be willing to do you a service for nothing" — and Agnes reluctantly replaced the half-guinea. But then a fresh source of altercation began; the cottager insisted on seeing Agnes to the town, and she insisted on going by herself: at last she agreed he should go with her as far as the street where her friends lived, wait for her at the end of it, and if they were not living, or were removed, she was to return, and sleep at the cottage.

Then, with a beating heart and dejected countenance, Agnes took her child in her arms, and, leaning on her companion, with slow and unsteady steps she began her walk to her native place, once the scene of her happiness and her glory, but now about to be the witness of her misery and her shame.

As they drew near the town, Agnes saw, on one side of the road, a new building, and instantly hurried from it as fast as her trembling limbs could carry her. — "Did you hear them?" asked the cottager. — "Hear whom?" said Agnes. — "The poor creatures," returned her companion, "who are confined there. — That is the new bedlam — and — hark! What a loud scream that was!" — Agnes, unable to support herself, staggered to a bench that projected from the court surrounding the building, while the cottager, unconscious why she stopped, observed it was strange she should like to stay and hear the poor creatures — For his part he thought it shocking to hear them shriek, and still more so to hear them laugh — "for it is so piteous," said he, "to hear those laugh who have so much reason to cry."

Agnes had not power to interrupt him, and he went on: —

"This house was built by subscription; and it was begun by a kind gentleman of the name of Fitzhenry, who afterwards, poor soul, being made low in the world by losses in trade, and by having his brain turned by a good-for-nothing daughter, was one of the first patients in it himself."[1] — Here Agnes, to whom this recollection had but too forcibly occurred already, groaned aloud. — "What, tired so soon?" said her companion. "I doubt you have not been used to stir about — you have been too tenderly brought up. Ah! tender parents often spoil children, and they never thank them for it when they grow up neither, and often come to no good besides."

Agnes was going to make some observation wrung from her by the poignancy of self-upbraiding, when she heard a loud cry as of one in agony: and fancying it her father's voice, she started up, and, stopping her ears, ran towards the town so fast that it was with difficulty that the cottager could overtake her. When he did so, he was surprised at the agitation of her manner. — "What, I suppose you thought they were coming after you?" said he. "But there was no danger — I dare say it was only an unruly one whom they were beating." — Agnes, on hearing this, absolutely screamed with agony; and seizing the cottager's arm, "Let us hasten to the town," said she in a hollow and broken voice, "while I have strength enough left to carry me thither."

At length they entered its walls, and the cottager said, "Here we are at last. — A welcome home to you, young woman." — "Welcome! and home to me!" cried Agnes wildly — "I have no home now — I can expect no welcome! Once indeed —" Here, overcome with recollections almost too painful to be endured, she turned from him and sobbed aloud, while the kind-hearted man could scarcely forbear shedding tears at sight of such mysterious, yet evidently real distress.

In happier days, when Agnes used to leave home on visits to her distant friends, anticipation of the welcome she should receive on her return was, perhaps, the greatest pleasure she

---

1 Despite the earlier comment that Fitzhenry was taken to a private madhouse, this and subsequent details of the asylum's governance make clear that he is placed in a charitably funded public asylum.

enjoyed during her absence. As the adventurer to India, while toiling for wealth, never loses sight of the hope that he shall spend his fortune in his native land; so Agnes, whatever company she saw, whatever amusements she partook of, looked eagerly forward to the hour when she should give her expecting father, and her affectionate companions, a recital of all she had heard and seen. For, though she had been absent a few weeks only, "her presence made a little holiday,"[1] and she was received by Fitzhenry with delight too deep to be expressed; while, even earlier than decorum warranted, her friends were thronging to her door to welcome home the heightener of their pleasures, and the gentle soother of their sorrows; (for Agnes "loved and felt for all:"[2] she had a smile ready to greet the child of prosperity, and a tear for the child of adversity)— As she was thus honoured, thus beloved, no wonder the thoughts of home, and of returning home, were wont to suffuse the eyes of Agnes with tears of exquisite pleasure; and that, when her native town appeared in view, a group of expecting and joyful faces used to swim before her sight, while, hastening forward to have the first glance of her, fancy used to picture her father! — Now, dread reverse! after a *long* absence, an absence of years, she was returning to the same place, inhabited by the same friends: but the voices that used to be loud in pronouncing her welcome, would now be loud in proclaiming indignation at her sight; the eyes that used to beam with gladness at her presence, would now be turned from her with disgust; and the fond father, who used to be counting the moments till she arrived, was now — I shall not go on — suffice, that Agnes felt, to "her heart's core,"[3] all the bitterness of the contrast.

When they arrived near the place of her destination, Agnes stopped, and told the cottager that they must part. — "So much the worse," said the good man. "I do not know how it is, but

---

1 Untraced.

2 Slightly altered reference to "The Deserted Village" (1770), where Goldsmith describes the village preacher: "Thus to relieve the wretched was his pride, / And even his failings leaned to Virtue's side; / But in his duty prompt at every call, / He watched and wept, he prayed and felt, for all" (ll.163-166).

3 Shakespeare, *Hamlet,* Act 3, scene 2, ll. 75-78: "Give me that man / That is not passion's slave, and I will wear him / In my heart's core, ay in my heart of hearts / As I do thee."

you are so sorrowful, yet so kind and gentle, somehow, that both my wife and I have taken a liking to you: — you must not be angry, but we cannot help thinking you are not one of us, but a lady, though you are so disguised and so humble—but misfortune spares no one, you know."

Agnes, affected and gratified by these artless expressions of good will, replied,—"I have, indeed, known better days"— "And will again, I hope with all my heart and soul," interrupted the cottager with great warmth. — "I fear not," replied Agnes, "my dear worthy friend." — "Nay, young lady," rejoined he, "my wife and I are proper to be your servants, not friends." — "You are my friends, perhaps my only friends," returned Agnes mournfully: "perhaps there is not, at this moment, another hand in the universe that would not reject mine, or another tongue that would not upbraid me." — "They must be hard-hearted wretches, indeed, who could upbraid a poor woman for her misfortunes," cried the cottager: "however, you shall never want a friend while I live. You know I saved your life; and, somehow, I feel now as if you belonged to me. I once saved one of my pigeons from a hawk, and I believe, were I starving, I could not now bear to kill the little creature; it would seem like eating my own flesh and blood—so I am sure I could never desert you." — "You have not yet heard my story," replied Agnes; "but you shall know who I am soon, and then, if you still feel disposed to offer me your friendship, I shall be proud to accept it."

The house to which Agnes was hastening was that of her nurse, from whom she had always experienced the affection of a mother, and hoped now to receive a temporary asylum; but she might not be living—and, with a beating heart, Agnes knocked at the door. It was opened by Fanny, her nurse's daughter, the play fellow of Agnes's childhood. — "Thank Heaven!" said Agnes, as she hastened back to the cottager, "I hope I have, at least, one friend left;" and telling him he might go home again, as she was almost certain of shelter for the night, the poor man shook her heartily by the hand, prayed God to bless her, and departed.

Agnes then returned to Fanny, who was still standing by the door, wondering who had knocked at so late an hour, and displeased at being kept so long in the cold—"Will you admit me, Fanny, and give me shelter for the night?" said Agnes in a faint and broken voice.—"Gracious heaven! who are you?" cried Fanny, starting back. "Do you not know me?" she replied, looking earnestly in her face.—Fanny again started; then bursting into tears, as she drew Agnes forward, and closed the door—"O God! it is my dear young lady!"—"And are you sorry to see me?" replied Agnes.—"Sorry!" answered the other.—"Oh, no! but to see you thus!—O! my dear lady, what you must have suffered! Thank Heaven my poor mother is not alive to see this day!"

"And is she dead?" cried Agnes, turning very faint, and catching hold of a chair to keep her from falling. "Then is the measure of my affliction full: I have lost my oldest and best friend!"—"I am not dead," said Fanny respectfully.—"Excellent, kind creature!" continued Agnes, "I hoped so much alleviation of my misery from her affection!"—"Do you hope none from mine?" rejoined Fanny in a tone of reproach—"Indeed, my dear young lady, I love you as well as my mother did, and will do as much for you as she would have done. Do I not owe all I have to you? and now that you are in trouble, perhaps in want too—But no, that cannot and shall not be," wringing her hands and pacing the room with frantic violence: "I can't bear to think of such a thing. That ever I should live to see my dear young lady in want of the help she was always so ready to give!"

Agnes tried to comfort her; but the sight of her distress notwithstanding was soothing to her, as it convinced her she was still dear to one pure and affectionate heart.

During this time little Edward remained covered up so closely that Fanny did not know what the bundle was that Agnes held in her lap; but when she lifted up the cloak that concealed him, Fanny was in an instant kneeling by his side, and gazing on him with admiration—"Is it—is it—" said Fanny with hesitation—"It is my child," replied Agnes, sighing; and Fanny lavished on the unconscious boy the caresses which respect forbade her to bestow on the mother.

"Fanny," said Agnes, "you say nothing of your husband?"—

"He is dead," replied Fanny with emotion. — "Have you any children?" — "None." — "Then will you promise me, if I die, to be a mother to this child?" — Fanny seized her hand, and, in a voice half choked by sobs, said, "I promise you." — "Enough," cried Agnes; then holding out her arms to her humble friend, Fanny's respect yielded to affection, and, falling on Agnes's neck, she sobbed aloud.

"My dear Fanny," said Agnes, "I have a question to ask, and I charge you to answer it truly." — "Do not ask me, do not ask me, for indeed I dare not answer you," replied Fanny in great agitation. Agnes guessed the cause, and hastened to tell her that the question was not concerning her father, as she was acquainted with his situation already, and proceeded to ask whether her elopement and ill conduct had at all hastened the death of her nurse, who was in ill health when she went away. — "Oh no," replied Fanny, "she never believed that you could be gone off willingly, but was sure you were spirited away, and she died expecting you would someday return, and take the law of the villain; and no doubt she was right, though nobody thinks so now but me, for you were always too good to do wrong."

Agnes was too honourable to take to herself the merit she did not deserve: she therefore owned she was indeed guilty; "nor should I," she added, "have dared to intrude myself on you, or solicit you to let me remain under your roof, were I not severely punished for my crime, and resolved to pass the rest of my days in solitude and labour." — "You should not presume to intrude yourself on me!" replied Fanny — "Do not talk thus, if you do not mean to break my heart." — "Nay, Fanny," answered Agnes, "it would be presumption in any woman who has quitted the path of virtue to intrude herself, however high her rank might be, on the meanest of her acquaintance whose honour is spotless. Nor would I thus throw myself on your generosity were I not afraid that, if I were to be unsoothed by the presence of a sympathizing friend, I should sink beneath my sorrows, and want resolution to fulfil the hard task my duty enjoins me."

I shall not attempt to describe the anguish of Fanny when she thought of her young lady, the pride of her heart, as she used to call her, being reduced so low in the world, nor the sudden bursts of joy she gave way to the next moment when she reflected that Agnes was returned, never perhaps to leave her again.

Agnes wore away [a] great part of the night in telling Fanny her mournful tale, and in hearing from her a full account of her father's sufferings, bankruptcy, and consequent madness. At day-break she retired to bed, not to sleep, but ruminate on the romantic yet in her eyes feasible plan she had formed for the future—while Fanny, wearied out by the violent emotions she had undergone, sobbed herself to sleep by her side.

The next morning Agnes did not rise till Fanny had been up some time; and when she seated herself at the breakfast-table, she was surprised to see it spread in a manner which ill accorded with her or Fanny's situation. On asking the reason, Fanny owned she could not bear her dear young lady should fare as she did only, and had therefore provided a suitable breakfast for her. — "But you forget," said Agnes, "that if I remain with you, neither you nor I can afford such breakfasts as these." — "True," replied Fanny mournfully, "then you must consider this as only a welcome, madam." — "Aye," rejoined Agnes, "the prodigal is returned, and you have killed the fatted calf."[1] Fanny burst into tears; while Agnes, shocked at having excited them by the turn she unguardedly gave to her poor friend's attention, tried to sooth her into composure, and affected a gaiety which she was far from feeling.

"Now then to my first task," said Agnes, rising as soon as she had finished her breakfast: "I am going to call on Mr. Seymour; you say he lives where he formerly did." — "To call on Mr. Seymour!" exclaimed Fanny; "O! my dear madam, do not go near him, I beseech you; he is a very severe man, and will affront you, depend upon it." — "No matter," rejoined Agnes, "I have deserved humiliation, and will not shrink from it: but his daughter Caroline, you know, was once my dearest friend, and she will not suffer him to trample on the fallen: and, it is necessary I should apply to him in order to succeed in my

---

1 A reference to the parable of the prodigal son, Luke 15.20-24, illustrating true repentance and unconditional forgiveness.

scheme." — "What scheme?" replied Fanny. "You would not approve it, Fanny, therefore I shall not explain it to you at present; but, when I return, perhaps I shall tell you all." — "But you are not going so soon? not in day-light, surely? If you should be insulted!"

Agnes started with horror at this proof which Fanny had unguardedly given, how hateful her guilt had made her in a place that used to echo with her praises[1]—but recovering herself, she said she should welcome insults as part of the expiation she meant to perform. "But if you will not avoid them for your own sake, pray, pray do for mine," exclaimed Fanny. "If you were to be ill used, I am sure I should never survive it: so, if you must go to Mr. Seymour's, at least oblige me in not going before dark:" and, affected by this fresh mark of her attachment, Agnes consented to stay.

At six o'clock in the evening, while the family was sitting round the fire, and Caroline Seymour was expecting the arrival of her lover, to whom she was to be united in a few days, Agnes knocked at Mr. Seymour's door, having positively forbidden Fanny to accompany her. Caroline, being on the watch for her intended bridegroom, started at the sound; and though the knock which Agnes gave did not much resemble that of an impatient lover, still "it might be he" — "he might mean to surprise her—" and, half opening the parlour door, she listened with a beating heart for the servant's answering the knock.

By this means she distinctly heard Agnes ask whether Mr. Seymour was at home. The servant started, and stammered out that he believed his master was within — while Caroline, springing forward, exclaimed, "I know that voice — O yes! It must be she!" — But her father, seizing her arm, pushed her back into the parlour, saying, "I also know that voice, and I command you to stay where you are." — Then going up to Agnes, he desired her to leave his house directly, as it should be no harbour for abandoned women and unnatural children.

"But will you not allow it to shelter for one moment the wretched and the penitent?" she replied. "Father, my dear, dear

---

1   The phrase "in a place that used to echo with her praises" is omitted in the 1843 edition.

father," cried Caroline, again coming forward, but was again driven back by Mr. Seymour, who, turning to Agnes, bade her claim shelter from the man for whom she had left the best of parents; and desiring the servant to shut the door in her face, he re-entered the parlour, whence Agnes distinctly heard the sobs of the compassionate Caroline.

But the servant was kinder than the master, and could not obey the orders he had received. — "O madam! miss Fitzhenry, do you not know me?" said he. "I once lived with you; have you forgotten little William? I shall never forget you; you were the sweetest tempered young lady — That ever I should see you thus!"

Before Agnes could reply, Mr. Seymour again angrily asked why his orders were not obeyed; and Agnes, checking her emotion, besought William to deliver a message to his master. "Tell him," said she, "all I ask of him is, that he will use his interest to get me the place of servant in the house, the bedlam I would say, where — he will know what I mean," she added, unable to utter the conclusion of the sentence — and William, in a broken voice, delivered the message.

"O my poor Agnes!" cried Caroline passionately — "A servant! she a servant! and in such a place too!" William adding in a low voice — "Ah! miss! and she looks so poor and wretched!"

Meanwhile Mr. Seymour was walking up and down the room hesitating how to act; but, reflecting that it was easier to forbid any communication with Agnes than to check it if once begun, he again desired William to shut the door against her. "You must do it yourself then," replied William, "for I am not hard-hearted enough;" — and Mr. Seymour, summoning up resolution, told Agnes there were other governors to whom she might apply, and then locked the door against her himself — while Agnes slowly and sorrowfully turned her steps towards Fanny's more hospitable roof.

She had not gone far, however, when she heard a light footstep behind her, and her name pronounced in a gentle, faltering voice — and turning round she beheld Caroline Seymour, who, seizing her hand, forced something into it, hastily pressed it to her lips, and, without saying one word, suddenly disappeared, leaving Agnes motionless as a statue, and, but for the parcel she held in her hand, disposed to think she was dreaming. —Then, eager to see what it contained, she hastened back to Fanny, who heard with indignation the reception she had met from Mr. Seymour, but on her knees invoked blessings on the head of Caroline, when on opening the parcel she found it contained twenty guineas inclosed in a paper, on which was written, but almost effaced with tears, "For my still dear Agnes—would I dare say more!"[1]

This money the generous girl had taken from that allowed her for wedding-clothes, and felt more delight in relieving with it the wants even of a guilty fellow-creature, than purchasing the most splendid dress could have afforded her. And her present did more than she expected; it relieved the mind of Agnes: she had taught herself to meet without repining the assaults of poverty, but not to encounter with calmness the scorn of the friends she loved.

But Caroline and her kindness soon vanished again from her mind, and the idea of her father, and her scheme, took entire possession of it—"But it might not succeed—no doubt Mr. Seymour would be her enemy—still he had hinted she might apply to the other governors;" and Fanny having learnt that they were all to meet at the bedlam on business the next day, she resolved to write a note, requesting to be allowed to appear before them.[2]

This note, Fanny, who was not acquainted with its contents, undertook to deliver, and, to the great surprise of Agnes (as she expected Mr. Seymour would oppose it), her request was instantly granted. Indeed it was Mr. Seymour himself who urged the compliance.

There was not a kinder-hearted man in the world than Mr. Seymour; and in his severity towards Agnes he acted more from

---

1 Caroline's generosity marks her as type of Macaulay's idealized woman "whose justice will incline her to extend her benevolence to the frailties of the fair as circumstances invite" (Appendix H.2).

2 Roy Porter points out that in charitable asylums "A substantial gift bought a 'governorship,' and governors donated their time and services *gratis*" in administering the institution (129).

what he thought his duty, than from his inclination. He was the father of several daughters; and it was his opinion that a parent could not too forcibly inculcate on the minds of young women the salutary truth, that loss of virtue must be to them the loss of friends. Besides, his eldest daughter, Caroline, was going to be married to the son of a very severe, rigid mother, then staying at the house, and he feared that, if he took any notice of the fallen Agnes, the old lady might conceive a prejudice against him and her daughter-in-law. Added to these reasons, Mr. Seymour was a very vain man, and never acted in any way without saying to himself, "What will the world say?" Hence, though his first impulses were frequently good, the determinations of his judgement were often contemptible.

But, however satisfied Mr. Seymour might be with his motives on this occasion, his feelings revolted at the consciousness of the anguish he had occasioned Agnes. He wished, ardently wished, he had dared to have been kinder: and when Caroline, who was incapable of the meanness of concealing any action which she thought it right to perform, told him of the gift she had in person bestowed on Agnes, he could scarcely forbear commending her conduct; and, while he forbade any future intercourse between them, he was forced to turn away his head to hide the tear of gratified sensibility, and the smile of parental exultation: nevertheless, he did not omit to bid her keep her own counsel, "for, if your conduct were known," added he, "what would the world say?"

No wonder then, that, softened as he was by Agnes's application, though he deemed the scheme wild and impracticable, and afraid he had treated her unkindly, he was pleased to have an opportunity of obliging her, without injuring himself, and that her request to the governors was strengthened by his representations; nor is it extraordinary, that, alive as he always was to the opinion of every one, he should dread seeing Agnes after the reception he had given her, more than Agnes dreaded to appear before the board.

Agnes, who had borrowed of Fanny the dress of a respectable maid servant, when summoned to attend the governors, entered the room with modest but dignified composure, prepared to expect contumely, but resolved to endure it as became a contrite heart. But no contumely awaited her.

In the hour of her prosperity she had borne her faculties so meekly, and had been so careful never to humble any one by showing a consciousness of superiority, that she had been beloved even more than she had been admired; and hard indeed must the heart of that man have been, who could have rejoiced that she herself was humbled.

A dead, nay a solemn silence took place on her entrance. Every one present beheld with surprise, and with *stolen* looks of pity, the ravages which remorse and anguish had made in her form, and the striking change in her apparel; for every one had often followed with delight her graceful figure through the dance, and gazed with admiration on the tasteful varieties of her dress; every one had listened with pleasure to the winning sound of her voice, and envied Fitzhenry the possession of such a daughter. As they now beheld her, these recollections forcibly occurred to them: — they agonized — they overcame them. — They thought of their own daughters, and secretly prayed Heaven to keep them from the voice of the seducer: — away went all their resolutions to receive Agnes with that open disdain and detestation which her crime deserved; the sight of her disarmed them; and not one amongst them had, for some moments, firmness enough to speak. At last, "Pray sit down, miss Fitzhenry," said the president in a voice hoarse with emotion: "Here is a chair," added another: and Mr. Seymour, bowing as he did it, placed a seat for her near the fire.

Agnes, who had made up her mind to bear expected indignity with composure, was not proof against unexpected kindness; and, hastily turning to the window, she gave vent to her sensations in an agony of tears. But, recollecting the importance of the business on which she came, she struggled with her feelings; and on being desired by the president to explain to the board what she wanted, she began to address them in a faint and faltering voice: however, as she proceeded, she gained courage, remembering it was her interest to affect her auditors, and make them enter warmly into her feelings and designs. She told her whole story, in as concise a manner as possible, from the time of her leaving Clifford to her rencontre with her father in the forest, and his being torn from her by the keepers; and when she was unable to go on, from the violence of her emotions, she had the satisfaction of seeing that the tears of her auditors kept pace with her own. When her narrative was ended, she proceeded thus: —

"I come now, gentlemen, to the reason of my troubling you. From the impression the sight of me made on my father, I feel a certain conviction that, were I constantly with him, I might in time be able to restore to him that reason my guilt has deprived him of. To effect this purpose, it is my wish to become a servant in this house: if I should not succeed in my endeavours, I am so sure he will have pleasure in seeing me, that I feel it my duty to be with him, even on that account; and, if there be any balm for a heart and conscience so wounded as mine, I must find it in devoting all my future days to alleviate, though I cannot cure, the misery I have occasioned. And if," added she with affecting enthusiasm, "it should please Heaven to smile on my endeavours to restore him to reason, how exquisite will be my satisfaction in labouring to maintain him!"

To this plan, it is to be supposed, the governors saw more objection than Agnes did; but, though they rejected the idea of her being a servant in the house, they were not averse to giving her an opportunity of making the trial she desired, if it were only to alleviate her evident wretchedness; and, having consulted the medical attendants belonging to the institution, they ordered that Agnes should be permitted two hours at a time, morning and evening, to see Fitzhenry. And she, who had not dared to flatter herself she should obtain so much, was too full of emotion to show, otherwise than by incoherent expressions and broken sentences, her sense of the obligation.[1]

"Our next care," observed the president, "must be, as friends of your poor father, to see what we can do for your future support." — "That, sir, I shall provide for myself," replied Agnes;

---

1 Close contact with family members was often discouraged as part of the treatment of the illness, so the governors are indeed liberal with Agnes. See Battie (Appendix J.3.ii) and Cullen (Appendix J.5.ii) for recommendations against visits from family, and Harper (Appendix J.6.iv) for recommendations in favour.

"I will not eat the bread of idleness, as well as of shame and affliction,[1] and shall even rejoice in being obliged to labour for my support, and that of my child—happy, if, in fulfilling well the duties of a mother, I may make some atonement for having violated those of a daughter."

"But, miss Fitzhenry," answered the president, "accept at least some assistance from us till you can find means of maintaining yourself." — "Never, never," cried Agnes: "I thank you for your kindness, but I will not accept it; nor do I need it. I have already accepted assistance from one kind friend, and merely because I should, under similar circumstances, have been hurt at having a gift of mine refused: but, allow me to say that, from the wretchedness into which my guilt has plunged me, nothing henceforward but my industry shall relieve me."

So saying, she curtsied to the gentlemen, and hastily withdrew, leaving them all deeply affected by her narrative, and her proposed expiatory plan of life, and ready to grant her their admiration, should she have resolution to fulfil her good intentions, after the strong impression which the meeting with her father in the forest had made on her mind, should have been weakened by time and occupation.

Agnes hastened from the governors' room to put in force the leave which she had obtained, and was immediately conducted to Fitzhenry's cell. She found him with his back to the door, drawing with a piece of coal on the wall; and as he did not observe her entrance, she had an opportunity of looking over his shoulder, and she saw that he had drawn the shape of a coffin, and was then writing on the lid the name of Agnes.[2]

A groan which involuntarily escaped her made him turn round: at sight of her he started, and looked wildly as he had done in the forest; then, shaking his head and sighing deeply, he resumed his employment, still occasionally looking back at

---

1 Agnes conflates two biblical references. Proverbs 31.27: "she looketh well to the ways of her household, and eateth not the bread of idleness" and 1 Kings 22:27: "And say, thus saith the king, Put this *fellow* in the prison, and feed him with bread of affliction, and with water of affliction, until I come in peace."

2 The frontispiece to the second and subsequent editions of the novel gives John Opie's rendering of this scene. See figure 3.

Agnes; who, at length overcome by her feelings, threw herself on the bed beside him, and burst into tears.

Hearing her sobs, he immediately turned round again, and, patting her cheek as he had done on their first meeting, said, "Poor thing! poor thing!" and, fixing his eyes steadfastly on her face, while Agnes turned towards him and pressed his hand to her lips, he gazed on her as before with a look of anxious curiosity; then, turning from her, muttered to himself, "She is dead, for all that."

Soon after, he asked her to take a walk with him; adding, in a whisper, "We will go find her grave;" and, taking her under his arm, he led her to the garden, smiling on her from time to time, as if it gave him pleasure to see her; and sometimes laughing, as if at some secret satisfaction which he would not communicate. When they had made one turn round the garden, he suddenly stopped, and began singing—"Tears such as tender fathers shed," that pathetic song of Handel's, which he used to delight to hear Agnes sing:[1] "I can't go on," he observed, looking at Agnes; "can you?" as if there were in his mind some association between her and that song; and Agnes, with a bursting heart, took up the song where he left off.

Fitzhenry listened with restless agitation; and when she had finished, he desired her to sing it again. "But say the words first," he added: and Agnes repeated —

> "Tears such as tender fathers shed,
> Warm from my aged eyes descend,
> For joy, to think, when I am dead,
> My son will have mankind his friend."

"No, no," cried Fitzhenry with quickness, "'for joy to think when I am dead, Agnes will have mankind her friend.' I used to sing it so; and so did she, when I bade her to do so. O! she sung it so well!—But she can sing it no more now, for she is dead; and we will go look for her grave."

---

1 Handel's *Deborah*. See also Harper's comments on the use of music in treatment (Appendix J.6.iv).

Then he ran hastily round the garden, while Agnes, whom the words of this song, by recalling painful recollections, had almost deprived of reason, sat down on a bench, nearly insensible, till he again came to her, and, taking her hand, said, in a hurried manner, "You will not leave me, will you?" And on her answering No, in a very earnest and passionate manner, he looked delighted; and, saying "Poor thing!" again gazed on her intently; and again Agnes's hopes that he would in time know her returned. — "Very pale, very pale!" cried Fitzhenry the next moment, stroking her cheek; "and *she* had such a bloom! — Sing again; for the love of God, sing again:" — and in a hoarse, broken voice, Agnes complied. "She sung better than you," rejoined he when she had done;— "so sweet, so clear it was! — But she is gone!" So saying, he relapsed into total indifference to Agnes, and every thing around him — and again her new-raised hopes vanished.

The keeper now told her it was time for her to depart; and she mournfully arose: but, first seizing her father's hand, she leaned for a moment her head on his arm; then, bidding God bless him, walked to the door with the keeper. But on seeing her about to leave him, Fitzhenry ran after her, as fast as his heavy irons would let him, wildly exclaiming, "You shall not go — you shall not go."

Agnes, overjoyed at this evident proof of the pleasure her presence gave him, looked at the keeper for permission to stay; but as he told her it would be against the rules, she thought it more prudent to submit; and before Fitzhenry could catch hold of her in order to detain her by force, she ran through the house, and the grated door was closed on her.

"And this," said Agnes to herself, turning round to survey the melancholy mansion she had left, while mingled sounds of groans, shrieks, shouts, laughter, and the clanking of irons, burst upon her ears, "this is the abode of my father! and provided for him by me! — This is the recompense bestowed on him by the daughter whom he loved and trusted, in return for years of unparalleled fondness and indulgence!"

The recollection was too horrible; and Agnes, calling up all the energy of her mind, remembered the uselessness of regret for the past, but thought with pleasure on the advantages of amendment for the present and the future: and by the time she reached Fanny's door, her mind had recovered its sad composure.

Her countenance, at her return, was very different to what it had been at her departure. Hope animated her sunk eye, and she seemed full of joyful though distant expectations: nay, so much was she absorbed in pleasing anticipations, that she feebly returned the caresses of her child, who climbed up her knees to express his joy at seeing her; and even while she kissed his ruddy cheek, her eye looked beyond it with the open gaze of absence.

"I have seen him again," she cried, turning to Fanny; "and he almost knew me! He will know me entirely, in time; and next, he will know every thing; and then I shall be happy!"

Fanny, to whom Agnes had given no clue to enable her to understand this language, was alarmed for her intellects, till she explained her plans, and her hopes; which Fanny, though she could not share in them, was too humane to discourage.

"But now," continued Agnes, "let us consult on my future means of gaining a livelihood;" and finding that Fanny, besides keeping a day-school, took in shawl-work,[1] a considerable shawl manufacture being carried on in the town, it was settled that she should procure the same employment for Agnes; and that a small back room in Fanny's little dwelling should be fitted up for her use.

In the mean while the governors of the bedlam had returned to their respective habitations, with feelings towards Agnes very different to those with which they had assembled. But too prudent to make even a penitent sinner the subject of praise in their own families, they gave short, evasive answers to the inquiries that were made there.

Mr. Seymour, on the contrary, thought it his duty to relieve the generous and affectionate heart of his daughter, by a minute detail of what had passed at the meeting; but he had no opportunity of doing this when he first returned home, as he found

---

1   Cottage-industry textile-work was one of the few means of earning a living available to women in this period.

there a large party assembled to dinner. Caroline, however, watched his countenance and manner; and seeing on the first an expression of highly-awakened feelings, and in the latter a degree of absence, and aversion to talking, which it always displayed whenever his heart had been deeply interested, she flattered herself that Agnes was the cause of these appearances, and hoped to hear of something to her advantage.

During dinner, a lady asked Caroline which of her young friends would accompany her to church, in the capacity of bride-maid. Caroline started, and turned pale at the question — for melancholy were the reflections it excited in her mind. It had always been an agreement between her and Agnes, that which ever of the two was married first should have the other for her bride-maid; and the question was repeated before Caroline could trust her voice to answer it. "I shall have no bride-maids, but my sisters," she replied at length with a quivering lip; "I cannot; indeed I wish to have no other now." Then, looking at her father, she saw his eyes were filled with tears; and unable to suppress, but wishing to conceal his emotion, he abruptly left the room.

There is scarcely any human being whose heart has not taught him that we are never so compassionate and benevolent towards others, as when our own wishes are completely gratified — we are never so humble as then. This was the case with Mr. Seymour; he was about to marry his eldest daughter in a manner even superior to his warmest expectations, and his paternal care, therefore, was amply rewarded. But his heart told him that his care and his affection had not exceeded, perhaps not equalled, that of Fitzhenry; nor had the promise of his daughter's youth, fair as it was, ever equalled that of the unhappy Agnes; yet Caroline was going to aggrandize her family, and Agnes had disgraced hers. She was happy — Agnes miserable. He was the possessor of a large fortune, and all the comforts of life; and Fitzhenry was in a madhouse.

This contrast between their situations was forcibly recalled to his mind by the question addressed to Caroline; and already softened by the interview of the morning, he could not support his feelings, but was obliged to hasten to his chamber to vent in tears and thanksgivings the mingled sensations of humility and gratitude. Caroline soon followed him; and heard, with emotions as violent, her father's description of Agnes's narration, and her conduct before the governors.

"But it is not sufficient," said she, "that you tell me this: you must tell it wherever you hear the poor penitent's name mentioned, and avow the change it has made in your sentiments towards her; you must be her advocate."

"Her advocate! What would the world say?"

"Just what you wish it to say. Believe me, my dear father, the world is in many instances like a spoiled child, who treats with contempt the foolish parent that indulges his caprices, but behaves with respect to those, who, regardless of his clamours, give the law to him, instead of receiving it."

"You speak from the untaught enthusiasm and confidence of youth, Caroline — but experience will teach you that no one can with impunity run counter to the opinions of the world."

"My experience has taught me that already; but, in this case, you do not seem to do the world justice. The world would blame you, and justly too, if, while talking of the unhappy Agnes, you should make light of her guilt; but why not, while you acknowledge that to be enormous, descant with equal justice on the deep sense she entertains of it, and on the excellence of her present intentions? To this, what can the world say, but that you are a just judge? And even suppose they should think you too lenient a one, will not the approbation of your own conscience be an ample consolation for such a condemnation? O! my dear father! were you not one of the best, and most *unspoilable* of men, your anxious attention to what the world will say of your actions, must long ere this have made you one of the worst."

"Enough, enough," cried Mr. Seymour, wounded self-love contending in his bosom with parental pride, for he had some suspicion that Caroline was right, "what would the world say, if it were to hear you schooling your father?"

"When the world hears me trying to exalt my own wisdom by doubting my father's, I hope it will treat me with the severity I shall deserve."

Mr. Seymour clasped her to his bosom as she said this, and involuntarily exclaimed, "O! poor Fitzhenry!" — "And poor Agnes too!" retorted Caroline, throwing her arms round his neck: "it will be my parting request, when I leave my paternal roof, that you will do all the justice you can to my once honoured friend — and let the world say what it pleases." — "Well, well, I will indulge you, by granting your request," cried Mr. Seymour; "or rather I will indulge myself." And then, contented with each other, they returned to the company.

A few days after this conversation Caroline's marriage took place, and was celebrated by the ringing of bells and other rejoicings. "What are the bells ringing for to-day?" said Agnes to Fanny, as she was eating her breakfast with more appetite than usual. Fanny hesitated; and then, in a peevish tone, replied, that she supposed they rang for miss Caroline Seymour, as she was married that morning: — adding, "Such a fuss, indeed! such preparations! one would think nobody was ever married before!"

Yet, spitefully as Fanny spoke this, she had no dislike to the amiable Caroline; her pettishness proceeded merely from her love for Agnes. Just such preparations, just such rejoicings, she had hoped to see one day for the marriage of her dear young lady; — and though Agnes had not perceived it, Fanny had for the last two days shed many a tear of regret and mortification, while news of the intended wedding reached her ear on every side: and she had not courage to tell Agnes what she heard, lest the feelings of Agnes on the occasion should resemble hers, but in a more painful degree. "Caroline Seymour married!" cried Agnes, rising from her unfinished meal; "well married, I hope?" — "O yes, very well indeed — Mr. Seymour is so proud of the connection!" "Thank God!" said Agnes fervently: "May she be as happy as her virtues deserve!" — and then with a hasty step she retired to her own apartment.

It is certain that Agnes had a mind above the meanness of envy, and that she did not repine at the happiness of her friend; yet, while with tears trickling down her cheek she faltered out the words "Happy Caroline! — Mr. Seymour proud! Well may he be so!" her feelings were as bitter as those which envy excites. "O! my poor father! I once hoped—" added she; but, overcome with the acuteness of regret and remorse, she threw herself on the bed in speechless anguish.

Then the image of Caroline, as she last saw her, weeping for her misfortunes, and administering to her wants, recurred to her mind, and, in a transport of affection and gratitude, she took the paper that contained the gift from her bosom, kissed the blotted scrawl on the back of it, and prayed fervently for her happiness.

"But surely," cried she, starting up, and running into the next room to Fanny, "I should write a few lines of congratulation to the bride?" Fanny did not answer; indeed she could not; for the affectionate creature was drowned in tears, which Agnes well understood, and was gratified, though pained, to behold. At length, still more ashamed of her own weakness when she saw it reflected in another, Agnes gently reproved Fanny, telling her it seemed as if she repined at miss Seymour's happiness.

"No," replied Fanny, "I only repine at your misery. Dear me, she is a sweet young lady, to be sure, but no more to be compared to you—"—"Hush! Fanny; 'tis I who am now not to be compared to her;—remember, my misery is owing to my guilt."—"It is not the less to be repined at on that account," replied Fanny.

To this remark, unconsciously severe, Agnes with a sigh assented; and, unable to continue the conversation in this strain, she again asked whether Fanny did not think she ought to congratulate the generous Caroline. "By all means," replied Fanny: but, before she answered, Agnes had determined that it would be kinder in her not to damp the joy of Caroline, by calling to her mind the image of a wretched friend. "True," she observed, "it would gratify my feelings to express the love and gratitude I bear her, and my self-love would exult in being recollected by her with tenderness and regret, even in the hour of her bridal splendour; but the gratification would only be a selfish one, and therefore I will reject it."

Having formed this laudable resolution, Agnes, after trying

to compose her agitated spirits by playing with her child, who was already idolized by the faithful Fanny, bent her steps as usual to the cell of her father. Unfortunately for Agnes, she was obliged to pass the house of Mr. Seymour, and at the door she saw the carriages waiting to convey the bride and her train to the country seat of her mother-in-law. Agnes hurried on as fast as her trembling limbs could carry her; but, as she cast a hasty glance on the splendid liveries, and the crowd gazing on them, she saw Mr. Seymour bustling at the door, with all the pleased consequence of a happy parent in his countenance; and not daring to analyse her feelings, she rushed forward from the mirthful scene, and did not stop again till she found herself at the door of the bedlam.

But when there, and when, looking up at its grated windows, she contemplated it as the habitation of her father — so different to that of the father of Caroline — and beheld in fancy the woe-worn, sallow face of Fitzhenry, so unlike the healthy, satisfied look of Mr. Seymour — "I can't go in, I can't see him to-day," she faintly articulated, overcome with a sudden faintness — and, as soon as she could recover her strength, she returned home; and, shutting herself up in her own apartment, spent the rest of the day in that mournful and solitary meditation that "maketh the heart better."[1]

It would no doubt have gladdened the heart of the poor mourner to have known, that, surrounded by joyous and congratulating friends, Caroline sighed for the absent Agnes, and felt the want of her congratulations — "Surely she will write to me!" said she mentally, "I am sure she wishes me happy! and one of my greatest pangs at leaving my native place is, the consciousness that I leave her miserable."

The last words that Caroline uttered, as she bade adieu to the domestics, were, "Be sure to send after me any note or letter that may come." But no note or letter from Agnes arrived; and had Caroline known the reason, she would have loved her once happy friend the more.

---

1 Probably a memorial reference Ecclesiastes 7.3: "Sorrow is better than laughter: for by the sadness of the countenance the heart is made better." Perhaps also, given the situation, with the opening lines of this chapter in mind: "A good name *is* better than precious ointment."

The next day, earlier than usual, Agnes went in quest of her father. She did not absolutely flatter herself that he had missed her the day before, still she did not think it absolutely *impossible* that he *might*. She dared not, however, ask the question; but luckily for her, the keeper told her, unasked, that Fitzhenry was observed to be restless, and looking out of the door of his cell frequently, both morning and evening, as if expecting somebody; and that at night, as he was going to bed, he asked whether the lady had not been there.

"Indeed!" cried Agnes, her eyes sparkling with pleasure — "Where is he? — Let me see him directly." But, after the first joyful emotion which he always showed at seeing her had subsided, she could not flatter herself that his symptoms were more favourable than before.

The keeper also informed her that he had been thrown into so violent a raving fit, by the agitation he felt at parting with her the last time she was there, that she must contrive to slip away unperceived whenever she came: and this visit having passed away without any thing material occurring, Agnes contrived to make her escape unseen.

On her return she repeated to Fanny several times, with a sort of pathetic pleasure, the question her father had asked — "He inquired whether the lady had not been there; — think of that, Fanny:" while so incoherent was her language and so absent were her looks, that Fanny again began to fear her afflictions had impaired her reason.

After staying a few days with the new-married couple, Mr. Seymour returned home, Caroline having before he left her again desired him to be the friend of the penitent Agnes, whenever he heard her unpityingly attacked; and an opportunity soon offered of gratifying his daughter's benevolence, and his own.

Mr. Seymour was drinking tea in a large party, when a lady, to whose plain, awkward, uninteresting daughters, the once beautiful, graceful, and engaging Agnes had formerly been a powerful rival, said, with no small share of malignity, "So! —fine impudence indeed! — I hear that good for nothing minx, Fitzhenry's daughter, is come to town: I wonder for my part she dares show her face here — But the assurance of those creatures is amazing."

"Aye, it is indeed," echoed from one lady to another. "But this girl must be a hardened wretch indeed," resumed Mrs. Macfiendy, the first speaker. "I suppose her fellow is tired of her, and she will be on the town soon—"

"In the church-yard rather," replied Mr. Seymour, whom a feeling of resentment at these vulgar expressions of female spite had hitherto kept silent:—"Miss Fitzhenry has lost all power of charming the eye of the libertine, and even the wish;—but she is an object whom the compassionate and humane cannot behold, or listen to, without the strongest emotion."

"No, to be sure," replied Mrs. Macfiendy bridling—"the girl had always a plausible tongue of her own—and as to her beauty, I never thought that was made for lasting. —What then you have seen her, Mr. Seymour? I wonder you could condescend to *look* at such trash."

"Yes, madam, I have seen, and heard her too;—and if heartfelt misery, contrition, and true penitence, may hope to win favour in the sight of God, and expiate past offences, 'a ministering angel might this frail one be, though we lay howling.'"[1]

"I lie howling, indeed!" screamed out Mrs. Macfiendy: "speak for yourself, if you please, Mr. Seymour; for my part, I do not expect when I go to another world to keep such company as miss Fitzhenry."

"If with the same measure you mete it should be meted to you again, madam, I believe there is little chance in another world that you and miss Fitzhenry will be visiting acquaintance." Then, bespeaking the attention of the company, he gave that account of Agnes, her present situation, and her intentions for the future, which she gave the governors; and all the company, save the outrageously virtuous mother and her daughters, heard it with as much emotion as Mr. Seymour felt in relating it. —Exclamations of "Poor unfortunate girl! what a pity she should have been guilty! —But, fallen as she is, she is still Agnes Fitzhenry," resounded through the room.[2]

Mrs. Macfiendy could not bear this in silence; but, with a

---

1   Shakespeare, *Hamlet*, Act V, scene i, 265.
2   The final sentence of this paragraph is omitted in the second and subsequent editions.

cheek pale, nay livid, with malignity, and in a voice sharpened by passion, which at all times resembled the scream of a pea-hen, she exclaimed, "Well, for my part, some people may do any thing, yet be praised up to the skies; other people's daughters would not find such mercy. Before she went off, it was miss Fitzhenry this, and miss Fitzhenry that,—though other people's children could perhaps do as much, though they were not so fond of showing what they could do."

"No," cried one of the miss Macfiendys, "miss Fitzhenry had courage enough for any thing."

"True, child," resumed the mother; "and what did it end in? Why, in becoming a—what I do not choose to name."

"Fie, madam, fie," cried Mr. Seymour; "Why thus exult over the fallen?"

"O! then you do allow her to be fallen?"

"She is fallen indeed, madam," said Mr. Seymour; "but even in her proudest hour, miss Fitzhenry never expressed herself towards her erring neighbours with unchristian severity;—but set you an example of forbearance, which you would do well to follow."

"She set *me* an example!" vociferated Mrs. Macfiendy— "she indeed! a creature!—I will not stay, nor shall my daughters, to hear such immoral talk. But 'tis as I said—some people may do any thing—for, wicked as she is, miss Fitzhenry is still cried up as something extraordinary, and is even held up as an example to modest women."

So saying, she arose; but Mr. Seymour rose also, and said, "There is no necessity for *your* leaving the company, madam, as I will leave it; for I am tired of hearing myself so grossly misrepresented. No one abhors more than I do the crime of miss Fitzhenry; and no one would more strongly object, for the sake of other young women, to her being again received into general company; but, at the same time, I will always be ready to encourage the penitent by the voice of just praise; and I feel delight in reflecting that, however the judges of this world may be fond of condemning her, she will one day appeal from them to a merciful and long-suffering judge."

Then, bowing respectfully to all but Mrs. Macfiendy, he

withdrew, and gave her an opportunity of remarking that Mr. Seymour was mighty warm in the creature's defence. She did not know he was so interested about her; but she always thought him a *gay man*, and she supposed *miss Fitzhenry*, as he called her, would be glad to take up with any thing *now*.[1]

This speech, sorry am I to say, was received with a general and complaisant smile, though it was reckoned unjust; for there are few who have virtue and resolution enough to stand forward as champions for an absent and calumniated individual, if there be any thing ludicrous in the tale against him;—and the precise, careful, elderly Mr. Seymour, who was always shrinking, like a sensitive plant, from the touch of censure,[2] accused by implication of being the private friend of the youthful Agnes, excited a degree of merry malice in the company not unpleasant to their feelings.

But, in spite of the efforts of calumny, the account Mr. Seymour had given of Agnes and her penitence became town talk; and, as it was confirmed by the other governors, every one, except the ferociously chaste, was eager to prevent Agnes from feeling pecuniary distress, by procuring her employment.

Still she was not supplied with work as fast as she executed it; for, except during the hours which she was allowed to spend with her father, she was constantly employed; and she even deprived herself of her usual quantity of sleep, and was never in bed before one, or after four.

In proportion as her business and profits increased, were her spirits elevated; but the more she gained, the more saving she became: she would scarcely allow herself sufficient food or clothing; and, to the astonishment of Fanny, the once generous Agnes appeared penurious, and a lover of money. "What does this change mean, my dear lady?" said Fanny to her one day.

---

1   See Hannah More (Appendix H.4) for the embodiment of female criticism of lapses from chastity, and Catharine Macaulay (Appendix H.2) for the rebuke of women as the fiercest critics of such lapses, and the equation of any lapse with prostitution.

2   Markman Ellis point out that "in mid-eighteenth century there was much conjecture about vegetable sensitivity, especially the example of the sensitive plant, mimosa, which shrank from the touch" (*The Politics of Sensibility*, 20). Indeed, the plant became an emblem of extreme sensibility, appearing in Romney's painting "Sensibility" (1786).

"I have my reasons for it," replied Agnes coldly; then changed the subject; and Fanny respected her too much to urge an explanation.

But Agnes soon after began to wonder at an obvious change in Fanny. At first, when Agnes returned from visiting her father, Fanny used to examine her countenance: and she could learn from that, without asking a single question, whether Fitzhenry seemed to show any new symptoms of amendment, or whether his insanity still appeared incurable. If the former, Fanny, tenderly pressing her hand, would say, "Thank God!" and prepare their dinner or supper with more alacrity than usual: if the latter, Fanny would say nothing; but endeavour, by bringing little Edward to her, or by engaging her in conversation, to divert the gloom she could not remove; and Agnes, though she took no notice of these artless proofs of affection, observed and felt them deeply; and as she drew near the house, she always anticipated them as one of the comforts of her home.

But, for some days past, Fanny had discontinued this mode of welcome so grateful to the feelings of Agnes, and seemed wholly absorbed in her own. She was silent, reserved, and evidently oppressed with some anxiety which she was studious to conceal. Once or twice, when Agnes came home rather sooner than usual, she found her in tears; and, when she affectionately asked the reason of them, Fanny pleaded mere lowness of spirits as the cause.

But the eye of anxious affection is not easily blinded. Agnes was convinced that Fanny's misery had some more important origin; and, secretly fearing that it proceeded from her, she was on the watch for something to confirm her suspicions.

One day, as she passed through the room where Fanny kept her school, Agnes observed that the number of her scholars was considerably diminished; and, when she asked Fanny where the children whom she missed were, there was a confusion and hesitation in her manner, while she made different excuses for their absence, which convinced Agnes that she concealed from her some unwelcome truth.

A very painful suspicion immediately darted across her

mind, the truth of which was but too soon confirmed. A day or two after, while again passing through the school-room, she was attracted by the beauty of a little girl, who was about eight years old; and, smoothing down her curling hair, she stooped to kiss her ruddy cheek; but the child, uttering a loud scream, sprung from her arms, and, sobbing violently, hid her face on Fanny's lap. Agnes, who was very fond of children, was much hurt by symptoms of a dislike so violent towards her, and urged the child to give a reason for such strange conduct: on which the artless girl owned that her mother had charged her never to touch or go near miss Fitzhenry, because she was the most wicked woman that ever breathed.

Agnes heard this new consequence of her guilt with equal surprise and grief; but, on looking at Fanny, though she saw grief in her countenance, there was no surprise in it; and she instantly told her she was convinced the loss of her scholars was occasioned by her having allowed her to reside with her. Fanny, bursting into tears, at last confessed that her suspicions were just, while to the shuddering Agnes she unfolded a series of persecutions which she had undergone from her employers, because she had declared her resolution of starving, rather than drive from her house her friend and benefactress.

Agnes was not long in forming her resolution; and the next morning, without saying a word to Fanny on the subject, she went out in search of a lodging for herself and child—as gratitude and justice forbade her to remain any longer with her persecuted companion.

But after having in vain tried to procure a lodging suitable to the low state of her finances, or rather to her saving plan, she hired a little cottage on the heath above the town, adjoining to that where she had been so hospitably received in the hour of her distress; and, having gladdened the hearts of the friendly cottager and his wife by telling them she was coming to be their neighbour, she went to break the unwelcome tidings to Fanny.

Passionate and vehement indeed was her distress at hearing her young lady, as she still persisted to call her, was going to leave her; but her expostulations and tears were vain; and Agnes, after promising to see Fanny every day, took possession that very evening of her humble habitation.

But her intention in removing was frustrated by the honest indignation and indiscretion of Fanny. She loudly raved against the illiberality which had robbed her of the society of all she held dear, and, as she told every one that Agnes left her by her own choice and not at her desire, those children, who had been taken away because Agnes resided with her, were not sent back to her on her removal. At last, the number of her scholars became so small, that she gave up school-keeping, and employed herself in shawl-working only; while her leisure time was spent in visiting Agnes, or in inveighing, to those who would listen to her, against the cruelty that had driven her young lady from her house.

Fanny used to begin by relating the many obligations her mother and she had received from Agnes and her father, and always ended with saying, "Yet to this woman, who saved me and mine from a workhouse, they wanted me to refuse a home when she stood in need of one! They need not have been afraid of her being too happy! Such a mind as hers can never be happy under the consciousness of having been guilty; and could she ever forget her crime, one visit to her poor father would make her remember it again."

Thus did Fanny talk, as I said before, to those who would listen to her; and there was one auditor who could have listened to her for ever on this subject, and who thought Fanny looked more lovely while expressing her love for her penitent mistress, and pleading her cause with a cheek flushed with virtuous indignation, and eyes suffused with the tears of artless sensibility, than when, attended by the then happy Agnes, she gave her hand in the bloom of youth and beauty to the man of her heart.

This auditor was a respectable tradesman who lived in Fanny's neighbourhood, to whom her faithful attachment to Agnes had for some time endeared her; while Fanny, in return, felt grateful to him for entering with such warmth into her feelings, and for listening so patiently to her complaints; and it was not long before he offered her his hand.

To so advantageous an offer, and to a man so amiable, Fanny could make no objection; especially as Agnes advised her accepting the proposal. But Fanny declared to her lover that she would not marry him, unless he would promise that Agnes and her child should, whenever they chose, have a home with her. To this condition the lover consented; telling Fanny he loved her the better for making it; and Agnes had soon the satisfaction of witnessing the union of this worthy couple.

But they tried in vain to persuade Agnes to take up her residence with them. She preferred living by herself. To her, solitude was a luxury; as, while the little Edward was playing on the heath with the cottager's children, Agnes delighted to brood in uninterrupted silence over the soothing hope, the fond idea, that alone stimulated her to exertion, and procured her tranquillity. All the energies of her mind and body were directed to one end; and while she kept her eye steadfastly fixed on the future, the past lost its power to torture, and the present had some portion of enjoyment.

But were not these soothing reveries sometimes disturbed by the pangs of ill-requited love? and could she, who had loved so fondly as to sacrifice to the indulgence of her passion every thing she held most dear, rise superior to the power of tender recollection, and at once tear from her heart the image of her fascinating lover? It would be unnatural to suppose that Agnes could entirely forget the once-honoured choice of her heart, and the father of her child; or that, although experience had convinced her of its unworthiness, she did not sometimes contemplate, with the sick feelings of disappointed tenderness, the idol which her imagination had decked in graces all its own.

But these remembrances were rare. She oftener beheld him as he appeared before the tribunal of her reason—a cold, selfish, profligate, hypocritical deceiver, as the unfeeling destroyer of her hopes and happiness, and as one who, as she had learned from his own lips, when he most invited confidence, was the most determined to betray. She saw him also as a wretch so devoid of the common feelings of nature and humanity, that, though she left her apartments in London in the dead of night, and in the depth of a severe winter, an almost helpless child in her arms, and no visible protector near, he had never made a single inquiry concerning her fate, or that of his offspring.

At times, the sensations of Agnes bordered on phrensy, when in this heartless, unnatural wretch she beheld the being for whom she had resigned the matchless comforts of her home, and destroyed the happiness and reason of her father. — At these moments, and these only, she used to rush wildly forth in search of company, that she might escape from herself: but more frequently she directed her steps to the abode of the poor; to those who, in her happier hours, had been supported by her bounty, and who now were eager to meet her in her walks, to repay her past benefactions by a "God bless you, lady!" uttered in a tone of respectful pity.

When her return was first known to the objects of her benevolence, Agnes soon saw herself surrounded by them; and was, in her humble apparel and dejected state, followed by them with more blessings and more heartfelt respect than in the proudest hour of her prosperity.

"Thank God!" ejaculated Agnes, as she turned a glistening eye on her ragged followers; "there are yet those whose eyes mine may meet with confidence. There are some beings in the world towards whom I have done my duty." But the next minute she recollected that the guilty flight which made her violate the duty she owed her father, at the same time removed her from the power of fulfilling her duty to the poor; for it is certain, that our duties are so closely linked together, that, as the breaking one pearl from a string of pearls hazards the loss of all, so the violation of one duty endangers the safety of every other.

"Alas!" exclaimed Agnes, as this melancholy truth occurred to her, "it is not for me to exult; for, even in the squalid, meagre countenances of these kind and grateful beings, I read evidences of my guilt — They looked up to me for aid, and I deserted them!"

In time, however, these acute feelings wore away; and Agnes, by entering again on the offices of benevolence and humanity towards the distressed, lost in a consciousness of present usefulness the bitter sensations of past neglect.

True, she could no longer feed the hungry or clothe the naked, but she could soften the pangs of sickness by expressing sympathy in its sufferings. She could make the nauseous medicine more welcome, if not more salutary, by administering it herself; for, though poor, she was still superior to the sufferers she attended; and it was soothing to them to see such a lady take so much trouble for those so much beneath her—and she could watch the live-long night by the bed of the dying, join in the consoling prayer offered by the lips of another, or, in her own eloquent and impassioned language, speak peace and hope to the departing soul.

These tender offices, these delicate attentions, so dear to the heart of every one, but so particularly welcome to the poor from their superiors, as they are acknowledgements of the relationship between them, and confessions that they are of the same species as themselves, and heirs of the same hopes, even those who bestow money with generous profusion do not often pay. But Agnes was never content to give relief unaccompanied by attendance: she had reflected deeply on the nature of the human heart, and knew that a participating smile, a sympathizing tear, a friendly pressure of the hand, the shifting of an uneasy pillow, and patient attention to an unconnected tale of twice-told symptoms, were, in the esteem of the indigent sufferer, of as great value as pecuniary assistance.

Agnes, therefore, in her poverty, had the satisfaction of knowing that she was as consoling to the distressed, if not as useful, as she was in her prosperity; and if there could be a moment when she felt the glow of exultation in her breast, it was when she left the habitation of indigence or sorrow, followed by the well-earned blessings of its inhabitants.

Had Agnes been capable of exulting in a consciousness of being revenged, another source of exultation might have been hers, provided she had ever deigned to inquire concerning her profligate seducer, whom she wrongfully accused of having neglected to make inquiries concerning her and her child. Agnes saw, two months after her return from London, an account of Clifford's marriage in the paper, and felt some curiosity to know what had so long retarded an union which, when she left town, was fixed for the Monday following; and Fanny observed an increased degree of gloom and abstraction in her appearance all that day. But, dismissing this feeling from her mind as unworthy of it, from that moment she resolved, if possible, to recall Clifford to her imagination, as one who, towards her, had been guilty not of perfidy and deceit only, but of brutal and unnatural neglect.

In this last accusation, however, as I said before, she was unjust. When Clifford awoke the next morning after his last interview with Agnes, and the fumes of the wine he had drunk the night before were entirely dissipated, he recollected, with great uneasiness, the insulting manner in which he had justified his intended marriage, and the insight into the baseness of his character which his unguarded confessions had given to her penetration.

The idea of having incurred the contempt of Agnes was insupportable. Yet, when he recollected the cold, calm, and dignified manner in which she spoke and acted when he bade her adieu, he was convinced that he had taught her to despise him; and, knowing Agnes, he was also certain, that she must soon cease to love the man whom she had once learned to despise.

"But I will go to her directly," exclaimed he to himself, ringing his bell violently; "and I will attribute my infernal folly to drunkenness." He then ordered his servant to call a coach, finding himself too languid, from his late intemperance, to walk; and was just going to step into it when he saw Mrs. Askew, pale and trembling, and heard her, in a faltering voice, demand to see him in private for a few minutes.

I shall not attempt to describe his rage and astonishment when he heard of the elopement of Agnes. But these feelings were soon followed by those of terror for her safety, and that of his child; and his agitation for some moments was so great as to deprive him of the power of considering how he should proceed, in order to hear some tidings of the fugitives, and endeavour to recall them.

It was evident that Agnes had escaped the night before, because a servant, sitting up for a gentleman who lodged in the house, was awakened from sleep by the noise she made in opening the door; and, running into the hall, she saw the tail of Agnes's gown as she shut it again; and looking to see who was gone out, she saw a lady who she was almost certain was miss Fitzhenry, running down the street with great speed. But to put its being Agnes beyond all doubt, she ran up to her room, and finding the door open, went in, and could see neither her nor her child.

To this narration Clifford listened with some calmness; but when Mrs. Askew told him that Agnes had taken none of her clothes with her, he fell into an agony amounting to phrensy, and exclaiming, "Then it must be so — she has destroyed both herself and the child!" his senses failed him, and he dropped down insensible on the sofa. This horrible probability had occurred to Mrs. Askew; and she had sent servants different ways all night, in order to find her if she were still in existence, that she might spare Clifford, if possible, the pain of conceiving a suspicion like her own.

Clifford was not so fortunate as to remain long in a state of unconsciousness, but soon recovered to a sense of misery and unavailing remorse. At length, he recollected that a coach set off that very night for her native place, from the White-horse Cellar,[1] and that it was possible that she might have obtained a lodging the night before, where she meant to stay till the coach was ready to set off the following evening. He immediately went to Piccadilly, to see whether places for a lady and child had been taken—but no such passengers were on the list. He then inquired whether a lady and child had gone from that inn the night before in the coach that went within a few miles of the town of ———. But, as Agnes had reached the inn just as the coach was setting off, no one belonging to it, but the coachman, knew she was a passenger.

---

1   See note 2, p. 86

"Well, I flatter myself," said Clifford to Mrs. Askew, endeavouring to smile, "that she will make her appearance here at night, if she does not come to-day; and I will not stir from this spot till the coach sets off, and will even go in it some way, to see whether it does not stop to take her up on the road."

This resolution he punctually put in practice. All day Clifford was stationed at a window opposite to the inn, or in the book-keeper's office; but night came, the coach was ready to set off, and still no Agnes appeared. However, Clifford, having secured a place, got in with the other passengers, and went six miles or more before he gave up the hope of hearing the coachman ordered to stop, in the soft voice of Agnes.

At last, all expectation failed him; and, complaining of a violent headach, he desired to be set down, sprang out of the carriage, and relieved the other passengers from a very restless and disagreeable companion: and Clifford, without a great coat and in a violent attack of fever, was wandering on the road to London, in hopes of meeting Agnes, at the very time when his victim was on the road to her native place, in company with her unhappy father.

By the time Clifford reached London, he was bordering on a state of delirium—but had recollection enough to desire his confidential servant to inform his father of the state he was in, and then take the road to ———, and ask at every inn on the road whether a lady and child (describing Agnes and little Edward) had been there. The servant obeyed; and the anxious father, who had been informed of the cause of his son's malady, soon received the following letter from Wilson, while he was attending at his bedside:

"My Lord,

"Sad news of miss Fitzhenry and the child; and reason to fear they both perished with cold. For being told at one of the inns on this road that a young woman and child had been found frozen to death last night, and carried to the next town to be owned, I set off for there directly: and while I was taking a drap of brandy to give me spirits to see the bodies, for a qualm came over me, when I thought of what can't be helped, and how pretty, and good-natured, and happy she once was, a woman came down with a silk wrapper and a shawl that I knew belonged to the poor lady, and said the young woman found dead had those things on. This was proof positive, my lord,—and it turned me sick. Still it is better so than self-murder; so my master had best know it, I think; and humbly hoping your lordship will think so too, I remain your lordship's

"Most humble servant to command,

"J. WILSON.

"P.S. If I gain more particulars shall send them."

Dreadful as the supposed death of Agnes and her child appeared to the father of Clifford, he could not be sorry that so formidable a rival to his future daughter-in-law was no longer to be feared; and as Clifford, in the ravings of his fever, was continually talking of Agnes as self-murdered, and the murderer of her child, and of himself as the abandoned cause; and as that idea seemed to haunt and terrify his imagination, he thought with his son's servant that he had better take the first opportunity of telling Clifford the truth, melancholy as it was. When, therefore, a proper occasion offered he had done so, before he received this second letter from Wilson:

"My lord,

"It was all fudge;—miss Fitzhenry is alive, and alive like, at ————. She stopped at an inn on the road and parted with her silk coat and shawl for some things she wanted, and a hussey of a chambermaid stole them and went off in the night with them, and her little by-blow:[1]—but justice overtakes us sooner or later. I suppose his honour, my master, will be cheery at this;—but, as joy often distracts as much as grief, they say, though I never believed it, I take it you will not tell him this good news hand-over-head,—and am

"Your lordship's

"Most humble to command,

"J. WILSON.

"P.S. I have been to ———— and have heard for certain miss F. and her child are there."

---

1 Illegitimate child.

His lordship was even more cautious than Wilson wished him to be; for he resolved not to communicate the glad tidings to Clifford, cautiously or incautiously, as he thought there would be no chance of his son's fulfilling his engagements with miss Sandford, if he knew Agnes was living: —especially, as her flight and her supposed death had proved to Clifford how necessary she was to his happiness. Nay, his lordship went still further; and he resolved Clifford should never know, if he could possibly help it, that the report of her death was false.

How to effect this was the difficulty; but wisely conceiving that Wilson was not inaccessible to a bribe, he offered him so much a year, on condition he suffered his master to remain convinced of the truth of the story that Agnes and her child had perished in the snow, and of intercepting all letters that he fancied came from Agnes; telling him at the same time that if he ever found he had violated the conditions, the annuity should immediately cease.

To this Wilson consented; and, when Clifford recovered, he made his compliance with the terms more easy, by desiring Wilson, and the friends to whom his connection with Agnes had been known, never to mention her name in his presence again, if they valued his health and reason, and as the safety of both depended on his forgetting a woman, of whom he had never felt the value sufficiently till he had lost her for ever.

Soon after, he married;—and the disagreeable qualities of his wife made him recollect, with more painful regret, the charms and virtues of Agnes. The consequence was that he plunged deeper than ever into dissipation, and had recourse to intoxication in order to banish care and disagreeable recollections: —and, while year after year passed away in fruitless expectation of a child to inherit the estate and the long-disputed title, he remembered, with agonizing regrets, the beauty of his lost Edward; and reflected that, by refusing to perform his promises to the injured Agnes, he had deprived himself of the heir he so much coveted, and of a wife who would have added dignity to the title she bore, and been the delight and ornament of his family.

Such were the miserable feelings of Clifford—such the cor-roding cares that robbed his mind of its energy, and his body of health and vigour. Though courted, caressed, flattered, and sur-rounded by affluence and splendour, he was disappointed and self condemned. And while Agnes, for the first time condemn-ing him unjustly, attributed his silence and neglect of her and her offspring to a degree of indifference and hard-heartedness which human nature shudders at, Clifford was feeling all the horrors of remorse, without the consolations of repentance.

I have before observed, that one idea engrossed the mind and prompted the exertions of Agnes;—and this was the prob-able restoration of her father to reason.—"Could I but once more hear him call me by my name, and bless me with his for-giveness, I should die in peace; and something within me tells me my hopes will not be vain: and who knows but we may pass a contented, if not a happy life together, yet?—So toil on, toil on, Agnes, and expect the fruit of thy labours."

These words she was in the habit of repeating not only to Fanny and her next door neighbours (whom she had acquaint-ed with her story), but to her self as she sat at work or traversed the heath. Even in the dead of night she would start from a troubled sleep, and repeating these words, they would operate as a charm on her disturbed mind; and as she spoke the last sen-tence, she would fall into a quiet slumber, from which she awoke the next morning at day-break to pursue with increased alacrity the labours of the day.

Meanwhile Agnes and her exemplary industry continued to engage the attention and admiration of the candid and liberal in the town of ———.

Mr. Seymour, who did not venture to inquire concerning her of Fanny while she lived at her house, now often called there to ask news of Agnes and her employments; and his curiosity was excited to know to what purpose she intended to devote the money earned with so much labour, and hoarded with such parsimonious care.

But Fanny was as ignorant on this subject as himself, and the only new information she could give him was, that Agnes had begun to employ herself in fancy-works, in order to increase her gains; and that it was her intention soon to send little Edward (then four years old) to town, to offer artificial flowers, painted needle-books,[1] work bags, &c. at the doors of the opulent and humane.

Nor was it long before this design was put in execution; and Mr. Seymour had the satisfaction of buying the first time all the lovely boy's store, himself, for presents to his daughters. The little merchant returned to his anxious mother, bounding with delight, not at the good success of his first venture, for its importance he did not understand, but at the kindness of Mr. Seymour, who had met him on the road, conducted him to his house, helped his daughters to load his pockets with cakes, &c. and put in his basket, in exchange for his merchandize, tongue, chicken, &c. to carry home to his mother.

Agnes heard the child's narration with more pleasure than she had for some time experienced. — "They do not despise me, then," said she, "they even respect me too much to offer me pecuniary aid, or presents of any kind but in a way that cannot wound my feelings."

But this pleasure was almost immediately checked by the recollection that he whose wounded spirit would have been soothed by seeing her once more an object of delicate attention and respect, and for whose sake alone she could now ever be capable of enjoying them, was still unconscious of her claims to it, and knew not they were so generally acknowledged. In the words of Jane de Montfort she could have said,

> "He to whose ear my praise most welcome was,
> Hears it no more!"[2]

"But I will still hope on," Agnes used to exclaim as these thoughts occurred to her; and again her countenance assumed the wild expression of a dissatisfied but still expecting spirit.

---

1 Needle books were decorated folders of heavy paper designed to hold sewing or embroidery needles. Like needlework, this type of artistic craft offered a way to earn money to the impoverished woman.

2 Joanna Baillie, *De Monfort: A Tragedy*, Act V, scene iv, 97–98. The lines are spoken by the character Jane de Monfort. The play was first published in 1798.

Three years had now elapsed since Agnes first returned to her native place. "The next year," said Agnes to Fanny with unusual animation, "cannot fail of bringing forth good to me. You know that, according to the rules of the new bedlam, a patient is to remain five years in the house: at the end of that time, if not cured, he is to be removed to the apartments appropriated to incurables, and kept there for life, his friends paying a certain annuity for his maintenance; or he is, on their application, to be returned to their care—"—"And what then?" said Fanny, wondering at the unusual joy that animated Agnes's countenance. "Why then," replied she, "as my father's time for being confined expires at the end of the next year, he will either be cured by that time, or he will be given up to my care; and then, who knows what the consequences may be!"—"What indeed!" returned Fanny, who foresaw great personal fatigue and anxiety, if not danger, to Agnes in such a plan, and was going to express her fears and objections; but Agnes, in a manner overpoweringly severe, desired her to be silent, and angrily withdrew.

Soon after, Agnes received a proof of being still dear to her friend Caroline; which gave her a degree of satisfaction amounting even to joy.

Mr. Seymour, in a letter to his daughter, had given her an account of all the proceedings of Agnes, and expressed his surprise at the eagerness with which she laboured to gain money, merely, as it seemed, for the sake of hoarding it, as she had then only herself and child to maintain; and it was certain her father would always be allowed to remain, free of all expenses, an inhabitant of an asylum which owed its erection chiefly to his benevolent exertions.

But Caroline, to whom the mind of Agnes was well known, and who had often contemplated with surprise and admiration her boldness in projecting, her promptness in deciding, and her ability in executing the projects she had formed; and above all that sanguine temper which led her to believe probable what others only conceived to be possible, found a reason immediately for the passion of hoarding which seemed to have taken possession of her friend—and, following the instant impulse of friendship and compassion, she sent Agnes the following letter, in which was inclosed a bank note to a considerable amount:

"I have divined your secret, my dear Agnes. I know why you are so anxious to hoard what you gain with such exemplary industry. In another year your father will have been the allotted time under the care of the medical attendants in your part of the world; and you are hoarding that you may be able, when that time comes, to procure for him elsewhere the best possible advice and assistance. Yes, yes, I know I am right: — therefore, lest your own exertions should not, in the space of a twelve-month, be crowned with sufficient success, I conjure you, by our long friendship, to appropriate the inclosed to the purpose in question; and should the scheme which I impute to you be merely the creature of my own brain, as it is a good scheme, employ the money in executing it.

"To silence all your scruples, I assure you that my gift is sanctioned by my husband and my father, who join with me in approbation of your conduct, and in the most earnest wishes that you may receive the reward of it in the entire restoration of your afflicted parent. Already have the candid and enlightened paid you their tribute of recovered esteem.

"It is the *slang* of the present day, if I may be allowed this vulgar but forcible expression, to inveigh bitterly against society for excluding from its circle, with unrelenting rigour, the woman who has once transgressed the salutary laws of chastity; and some brilliant and persuasive, but, in my opinion, mistaken writers, of both sexes, have endeavoured to prove that many an amiable woman has been for ever lost to virtue and the world, and become the victim of prostitution, merely because her first fault was treated with ill-judging and criminal severity.[1]

---

1 Mary Wollstonecraft writes in *A Vindication of the Rights of Woman* (1792): "A woman who has lost her honour, imagines that she cannot fall lower, and as for recovering her former station, it is impossible; no exertion can wash this stain away. Losing thus every spur, and having no other means of support, prostitution becomes her only refuge, and the character is quickly depraved by circumstances over which the poor wretch has little power, unless she possesses an uncommon portion of sense and loftiness of spirit" (Chapter IV, "Observations on the State of Degradation to Which Woman is Reduced by Various Causes," 71-72). But Macaulay argues

"This assertion appears to me to be fraught with mischief; as it is calculated to deter the victim of seduction from penitence and amendment, by telling her that she would employ them in her favour in vain. And it is surely as false as it is dangerous. I know many instances; and it is fair to conclude that the experience of others is similar to mine, of women restored by perseverance in a life of expiatory amendment, to that rank in society which they had forfeited by one false step, while their fault has been forgotten in their exemplary conduct, as wives and mothers.

"But it is not to be expected that society should open its arms to receive its prodigal children till they have undergone a long and painful probation,—till they have practised the virtues of self-denial, patience, fortitude, and industry. And she whose penitence is not the mere result of wounded pride and caprice, will be capable of exerting all these virtues, in order to regain some portion of the esteem she has lost. What will difficulties and mortifications be to her? Keeping her eye steadily fixed on the end she has in view, she will bound lightly over them all; nor will she seek the smiles of the world, till, instead of receiving them as a favour, she can demand them as a right.

"Agnes, my dear Agnes, do you not know the original of the above picture? You, by a life of self-denial, patience, fortitude, and industry, have endeavoured to atone for the crime you committed against society; and I hear her voice saying, 'Thy sins are forgiven thee!' and ill befall the hand that would uplift the sacred pall which penitence and amendment have thrown over departed guilt!"

Such was the letter of Caroline: —a letter intended to speak peace and hope to the heart of Agnes; to reconcile the offender to herself; and light up her dim eye with the beams of self-approbation. Thus did she try to console her guilty and unhappy friend in the hour of her adversity and degradation. But Caroline had given a still *greater* proof of the sincerity of her friendship: —she had never wounded the feelings, or endeav-

---

somewhat differently, referring to "the trite and foolish observation, that the first fault against chastity in woman has a radical power to deprave the character. But no such frail beings come out of the hands of Nature" (see Appendix I.4).

oured to mortify the self-love of Agnes in the hour of her prosperity and acknowledged superiority; she had seen her attractions, and heard her praises, without envy; nor ever with seeming kindness but real malignity related to her, in the accents of pretended wonder and indignation, the censures she had incurred, or the ridicule she had excited,—but in every instance she had proved her friendship;—a memorable exception to what are sarcastically termed the friendships of women.

"Yes,—she has indeed divined my secret," said Agnes when she had perused the letter, while tears of tenderness trickled down her cheeks, "and she deserves to assist me in procuring means for my poor father's recovery,—an indulgence which I should be jealous of granting to any one else, except you, Fanny," she added, seeing on Fanny's countenance an expression of jealousy of this richer friend; "and on the strength of this noble present," looking with a smile at her darned and pieced, though neat apparel, "I will treat myself with a new gown." — "Not before it was wanted," said Fanny peevishly. — "Nay," replied Agnes with a forced smile, "surely I am well dressed enough for a runaway daughter. 'My father loved to see me fine,' as poor Clarissa says,[1] and had I never left him, I should not have been forced to wear such a gown as this: — but, Fanny, let me but see him once more capable of knowing me, and of loving me, if it be possible for him to forgive me," added she in a faltering voice, "and I will then, if he wishes it, be fine again, though I work all night to make myself so."

"My dear, dear lady," said Fanny sorrowfully, "I am sure I did not mean any thing by what I said; but you have such a way with you, and talk so sadly! — Yet, I can't bear, indeed I can't, to see such a lady in a gown not good enough for me; and then to see my young master no better dressed than the cottager's boys next door;—and then to hear them call master Edward little Fitzhenry, as if he was not their betters;—I can't bear it—it does not signify talking, I can't bear to think of it."

---

1 Clarissa is the central character in Samuel Richardson's novel *Clarissa, or The History of a Young Lady* (1747-8). In the first edition of the novel this phrase appears in Volume 6, letter 40, 154.

"How, then," answered Agnes in a solemn tone, and grasping her hand as she spoke, "how can I bear to think of the guilt which has thus reduced so low both me and my child? O! would to God! my boy could exchange situation with the children whom you think his inferiors! I have given him life, indeed, but not one legal claim to what is necessary to the support of life, except the scanty pittance I might, by a public avowal of my shame, wring from his father."

"I would beg my bread with him through the streets before you should do that," hastily exclaimed Fanny, "and, for the love of God, say no more on this subject;—He is *my child*, as well as yours," she continued, snatching little Edward to her bosom, who was contentedly playing with his top at the door; and Agnes, in contemplating the blooming graces of the boy, forgot he was an object of compassion.

The next year passed away as the former had done; and at the end of it Fitzhenry being pronounced incurable, but perfectly quiet and harmless, Agnes desired, in spite of the advice and entreaties of the governors, that he might be delivered up to her, that she might put him under the care of Dr. W——.

Luckily for Agnes the assignees of her father recovered a debt of a hundred pounds, which had long been due to him; and this sum they had great pleasure in paying Agnes, in order to further the success of her last hope.[1]

On the day fixed for Fitzhenry's release, Agnes purchased a complete suit of clothes for him, such as he used to wear in former days, and dressed herself in a manner suited to her birth, rather than her situation; then set out in a post-chaise, attended by the friendly cottager, as it was judged imprudent for her to travel with her father alone, to take up Fitzhenry at the bedlam, while Fanny was crying with joy to see her dear lady looking like herself again, and travelling like a *gentlewoman*.

But the poor, whom gratitude and affection made constantly

---

1   Private madhouses could be extremely expensive, hence the need for Agnes's savings, Caroline's substantial bank-note, and the recovery of part of Fitzhenry's debt. Roy Porter notes that they appeared in profusion in eighteenth-century England and that "they were to prove running sores of scandal: but they also became sites of therapeutic innovation" (*Mind-Forged Manacles* 131).

observant of the actions of Agnes, were full of consternation, when some of them heard, and communicated to the others, that a post-chaise was standing at miss Fitzhenry's door. "O dear! she is going to leave us again; what shall we do without her?" was the general exclamation; and when Agnes come out to enter her chaise, she found it surrounded by her humble friends, lamenting and inquiring, though with cautious respect, whether she ever meant to come back again. "Fanny will tell you every thing," said Agnes, overcome with grateful emotion at observing the interest she excited. Unable to say more, she waved her hand as a token of farewell to them, and the chaise drove off.

"Is miss Fitzhenry grown *rich* again?" was the general question addressed to Fanny; and I am sure it was a disinterested one, and that, at the moment, they asked it without a view to their profiting by her change of situation, and merely as anxious for her welfare;—and when Fanny told them whither and wherefore Agnes was gone, could prayers, good wishes, and blessings, have secured success to the hopes of Agnes, her father, even as soon as she stopped at the gate of the bedlam, would have recognised and received her with open arms. But when she arrived, she found Fitzhenry as irrational as ever, though delighted to hear he was going to take a ride with "*the lady*," as he always called Agnes; and she had the pleasure of seeing him seat himself beside her with a look of uncommon satisfaction. Nothing worth relating happened on the road. Fitzhenry was very tractable, except at night, when the cottager, who slept in the same room with him, found it difficult to make him keep in bed, and was sometimes forced to call Agnes to his assistance: at sight of her he always became quiet, and obeyed her implicitly.

The skilful and celebrated man to whom she applied, received her with sympathizing kindness, and heard her story with a degree of interest and sensibility peculiarly grateful to the afflicted heart. Agnes related with praise-worthy ingenuousness the whole of her sad history, judging it necessary that the doctor should know the cause of the malady for which he was to prescribe.

It was peculiarly the faculty of Agnes to interest in her welfare those with whom she conversed; and the doctor soon experienced a more than ordinary earnestness to cure a patient so interesting from his misfortunes, and recommended by so interesting a daughter. "Six months," said he, "will be a sufficient time of trial, and in the mean while you shall reside in a lodging near us." Fitzhenry then became an inmate of the doctor's house; Agnes took possession of apartments in the neighbourhood; and the cottager returned to ———.

The ensuing six months were passed by Agnes in the soul-sickening feeling of hope deferred:[1] and, while the air of the place agreed so well with her father that he became fat and healthy in his appearance, anxiety preyed on her delicate frame, and made the doctor fear that when he should be forced to pronounce his patient beyond his power to cure, she would sink under the blow; unless the hope of being still serviceable to her father should support her under its pressure. He resolved, therefore, to inform her, in as judicious and cautious a manner as possible, that he saw no prospect of curing the thoroughly-shattered intellect of Fitzhenry.

"*I* can do nothing for your father," said he to Agnes (when he had been under his care six months), laying great stress on the word *I*;—(Agnes, with a face of horror, started from her seat, and laid her hand on his arm)—"but *you* can do a great deal." —

"Can I? can I?" exclaimed Agnes, sobbing convulsively — "Blessed hearing! But the means — the means?"

"It is very certain," he replied, "that he experiences great delight when he sees you, and sees you too employed in his service;—and when he lives with you, and sees you again where he has been accustomed to see you —"

"You advise his living with me then?" interrupted Agnes with eagerness. —

"I do, most strenuously," replied the doctor.

"Blessings on you for those words!" answered Agnes: "they said you would oppose it! You are a wise and a kind-hearted man!"

---

1 Proverbs 13.2: "Hope deferred maketh the heart sick."

"My dear child," rejoined the doctor, "when an evil can't be cured, it should at least be alleviated."

"You think it can't be cured, then?" again interrupted Agnes.

"Not absolutely so: — I know not what a course of medicine, and living with you as much in your old way as possible, may do for him. Let him resume his usual habits, his usual walks, live as near your former habitation as you possibly can; let him hear his favourite songs, and be as much with him as you can contrive to be; and if you should not succeed in making him rational again, you will at least make him happy."[1]

"Happy! — I make him happy, now!" exclaimed Agnes, pacing the room in an agony: — "I made him happy once! — but now! —"

"You must hire some one to sleep in the room with him," resumed the doctor.

"No, no," cried Agnes impatiently;— "no one shall wait on him but myself;— I will attend him day and night."

"And should your strength be worn out by such incessant watching, who would take care of him then? — Remember, you are but mortal." — Agnes shook her head, and was silent. — "Besides, the strength of a man may sometimes be necessary, and, for his sake as well as yours, I must insist on being obeyed."

"You shall be obeyed," said Agnes mournfully.

"Then now," rejoined he, "let me give you my advice relative to diet, medicine, and management." This he did in detail, as he found Agnes had a mind capacious enough to understand his system; and promising to answer her letters immediately, whenever she wrote to him for advice, he took an affectionate farewell of her; and Agnes and her father, accompanied by a man whom the doctor had procured for the purpose, set off for ———.

Fanny was waiting at the cottage with little Edward to receive them,—but the dejected countenance of Agnes precluded all necessity of asking concerning the state of Fitzhenry.

---

1 Dr. W———'s recommendations suggest he is a practitioner of "moral therapy," a more benign approach to the treatment of insanity. For similar recommendations see Harper (Appendix J.6.iv).

Scarcely could the caresses and joy her child expressed at seeing her call a smile to her lips; and, as she pressed him to her bosom, tears of bitter disappointment mingled with those of tenderness.

In a day or two after, Agnes, in compliance with the doctor's desire, hired a small tenement very near the house in which they formerly lived; and in the garden of which, as it was then empty, they obtained leave to walk. She also procured a person to sleep in the room with her father instead of the man who came with them; and he carried back a letter from her to the doctor, informing him that she had arranged every thing according to his directions.

It was a most painfully pleasing sight to behold the attention of Agnes to her father. She knew it was not in her power to repair the enormous injury she had done him, and that all she could now do, was but a poor amends; still it was affecting to see how anxiously she watched his steps whenever he chose to wander alone from home, and what pains she took to make him neat in his appearance, and cleanly in his person. Her child and herself were clothed in coarse apparel, but she bought for her father every thing of the best materials; and, altered as he was, Fitzhenry still looked like a gentleman.

Sometimes he seemed in every respect so like himself, that Agnes, hurried away by her imagination, would, after gazing on him some minutes, start from her seat, seize his hand, and, breathless with hope, address him as if he were a rational being;— when a laugh of vacancy, or a speech full of the inconsistency of phrensy, would send her back to her chair again, with a pulse quickened, and a cheek flushed with the fever of disappointed expectation.

However, he certainly was pleased with her attentions,— but, alas! he knew not who was the bestower of them: he knew not that the child whose ingratitude or whose death he still lamented in his ravings in the dead of night, was returned to succour, to sooth him, and to devote herself entirely to his service. He heard her, but he knew her not; he saw her, but in her he was not certain he beheld his child: and this was the pang that preyed on the cheek and withered the frame of Agnes: but she persisted to hope, and patiently endured the pain of to-day, expecting the joy of to-morrow; nor did her hopes always appear ill founded.

The first day that Agnes led him to the garden once his own, he ran through every walk with eager delight; but he seemed surprised and angry to see the long grass growing in the walks, and the few flowers that remained choked up with weeds,—and began to pluck up the weeds with hasty violence.

"It is time to go home," said Agnes to him just as the day began to close in; and Fitzhenry immediately walked to the door which led into the house, and, finding it locked, looked surprised: then, turning to Agnes, he asked her if she had not the key in her pocket; and on her telling him that was not his home, he quitted the house evidently with great distress and reluctance, and was continually looking back at it, as if he did not know how to believe her.

On this little circumstance poor Agnes lay ruminating the whole night after, with joyful expectation; and she repaired to the garden at day-break, with a gardener whom she hired, to make the walks look as much as possible as they formerly did. But they had omitted to tie up some straggling flowers;—and when Agnes, Fanny, and the cottager, accompanied Fitzhenry thither the next evening, he, though he seemed conscious of the improvement that had taken place, was disturbed at seeing some gilliflowers[1] trailing along the ground; and suddenly turning to Agnes he said, "Why do you not bind up these?"

To do these little offices in the garden, and keep the parterre[2] in order, was formerly Agnes's employment. What delight, then, must these words of Fitzhenry, so evidently the result of an association in his mind between her and his daughter, have excited in Agnes! With a trembling hand and a glowing cheek she obeyed; and Fitzhenry saw her, with manifest satisfaction, tie up every straggling flower in the garden, while he eagerly followed her, and bent attentively over her.

At last, when she had gone the whole round of the flower-

---

1 Gillyflowers are any clove-scented flower, but especially pinks or carnations.
2 A flat space in a garden filled by ornamental beds of different sizes and shapes, symmetrically patterned.

beds, he exclaimed, "Good girl! Good girl!" and, putting his arm round her waist, suddenly kissed her cheek.

Surprise, joy, and an emotion difficult to be defined, overcame the irritable frame of Agnes, and she fell senseless to the ground. But the care of Fanny soon recovered her again;—and the first question she asked was, how her father (whom she saw in great agitation running round the garden) behaved when he saw her fall.

"He raised you up," replied Fanny, "and seemed so distressed! he would hold the salts[1] to your nose himself, and would scarcely suffer me to do any thing for you; but, hearing you mutter 'Father! dear father!' as you began to come to yourself, he changed colour, and immediately began to run round the garden, as you now see him."

"Say no more, say no more, my dear friend," cried Agnes; "it is enough. I am happy, quite happy;—it is clear that he knew me;—and I have again received a father's embrace: — Then his anxiety too while I was ill;—O! there is no doubt now that he will be quite himself in time."

"Perhaps he may," replied Fanny;— "but —"

"But! and perhaps!" cried Agnes pettishly;— "I tell you he will, he certainly will recover; and those are not my friends who doubt it." So saying, she ran hastily forward to meet Fitzhenry, who was joyfully hastening towards her, leaving Fanny grieved and astonished at her petulance; but few are the tempers proof against continual anxiety, and the souring influence of still renewed and still disappointed hope: and even Agnes, the once gentle Agnes, if contradicted on this one subject, became angry and unjust.

But she was never conscious of having given pain to the feelings of another, without bitter regret and an earnest desire of healing the wound she had made; and when, leaning on Fitzhenry's arm, she returned towards Fanny, and saw her in tears, she felt a pang severer than she had inflicted, and said every thing that affection and gratitude could dictate, to restore her to tranquillity again. Her agitation alarmed Fitzhenry; and,

---

1   Smelling salts (usually ammonium carbonate), used to restore consciousness to people feeling faint.

exclaiming "Poor thing!" he held the smelling-bottle, almost by force, to her nose, and seemed terrified lest she was going to faint again.

"You see, you see," said Agnes triumphantly to Fanny: and Fanny, made cautious by experience, declared her conviction that her young lady must know more of all matters than she did.

But month after month elapsed, and no circumstances of a similar nature occurred to give new strength to the hopes of Agnes; however, she had the pleasure to see that Fitzhenry not only seemed attached to her, but to be pleased with little Edward.

She had indeed taken pains to teach him to endeavour to amuse her father,—but sometimes she had the mortification of hearing, when fits of loud laughter from the child reached her ear, "Edward was only laughing at grandpapa's odd faces and actions, mamma:" and having at last taught him it was wicked to laugh at such things, because his grandfather was not well when he distorted his face, her heart was nearly as much wrung by the pity he expressed; for whenever these occasional slight fits of phrensy attacked Fitzhenry, little Edward would exclaim, "Poor grandpapa! He is not well now;—I wish we could make him well, mamma!" But, on the whole, she had reason to be tolerably cheerful.

Every evening, when the weather was fine, Agnes, holding her father's arm, was seen taking her usual walk, her little boy gamboling before them; and never, in their most prosperous hours, were they met with curtsies more low, or bows more respectful, than on these occasions; and many a one grasped with affectionate eagerness the meagre hand of Fitzhenry, and the feverish hand of Agnes; for even the most rigid hearts were softened in favour of Agnes, when they beheld the ravages grief had made in her form, and gazed on her countenance, which spoke in forcible language the sadness yet resignation of her mind. She might, if she had chosen it, have been received at many houses where she had formerly been intimate; but she declined it, as visiting would have interfered with the necessary labours of the day, with her constant attention to her father, and with the education of her child. "But when my father recovers," said she to Fanny, "as he will be pleased to find I am not deemed wholly unworthy of notice, I shall have great satisfaction in visiting with him."

To be brief: — Another year elapsed, and Agnes still hoped; and Fitzhenry continued the same to every eye but hers: — she every day fancied his symptoms of returning reason increased, and no one of her friends dared to contradict her. But in order, if possible, to accelerate his recovery, she had resolved to carry him to London, to receive the best advice the metropolis afforded, when Fitzhenry was attacked by an acute complaint which confined him to his bed. This event, instead of alarming Agnes, redoubled her hopes. She insisted that it was the crisis of his disorder, and expected health and reason would return together. Not for one moment, therefore, would she leave his bedside, and she would allow herself neither food nor rest, while with earnest attention she gazed on the fast sinking eyes of Fitzhenry, eager to catch in them an expression of returning recognition.

One day, after he had been sleeping some time, and she, as usual, was attentively watching by him, Fitzhenry slowly and gradually awoke; and, at last, raising himself on his elbow, looked round him with an expression of surprise, and, seeing Agnes, exclaimed, "My child! are you there? Gracious God! is this possible?"

Let those who have for years been pining away life in fruitless expectation, and who see themselves at last possessed of the long-desired blessing, figure to themselves the rapture of Agnes. — "He knows me! He is himself again!" burst from her quivering lips — unconscious that it was too probable, restored reason was here the forerunner of dissolution.

"O! my father!" she cried, falling on her knees, but not daring to look up at him, "O! my father, forgive me, if possible: — I have been guilty, but I am penitent!"

Fitzhenry, as much affected as Agnes, faltered out, "Thou art restored to me, — and God knows how heartily I forgive thee!" Then raising her to his arms, Agnes, happy in the fulfilment of her utmost wishes, felt herself once more pressed to the bosom of the most affectionate of fathers.

"But surely you are not now come back?" asked Fitzhenry. "I have seen you before, and very lately." — "Seen me! O yes!" replied Agnes with passionate rapidity;— "for these last five years I have seen you daily; and for the last two years you have lived with me, and I have worked to maintain you!" — "Indeed!" answered Fitzhenry: — "but how pale and thin you are! you have worked too much: — Had you no *friends*, my child?"

"O yes! and guilty as I have been, they pity, nay, they respect me, and we may yet be happy! as Heaven restores you to my prayers! — True, I have suffered much; but this blessed moment repays me;— this is the only moment of true enjoyment I have known since I left my home and you!"

Agnes was thus pouring out the hasty effusions of her joy, unconscious that Fitzhenry, overcome with affection, emotion, and, perhaps, sorrowful recollections, was struggling in vain for utterance: — At last,— "For so many years,— and I knew you not! — worked for me,— attended me! — Bless, bless her, Heaven!" he faintly articulated; and, worn out with illness, and choked with contending emotions, he fell back on his pillow and expired!

Thus, that blessing, the hope of obtaining which alone gave Agnes courage to endure contumely, poverty, fatigue, and sorrow, was for one moment her own, and then snatched from her for ever!

No wonder, then, that when convinced her father was really dead, she fell into a state of stupefaction, from which she never recovered;—and, at the same time, were borne to the same grave, the father and daughter.[1]

The day of their funeral was indeed a melancholy one: — They were attended to the grave by a numerous procession of respectable inhabitants of both sexes,— while the afflicted and lamenting poor followed mournfully at a distance. Even those who had distinguished themselves by their violence against Agnes at her return, dropped a tear as they saw her borne to her long home. Mrs. Macfiendy forgot her beauty and accom-

---

1 Life imitates art: on her death in 1853 Amelia Opie was buried in her father's grave in the Friends' burying ground in Norwich.

plishments in her misfortunes and early death; and the mother of the child who had fled from the touch of Agnes, felt sorry that she had ever called her the wickedest woman in the world.

But the most affecting part of the procession was little Edward, as chief mourner, led by Fanny and her husband, in all the happy insensibility of childhood, unconscious all the while that he was the pitiable hero of that show, which, by its novelty and parade, so much delighted him,—while his smiles, poor orphan! excited the tears of those around him.

Just before the procession began to move, a post-chariot and four, with white favours,[1] drove into the yard of the largest inn in the town. It contained lord and lady Mountcarrol, who were married only the day before, and were then on their way to her ladyship's country seat.

His lordship, who seemed incapable of resting in one place for a minute together, did nothing but swear at the postillions[2] for bringing them that road, and express an earnest desire to leave the town again as fast as possible.

While he was gone into the stable, for the third time, to see whether the horses were not sufficiently refreshed to go on, a waiter came in to ask lady Mountcarrol's commands, and at that moment the funeral passed the window. The waiter (who was the very servant that at Mr. Seymour's had refused to shut the door against Agnes) instantly turned away his head, and burst into tears. This excited her ladyship's curiosity; and she drew from him a short but full account of Agnes and her father.

He had scarcely finished his story when lord Mountcarrol came in, saying the carriage was ready; and no sooner had his bride begun to relate to him the story she had just heard, than he exclaimed in a voice of thunder, "It is as false as hell, madam! Miss Fitzhenry and her child both died years ago." Then rushing into the carriage, he left lady Mountcarrol terrified and amazed at his manner. But when she was seating herself by his side, she could not help saying that it was impossible for a story

---

1   Favours are ribbons, cockades, or plumes used to decorate the harness.
2   Riders who guide the horses. Rather than placing a driver on the coach, it was common for carriage teams to be directed by men mounted on the near (left) horse of each pair.

to be false, which all the people in the inn averred to be true: then, as he did not offer to interrupt her, she went through the whole story of Agnes and her sufferings; and she was going to comment on them, when the procession, returning from church, crossed the road in which they were going, and obliged the postillions to stop.

Foremost came the little Edward, with all his mother's beauty in his face. "Poor little orphan!" said lady Mountcarrol, giving a tear to the memory of Agnes: "See, my lord, what a lovely boy!" As she spoke, the extreme elegance of the carriage attracted Edward's attention, and springing from Fanny's hand, who in vain endeavoured to hold him back, he ran up to the door to examine the figures on the pannel. At that instant lord Mountcarrol opened the door, lifted the child into the chaise, and, throwing his card of address to the astonished mourners, ordered the servants to drive on as fast as possible.

They did so in despite of Mr. Seymour and others, for astonishment had at first deprived them of the power of moving; and the horses, before the witnesses of this sudden and strange event had recovered their recollection, had gone too far to allow themselves to be stopped.

The card with lord Mountcarrol's name explained what at first had puzzled and confounded, as well as alarmed them; and Fanny, who had fainted at sight of his lordship, because she knew him, altered as he was, to be Edward's father, and the bane of Agnes, now recovering herself, conjured Mr. Seymour to follow his lordship immediately, and tell him Edward was bequeathed to her care.

Mr. Seymour instantly ordered post-horses, and in about an hour after set off in pursuit of the ravisher.

But the surprise and consternation of Fanny and the rest of the mourners, were not greater than that of lady Mountcarrol at sight of her lord's strange conduct. — "What does this outrage mean, my lord?" she exclaimed in a faltering voice; "and whose child is that?" — "It is *my child*, madam," replied he; "and I will never resign him but with life." Then pressing the astonished child to his bosom, he for some minutes sobbed aloud, — while lady Mountcarrol, though she could not help feeling compassion for the agony which the seducer of Agnes must experience at such a moment, was not a little displeased and shocked at finding herself the wife of that Clifford, whose name she had so lately heard coupled with that of a villain.

But her attention was soon called from reflections so unpleasant by the cries of Edward, whose surprise at being seized and carried away by a stranger now yielded to terror, and who, bursting from lord Mountcarrol, desired to go back to his mamma Fanny, and Mr. Seymour.

"What! and leave your own father, Edward?" asked his agitated parent. — "Look at me, — I am your father; — but, I suppose, your mother, as well she might, taught you to hate me?" — "My mamma told me it was wicked to hate any body; and I am sure I have no papa: I had a grandpapa, but he is gone to heaven along with my mamma, Fanny says, and she is my mamma now." And again screaming and stamping with impatience, he insisted on going back to her.

But at length, by promises of riding on a fine horse, and of sending for Fanny to ride with him, he was pacified. Then with artless readiness he related his mother's way of life, and the odd ways of his grandpapa; and thus by acquainting lord Mountcarrol with the sufferings and the virtuous exertions of Agnes, he increased his horror of his own conduct, and his regret at not having placed so noble-minded a woman at the head of his family. But whence arose the story of her death he had yet to learn.

In a few hours they reached the seat which he had acquired by his second marriage; and there too, in an hour after, arrived Mr. Seymour and the husband of Fanny.

Lord Mountcarrol expected this visit, and received them courteously; while Mr. Seymour was so surprised at seeing the once healthy and handsome Clifford changed to an emaciated valetudinarian, and carrying in his face the marks of habitual intemperance, that his indignation was for a moment lost in pity. But recovering himself, he told his lordship that he came to demand justice for the outrage which he had committed, and in the name of the friend to whom miss Fitzhenry had, in case of her sudden death, bequeathed her child, to insist on his being restored to her.

"We will settle that point presently," replied lord Mountcarrol; "but first I conjure you to tell me all that has happened to her since we parted, whose name I have not for years been able to repeat, and who, as well as this child, I have also for years believed dead."

"I will, my lord," answered Mr. Seymour; "but I warn you, that if you have any feeling, it will be tortured by the narration."

"If I have any feeling!" cried his lordship: "but go on, sir; from you, sir—from you, as as—*her friend*, I can bear any thing."

Words could not do justice to the agonies of lord Mountcarrol, while Mr. Seymour, beginning with Agnes's midnight walk to ———, went through a recital of her conduct and sufferings, and hopes and anxieties, and ended with the momentary recovery and death-scene of her father.

But when lord Mountcarrol discovered that Agnes supposed his not making any inquiries concerning her or the child proceeded from brutal indifference concerning their fate, and that, considering him as a monster of inhumanity, she had regarded him not only with contempt, but abhorrence, and seemed to have dismissed him entirely from her remembrance, he beat his breast, he rolled on the floor in frantic anguish, lamenting, in all the bitterness of fruitless regret, that Agnes died without knowing how much he loved her, and without suspecting that while she was supposing him unnaturally forgetful of her and her child, he was struggling with illness, caused by her desertion, and with a dejection of spirits which he had never, at times, been able to overcome; execrating at the same time the memory of his father, and Wilson, whom he suspected of having intentionally deceived him.

To conclude.—Pity for the misery and compunction of lord Mountcarrol, and a sense of the advantages both in education and fortune that would accrue to little Edward from living with his father, prevailed on Mr. Seymour and the husband of Fanny to consent to his remaining where he was;—and from that day Edward was universally known as his lordship's son,—who immediately made a will bequeathing him a considerable fortune.

Lord Mountcarrol was then sinking fast into his grave, the victim of his vices, and worn to the bone by the corroding consciousness that Agnes had died in the persuasion of his having brutally neglected her. — That was the bitterest pang of all! She had thought him so vile, that she could not for a moment regret him!

His first wife he had despised because she was weak and illiterate, and hated because she had brought him no children. His second wife was too amiable to be disliked; but, though he survived his marriage with her two years, she also failed to produce an heir to the title. And while he contemplated in Edward the mind and person of his mother, he was almost frantic with regret that he was not legally his son; and he cursed the hour when with short-sighted cunning he sacrificed the honour of Agnes to his views of family aggrandizement.

But, selfish to the last moment of his existence, it was a consciousness of his own misery, not of that which he had inflicted, which prompted his expressions of misery and regret; and he grudged and envied Agnes the comfort of having been able to despise and forget him. [1]

Peace to the memory of Agnes Fitzhenry! — And may the woman who, like her, has been the victim of artifice, self-confidence, and temptation, like her endeavour to regain the esteem of the world by patient suffering and virtuous exertion; and look forward to the attainment of it with confidence! But may she whose innocence is yet secure, and whose virtues still boast the stamp of chastity, which can alone make them current in the world, tremble with horror at the idea of listening to the voice of the seducer! — For, though the victim of seduction may in time recover the approbation of others, she must always despair of recovering her own.[2]— The image of a father, a

---

1 Though Opie insists on Clifford's irredeemable nature, dramatic adaptations of the novel offer a more penitent seducer. See Appendix E.1.iii and Appendix F.4.

2 The sentence "For, though the victim of seduction ... must always despair of recovering her own" is omitted in the second and subsequent editions.

mother, a brother, a sister, or some other fellow-being, whose peace of mind has been injured by her deviation from virtue, will probably haunt her path through life; and she who might, perhaps, have contemplated with fortitude the wreck of her own happiness, is doomed to pine with fruitless remorse at the consciousness of having destroyed that of another. — For, where is the mortal who can venture to pronounce that his actions are of importance to no one, and that the consequences of his virtues or his vices will be confined to himself alone?

END OF THE TALE.

POEMS.

Epistle supposed to be Addressed by Eudora, The Maid of Corinth, to Her Lover Philemon, Informing him of her having traced his SHADOW on the Wall while he was sleeping, the Night before his Departure: Together with the joyful Consequences of this Action.

THE ARGUMENT.

Dibutades, a potter of Sicyon, first formed likenesses in clay at Corinth, but was indebted to his daughter for the invention.... The girl, being in love with a young man who was soon going from her into some remote country, traced out the lines of his face from his shadow on the wall by candle-light.... Her father filling up the lines with clay formed a bust, and hardened it in the fire with the rest of his earthen ware.

PLINY. Lib. xxxv.[1]

EPISTLE FROM EUDORA, THE MAID OF CORINTH, TO HER LOVER PHILEMON.

> O Love! it was thy glory to impart
> Its infant being to this magic art;
> By thee inspired, the soft Corinthian maid
> Her graceful lover's sleeping form pourtray'd.
> HAYLEY.[2]

YES, I must write—applause to me is vain,
Tho' by admiring multitudes bestow'd,
While my proud triumphs still unknown remain
To thee, dear source from which the blessings flow'd.

5   Then let me breathe the tidings in thine ear;
Learn, how to bless me Love and Fame agree!

---

1   From Pliny's *Natural History*, Book XXXV, Section xliii.
2   William Hayley (1745-1820), "An Essay on Painting in two Epistles to Mr. Romney," ll.125-128.

Why art thou absent at an hour so dear?
I hate e'en glory, if unshar'd by thee.

On the sad eve of that unwelcome day
Ordain'd to tear thee from Eudora's arms,   10
My sinking heart, to various fears a prey,
Felt all a lover's exquisite alarms.

Now with slow step, and now with frantic speed,
Thro' public scenes or lonely shades I rov'd,
When, lo! a favouring, pitying Power decreed   15
That I asleep should find the youth I lov'd.

Yes....I beheld thee (hour with blessings fraught!)
As on thy hand thy sleep-flush'd cheek repos'd:
Yet I, at first, by cold decorum taught,
Fled, and with blushing haste the portal clos'd.   20

But soon Affection fondly check'd my flight:
She whisper'd, "View that winning form once more:
Remember, he who lately charm'd thy sight
Will seek at morning's dawn a distant shore."

At that idea, frigid caution fled;   25
To passion's sway resigning all my soul,
And hurrying back, with timid, trembling tread,
With breath suspended, to thy couch I stole.

Long time I stood in tender thoughts entranc'd,
Gazing uncheck'd,....a new unwonted bliss....   30
Now to thy cheek my trembling lips advanc'd,
Nor quite bestow'd, nor quite withheld the kiss.

"And must that form delight my eyes no more?"
I softly murmur'd, as regret impell'd,
When, lo! with rapture never felt before,   35
I thy dear shadow on the wall beheld.

That moment, Love upon his votary smil'd,
My hand his sceptre, and his throne my breast;
He fired the thought which then my grief beguil'd,
And which to future times will make me blest.

With eager haste I seiz'd a slender wand
Which near the couch a friendly Power had plac'd,
And with a beating heart, a trembling hand,
Along the wall the faithful shadow trac'd.

O happy moment! how my bosom burn'd
With transport, rich reward for all my pain,
When, tho' thy head in various postures turn'd,
I saw the outline still unchang'd remain!

But 'midst my rapture as I heard thee sigh,
And half awak'ning speak Eudora's name,
Beheld thee throw thy languid arms on high,
As recollection o'er thy senses came,

Asham'd to meet thy fond, inquiring eyes,
Asham'd my strong emotion to reveal,
Again I fled....resolv'd my new-found prize
E'en from thy knowledge I'd with care conceal....

But when I reach'd my home, to Memory's eye
So dear, so precious seem'd the mimic line,
"Hence, hence, reserve!" I cried, "vain scruples, fly!
Philemon's heart shall share the joy of mine!"

Ah me! that promis'd pleasure Fate denied....
When next we met, thou cam'st to bid farewell!
And I forgot the invention late my pride,
While on thy neck in speechless grief I fell.

But when, dear youth! thy last farewell I heard,
Nor more my living lover met my view,

Thy lifeless semblance to my mind recurr'd,
And to the prize with breathless speed I flew.

Then, as Aurora,[1] while o'er sinking night
Her radiant hand assumes a sudden sway,   70
In one vast urn collecting all her light,
Pours in full stream at once the flood of day,

So in a moment, skill'd the gloom to chase
Which absence (lovers' night) around me spread,
Upon the wall beam'd forth thy well-known face,   75
And from my mind Affliction's darkness fled.

What tho' I could not on that wall survey
The youthful crimson mantling on thy cheek,
Nor bid the sorrow-soothing line pourtray
Those looks which passion, valour, genius speak....   80

Yet, as I gaze, see Fancy's friendly art
The charms they wanted to my lines supply,
See the soft magic of her touch impart
Bloom to thy cheek, and lustre to thine eye:

Thus, tho' the orb that gilds the face of night   85
Is, sages say, a gloomy mass alone,
When Phœbus[2] fills her with his radiant light,
She charms our eyes with splendour not her own.

But soon new hopes my throbbing bosom sway....
I with quick footsteps to my father press....   90
Exclaiming, "Haste! the mimic lines survey,
Whose magic power has sooth'd my fond distress."

And as he wond'ring gaz'd, I cried, "Thy art
Shall stronger yet Philemon's graces show,

---

1 The goddess of the dawn.
2 Phoebus Apollo, the god of light and youth.

95   Bid his crisp'd curls upon his forehead part,
And speak the grandeur of his swelling brow."

At my entreaty, then with humid clay
The lines he copied which my hand had made,
And to his furnace bore the prize away,
100   While I the process, fir'd with hope, survey'd.

But not Deucalion felt more joy to see
Men spring to being from the stones he threw,[1]
Than I experienc'd, when a bust of thee
From the Promethean fire my father drew!

105   Feebly would words that burst of joy reveal,
The image seem'd my lover to restore!
And sure thy heart this tender truth can feel;
Till thou return, 'twill charm me more and more.

The breath of absence bids faint flames expire,
110   But fiercer makes a real passion burn:
Long separation feeds a lover's fire,
Yet still, too tardy youth, return! return!

Now hear my triumphs....Soon the tale transpir'd,
Soon was it borne upon the wing of Fame,
115   Till e'en my inmost soul of praise was tir'd,....
For to our roof assembled Corinth came.

Grave sages....heroes with the laurel'd brow,....
E'en gifted bards who breathe the lofty lay
Feel their glad hearts with new ambition glow,
120   And bid me haste their features to portray.

---

1   Deucalion, in Greek mythology, was the son of Prometheus. When his father's theft
of fire from the gods angered Zeus so much that he sent a flood, Deucalion, fore-
warned by Prometheus, built a boat and so escaped the deluge. After they landed
on Parnassus, they were told by an oracle to throw over their shoulders "the bones
of their mother." Interpreting this correctly as the bones of Mother Earth, they
threw stones behind them: from those thrown by Prometheus there arose women,
from those by Deucalion, men.

My father's art then forms the mimic head,
While to the lyre my honour'd name is breath'd,
While nymphs and swains my path with roses spread,
While round my brow are votive garlands wreath'd.

"And, when thy limbs the funeral pile shall press,   125
Think not (they cry) thy glory will expire:
Know, future ages shall Eudora bless,
And hail the art that sprang from chaste desire.

Yes....Corinth's pride! till Time itself be o'er,
Throughout the world be thy dear name convey'd,   130
And let the lover, hero, sage, adore
The tender skill of the Corinthian maid."

Such homage Corinth to Eudora pays....
But well thou know'st I shun, not covet fame;
From the fond breast that genuine passion sways   135
For ever distant be Ambition's flame!

Ah! not with pride, but tenderness I glow,
When I this offspring of my love behold;
And round my heart warm tides of transport flow,
To which Ambition's boasted fire is cold.   140

'Tis mine to know, it glads my father's breast,
His lov'd Eudora's spreading fame to see;
'Tis mine to feel, thus honour'd, thus caress'd,
I grow more worthy, matchless youth! of thee.

But, dearest boast! I've circumscrib'd the sway   145
Of stern-brow'd Death, the world's relentless king,....
Unhonour'd god! to whom none homage pay,
To whom no voices grateful pæans sing.

Yes....now no more this tyrant of mankind
Shall proudly tear from our encircling arms   150
The forms we love....and leave no trace behind
Of childhood, youth, or manhood's glowing charms.

Sav'd by my power from his rapacious hand,
Their image still shall charm in breathing clay;
With gentle force shall Memory's sighs command,
And spite of fate prolong its pleasing sway.

By this blest art succeeding chiefs shall know
What noble features Corinth's heroes bore,
Then, rous'd to valour by each dauntless brow,
Shall be themselves the heroes they adore.

Besides....(for what Invention's wings can bind?)....
Some gentle maid, inspir'd by love like mine,
In times to come may bright devices find
On the pale clay to bid warm colours shine.

Creative art improves by slow degrees;
When first a mortal's weight stern Ocean bore,
No fluttering canvas caught the swelling breeze,
But on a raft he ventur'd from the shore.

Sure Love alone could urge so bold a feat!
And he who first such wondrous danger prov'd,
Was some fond, faithful youth, resolv'd to meet,
Spite of opposing seas, the maid he lov'd.

Then, in succeeding years, Love's godhead sought
The art to perfect which to him we ow'd,
And in a votary's ear he breath'd the thought
That on the bark the useful sail bestow'd.

Once on a time two faithful lovers dar'd
The varied dangers of the treacherous main,
And sought an island where the priest prepar'd
To join their hands in Hymen's[1] silken chain:

But, as their bark too slowly seem'd to move

---

1   The god of marriage in Greek mythology.

For lovers' wishes o'er the restless wave,
The impatient youth invok'd the God of Love,
Who soon the aid he ask'd in pity gave.

Inspir'd by him, the eager lover tied   185
Fast to his vessel's head his fair-one's veil,
And lo! to land they flew!....Hence others tried
Their mimic art, and form'd the swelling sail.

Thus Fancy (playful power!) the story tells;
And as her airy heights I fondly climb,   190
Urg'd by the magic of her potent spells,
I boldly bound across the gulph of Time;

And as the future blazes on my sight,
I scorn the present, I forget the past.
Stay, radiant visions! still my eyes delight!   195
Scene following scene, each lovelier than the last.

Lo there! the maid by love like mine inspir'd,
Not only colour to my lines imparts,
See her bold hand to greater deeds is fir'd,
See the whole form to mimic being starts!   200

Hail! fair creations, bursting on my view!
Kings, heroes, sages, even gods appear,
At Art's bold touch, assuming Nature's hue!
Jove grasps his lightning, Pallas lifts her spear![1]

See, to their temples wond'ring votaries throng;   205
The breathing forms they view with timid eye;
Till, bolder grown, they raise the exulting song,
And "Lo! a present deity!" they cry.

---

1   Jove or Jupiter was the Roman equivalent of Zeus, the chief sky god; he is associat-
    ed with thunder-bolts or lightning, all places struck by lightning being sacred to
    him. Pallas, meaning "maiden," was a common epithet for Athena, the warrior-
    goddess daughter of Zeus, who was not born but rather sprang fully armed from his
    head—hence the spear as her chief emblem.

But when shall mortals realize the scene?
210   Not till some virgin learn to love like me:
And such, Philemon, is thy mind, thy mien,
Ages may pass, yet no youth charm like thee.

Meanwhile my humbler art shall please, shall bless,
Shall make thy charms and my affection known,
215   Shall calm the mourner's grief o'er those who press
Death's awful bier....shall softly sooth my own.

For when my father's ashes drink my tears,
I to his reverend image still may kneel,
Still think he all my vows of duty hears,
220   Still deigns to share each heart-felt joy I feel.

And oh! should Fate thy early death decree!....
Hence, false idea! traitor to my heart!
When on thy cheek I Death's pale ensign see,
In one embrace we'll meet, no more to part.

225   Yet, for thy country shouldst thou yield thy breath,
I'd try to bid my selfish sorrow cease....
A Grecian maid should bless her lover's death,
If that he fell for Liberty and Greece.

But oh! return, Philemon! round thy head
230   I'd rather lovers' wreaths than heroes' twine;
I dare not grieve if thou shouldst glory wed,
Yet still, lov'd youth, I'd rather call thee mine.

What tho' consoling Fancy paints thee near,
And thee I view tho' seas between us roll;
235   Tho' thy fond parting accents still I hear,
And tho' thy long, last look thrills thro' my soul:

Yet still thy absence prompts my ceaseless sigh,
Thy smiles alone can cheer my drooping heart:

For oh! when Fame my humble roof drew nigh,
Friendship I saw by slow degrees depart. 240

The fair companions of my lowly youth
With coldness praise me, or with malice blame,
And on my heart impress this mournful truth,
They forfeit friendship, who are dear to fame.

But thou canst make me e'en this loss despise, 245
Blest shall I be tho' 'reft of every friend,
For still Philemon's and my father's eyes
On me the looks of fond affection bend.

Our surest joys Jove's wisdom has decreed,
From Love's best, nearest, tenderest ties shall come; 250
They of true bliss the sacred lamp must feed,
They, her sole priests....her only altar, home.

Come then, dear youth! nor fear the wint'ry wind,
But dauntless venture on the foaming tide;
For such strong fetters Danger's power will bind! 255
And such a pilot will thy vessel guide!

Know, that last night when Sleep in silence reign'd,
And I in restless, feverish slumbers dream'd,
Beside my couch a gentle voice complain'd,
While round me more than morning's splendour beam'd. 260

Starting I woke; when, lo! my dazzled eyes
A figure rich in youth's first charms survey'd,
Like thine his features, such his cheek's rich dyes,
Like thee the wondrous vision seem'd array'd.

Then, with arch smiles, he cried, "Sleep, wooing fair! 265
At last I've made that rival power remove....
Know'st thou not me? This fond, voluptuous air,
This smile, these darts, proclaim the God of Love.

And hark! the wint'ry winds that loudly roar'd,
270   Hush'd by my presence, seem to murmur now;
To these chill plains by my warm breath restor'd,
See round thy couch the flowers of summer blow!

Now hear, blest maid! the joyful news I bring:
Long had I known the tumults of thy heart,
275   Long hover'd o'er thee with delighted wing,
O'erjoy'd to mark a passion void of art;

And when thy breast with boding anguish swell'd,
'Now, now (I cried), her homage I'll repay,'
Then flew to earth….and I thy feet impell'd
280   To seek the couch where thy Philemon lay.

I, on the wall the deep'ning shadow threw….
The slender wand beside the couch I plac'd….
I, with nice art the faithful outline drew,
And the lov'd youth with added beauty grac'd.

285   Nor, maid most favour'd! ceases yet my smile;
I come to tell thee, safe from all alarms,
For of its power I will the wind beguile,
I'll bring Philemon to thy constant arms.

The halcyon,[1] tamer of the tyrant flood,
290   By her sad note and azure plumage known,
Shall, at my bidding, on the billows brood,
And guard thy heart from sorrows like her own.

For this new proof of favour, let thy hand
Exert its skill my bounty to repay;
295   Upon my altar bid my image stand,
And try Love's glowing features to pourtray."

This said, away he wing'd his graceful flight….

---

1   A mythical bird said to have the power to calm the waters of the ocean where it
nested at the winter solstice.

His rustling pinions softest music breath'd....
And as he flew, around the brow of Night
His twining figure spires of radiance wreath'd.   300

Then from my couch I sprang with grateful haste,
Eager the lovely vision to pourtray:
But tho' I thought I Love's own features trac'd,
Thine, and thine only, could my eyes survey.

Yet wherefore not? Like thee he seem'd to move,   305
Save that his form with younger graces glow'd,
And my bold fingers on the God of Love
Thy matchless semblance have at last bestow'd:

But, waving richly, o'er his shoulder spreads
One of the fleecy, bounding, shining wings,   310
On which he hovers o'er true votaries' heads,
And to their aid divine assistance brings.

Those radiant pinions now for thee expand....
Then why, lov'd youth, thy wish'd return delay?
Come, see the wonders of Eudora's hand,   315
Come, at Love's breathing semblance homage pay.

Yes....when exulting in his kind decree
Thou com'st triumphant o'er the conquer'd wind,
We'll seek Love's altar....and, on bended knee,
Around his head will votive garlands bind.   320

O! thou hast much to see! no longer poor,
Our alter'd state our alter'd dwelling speaks;
And when the needy stranger opes our door,
We now can give the friendly aid he seeks.

Now, sight most pleasing to his daughter's eyes,   325
Coarse robes no more obscure my father's mien;
His ample tunic glows with Tyrian dyes,
And all his native dignity is seen....

While down his robe his silver ringlets flow,
330   Their white contrasted with its glowing red,....
So look bright clouds upon the mountain's brow,
When with the sun's last crimson rays o'erspread:

And both from poverty and pomp remote,
My vest....But why such trivial tales impart?
335   Haste to behold the change my words denote!
All, all is alter'd here....except....my heart.

Come....and tho' absence now my bliss alloys,
More bright 'twill make the hour of meeting glow;
Past pains sometimes create our present joys....
340   The rainbow's beauties to the storm we owe.

But till we meet, believe the fond distress
That absence brings, in all its force I prove,
Save when against my throbbing heart I press
The faithful semblance of the youth I love.

SONGS, AND OTHER POETICAL PIECES.

THE MOURNER.

COME, smiles! come, gay attire! and hide
The secret fang that tears my breast!
I'll lay my sable garb aside,
And seem to cold inquirers blest.
5   Yes,—I will happy triflers join,
As when grief's dart beside me flew,
And love and all its joys were mine,
And sorrow but by name I knew:
        For health I saw in Henry's bloom,
10   Nor knew it mark'd him for the tomb.

Hard was the stroke,—but O! I hate
The sacred pomp of grief to show;

Thron'd in my breast, in secret state,
Shall live the reverend form of woe:
For observation would degrade   15
The homage to her empire paid.

I hate the tear which pity gives,
I'm jealous of her curious eye;
The only balm my wound receives,
Is from my own unheeded sigh.   20
A face of smiles, a heart of tears!
So in the church-yard (realm of death)
The turf increasing verdure wears,
While all is pale and dead beneath.

TO THE GLOW-WORM.

GEM of this lone and silent vale,
Treasure of evening's pensive hour,
I come thy fairy rays to hail,
I come a votive strain to pour.

Nor chilly damps, nor paths untrod,   5
Shall from thy shrine my footsteps fright;
Thy lamp shall guide me o'er the sod,
And cheer the gathering mists of night.

Again thy yellow fire impart,
Lo! planets shed a mimic day;   10
Lo! vivid meteors round me dart,
On western clouds red lightnings play!

But I disdain these garish fires,
Sporting on evening's sultry wing;
Thy humbler light my eye admires,   15
Thy soft, retiring charms I sing.

Thine is an unobtrusive blaze,
Content in lowly shades to shine;

And much I wish, while thus I gaze,
To make thy modest merit mine.

For, long by youth's wild wishes cast
On the false world's tempestuous sea,
I seek retirement's shore at last,
And find a monitor in thee.

SONG OF AN INDOSTAN GIRL.

This Song was occasioned by the following circumstance: — Mr. BIGGS, the composer and editor of many beautiful Airs, gave me some time ago a plaintive melody, said to have been composed and sung by an Indostan girl on being separated from the man she loved.

She had lived several years in India with an English gentleman to whom she was tenderly attached; but he, when about to marry, sent his Indian favourite up the country; and as she was borne along in her palanquin,[1] she was heard to sing the above-mentioned melody. To this melody I wrote the following words; and they have been already given to the public, with the original music, in a second set of Hindoo airs, arranged and harmonized by Mr. BIGGS.[2]

'TIS thy will, and I must leave thee,
O! then, best belov'd, farewell!

---

1   "A covered litter or conveyance, usually for one person, used in India and other eastern countries, consisting of a large box with wooden shutters like Venetian blinds, carried by four or six (rarely two) men by means of poles projecting before and behind" (OED).

2   First published as "A Hindustàni Girl's Song," Air III of *A Second Set of Hindoo Airs with English Words adapted to them by Mrs. Opie*; also sold separately as a single song. The music was arranged by Edward Biggs, based on *The Oriental Miscellany* (a collection of airs published in Calcutta), and printed by Robert Birchall. Exact dating of printed music of this period is difficult, but these songs must have been published between May 1798, when marriage rendered Amelia Alderson Mrs. Opie, and March 1801, which marks the first publication of *The Father and Daughter*. The song also exists as "The Poor Hindoo," with music composed by Mrs. Alsop, published in 1824 in Baltimore.

I forbear, lest I should grieve thee,
  Half my heartfelt pangs to tell.
Soon a British fair will charm thee,   5
  Thou her smiles wilt fondly woo;
But tho' she to rapture warm thee,
  Don't forget THY POOR HINDOO.

Well I know this happy beauty
  Soon thy envied bride will shine;   10
But will she, by anxious duty,
  Prove a passion warm as mine?
If to rule be her ambition,
  And her own desires pursue;
Thou'lt recall my fond submission,   15
  And regret THY POOR HINDOO.

Born herself to rank and splendour,
  Will she deign to wait on thee;
And those soft attentions render,
  Thou so oft hast prais'd in me?   20
Yet, why doubt her care to please thee?
  Thou must every heart subdue;
I am sure, each maid that sees thee
  Loves thee like THY POOR HINDOO.

No, ah! no!—tho' from thee parted,   25
  Other maids will peace obtain;
But thy Zayda, broken-hearted,
  Ne'er, O! ne'er, will smile again.
O! how fast from thee they tear me!
  Faster still shall death pursue: 30
But 'tis well—death will endear me,
  And thou'lt mourn THY POOR HINDOO.

SONG*.

Yes, Mary Anne, I freely grant,
The charms of Henry's eyes I see;
But while I gaze, I something want,
I want those eyes — to gaze on me.

5   And I allow, in Henry's heart
Not Envy's self a fault can see:
Yet still I must one wish impart,
I wish that heart — to sigh for me.

SONG.[1]

A youth for Jane with ardour sigh'd,
The maid with sparkling eye;
But to his vows she still replied,
"I'll hear you by and by."

5   "Suspense (he cries) my bloom decays,
"And bids my spirits fly;
"*Now* hear my vows," — but still she says,
"I'll hear you by and by."

At length her frowns his love subdue,
10   He shuns her scornful eye,
And Emma seeks, who'll hear him woo
Both now, and by and by.

And soon to church he leads the maid,
When lo! he sees draw nigh,
15   The now repentant fair, who said
She'd hear him by and by.

---

* This and the three following Songs belong to a set of Songs composed by Mr. Biggs, which are now published [Opie's footnote]. Opie refers to *Six Songs ... Dedicated to the Right Honourable Lady Willoughby de Eresby*. This was "Song II."
1   Song V from *Six Songs*.

"Hear me (she cries): no more in vain
    "Thy heart for me shall sigh!"—
"I'm busy now (said he)—but, Jane!
    "I'll hear you by and by."

A MAD-SONG.[1]

HA! what is this that on my brow
Presses with such o'erwhelming power?
My love to heav'n is gone, I know;
But 'tis to fix our bridal hour.
Then on his tomb why should I sorrow?   5
He's gone, but he'll return to-morrow.

Ah! then yon lofty hill I'll mount,
And seize on morning's brightest cloud;
On that I'll wait my love, and count
The moments till he leaves his shrowd: 10
And he the rainbow's vest shall borrow,
To grace our bridal day to-morrow.

But all's not right in this poor heart,—
Yet why should I his loss deplore?
It was indeed a pang to part,   15
But when he comes, he'll rove no more:
And all to day can laugh at sorrow,
When sure of being bless'd to-morrow.

Then why am I in black array'd?
And why is Henry's father pale?   20
And why do I, poor frantic maid,
Tell to the winds a mournful tale?
Alas! the weight I feel is sorrow....
No, no—he cannot come to-morrow.

---

1   Song VI from *Six Songs*; also sold separately as a single song.

SONG.[1]

I ONCE rejoic'd, sweet Evening gale,
To see thy breath the poplar wave;
But now it makes my cheek turn pale,
It waves the grass o'er Henry's grave.

Ah! setting sun! how chang'd I seem!
I to thy rays prefer deep gloom,—
Since now, alas! I see them beam
Upon my Henry's lonely tomb.

Sweet Evening gale! howe'er I seem,
I wish thee o'er my sod to wave;
Ah! setting sun! soon mayst thou beam
On mine, as well as Henry's grave!

EPIGRAM

On reading the *Pleadings* of Count LALLY TOLENDAL for his
Father the late Count LALLY.[2]

---

1   Song III from *Six Songs*.
2   Count Lally was Thomas-Arthur, Comte de Lally, a French general who surren-
    dered to the British after being besieged at Pondicherry in India in January 1761.
    He returned to France where he stood trial, charged with treason, was convicted
    and subsequently beheaded May 9, 1766. Lally-Tollendal was his son, an important
    figure in the French Revolution. Simon Schama, in *Citizens: A Chronicle of the
    French Revolution*, discusses the importance of the father-son connection: "Some
    young aristocrats became politicized precisely because they failed to see in the per-
    son of the court and the monarchy (especially in the last years of Louis XV) the
    virtues proper to patriotic severity. Indeed they sometimes accused the court of
    besmirching the reputation of patriots for reasons of base expediency and self-
    exculpation. The young Lally-Tollendale, for example, was set on course to become
    a revolutionary aristocrat by his crusade to vindicate the reputation of his father,
    who had been tried and executed as the scapegoat for French military failure in
    India. So awful was this disgrace that the boy was brought up in absolute ignorance
    of his father. Even his surname was altered to Trophime, his given name, as a way of
    sparing him the taint. At the age of fifteen, however, he inadvertently discovered
    the truth.... After a ten-year, dogged campaign to reverse the injustice, the new
    reign took heed" (31-32).

Oui, je conviens qu' Enée étoit digne d'envie,
Mais je crois que Lally le surpasse en bonheur:
Le Troyen à son Père a su sauver LA VIE,
Mais au sien le François a su sauver L'HONNEUR.[1]

LINES
ADDRESSED TO MR. BIGGS,

On his having set the MAD SONG, and "MY LOVE TO WAR IS
GOING."[2]

WHILE from your taste my humble lays acquire
Attractive charms to them till now unknown,
My muse deceiv'd exulting strikes her lyre,
And loves her strains for graces not their own.

FATHERLESS FANNY.[3]
A BALLAD.

KEEN and cold is the blast loudly whistling around:
As cold are the lips that once smil'd upon me,
And unyielding, alas! as this hard-frozen ground,
The arms once so ready my shelter to be.
Both my parents are dead, and few friends I can boast,   5
But few to console, and to love me, if any;
And my gains are so small,—a bare pittance at most
Repays the exertions of fatherless Fanny.

Once indeed I with pleasure and patience could toil,
But 'twas when my parents sat by, and approv'd;   10
Then my laces[4] to sell I went out with a smile,

---

1   "Yes, I concede that Aeneas was enviable,
        But I believe Lally surpassed him in happiness:
        The Trojan, of his father, knowing how to save his life,
        While of his, the Frenchman knew how to save his honour."
2   E.B. Schnapper, *British Union Catalogue of Early Music* (1957), lists this as "A Song
     [the words by Miss Alderson, afterwards Mrs. Opie]" and dates it c.1795.
3   Schnapper lists this as a song printed for Birchall c.1799.
4   The sale of fancy needlework, such as embroidery and bobbin-lace, was a common
     means of support for poor women.

Because my fatigue fed the parents I lov'd.
And at night when I brought them my hardly-earn'd gains,
Tho' small they might be, still my comforts were many;
For my mother's fond blessing rewarded my pains,
My father stood watching to welcome his Fanny.

But, ah! now that I work by their presence uncheer'd,
I feel 'tis a hardship indeed to be poor,
While I shrink from the labour no longer endear'd,
And sigh as I knock at the wealthy man's door.
Then, alas! when at night I return to my home,
No longer I boast that my comforts are many;
To a silent, deserted, dark dwelling I come,
Where no one exclaims "Thou art welcome, my Fanny."

That, that is the pang;—want and toil would impart
No pang to my breast, if kind friends I could see;
For the wealth I require is that of the heart,
The smiles of affection are riches to me.

Then, ye wealthy, O think when to you I apply
To purchase my goods, tho' you do not buy any,
If in accents of kindness you deign to deny,
You'll comfort the heart of poor fatherless Fanny.

SONG—TO LAURA.

MAID of the cold suspicious heart,
Ah! wherefore doubt thy Henry's love?
Imputing thus to practis'd art
The signs that real passion prove.

While thro' the sleepless night I sigh,
And jealous fears and anguish own,
At morn in restless slumbers lie,
Then, languid, rise to muse alone:

While harmony my soul disdains,
And beauties vainly round me shine,

Save when I hear thy fav'rite strains,
Or beauties see resembling thine:

While I in fix'd attention gaze,
If e'er thou breathe thy plaintive lay,
And while, tho' others loudly praise,   15
I deeply sigh, and nothing say:

While I reject thy offer'd hand,
And shun the touch which others seek,
Alone with thee in silence stand,
Nor dare, tho' chance befriend me, speak: —   20

Ah! Laura, while I thus impart
The ardent love in which I pine,
While all these symptoms speak *my* heart,
Say, why should doubt inhabit *thine*?

THE DESPAIRING WANDERER.

O! 'TIS an hour to misery dear!
No noise, but dashing waves, I hear,
Save hollow blasts that rush around,
For Midnight reigns with horrors crown'd.

Lo! clouds in swarthy grandeur sweep   5
Portentous o'er the troubled deep:
O'er the tall rocks' majestic heads,
Lo! billowy vapour slowly spreads,
While Fancy, as she marks its swell,
Around it throws her magic spell: —   10
And see! fantastic shapes seem near,
The rocks with added height appear,
And from the mist, to seek the tide,
Gigantic figures darkly glide;
While, with quick step and hurried mien,   15
Pale Terror leads the shadowy scene.
Again loud blasts I shudd'ring hear,

Which seem to Fancy's list'ning ear
To toll some shipwreck'd sailor's knell!
20 Of fear, of grief, of death, they tell.
Perhaps they bade yon foaming tide
Unheard-of misery scatter wide.
Hail! dread idea, fancy-taught,—
To me with gloomy pleasure fraught;
25 I should rejoice the world to see
Distress'd, distracted, lost, like me.

O! why is phrensy call'd a curse?
I deem the sense of misery worse:
Come, Madness, come! tho' pale with fear
30 Be joy's flush'd cheek when thou art near,
On thee I eager glances bend;
Despair, O Madness! calls thee friend!
Come, with thy visions cheer my gloom,—
Spread o'er my cheek thy feverish bloom!
35 To my weak form thy strength impart,
From my sunk eye thy lightnings dart!
Oh! come, and on the troubled air
Throw rudely my disorder'd hair;
Arm me with thy supporting pride,
40 Let me all ills, all fears deride!
Oh! bid me roam in tatter'd vest,
Bare to the wint'ry wind my breast,
Horrors with dauntless eye behold,
And stalk in fancied greatness bold!
45 Let me, from yonder frowning rock,
With thy shrill scream the billows mock;
With fearless step ascend the steep,
That totters o'er th' encroaching deep;
And while the swelling main along
50 Blue lightning's awful splendours throng;
And while upon the foaming tide
Danger and Death in triumph ride,
And thunder rends the ear of Night,

Rousing the form of pale Affright,
Let me the mountain torrent quaff,   55
And 'midst the war of nature—laugh!

THE ORPHAN BOY'S TALE.[1]

STAY! lady, stay, for mercy's sake,
And hear a helpless orphan's tale!
Ah! sure my looks must pity wake,—
'Tis want that makes my cheek so pale.
Yet I was once a mother's pride,   5
And my brave father's hope and joy;
But in the Nile's proud fight[2] he died,
And I am now an ORPHAN BOY.

Poor foolish child! how pleas'd was I,
When news of Nelson's victory came,   10
Along the crowded streets to fly
And see the lighted windows flame!—
To force me home my mother sought,
She could not bear to see my joy;
For, with my father's life 'twas bought,   15
And made me a poor ORPHAN BOY.

The people's shouts were long and loud,—
My mother, shudd'ring, clos'd her ears,—
"Rejoice! rejoice!" still cried the crowd:
My mother answer'd with her tears.   20
"Why are you crying thus," said I,
"While others laugh and shout with joy?"

---

1   Published as a separate song, as listed in "A Catalogue of the Music Arranged, Har-
    monized, or Composed by Mr. Biggs" printed at the front of *Six Songs*. We have
    been unable to locate the version composed by Biggs. We have, however, found
    copies of a version composed by Thomas Wright at both the British Library and
    the Beinecke Library. See Appendix G.
2   The Battle of the Nile, fought between the French and British navies at Abu Q'ir
    Bay, near Alexandria in Egypt, August 1, 1798. It was considered one of Admiral
    Horatio Nelson's greatest victories, and served to keep Napoleon's army in Egypt
    by securing British naval control over the Mediterranean.

She kiss'd me — and with such a sigh!
She call'd me her poor ORPHAN BOY!

25 "What is an orphan boy?" I said, —
When suddenly she gasp'd for breath,
And her eyes clos'd; — I shriek'd for aid,
But, ah! her eyes were clos'd in death.
My hardships since I will not tell:
30 But, now no more a parent's joy,
Ah! lady, — I have learnt too well,
What 'tis to be an ORPHAN BOY.

O! were I by your bounty fed!
Nay, gentle lady, do not chide, —
35 Trust me, I mean to earn my bread;
The sailor's orphan boy has pride. —
Lady, you weep! — Ha! — this to me?
You'll give me clothing, food, employ? —
Look down, dear parents! look, and see
Your happy, happy, ORPHAN BOY.

THE END.

DANGERS

OF

COQUETRY.

A NOVEL.

On each fond fool beſtowing ſome kind glance,
Each conqueſt owing to ſome looſe advance :
Thus vain COQUETTES affect to be purſued,
And think they're virtuous, if not groſsly lewd.

IN TWO VOLUMES.

VOL. I.

LONDON:

Printed for W. LANE, Leadenhall-ſtreet.

M DCC XC.

Figure 4: Title page, first edition of *Dangers of Coquetry* (1790). Reproduced by permission of the British Library.

DANGERS OF COQUETRY.

A NOVEL.

On each fond fool bestowing some kind glance,
Each conquest owing to some loose advance:
Thus vain COQUETTES affect to be pursued,
And think they're virtuous, if not grossly lewd.[1]

---

1 Epigraph to volumes one and two of the novel. Catherine G. Jemmat, "The Lady's
Resolve," ll. 5–8; see Appendix I.2 for the complete poem.

VOL. I.

CHAPTER I.
THE COQUETTE.

LOUISA CONOLLY was the only child of a Baronet of large fortune, and at the age of seventeen she saw herself surrounded by
admirers, whom the fame of her beauty and the report of her
expectations, had assembled round the seat where her father
resided.

Louisa was more than beautiful: her countenance expressed
every emotion of her soul, and her voice was the tone of persuasion: when she walked, danced, or sung, every eye pursued,
and every tongue applauded her, and silent attention paid its
tribute of admiration. Rich, beautiful, and accomplished, she
was the envy of the women, and the idol of the men; happiness
seemed to have sown all its seeds in her path, and a little care
on her side, would have matured them to a plentiful harvest—
but Louisa was the slave of thoughtless indiscretion. Though
possessed of an understanding superior to that of most of her
sex, she was hurried by unguarded levity into the commission
of follies, which the weakest of it would have shunned and
condemned.

Vanity and the love of admiration had possession of her
heart, and tho' in her moments of reflection Louisa, listening to
the dictates of self-reproach, resolved on suppressing her indiscretion, and discarding the train of admirers whom she alternately encouraged, she still remained eager for admiration, even
from those whose understandings she despised: and though
shrinking with anguish from the thought of being regarded as
such, was at eighteen a finished coquette.

Still, however, Louisa had sensibility; "she lov'd and felt for
all:"[1] her ear was ever open to the tale of the distressed, and

---

[1] Slightly altered reference to "The Deserted Village" (1770), where Goldsmith
describes the village preacher:
> Thus to relieve the wretched was his pride,
> And even his failings leaned to Virtue's side;
> But in his duty prompt at every call,
> He watched and wept, he prayed and felt, for all. (l. 163-166)

those whom her thoughtlessness wounded, her heart bled to heal.[1] She was therefore constantly repenting of her errors, and she would retire from the assemblies where she was the idol of the crowd, to lament her broken resolutions, and to form fresh ones for the morrow.

The situation of Louisa was a dangerous one;[2] she had every thing to fear from the envy of her own sex, and while she wanted firmness to behave so as to defy censure, her self-love, and the delicacy of her mind were wounded, by the consciousness of deserving it. She was a prey to the quick feelings of an upbraiding heart, and though courted and caressed, she felt a void in her bosom, which self-approbation alone was able to fill.

CHAPTER II.
MISFORTUNES.

LOUISA had the misfortune to lose her mother at an early age, and was left to her own management, when restraint should have curbed the desire of being distinguished; and when entered into the world, with all her errors uncorrected, no friendly hand was stretched out to lead her into the path of prudence. Envy in her own sex, and design in the other, might perhaps with-hold the guidance she so much needed, as the rival and the admirer would certainly avoid amending imprudencies, by which they were both equally likely to profit.[3]

Yet in spite of her beauty, in spite of her errors, Louisa had a friend. — Caroline Egerton was the companion of her child-

---

1 In emphasizing the warmth and sensibility of Louisa's heart, Opie contrasts it with the iciness typical of the finished coquette: see Addison, Appendix I.1.

2 Catharine Macaulay notes that "coquettry in women is as dangerous as it is dishonourable" precisely because the desire for admiration leaves the coquette vulnerable to masculine seduction and social ostracism, despite any underlying virtues she may possess: see Appendix H.2.

3 Many writers are agreed on the role education plays in the formation of the coquette. Macaulay is critical of Rousseau's educational philosophy which sees all women as coquettes: see Appendix I.4. The author of the anonymous *Memoirs of a Coquet* is equally clear — "To a frivolous education, and to boarding-school accomplishments and connections, the present numerous race of coquets are owing": see Appendix I.3.i.

hood, and Louisa's sweetness of temper had interested her affection, before the faults in her character had made her forget her esteem.

Upon Louisa's entrance into the world, the ruin of Caroline's father occasioned a separation, and Miss Conolly saw her friend doomed to accompany a declining parent to a distant country, where the only prospect that awaited her was the certainty of struggling with increasing poverty, and of listening to complaints she was unable to remove.

This separation, and the cause of it, were the first sources of pain to the bosom of Louisa. To see her Caroline suffer, and not be able to relieve her, gave her the severest uneasiness. Conscious of her own failings, Louisa's heart was torn with the certainty of not deserving the blessings she enjoyed. She wondered at the decrees of Providence in having bestowed the smiles of fortune on the thoughtless and extravagant Louisa, while the prudent, truly generous Caroline, was the guiltless victim of the imprudencies of others.

Happy had it been for Louisa, if, in admiring the example of her friend, she had resolved to imitate it.

Caroline had all those perfections which Louisa wanted. She was not beautiful; she was not what the world calls accomplished; but she had endowments superior to beauty and accomplishments. She had an exquisite sense of propriety, which led her instantly to condemn and avoid every action which her reason disapproved. She was charitable more from principle than impulse; her temper was good from effort rather than nature; it had been tried in the school of unkindness, and resolution had made it equal to the trial.

While Louisa was the child of fortune, Caroline was the child of unhappiness. In infancy her temper had been injured by excessive indulgence: her mother, who doated on her (though her father, who had wished for a son, regarded her with indifference) gratified her in every wish of her heart. She died when Caroline had reached the age of thirteen, and left her, unsupported by maternal fondness, to endure the caprices and severity of an unfeeling parent.

Caroline's situation was rendered worse by her father's marrying again, and she soon found herself more cruelly a slave to the caprices and niggard bounty of a mother-in-law.[1]

Three years she dragged this heavy chain, unsoothed but by the attention of Louisa, and Death had but just relieved her from a yoke become insupportable to her father also, when this last stroke plunged her into new affliction, and obliterated for ever from her mind all traces of one flattering hope, which she had long delighted to indulge.

CHAPTER III.
THE HEIRESS.

AMONGST the many admirers that bowed at the shrine of Louisa's beauty, Edward Mountague was most worthy of notice. He was of the same age as Caroline, and had long distinguished her as the sharer of his pleasures, and the soother of his childish sorrows. As he grew up, and, introduced by Caroline, became the constant companion of Louisa, he felt the influence of her growing charms. His esteem, his reverence became every day more and more the due of Caroline, but his fancy was dazzled and captivated by the graces of Louisa.

Caroline, tall, pensive and majestic, at the same time that she excited his admiration, awakened a painful degree of deference towards her; while Louisa, unfixed in stature; and every day improving in attractions, alternately delighting him by the childish flightiness of youth, and the wonderful acquirements of superior genius, soon obtained over him the influence of a woman, while he thought he was only admiring the graces of a child, and ever most pleasing when on the brink of indiscretion, in exciting by turns his fears and his applauses, made the solid merit of Caroline pass almost unnoticed by him, except in his moments of serious reflection.

Different were the feelings of Miss Egerton towards him. Long accustomed to impart her cares to the affectionate bosom of Edward Mountague, his attention was necessary to her

---

1 Until the mid-nineteenth century this meant "step-mother."

peace, and whether gay or sad, her pleasure and her pains had their origin in him.

Miss Egerton had flattered herself that Edward's friendship for her would have ripened into love, and that she might one day supply his deficiency in fortune, by making him possessor of the wealth she was heiress to: for in expectancies of that kind, she had no reason to fear Louisa as a rival. She was also an only child, and as her father was engaged in an immense traffic, she was looked upon as the probable heiress of upwards of an hundred thousand pounds.[1]

Edward Mountague was descended from a noble family, but inherited its virtues only. He was therefore bent on turning his talents to profit, and while a small paternal estate placed him above present want, he determined on the profession of the bar, as a line best suited to his situation and inclinations.

With joy did Caroline look forward to having it one day in her power to make Edward Mountague possessor of a fortune equal to the liberality of his soul. Eagerly did she watch for some proof of a mutual regard, and she beheld, with painful emotion, the affection she would have died to possess, lavished on one who was too thoughtless to pity, too volatile to return, and too young to know the value of.

Hope, however, did not yet desert her: she knew Louisa would never return Mountague's passion, and she thought her inclination to coquetry, which he openly condemned, would in time disgust him, and make him turn his attention to one, whose disposition was more like his own.

Such were her hopes and expectations, when Edward Mountague set out to accompany an intimate friend of his on the tour of Europe.[2] Such they continued to be, when the total

---

1   Edward Copeland, in *Women Writing About Money: Women's Fiction in England 1790-1820*, notes, "Any lump sum is automatically calculated by the contemporary novel-reader for its annual, spendable income. A simple formula suffices: the amount of a lump sum inherited multiplied by five per cent, the annual yield a heroine can expect from the investment of that amount in the five per cent government funds" (23). Thus Caroline would have an annual income of £5000, a sum which places her resources on a par with those of the wealthy gentry.

2   "*The (grand) tour*, a journey through France, Germany, Switzerland, and Italy, formerly fashionable, esp. as a finishing course in the education of young men of rank" (*OED*).

ruin of Mr. Egerton, by the failure of most of his correspondents abroad, destroyed her prospects, and substituted the near approach of poverty for the pleasing phantom of future pleasure.

Such was the fate of Louisa's only friend; so tutored by the hand of sorrow, to learn the lesson of sympathy, was the bosom to whose tenderness Louisa constantly confided her sorrows and her joys.

Whatever were the occurrences she met with, she immediately sent an account of them to Lausanne, and the sincere hand of Caroline returned either the honest eulogium of friendship, or the kind reproof of unprejudiced reflection.

CHAPTER IV.
PORTRAIT OF A LOVER.

LOUISA was now eighteen, and immersed in all the gaieties which a large city, near which they resided, could produce. She had not yet visited the metropolis, as her father, to whose health air and exercise were necessary, could not bear the confinement of a town life; and as Louisa's vocal powers and vivacity cheer'd the retirement frequent attacks of the gout obliged him to, he could not bear the thought of her going thither without him.

This precaution our heroine regretted but little: the victims of her charms were many where she was, and as her love for admiration was gratified in the country, where she had no rivals, she did not like to run the risk of losing this gratification, by mixing in the gay world, where she would probably find many.

Louisa's heart was as yet untouched, and while a smile to one, a kind glance to another, some flattering attention to a third, made each hope that *he* was the happy man; Louisa thought that in time she should be capable of fixing, and that by encouraging many, she might find one at last entirely the object of her choice.

The object Louisa's fancy had painted as the only one capable of attaching her, was too amiable, too accomplished to exist in this dissolute age, and Louisa seemed destined, like another Pygmalion,[1] to sigh for the form her own fancy had created. But in every thing Heaven seemed ready to gratify her wishes, and an acquaintance she soon after formed with Henry Mortimer, realized the object she had long dwelt on in idea.

Henry Mortimer, both by birth and fortune, was authorized to address Louisa. His family was noble, and though his paternal estate was small, the large fortune of his uncle, which he was just become possessor of, made him a proper match for the daughter of Sir Charles Conolly.

In the pretensions nature had given him, he had no reason to fear a rival. His countenance at first sight impressed you with an idea of superior endowments, which a further acquaintance with his character served but to confirm. His eyes were dark and penetrating, but whether sparkling or languishing, it was not in the power of any one to determine, as they were the constant indexes of his mind, and as the feelings of that varied, the cast of his countenance also changed. In short, his face was formed for expression, and every feature was designed to strengthen the influence of the whole.

Had nature intended him for a beauty, she would have lessened and softened off some of his leading features; but, satisfied with giving him a countenance that spoke the manly soul which informed it; she contented herself with only heightening the interest his appearance occasioned, by spreading that mantling blush of health upon his cheek, without which regularity of features is vain, and strength of stature an apparent contradiction.

His figure was much above the common height, but proportionate stoutness, and perfect symmetry of form, entirely forbade that aukwardness of appearance so often attendant upon superior stature. He excelled in every fashionable exercise, and having been early introduced into high life, his manners were those of a finished man of the world, though his morals were as pure as if he had never mixed with it.

The tutor to whom the care of his education had been com-

---

1 In Greek mythology, a king of Cypress who fell in love with a statue (said in some versions to have been his own handiwork). Aphrodite answered his prayer for a wife who looked like the beloved object by bringing the statue itself to life.

mitted, had early impressed upon his mind a strong sense of the restraint religion and morality lay upon the passions; and the death of his most intimate friend, just as he was entering into life, the blooming darling of a father's care, whilst it convinced him of the frail tenure of mortal expectations, gave a melancholy cast to his temper, which preserved him from many incentives to vice, to which thoughtless vivacity so often falls a victim.

He was generous to a fault, and tho' severe to mark his own errors, he was but too indulgent to those of others. From a want of resolution to wound, though the only means of effecting a cure, he pitied and countenanced imperfections in his friends, which a little severity might have led them to amend: "But the error that springs from virtue may be pardoned,"[1] and this one failing of his heart may be suffered to pass unnoticed.

It would be endless to dwell on the cultivation of his mind, and the extent of his genius; suffice it to say, that Louisa's warmest idea of perfection was realized in him, though his conceptions of female merit were not altogether gratified in her.

CHAPTER V.
THE INTERVIEW.

HENRY Mortimer had long heard of Louisa's beauty and accomplishments, but her disposition to coquetry, which he had always heard mentioned at the same time, damped his eagerness to be eye-witness of her charms: for a coquette was his aversion, and, like many theorists on the same subject, he required charms in a woman, without their, often necessary, alloys.

In an acquaintance with Louisa, therefore, he was not likely to be gratified; at length, however, her repeated praises got the better of his repeated resolutions, and he determined to run the risk of having his heart deluded by the attractions which he was sure his reason could not fail to despise.

---

1   Henry Mackenzie, *Julia de Roubigné* (1777). Letter 10, vol. 1, 81.

He heard Louisa was spending a few days at the house of an amiable widow of his acquaintance; thither he determined to go; and, full of the idea of a volatile coquette, he painted Miss Conolly in his mind as a fine woman, fashioned into a beauty by the help of unlimited art, and modish extravagance of dress; while a pair of bright eyes, widened by the stare of conscious triumph, were continually in motion, seeking proper objects to exercise their power on.[1]

Louisa had been for many days indisposed, but her disorder was of so slight a nature, as only served to give an interesting languor to her charms, sometimes more dangerous than beauty itself.

The retirement Mrs. Mordaunt's house afforded was at this time peculiarly grateful to her feelings, and the pensiveness occasioned by her illness led her seriously to reflect on the impropriety of her conduct, and the value of the time she so thoughtlessly wasted. She was so much engrossed by these reflections, that she had neglected the study of the toilet, and for once in her life, Louisa was dressed for conquest, without designing to be so.

A profusion of pale brown hair flowed in ringlets down her shoulders, and was combed carelessly round her face entirely devoid of ornament; a white gown made close to her shape, and fastened by a blue girdle, the colour of her eyes, marked and did justice to the elegance of her form. A black teresa,[2] thrown round her shoulders, set off the dazzling whiteness of a neck, rounded by the hands of the graces. Her cheeks were suffused with a pale flush, arising from the agitation of her mind, and her eyes, darting a languid lustre thro' long dark lash-

---

1 The expression of both coquetry and chastity resided in the eye. Addison's coquette makes all men believe she regards them "with an Eye of Kindness," and the nerves of her heart descend not from the brain, but from the eye; see Appendix I.1. This use of the eye should be understood in contrast with the downcast eyes of modesty, or the forbidding gaze of chastity. Mandeville, in *The Fable of the Bees* writes: "But the wise sort of mankind are well assured, that the free and open countenance of the smiling fair, is more inviting, and yields greater hopes to the seducer, than the ever-watchful look of a forbidding eye" (vol. 1).

2 "A light gauze kerchief worn over the ladies' head-dress about 1786," probably named for the Empress Maria-Theresa (1717-80) (*OED*).

es, and sometimes made still more interesting in their expression by a swelling tear, portended more danger to a man of nice feelings, than when animated by the rage of conquest, and bestowing on all indiscriminate glances of flattering encouragement.

Such was the lovely figure, that, absorbed in painful thought, was bending over a frame of embroidery, Mrs. Mordaunt, reading by her side; when the latter suddenly exclaimed, "See, Louisa, a carriage is driving up to the gate, who can it be!" then running to the window, as the visitor alighted, "Come, child, call up some of your dangerous powers, here is a prize worth trying for; Harry Mortimer, by all that is fortunate; the best and most accomplished young man in England."

The handsomest too thought Louisa, as she raised her expressive eyes from her work, and met the most penetrating pair in the world fixed upon her. Louisa cast hers down again in confusion, while a blush of timid pleasure glowed on her cheek, from the animated admiration Mr. Mortimer's look expressed; but gracefully recovering herself, with an unseeming dignity, she received Mr. Mortimer's self congratulations, upon having met, at last, with an opportunity of forming an acquaintance with Miss Conolly.

The conversation soon became interesting. Louisa's share in it displayed a brilliant imagination, so tempered by judgement; feelings so alive to compassion, and a sense of propriety, so far removed from levity; that Mortimer began to think, that envy alone had stigmatized her with the name of coquette; and when, at the earnest entreaty of Mrs. Mordaunt she sung a plaintive air of Parsiello's,[1] with a pathos and expression which her feelings at the moment made perfectly natural to her, he found his whole heart melted into tenderness, and he determined to make her amends for the injustice he had done her, by an unlimited belief in her virtues, constancy and perfections.

Louisa, on her side, felt an emotion unknown before; whenever Mr. Mortimer addressed his conversation to her, and her eyes which were not accustomed to shrink from the eager look

---

1   A typographical error for Giovanni Paisiello (1740-1816), an Italian composer popular in the last 20 years of the 18th century.

of observation, now bent their timid glances to the ground, unable to bear the expressive ones of Mortimer: and her apparent timidity while it added to her charms, spoke a forcible language to the heart of Mr. Mortimer. His vanity was gratified by her confusion, and his penetration read in it omens favourable to his love.

The day insensibly passed, and Mr. Mortimer had readily accepted Mrs. Mordaunt's invitation to stay the evening; when the latter exclaimed, with good humoured earnestness; "I wonder, Mortimer, you are yet single! Amongst all the fair ones who have courted the honor of your smiles, have you not seen one capable of attaching you? Miss Beaumont, for instance; surely you cannot be insensible to her charms!" Louisa's heart died within her at this discourse, and she waited, with ill conceal'd confusion, for Mr. Mortimer's reply.

"You know, Madam," said Mr. Mortimer; "I have always said, to touch my heart a woman must first engage my esteem; now tho' I allow Miss Beaumont's attractions great, she can never captivate me; all who see her must pronounce her a finished coquette, a character which I hold in the greatest detestation."

"You are a strange young man," returned Mrs. Mordaunt, "your sex, in this age, seem to idolize coquetry, for when were they more attentive to ours? Search throughout the beau monde,[1] and you will scarcely see a woman that is not versed in every art of it. Surely, then, you ought to excuse an error your indulgence has encouraged."

"I can excuse nothing," replied Mortimer, "which bespeaks mental depravity, however tolerated by fashion, or glossed by situation. A coquette in your sex is, in my opinion, as detestable as a libertine in ours, and has certainly less excuse for her fault than the latter can boast. The libertine has passion for his excuse, and those who know the force of it, in the bosom of youth, should make some allowances for its effects; but in cool blood to take pains to destroy the happiness of others, to wound an inexperienced heart for the sake of wounding it, as an unwhip'd urchin torments a worm for the pleasure of seeing

---

1   "The fashionable world, society" (*OED*).

it writhe about in torture;[1] to seduce lovers from their affianced brides, husbands from their wives, and all to gratify a thirst of admiration, and a despicable vanity, with but a grain of passion to plead her excuse; this is the conduct of a finished coquette, and this is the character, tho' gilded over by beauty and accomplishments, which will ever deserve and ever meet my abhorrence!"

CHAPTER VI.
THE COQUETTE PUNISHED—
A STRATAGEM.

LOUISA, who, conscious of her resemblance to the character Mr. Mortimer had depicted, had but ill born the commencement of this conversation, could sit it no longer, and hastily throwing up the sash, complained of the intense heat of the room.

Mrs. Mordaunt, who had seen her colour change, earnestly pressed her to retire to bed: but Mr. Mortimer, more knowing, because more interested in the cause of her illness, and who judged his discourse had in some measure occasioned it, though he felt all his suspicions awakened and confirmed, and though he considered Louisa as deserving the detestation he had just expressed, could not bear the thoughts of losing her company; and begging Mrs. Mordaunt would wait the effect of the fresh air, before she repeated her advice, kindly approached Miss Conolly, and taking her hand, expressed his concern for her illness in so soothing a manner, and in a tone of voice so full of tender sympathy, that Louisa, stung to the soul at the thought of being unworthy and incapable of possessing the esteem of the only man she ever saw worthy of possessing hers, was overcome with contending emotions, and bursting into a

---

1 Mortimer emphasizes the coldness attributed to the coquette's heart (see Addison, Appendix I.1), finding it more culpable than the heat of passion that he supposes drives the libertine male. Though no libertine himself, Mortimer does articulate the double standards governing sexual conduct in the eighteenth century. As the anonymous author of *Woman Triumphant* (1721) phrases it, "If a woman falls into your snares … you can find an hundred excuses to extenuate the crimes of your own sex, you call them slips, tricks of youth, heat of young blood, or the like…" (quoted in Bridget Hill 32.)

violent flood of tears, she hid her face in Mrs. Mordaunt's bosom; insensible to every thing but the reproaches of her own heart.

As soon as she recovered, her consciousness of the cause of her disorder made her gladly consent to Mrs. Mordaunt's proposal of retiring, as she feared Mr. Mortimer's penetrating eyes would read in hers a confusion that would reveal a fault in her character, she was anxious to hide from his view. She withdrew, therefore, but not before Mr. Mortimer had obtained her permission to call next morning, to enquire after her health.

Louisa retired to bed, but to sleep was impossible. She now began seriously to wish she had followed the advice of her Caroline, to check every propensity to coquetry; and she now saw her error, when it was too late to amend it: she found herself at last punished for her misconduct, in being forced to forego every hope of gaining the heart of the only man she now thought herself ambitious of captivating. These thoughts kept her awake all night, and she arose in the morning, little refreshed by the repose which she had retired so early to obtain.

Mr. Mortimer also had spent a sleepless night, but joyful expectation was the cause of his watchfulness, and had the same effect on him despair had on Louisa.

He rightly judged self-accusation had a great share in Louisa's indisposition, and he could not help flattering himself, that anxiety for his entertaining a favorable opinion of her, had added force to her feelings, and produced the emotion to which he had been witness. This idea delighted him. Though Louisa was a coquette, he saw she abounded in sensibility and understanding, and could she once be induced to call in these better powers to subdue her propensity to coquetry, he was certain her follies would fade before the light of her reason, and that she would become in time an estimable character. Her reformation, therefore, he thought, would with ease be effected, if her heart were attached, without the certainty of its attachment being returned; and attached too to one, whose esteem she found it necessary for her to gain, before she could engage his affection.

Hope and self-flattery whispered he himself was likely to become the object of Louisa's choice; and tho' the thought gratified his feelings, he determined his conduct should not betray them, and resolved to pay Miss Conolly only those general attentions which a fine woman receives from every one.

Mr. Mortimer immediately put his resolution in practice. He was constant, indeed, in his visits to Mrs. Mordaunt, while Louisa was with her, and on her return home, which happened soon after, he became a visitor at her father's; but he kept so constant a guard over his eyes, when they met those of Louisa, that she had no suspicion of his attachment; and she imagined the impression her external charms had occasioned had been counteracted by the contempt her character excited.

These thoughts, and the apprehensions that gave birth to them, had soon a visible effect upon the conduct of Louisa. She was no longer volatile, but pensive; absent in every company, where Mortimer was not present, and when with him, her eyes no longer roved in search of admiration, but confined their stolen glances to him alone; while a cautious reserve, and a painful consciousness, gave added softness to her voice, and unknown to herself riveted the chains in which her beauty had entangled him. Mortimer secretly rejoiced in the effects of his resolution, for he clearly discerned the cause of this change in Louisa; he looked forward with rapturous expectation to the hour when Louisa, freed from the follies that disgraced her character, should amply recompense him, by the gift of her hand, for the cruel restraint, concern for her welfare had determined him to lay upon himself, in the concealment of a passion which he exulted in, and imagined she was not entirely averse to.

CHAPTER VII.
TREACHERY OF LOVE—
FILIAL AFFECTION.

LET not the heart, avowedly a slave to love, presume to value itself upon steady resolution. One moment overpowered Mr. Mortimer's, and destroyed his projects of concealment for ever.

Having alighted from his horse to pay a morning visit to Louisa, he was told by the servant she was in a favourite arbor at the bottom of the garden; thither he repaired, and as he approached the arbor, saw Louisa leaning on her arm, apparently absorbed in grief, while her frequent sobs and violent agitations soon destroyed the secret hope he at first entertained, that he was the cause of her dejection, and awakened his feelings into the tenderest apprehensions.

He hastily accosted her, and seizing her hand in the most passionate manner, begged to know the cause of her distress, Louisa, too much agitated to answer his questions fully, only pronounced the name of Caroline with reiterated bursts of grief.

Mortimer being acquainted with her friendship for Miss Egerton, and knowing from fatal experience what heart rending affliction the death of a beloved friend occasions, felt his whole soul melted into sorrow and compassion; all his resolutions were forgotten; he saw nothing but Louisa, and Louisa in despair; he was no longer master of his feelings, but avowing his attachment, he asserted his right to be a sharer in her grief.

Surprize and joy, united with the distress Louisa had just experienced, overpowered her now weak frame, and she fell senseless in the arms of Mr. Mortimer; but when, on recovering, she found herself supported by the affectionate attention of the man whom she had long vainly tried to look on with indifference, her satisfaction was so great, that the cause of the affliction which had brought on this discovery, was for the moment forgotten. It was not a time for disguise, and when Mortimer repeated his professions of attachment, and pressed for a return of it, the generous frankness of Louisa's answer delighted her lover, and did honour to herself.

When she became more composed, Mortimer again enquired into the cause of her distress. Louisa informed him that it proceeded from a letter she had just received from Caroline, in which she said, that wearied out with being a constant spectator of her father's misery, and with hearing complaints she was unable to remove, she had at length determined to sacrifice her own happiness to relieve his distress; or, rather, to endeavour to *find* peace in administering to *his*.

With this intention, she had resolved to gratify her father's wishes, in marrying an English gentleman, of considerable fortune, residing at Lausanne.

So far Louisa informed Mr. Mortimer, and he joined with her to admire the character of Caroline, and to lament the sacrifice she was about to make to filial affection.

Mortimer was so much interested for Miss Egerton, that he promised to think on means to prevent her resolutions being put in practice; and reminding Louisa of the permission she had given him to apply to Sir Charles for leave to address her, he left her, to go in search of her father.

The family and fortune, as well as character of Mr. Mortimer, insured him a welcome reception from Sir Charles. A father's sanction confirmed Louisa's choice, and preparations for their marriage were immediately begun.

Still resolved to save the friend of his Louisa from the painful task she had assigned herself, he purposed to carry his fair bride to Lausanne, hoping that the intreaties of Louisa, and his remonstrances, would not fail of effect—the one in prevailing on Caroline to relinquish her intention of fulfilling her promise, and the other persuade Mr. Egerton to give up his desire of claiming it.

That Caroline had no heart to bestow, Louisa had informed him, but the conclusion of her letter, which contained a full confession of her sentiments, she thought herself not at liberty to disclose. Caroline concluded thus:

"As my hopes of happiness, with the object that has for years engrossed the softest affections of my heart, are now for ever vanished, I must seek for comfort in beholding that of others—

I have been from my earliest hours a slave to love, though ever silent on the subject, even to you, Louisa, the chosen friend of my heart. — Alas! there were reasons for this concealment — but now I may unbosom my soul to you. Yet, surely my secret is already known, and you consider Edward Mountague as the object of my affection. Acquainted too as you are with his attachment to you, you can guess the reason of my secrecy.

"Pardon my presumption, Louisa, though I saw his senses dazzled, and his heart engrossed by your charms, I yet dared to hope he might one day be mine. — I thought I was more formed to make him happy in domestic life than you; and knowing you were not likely to return his affection, I hoped he would seek a refuge in mine, from the power of slighted love. — These dreams of bliss are fled for ever! — The struggle is over — and I am at length resigned. Through my means, my dear father may be happy, and I bless the Almighty hand that has vouchsafed to try me.

"Mr. Conway, though not the man of my heart, is amiable: he heard my tale of hopeless love with pity, and received my confidence with gratitude, for I thought it a duty I owed both to him and myself, to acquaint him with my prior engagement, though not with the object of it. That object, whose graceful image is ever present to my imagination — that object — but I must think of him no more! — yet while writing to one who esteems him as much as I do, how can I be silent in his praise!

"I will write again soon, but at present am too much agitated, and entreat your pardon for the freedom with which this letter is dictated. — Adieu, Louisa! Heaven seems to prepare a kinder fate for you, if you are careful to avoid the dangers your disposition exposes you to. Be prudent and be happy! and still continue to impart your pleasures and your pains to the faithful bosom of

"CAROLINE EGERTON."

CHAPTER VIII.
UNEXPECTED GOOD FORTUNE.

"A KINDER fate indeed!" said Louisa, bursting into tears, as she read the melancholy letter a second time, "and how have I deserved it!"

She compared Caroline's character and situation with her own, and was lost in the distress the comparison occasioned her, when, to her astonishment, Edward Mountague himself was announced! He was just returned from abroad, and returned, not as the youth whose abilities were obscured, and whose hopes were depressed by a scanty fortune, but as possessor of an high title, and a large estate.

By the death of a distant relation he became possessed of the title of Lord Fitzaubrey, and of the estate belonging to it. The news of his relation's decease reached him at Paris, where he was rejoicing in the victory he had gained over his boyish passion for Louisa, and was looking forward with pleasure to the dear society and gentle friendship of Caroline Egerton. For Louisa was most dangerous when present, Caroline still powerful when absent, as reflection could not recall her image without dwelling at the same time upon her virtues.

His hopes however of enjoying Miss Egerton's society were soon cruelly destroyed, by the news of her being gone to Lausanne, in consequence of her father's loss of fortune; and he hastened to Sir Charles's house, more impatient to gain some information concerning Caroline, than to behold the once adored Louisa.

In his way to the village where Sir Charles resided, he had heard Louisa was on the point of marriage, and as he heard it without emotion, he was convinced his heart was in no danger of a relapse, from the sight of her ripened beauty.

The situation of Louisa's mind at the time of his arrival has been before described; no wonder then the sight of one who was the chief cause of her friend's unhappiness should excite painful feelings in her heart, and that the kind and sisterly welcome with which she received Lord Fitzaubrey was embittered by the recollection of pleasures she might never taste again.

Fitzaubrey, was not less agitated; the sight of Louisa recalled to his mind the happy hours they had enjoyed together in the company of her friend, and his first enquiry was after the health of Caroline. This question entirely destroyed the composure Louisa had endeavoured to assume, a thousand tender remembrances crowded on her mind, and a violent flood of tears was her only answer. The sight of her distress awakened the most painful apprehensions in Lord Fitzaubrey's bosom, and with a faultering voice he again asked if Caroline was *dead*.

Shocked at the inference he had drawn, Louisa hastened to relieve his anxiety, but when she told him she was soon to be married, his feelings were but little improved. He had flattered himself Miss Egerton's friendship for him bordered upon a softer attachment, and he now found, from his disappointment and chagrin at the news of her engagements, that his affection for her might be easily mistaken for love. But his selfish feelings were rendered easier, when Louisa informed him, Caroline married more from duty than inclination, though his pity for her was encreased to a painful excess; he took his leave soon after in visible agitation, begging Louisa to present his kindest rememberance and best wishes, to the earliest and dearest friend of his heart. A thousand pleasing ideas arose in Louisa's mind, at sight of his emotion, and when she communicated what had passed to Mr. Mortimer, he joined with her in drawing from it omens favourable to the happiness of Caroline.

CHAPTER IX.
IN WHICH FITZAUBREY BETRAYS HIMSELF.

LORD Fitzaubrey, though unfitted for company, proceeded from Sir Charles's to the house of Lady Beaumont, where he had engaged himself to dine, and so great was his absence of mind, that though shewn into the drawing-room, he regarded not what the servant said, but went into Sir Henry Beaumont's apartment, where the first object that met his eyes, and recalled his scattered thoughts, was the picture of Caroline Egerton!

Fitzaubrey became motionless with surprize, but his reverie was soon interrupted by the entrance of Lady Beaumont, who immediately began to congratulate him upon his accession to the title and fortune of Fitzaubrey. She was so taken up with her eagerness to compliment his Lordship, that his confusion passed unnoticed by her.

"But, my Lord," continued she, "I fear your visit to me to-day will only be productive of disappointment to you. I suppose you expected to see my son, and came to his apartment in hopes of finding him there."

"You are right in your conjectures, Ma'am," replied Fitzaubrey, "and what makes my friend absent from this charming country, at a season so fitted for the diversions of the field?"[1]

"You are my son's friend, my Lord," rejoined Lady Beaumont, "I will therefore hide nothing from you. He is gone abroad in search of that peace which hopeless love has deprived him of." "Indeed!" exclaimed Fitzaubrey: "and who is the object of his attachment?" "*Your friend*," returned her Ladyship, with an arch smile, "Caroline Egerton."

Fitzaubrey's increased colour visibly betrayed his confusion, but recovering himself, he said, "my opinion of Sir Henry's discernment is confirmed; but whence comes it that Miss Egerton has forfeited all her pretensions to taste, by being insensible to his merit."

"For the best reason in the world," replied Lady Beaumont, "a prepossession in favour of the merit of another; Caroline is a noble girl, and deserves to be happy; her determination with regard to my son exalts her in my estimation, tho' I repine at it. But see (continued she) taking a letter out of a cabinet, here are her reasons for refusing Sir Henry, under her own hand; for refusing him too at a time when interest prompted the most ready consent; for when Mr. Egerton failed, Sir Henry immediately solicited my consent to his addressing Caroline, as he had then an opportunity of proving the disinterestedness of his passion. I approved his intention as warmly as he was eager to put it in execution. Caroline was an exemplary girl, and Sir

---

1 Hunting.

Henry had fortune enough to overlook the want of it in her; but I see you are impatient to read Miss Egerton's letter; you, as you were her bosom friend, may perhaps know the object she alludes to." Fitzaubrey took the letter. It was as follows:

"TO LADY BEAUMONT.

"My esteem for your Ladyship has always been unbounded, and my affection for you is now heightened by gratitude for the generous condescension you have shown, in giving your consent to the proposals Sir Henry Beaumont has honoured me by making. He has received my answer, and with a delicacy worthy of himself, has admitted my refusal of his offers without asking a reason for it. Indeed had he requested one, I must have denied it; but to your Ladyship I can be more explicit.

"Alas! Madam, I have not a heart to bestow. Perhaps I should hesitate to make this confession, if I were likely to be successful in my attachment, but every hope of its success is fled for ever. You have often commended my prudence, and have given it as your opinion, that Caroline Egerton would not soon yield to the influence of love, and that when she did own its power, she would 'let the spark drop from reason that lighted the flame.'[1] At that time I was cherishing the most tender passion for one whom I knew but too well was enamoured of another. I was so deluded by hope, and so blinded by self-flattery, that I looked forward with expectation to being the object of his choice.

"Nature had been liberal to him of her gifts, but fortune sparing, and it was the first wish of my heart to compensate for her neglect. — But the ruin of my father's fortune has destroyed all my hopes. He never can be mine, and all my chance of happiness from love is for ever gone. But though I resign all thoughts of him, I cannot think of marrying another, while my heart retains its first impression, and I trust I shall carry it to the grave with me.

"Sir Henry deserves a whole heart, and never can mine, wounded by hopeless love, and almost broken by affliction, be worthy to be tendered to his acceptance. No, Madam! we must

---

1   John Burgoyne, "The Heiress," Act II, scene iii, l. 186.

meet no more. I leave England, perhaps for ever, and I will spare you and myself the pain of parting; but allow me to assure you, that whithersoever I go, I shall carry with me the remembrance of your generous friendship, and my constant prayer shall be, that Sir Henry Beaumont may enjoy with another, that happiness he could never have known with the unfortunate

"CAROLINE EGERTON."

Fitzaubrey's countenance underwent many changes as he read the letter; he was convinced he was the object Caroline alluded to; gratitude for her generous intentions, and disinterested affection towards him, and despair from supposing she was now lost to him for ever, got the better of his prudence, and he feelingly exclaimed, "rash girl! why did you not keep your resolution, and remain constant to the man of your first choice! I had then been happy, but now I must be miserable for ever!"

"What do you mean," cried Lady Beaumont, terrified at his distress, "is Caroline married then? Though for my son's sake I wish it, yet for hers —"

"Married," interrupted Fitzaubrey, "Oh! no; my situation is not yet so desperate, but she is on the point of sacrificing herself to oblige her father! Oh! Lady Beaumont, I know I was the ungrateful object Caroline alluded to, but the charm is broken that blinded my reason, and my heart now is, and long has been irrecoverably hers. What is to be done? Thank heaven, she informs Miss Conolly, her marriage is delayed, on account of some writings not being ready — it may not yet be too late."

"Grant heaven it may not," replied her Ladyship; "but see! My Lord, methinks that picture has assumed a frown of displeasure, and chides you for even this short delay; she gave me that likeness of her just before her father's misfortunes."

Fitzaubrey fixed his eyes upon the faithful resemblance of his Caroline: the countenance admirably expressed the pensive tenderness of her soul. It spoke a subtile language to the heart of Fitzaubrey. I have been the cause of sorrow to her, said he, mentally, I may yet be the source of her happiness. — The idea hastened his departure, he threw himself into his carriage, and desired his postillions[1] to drive immediately to Dover. — He arrived there just as the pacquet[2] was about to sail, and a few hours landed him at Calais.

CHAPTER X.
IN WHICH CAROLINE APPEARS
TO ADVANTAGE.

In the mean while the preparations for Louisa's marriage were nearly concluded, and certain of being beloved by the man of her heart, she had regained her usual ease and vivacity.

Mr. Mortimer, though he rejoiced in the content her countenance expressed, was not pleased with the return of that gay thoughtlessness of disposition, which was one of the chief causes of her coquetry, and he began seriously to lament his not having possessed resolution enough to conceal his attachment, till suspence had cured Louisa's indiscretion, beyond the power of a relapse. Yet, tormented as he was with fears of the future, and dissatisfaction with the present, he had strength of mind enough to do justice to Louisa, in believing her heart entirely his own; and that however levity might obscure her virtue, real guilt would never disgrace it.

Louisa too was dissatisfied with herself; in spite of the joint efforts of reason and affection, her thoughts wandered to the expected pleasures of the metropolis, and she was still sensible of the hope of conquest, in the gay scene she was hastening to, though she was not to appear there, till she had assumed the respectable distinction of the wife of Mr. Mortimer.

In vain did Louisa resolve to confine all her future wishes to pleasing him alone; other objects glided before her fancy, and her prospects were clouded by her dread of not deserving them.

Such was the situation of her mind, when a pacquet arrived

---

1 Postillions are riders who guide the horses. Rather than placing a driver on the coach, it was common for carriage teams to be directed by men mounted on the near (left) horse of each pair.

2 A paquet-boat or vessel that sailed between two ports at regular intervals to carry mail as well as goods and passengers.

from Lausanne, and great were Louisa's surprize and joy when she beheld a letter in the hand writing of Lord Fitzaubrey. She broke the seal with the most eager impatience. He began with informing Louisa of what had passed at Lady Beaumont's, and of his resolution in consequence of it.

"I know not," continued he, "what my plans were at the moment, but the idea that engrossed my thoughts was the hope of arriving at Lausanne time enough to prevent Caroline's marriage with Mr. Conway, tho' without the prospect then of marrying her myself; but when I grew more composed, hope for myself, began to revive in my bosom.

"You had told me Mr. Conway was informed of her reluctance to give him her hand, and amiable as she described him to be, I thought he would not hesitate to give her to the man of her choice, when he appeared to claim his prior right. Difficult as I knew the task must be, I thought no man of delicacy would shrink from it, but would willingly resign all claim to the person of a woman, whose heart was in possession of another. Yet in spite of my self-flattery, my hopes were depressed by continual fears, and my heart so agitated by apprehensions of arriving too late to prevent the event I so much dreaded, that when I arrived at Lausanne, I could hardly make the necessary enquiries for the house of Mr. Egerton.

"I stayed a few minutes at the Inn to compose myself, and at length proceeded, with a beating heart, to a small but neat house, situated just out of the town. Here I was told I should find the object of my search. I knocked at the door and enquired for Miss Egerton. Being told she was at home, and alone, I begged leave to speak to her immediately, and went into a room, the door of which was open.

"Thank heaven, said I to myself, she is not yet married, as my enquiries for Miss Egerton are answered; and I was preparing myself for the interview, when I heard the voice of Caroline, who was singing to her guittar, that plaintive air of Jackson's, 'Oh! say, thou dear possessor of my breast!'[1] which I used to

---

1   William Jackson (1730-1803) published *Twelve Songs: opera quarta* in 1785. Among them was "O say thou dear possessor of my breast."

admire so much, when you were grave enough to do justice to it. I turned to see whence the sound proceeded, and I found it came from the next room. I immediately ascended a flight of stairs, that led to it — the door was half open — Caroline was seated on a sopha, and so intent upon her song, that she was unconscious of my being near her.

"As Caroline concluded, tears flowed down her cheeks, 'Ill fated tenderness!' she exclaimed, 'I will indulge it no longer, and this faithful likeness of one I must think of no more, I will destroy at once, (taking up a profile of me which I had given her.)' She rose up to put her threats in execution, but turning suddenly round, she discovered me, and with a shriek of terror fell senseless at my feet.

"To describe my sensations is impossible; love, fear and a thousand emotions almost bereft me of my faculties. I had just sense enough to carry her to the sopha, and was bending over her pale face, with a look of the tenderest apprehension, when a gentleman entered the room.

"'Great God!' he exclaimed, 'what do I see!' then fiercely advancing, 'resign that lady to my care, sir.'—'I will resign her to no one,' returned I, agitated with contending emotions, for I justly concluded this gentleman was Mr. Conway, and the ideas of rivalship and jealousy began to create violent disturbances in my bosom. —'By heaven!' replied Mr. Conway, 'you shall resign her.'— I took no notice of this threatning speech, for Caroline began to revive, and throwing my arms round her I addressed her in the most tender terms.

"When she became sensible of what had passed, she fixed her eyes on me with a look I shall never forget, and exclaimed, 'Has Louisa then betrayed me!' then springing from me, she staggered to a chair, and hid her face with her hand. Mr. Conway then approached her, and begged to know how far she authorized the familiarity of that gentleman, that he might know how far it became him to resent it.

"This speech rouzed her from her silence, and resuming that majesty of demeanour you and I have so often admired in her, 'You shall be satisfied immediately, sir,' she repeated, 'and do me the justice to suspend your judgment of my conduct, till Mr.

Mountague has explained his own.' Then with a dignity of voice and manner that would not admit of evasion, she desired to know what brought me to Lausanne?

"'Love and despair!' exclaimed I. Caroline faintly said, she never expected to hear such a declaration from me, and asked if I knew of her engagements? 'Yes, madam, I heard of them in England, and came hither in hopes of breaking them.' 'Of breaking them!' echoed Mr. Conway? My countenance did not promise a very gentle answer to this exclamation, which Caroline perceiving, her fears got the better of her assumed composure, and bursting into tears she cried, 'Oh, Edward! did you then come only to insult and terrify me!' Her distress immediately calmed us both; but when she addressed me by the familiar name of Edward, Mr. Conway changed colour, and with a voice scarcely audible, begged to know who that gentleman was, and what was his connection with her?"

CHAPTER XI.
BEING A CONTINUATION
OF THE FOREGOING.

"'THAT gentleman,' said Caroline, blushing, 'was the earliest friend I ever boasted, and I—' 'Tis enough,' said Mr. Conway, 'your former uneasiness has given me a clue to unravel this scene, my head is at present too confused, and my heart too full to suffer me to determine how I ought to behave; allow me to take my leave, for the present'; so saying, he bowed and left us.

"I should tire your patience, were I to relate what followed; suffice it to say, I drew from Caroline a reluctant confession of the interest I possessed in her heart, and obtained her pardon for coming to interrupt the composure she had been endeavouring to assume; but she still persisted in keeping her engagements.

"After an hour's absence, Mr. Conway returned, and addressing himself to me, he said, he was convinced from the scene he had been witness to, that I was the object of the early attachment Miss Egerton had confessed; he was also certain, from the emotion my unexpected presence had occasioned in her, that her affection for me was as ardent as ever. Convinced of this, delicacy and generosity both forbade him to accept the hand Caroline had promised him.

"'I have often assured Miss Egerton,' continued he, 'that it should be the study of my life to make her happy; I will keep that promise, by bestowing her on the man of her heart. I will ensure her happiness, even by the present loss of mine.' He then seized our hands, while we stood motionless with surprize, and joining them, he cried, 'Heaven bless you together,' and attempted to rush out of the room! This sudden action recalled us to ourselves — Caroline caught hold of his arm. 'Stay, most generous of men,' she exclaimed, 'and hear me resolve never to unite myself with any one but you, and I here promise to see Mr. Mountague no more!'

"'Stop, Caroline,' cried, I, almost frantic at her words, 'and let me speak, before you abandon me for ever.'

"'I will hear nothing,' she replied; 'you have made me weak, but shall not make me despicable. There is yet another reason, that were I free from all engagements would prevent my ever being yours; when I had the prospect of being an Heiress, it was the fond wish of my heart to bestow myself and fortune upon you, but when I became poor and friendless, I resolved never to be yours, though you should honour me with that regard you had before felt for me, as I could not bear to encrease your difficulties, by bringing beggary to your arms; that objection still remains in its full force; and, added to my esteem for Mr. Conway, and the many ties that bind me to him, forms an eternal bar between us.'

"'If my want of fortune,' said I, 'were all your objections to yielding to Mr. Conway's generosity, I should be happy indeed, for my fortune now is equal to my most sanguine wishes.'

"I saw Caroline turn pale at this unexpected removal of one important obstacle to my wishes, and I was just beginning to take advantage of her emotion to press my suit, when the entrance of Mr. Egerton prevented me. He was surprised at seeing me, but cordially shaking me by the hand, he begged know what led me into that part of the world; when perceiving his daughter's paleness and agitation, he begun, in not the most delicate manner in the world, to enquire what was the matter now?

"Mr. Conway undertook to explain matters, and having done so, in a manner that has bound me to him for ever, he retracted his promise to marry Miss Egerton, and begged her father to bestow her on me.

"Rage and disappointment now displayed themselves on the countenance of Mr. Egerton, 'And do you think,' exclaimed he, 'I shall indulge the folly of a ridiculous girl, and take her from a man of large property to bestow her on a beggar.'

"'If you mean me by the title of beggar,' said I, 'I can venture to assure you, sir, that my fortune is now such as Mr. Egerton, in his most prosperous hours, need not have rejected for his daughter.'

"'If this be true,' returned Mr. Egerton—'but fortunes are more easily lost than won, you know, young man.'

"'Dear sir,' said Mr. Conway, 'if Mr. Mountague be really inferior to me in point of fortune, is the happiness of such a child as Miss Egerton to be put in competition with a few acres!'

"'Why, indeed,' replied he, 'I think not; Caroline has been a good girl, and deserves to be rewarded; so if you gentlemen can settle it between you, she may have Mr. Mountague with all my heart.'

"Caroline then rose up and again persisted in her resolution of marrying Mr. Conway, but he as warmly refused her, and desired her candidly to own, that Mr. Mountague was still too dear to her heart, to suffer her to feel that warmth of affection for him his delicacy demanded. —

"Tears were her only answer. 'Then never,' continued he, 'will I accept your hand; and I again beg to join it with Mr. Mountague's.'

"Caroline still hesitated. 'Generous man,' said she, 'I am unwilling—' 'No more,' interrupted Mr. Conway, 'call me not generous, perhaps the title of selfish more properly belongs to me. Though not of a jealous temper, after such a scene as this, I should have distrusted your tenderest attention, and thought your warmest proofs of affection mere hypocrisy. Could I then hope for happiness with such prejudices in my bosom? Never—Therefore, to save myself, not you, from disquietude, I yield you to Mr. Mountague: long indeed will it be before I can look on you as a friend only, but when that time arrives, do not refuse to let me be an eye witness of the happiness I have endeavored to be instrumental to.' He then bowed and departed.

"Scarcely was he gone, when the servant came in, and enquired if Lord Fitzaubrey was there? 'No, no,' said Mr. Egerton, 'there are no Lords here,'—but I begged leave to contradict him, by assuring him his old friend Edward Mountague, and Lord Fitzaubrey were the same.

"'What!' replied Mr. Egerton in the utmost astonishment, 'does a gay young man, with a fine fortune, come hither after a broken merchant's daughter, without a penny? Well, well; but I say nothing.'

"I did not answer this fine speech, being too intent upon the looks of Caroline. 'This is too much,' said she; 'now there is another obstacle to our union. I can never consent to so disproportionate a match. —'Do you chuse then,' said I, reproachfully, 'to monopolize disinterested love: did you not intend to bestow yourself and fortune upon me, when poor, and will you not accept from me, what you would have bestowed upon me?' She was silent, but upon her father's quitting the room, I pleaded my cause so successfully, that she consented to be mine in a few days. The few days are elapsed, and this morning made me the happiest of men.

"You will perhaps think me too minute in my description, but Caroline desired me to be so; she intends writing herself in a day or two, but at present she is busy in preparing to set off for Montpelier, where we intend passing some time, as Lady Fitzaubrey's health is, in my opinion, much impaired. We shall spend the winter in Paris, and in the beginning of May, Caroline hopes to embrace the friend of her heart, and present to her in her happy husband, Miss Conolly's earliest, and most sincere friend,

"EDWARD MOUNTAGUE,
    "ALIAS FITZAUBREY."

CHAPTER XII.
THE FAREWELL.

THIS letter gave the warmest satisfaction to the affectionate heart of Louisa. She exulted in the happy lot of Caroline, and praised the justice of Heaven, in rewarding her superior virtue. But her joy was damped by the reflection that she should not make her first entrance into the dangerous scenes of high life, guarded by the advice and guided by the example of her friend. She regretted Lord Fitzaubrey's design of spending the winter at Paris; and when a few months after marriage, which took place soon after the pacquet arrived from Lausanne, Mr. Mortimer began to prepare for their removal to London, her natural vivacity was depressed by involuntary fears of the future, and she would gladly have consented, at the moment of departure, to have given up the idea of enjoying those scenes which her fancy before had delighted to anticipate.

Louisa took a mournful farewell of the companions of her youthful hours, visited and revisited the scenes of her childish pleasures; and as she viewed them for the last time, she secretly preferred a prayer, that she might return to them as happy as she left them.

Deeply as her sensibility was wounded by leaving these trifling objects of her regard, how much must she have suffered in bidding adieu to her father. She had never before been separated from him, and tho' she now left her paternal roof, under the care of a husband, dearer to her than life itself, she was a prey to the most poignant regret. She recollected his repeated indulgence to her follies and her errors, and she reflected, that in the world she was hastening to, the touch of partial affection would not soften the edge of censure, and her judges would be unlike a fond and doating parent.

Sir Charles was equally affected at parting with her, many times did he bid her adieu, and many times recall her to receive his blessing and embraces.

Mortimer did not behold this scene with indifference; by turns he wept with, and courted his Louisa, and as he bore her weeping on his bosom, from the abode of her ancestors he reflected with delight upon the warm affections of her heart, assuring himself that so affectionate a child must, in spite of the dangers of dissipation, make him happy as a wife.

I will leave her, said he, mentally, to the guidance of that heart whose sensibility I have experienced, and should she err, on its dictates only shall she depend for reformation; convinced of her affection, I desire no other security from jealousy, and while my confidence in her honour is unshaken, never shall a few foibles, arising from youthful indiscretion, induce me to run the risk of weakening her attachment, by the reproof of discontent, and the exertion of authority! I will guide by silken chains or not at all, and though she may lament my inability to make her happy, she shall not complain that my unkindness is the cause of it!

CHAPTER XIII.
NATURAL EFFECTS OF A COUNTRY EDUCATION.

ON the arrival of Mr. and Mrs. Mortimer in town, their house was crowded with morning visitors, of both sexes, the gentlemen eager to see the fair conqueror, who had captivated the well-guarded heart of Mortimer, and the ladies, ambitious of instructing the inexperienced, country-bred Louisa, in the important articles of dress and fashionable knowledge.

Aided by the strength of an understanding which only in a few instances she was incapable of using, Louisa received with cold civility, the attentions of the men, and with indifference heard the advice and proposals of the women. — But still their offers were in some things important to her. Dress was a necessary thing to be considered. Louisa put herself under the direction of some married ladies, of high rank, who carried her to the most fashionable milliners in town.

The display of finery and the preparations for scenes of gaiety which these places unfolded to her, awakened the desire of entering public life; which parting with her father had so much weakened. She longed for the hour of her entrance into the world, and impatiently waited to be presented at court. But the ceremony was, by some unlucky circumstances delayed, and Louisa was obliged to content herself at home, and to beguile the time by studying the characters of those visitors with whom her town life would chiefly be spent.

Accustomed to judge of manners and of morals, by the unerring rule of right, Louisa was surprized to find the arbitrary rule of judging that operated in the circles which assembled at her house. She found that fashion and caprice gave the word of command, and that as they dictated, the idol of the hour was either caressed and courted, or returned to the insignificance from which their voice had raised it.

Shocked at this depravity, Louisa secretly resolved to follow fashion in her manner and her dress, but never to let it influence her opinions; she thought herself incapable of being flattered by the attentions of a man she despised, because he was the reigning idol of the ton,[1] and she determined to scorn the offered acquaintance of any woman, distinguished for levity and imprudence, though countenanced by grandeur, and adorned by fashionable accomplishments.

Mrs. Mortimer imparted these resolutions to her husband, who agreed in their prudence, but feared her ability to keep them.

"I shall be but too happy," he replied, "if you have firmness enough to act up to the dictates of your reason."

"Do you then doubt me," said Louisa? He coldly answered, "no;" for he knew the fascinating power of fashion too well to look upon a young heart as ever sufficiently guarded against its influence.

Amongst the leaders of the ton, who were most frequently mentioned by the fashionable of both sexes, whom Mortimer was daily introducing to his bride, Louisa was surprized to hear the name of Mrs. Belmour. She remembered her when she lived in her neighbourhood, as one of her most frequent, though not most favoured companions, and she could hardly figure to herself Emily Hamilton as a favorite of the beaux, a rival of the belles,[2] and a leader of the fashion.

---

1   The fashionable world.

2   A beau was a man who gave particular, or excessive, attention to dress, bearing and social etiquette; similarly a belle was a handsome woman, especially one who dressed to set off her personal charms (*OED*).

In person she had always considered her as just not plain, and in understanding greatly inferior to many of her sex. Though possessed of a high spirit, eager to yield her opinion, when called in question by those she at all feared, and in manner, she was at twenty a complete Hoyden.[1] Louisa could not imagine how the original of such a picture should be respectable in high life, and even looked up to as a woman of taste and wit; and she heard, with some indignation, her dress quoted as genteel, her manner as elegant, and her pert sayings retailed as *bon mots*[2] of the first order.

Louisa however had a great deal to learn; she was as yet ignorant of the world, and its caprices, and meanly as she thought of Mrs. Belmour, it was to that lady she was chiefly indebted for an introduction into it.

CHAPTER XIV
A FASHIONABLE CHARACTER.

From the frequent accounts she heard of Mrs. Belmour's, elegance and stile,[3] Louisa was impatient to judge for herself, of the change in her old acquaintance, and she rejoiced to hear her name announced, while some of that lady's friends were paying her a morning visit.

Louisa received Mrs. Belmour very cordially, but took particular notice of her dress, her mode of entering a room, and her person. Her dress was elegant, last mourning for her husband, and her character was rather raised in Louisa's estimation, by her being told Mrs. Belmour was not insincere enough to grieve for the loss of a man whom interest only had induced her to marry.[4] Her person, though Louisa did not look to praise, appeared pleasing in her eyes. She was struck with a

---

1   A boisterous, noisy, ill-bred girl (*OED*).
2   Clever or witty sayings; witticism, repartée (*OED*).
3   Variant eighteenth-century spelling of style.
4   By the eighteenth century distinct degrees and phases of mourning had been established, especially for women, whose dress indicated the stage and level of the grieving process. Ann Buck notes : "For all except the shortest mourning, the period was divided, half deep and half second mourning, with the second period sometimes divided again to make a more relaxed final quarter before dress in full colours and

great improvement, in it; part of which, however, she attributed to the skillful use of rouge, and the addition of fashionable ornaments. Her manner was even in Louisa's opinion engaging; it was still familiar, but it was the familiarity of good breeding; and the acquired softness of her voice insensibly pleased her, while the openness of her behaviour invited her confidence.

Louisa could not help even joining in the laugh her lively sallies occasioned, and when Mrs. Belmour took her leave, Louisa cordially promised to be frequently of her parties, and she told Mortimer, that she felt more inclined to be intimate with Mrs. Belmour, than with any other of her acquaintance, as her former knowledge of her made an intimacy with her more proper than with strangers.

Mrs. Belmour was not behind hand with her in the observations of the morning, and her remarks were rather more just and accurate than Louisa's. One part of her character her young friend had not discovered. — Though her understanding was, as Louisa justly observed, inferior to that of many of her acquaintance, she possessed a quality which amply compensated for its deficiencies, namely, as Churchill phrases it

"— That low cunning which in fools supplies,
And amply too, the place of being wise."[1]

With this talent, it was easy for her to acquire a perfect knowledge of the foibles of her acquaintance, and that knowledge gained, she had sense and quickness enough to turn it to her own advantage. Besides, she had the happy art of adapting her manners and sentiments to the manners and sentiments of

---

trimmings was once more worn ... Of all mourning a widow's was the deepest and of longest duration" (60–61). By the nineteenth century widows were expected to wear deep mourning (unrelieved black dull fabric) for a year and a day, followed by six months of a shiny black fabric plus an additional year of half-mourning—black and white only, no colour. See Phillis Cunnington and Catherine Lucas, *Costume for Births, Marriages, and Deaths*. Mrs. Belmour drops deep mourning after the requisite six months, not, as Louisa suggests, from a rejection of hypocrisy but because she mistakenly believes that having been Ormington's mistress, she will be made his wife more quickly.

1   From Charles Churchill's "The Rosciad" (1761), a satire on the London stage, ll. 117-118.

those she conversed with. With the open and ingenuous, she was blunt and apparently unthinking; with the reserved, she was timid; with the young and volatile, lively and affectionate; with the vain, flattering; in short, she, Proteus like,[1] assumed all characters, while she kept her own concealed from every one.

Such was the woman who was now introduced to the acquaintance, and to the confidence of Louisa, even with the approbation of her husband, for so specious were her manners, they imposed upon all, and the giddy and the grave were equally the dupes of her softness and her art.

Greatly did Mrs. Belmour rejoice at the renewal of her acquaintance with Louisa; she beheld her beauty with satisfaction and delight, [and] the admiration she excited in the male part of her visitors[,] symptoms of vanity, and sensibility to praise, which gave her the most lively joy — for she fixed on Louisa as the future vehicle of her malice and revenge.

Louisa's wonder at Mrs. Belmour's being a leader of the ton, was well founded in justice, but not in a knowledge of the world. She was ignorant that it was in the power of a man of elegance and distinction to make any woman the fashion, however by nature unfitted for it, and such were the means by which Mrs. Belmour had acquired her superiority.

The gay world has generally a few reigning favourites, to whom opinion, taste, and admiration are sacrificed, whose dress is the standard of elegance, whose persons are the models of grace, and whose manners are the criterion of good-breeding.

CHAPTER XV.
CAPRICE OF FASHION.

The most favourite idol in power at the time of Louisa's initiation into the mysteries of high life, was Lord Ormington, a young nobleman, of a handsome fortune, and great expectations, the latter of which served to maintain him in possession of the superiority his charms had gained.

This young Lord was elegant in person, insinuating in man-

---

1 Proteus was a figure in classical Greek literature who had the power to assume different shapes.

ners, expensive in dress, commanding to the men, but all softness to the women. His title insured him a welcome, even
where his character was unknown, and with these native and
acquired endowments, he had gained the privilege of directing
the opinions of the young, of despising the indignation of the
old, of laughing at the abilities of the learned, and, in short, of
being universally acknowledged as the director of fashion.

But though his company and attentions were courted by the
young of both sexes, he was the terror of guardians and of parents—for his inconstancy was as great as his power to please,
and in the true spirit of coquetry, he neglected the deluded
object of his attentions, as soon as he was master of her heart.[1]

Numerous were the conquests he had thus gained and abandoned—when, tired at length of only shewing his power in
heightening the fame of the young and beautiful, by ranking
himself in the number of their conquests, he resolved to prove
the extent of his influence, by giving the reputation of grace
and beauty to some object whom nature seemed not to have
formed for admiration.

With surprize and gratitude did Mrs. Belmour receive Lord
Ormington's attentions, and with the warmest satisfaction she
beheld the change they produced in the conduct of her
acquaintance. Instead of the constrained notice of civility, she
received the prolonged addresses of *preference*, and the honour of
leading her to the carriage was warmly solicited by many
young men, ambitious of appearing as the rivals of Lord Ormington.

His Lordship secretly enjoyed his triumph, and while he
laughed at the caprice of taste, he continued to pay Mrs. Belmour such marked partiality, that in spite of her knowledge of
the world, she began to flatter herself the death of her husband,
which she daily expected, would remove the only obstacle to
her becoming the envied wife of Lord Ormington.

Full of this idea, she gave the most flattering encouragement
to the addresses of his Lordship, and she soon found her heart,

---

1 Rochefoucauld observes: "Coquets are those who studiously excite the passion of
   love, without meaning to gratify it. The male coquets are nearly as numerous as the
   female" (Maxim no. 67, 20).

as well as her vanity, was interested in the success of her wishes.

At length the happy time of her release arrived; Mr. Belmour was carried off by a rapid decline, and she beheld herself uncontrouled mistress of a splendid fortune.

As soon as her six months deep mourning was expired, during which time Lord Ormington's frequent visits had confirmed the long smothered hopes of her heart, she again launched forth into the fashionable world, eager to pave the way to new admiration, by exhibiting Lord Ormington as her captive. — But she appeared in vain, Lord Ormington no longer sought to gain her smiles, the fickle Peer was paying those attentions to a young beauty just entering high life, which she had vainly flattered herself were wholly hers.

Lady Jane Bertie, sister to Lord Charles Bertie, was in the bloom of eighteen, and had just left the convent in which she had been educated, to make her first entrance into the world under the fond protection of her only brother.

To the affection of his sister, and her influence over her father, Lord Bertie had been indebted for the old Earl's forgiveness, after he had spent a very handsome fortune in riot and dissipation, and when his dying parents bequeathed his orphan sister to his care, he resolved to reward her kindness, by watching over her with the unremitting attention of a tender father.

Lady Jane's portion was small, and as Lord Ormington's alliance was an amiable one, in point of fortune, as well as situation, Lord Bertie was delighted with the marked preference his Lordship gave his sister. But perceiving Lady Jane's heart was not insensible to his Lordship's assiduities, and knowing his general character, he judged it incumbent on him, as the protector of his sister, to hint to Lord Ormington the necessity of a decided declaration of his sentiments respecting Lady Jane.

Lord Ormington, though not capable of a real attachment, was so charmed with the artless graces of Lady Jane, that he mistook his admiration for love, and thinking a better opportunity had never offered of submitting to the marriage yoke, with dignity, he avowed his passion for her ladyship without hesitation, and solicited her brother's consent to his immediate union with her.

Ever ready to promote the happiness of his sister, Lord Bertie added his consent to the willing one Lord Ormington had obtained from Lady Jane, and every thing was in train for their marriage, at the time of Louisa's entrance into the gay and fashionable world.

END OF THE FIRST VOLUME.

VOLUME II.

CHAPTER XVII.
A VISIT TO RANELAGH.[1]

THE news of the approaching connection between Lord Ormington and Lady Jane Bertie, was a dagger in the breast of Mrs.
Belmour; but, well skilled in the art of disguising her feelings,
she frequented public amusements, apparently unhurt by the
desertion of her admirer, while she was secretly forming
schemes to destroy the projected happiness of her innocent
rival.

Such were her feelings and resolves, when she was introduced to Louisa, and from the moment she first beheld her, she
marked her as the future tool of her malice and revenge.

As scarcely a day passed without Mrs. Belmour's seeing
Louisa, she had a good opportunity of preparing her mind for
the impressions she wished it to receive, by talking to her of
Lord Ormington, and telling her his attentions had power to
make any woman the fashion; regretting, at the same time, that
such an insipid girl as Lady Jane Bertie, should engross the
regard of so enchanting a man as his Lordship.

This discourse did not fail of effect. Louisa secretly wished
to see Lord Ormington, and to engage his attention, and she
was disappointed at not seeing him the morning she was presented at Court.

"But you will see him at Ranelagh to-morrow," said Mrs.
Belmour, and Louisa's thoughtless heart beat high at the idea of
expected conquest.

After dropping in at several routs,[2] where she heard her
praises buzzed round the room, she set off for Ranelagh, her
eyes sparkling from the consciousness of triumph, and her
cheek flushed with the glow of expectation.

---

1 Popular pleasure gardens located in Chelsea, opened in 1742 and closed in 1805;
   described by Edward Gibbon as "the most convenient place for courtship of every
   kind—the best market we have in England" (see Weinreb and Hibbert 637).
2 A large evening party or reception, popular in the eighteenth and early nineteenth
   centuries (OED).

It was the first night of Ranelagh's being opened for the season, and the company was consequently brilliant—but wherever she passed, Louisa heard either the exclamation of wonder at her charms, or was forced to cast her eyes on the ground, to avoid the eager gaze her appearance occasioned.

Added to her beauty, Louisa had novelty to recommend her, and a new face, in the gay world, has frequently an advantage over a handsome one; but as here novelty and beauty were united, Louisa was the idol of the evening.

As she leant on the arm of Mortimer, she was known to be his bride; and "they are the handsomest couple in the room," echoed from every quarter, and reached the ears of Lord Ormington, upon his first entrance, from the lips of some titled beaux, who were thought great judges of personal beauty.

"Come this way, my Lord, and you will meet her," cried one. "I see her feathers[1] very near us," said another.

"I shall see her in time," replied his Lordship coldly, "and I am not impatient," looking tenderly at Lady Jane, who was hanging on Lord Bertie's arm, apparently inattentive to what passed, while her young heart fluttered with apprehension, from the unwelcome ideas of rivalship and jealousy.

Lord Ormington's composure was as artificial as her own. The idea of Louisa's being the most beautiful woman in the room, and the wife of the greatly admired Harry Mortimer, raised thoughts and wishes in his breast, which he was desirous of concealing from Lady Jane—to attach such a woman as Louisa was described to be, and rival such a man as her husband, was a task worthy of him, he thought—and "there, my Lord, that's she," caused some little perturbation in his bosom.

Louisa's emotions were similar to his. Mrs. Belmour, who was with her, gave her a signal of his approach, by a pressure of

---

1 Elaborate feather head-dresses were very much in fashion in the late eighteenth century. See Anne Buck, who quotes from *The Journals and Letters of Fanny Burney* for 1798: "charge the dear girls not to have their Feathers so long or so forward as to brush the royal cheek as they rise" (19-20). Opie herself was especially given to wearing them. Brightwell lists as part of her trousseau in 1798: "Blue satin bonnet russe with eight blue feathers; nine small feathers and a feather edge; three blue round feathers and two blue Scotch caps ... seven flat feathers and three curled ones" (67).

her arm, and Louisa's eyes sparkled with pleasure, when she found the look she honoured him with returned by one expressive of the warmest admiration. This look awoke all her dormant inclinations to coquetry. Her eyes were constantly turned towards his Lordship, when they met, and his as constantly spoke a language Louisa but too well understood.

CHAPTER XVIII.
THE DISSEMBLERS.

To see so fine a woman as Mrs. Mortimer without forming an acquaintance with her, was not at all agreeable to Lord Ormington's usual mode of proceeding; and, though somewhat awed by the presence of Lady Jane, he resolved to be immediately introduced to her. Though he knew Mrs. Belmour could not be much disposed to oblige him, he resolved to request her to introduce him to Louisa.

Accordingly, just as they passed, he told Lady Jane he had been so negligent as not to take any notice of his old acquaintance, Mrs. Belmour, that evening, and that he must leave her Ladyship a few minutes to apologize for his neglect.

Lady Jane's countenance discovered that she thought her lover had other reasons for leaving her than the desire of apologizing to Mrs. Belmour; but, begging he would make no excuses for leaving her, she turned from him, and left him at liberty to follow his inclinations.

With well-dissembled regard he accosted Mrs. Belmour, and with as much ease as if he had not been conscious she had reason to complain of him; but Mrs. Belmour was a woman of the world, and, as his Lordship seemed willing to forget what had passed, she determined to indulge him, and replied to his compliments with readiness and cordiality: besides, her views now were changed, and though, perhaps, a little hope for herself lurked in her heart, could she succeed in breaking off Lord Ormington's marriage with Lady Jane, her only idea now was of revenge upon her Ladyship and her lover, for she had penetration to see Louisa's heart was entirely in possession of her husband, and that a love of admiration, which she had too long indulged to be able to subdue it without great resolution, was the only feeling that could lead her to indulge the addresses of any man.

Convinced, therefore, that her virtue was impregnable, Mrs. Belmour delighted in the thought of being well revenged, by seeing Lady Jane enduring all the pangs of jealousy, and beholding Lord Ormington a prey to the quick feelings of mortified vanity and disappointed passion, by meeting with one gay woman whose heart he could not gain, and whose virtue he was unable to subdue.

This manœuver of Lord Ormington's to get acquainted with Louisa she had foreseen, and had pre-determined to grant his request whenever he should think proper to make it. — At length he ventured to express his admiration of Louisa, and intreated Mrs. Belmour to introduce him to her.

"Certainly, my Lord," she replied, "if you can assure me Lady Jane is not provided with a dagger or a poisoned nosegay; for, as I value my friend's life, and your Lordship is not famed for constancy, I cannot make you acquainted with her without this previous assurance."

"Your vivacity is charming, and your sarcasm unanswerable," rejoined his Lordship, rather disconcerted at her raillery; "but upon this occasion, unjust as well as ill-timed. Mrs. Mortimer is a fine woman — so is Lady Jane, and I cannot see why I may not admire both without being unjust to either."

"Granted, my Lord," replied Mrs. Belmour, "and, satisfied of your Lordship's intentions, I will willingly introduce you to my fair friend."

This introduction was highly welcome to Louisa, for, to her great surprize, Mortimer had quitted the party as soon as Lord Ormington joined it, and was paying his devoirs to Lady Jane Bertie — "A convincing proof," said Louisa, mentally, "that he is not jealous of me, as he leaves me exposed to the seducing arts of the most dangerous man in England!"

This desertion, which ought to have given her pleasure, as it was a proof of her husband's confidence in her affection, Louisa's wayward heart construed into indifference. Before the evening ended, she had in two instances erred against the dictates of reason; in the first, by doing Mortimer injustice, in supposing him capable of preferring any company to her's; and in the second, by giving encouragement to the presumptuous hopes of an avowed libertine.

CHAPTER XIX.
THE CONVERSATION—
ALMACK'S.[1]

As they returned home, Mortimer asked Louisa her opinion of Lord Ormington, and her reply was filled with encomiums on his person and manner.

"And what think you of his intended bride," rejoined he?

Hurried away by a feeling of indignation which she could not repress at the attention Mortimer had paid Lady Jane, and which she did not attribute to the right cause, namely, a compliance with the world's opinion which requires men to be attentive to other women than their wives, Louisa bestowed on Lady Jane the epithets insipid, unmeaning; adding, that her beauty was too childish and insignificant to engage attention long.

"You surprize me, Louisa," returned Mortimer. "Can the interesting and artless expressions of Lady Jane's countenance strike you as childish and insipid? and her delicate, but expressive features, deserve the name of insignificant? I think her the finest girl that has appeared for years in the gay world."

"The gay world has not abounded in beauty then," replied Louisa, (piqued at the warmth of his praises) "and, if Lady Jane's conversation be as inanimate as her look, she is fortunate, indeed, in having attached such a man as Lord Ormington."

"I never heard you speak so harshly of any one before, Louisa," said Mr. Mortimer; "and, had you ever been acquainted

---

1 A suite of fashionable assembly rooms opened in London by William Almack in 1765. Its guest lists were strictly controlled by a set of ladies of high rank, and admission to the weekly ball was a coveted ticket to mingle with the social elite (see Weinreb and Hibbert 20).

with Lady Jane, I should have supposed she had offended you. In a woman less likely to excite admiration than yourself, I should have attributed these remarks to envy; but, as that is impossible, I must think they proceed from a very blameable want of candour. You do not judge with your usual good-nature." —

"Nor you with your usual judgment," retorted Louisa, with quickness — but her voice was too expressive of her feelings to suffer her to continue the discourse, and she gave herself up to sullen silence.

It was the first time Mortimer had ever, in the slightest manner, disapproved her sentiments, or her mode of expressing them; and, in spite of herself, she felt an uncommon dislike to Lady Jane, whom she considered as the cause, in some measure, of her uneasiness. — In vain did Mortimer, by the most delicate attentions, and by seeming to overlook her ill humour, endeavour to draw her into conversation: she retired to rest dissatisfied with herself, and displeased with her husband. But the morning brought a new train of feelings with it, and Louisa bitterly reproached herself with the captiousness she had expressed towards her husband, and with her causeless dislike to the unoffending Lady Jane. She even felt pity for the uneasiness Lord Ormington's attention to her might have occasioned her Ladyship, and she resolved to make advances towards an acquaintance with her. To Mortimer she was all attention and tenderness; and, though secretly hurt at her behaviour the night before, he smothered his displeasure, and seemed not to remember she had ever been otherwise than kind.

Louisa prepared for Almack's in the evening with resolutions of prudence, which she thought herself incapable of departing from. She repented of the encouragement she had given Lord Ormington, and determined to endeavour to form an acquaintance with Lady Jane, though a coolness subsisting between Lord Bertie and her husband made this step rather impracticable.

Louisa entered the room after the dance was begun, and the first persons she saw were Lord Ormington and Lady Jane going down it. — She soon engaged Lord Ormington's attention, and he became incapable of attending either to the figure[1] or his partner.

Louisa saw the effect her presence produced, and prudently removed to another part of the room—but, when she saw them reach the bottom of the dance, and Lady Jane sit down rather overcome with the exercise and the heat, while her lover went in search of some refreshment for her, she resolved to take advantage of the opportunity, and endeavour to enter into conversation with her, by remarking the warmth of the room and the length of the dance.

Lady Jane, who entertained an aversion to Louisa far better founded than her's had been to her Ladyship, surveyed her with a look of surprise bordering upon insolence; and answering her in as cold and short a manner as possible, suddenly quitted her seat, and went to another part of the room.

Irritated at so rude and humiliating a return for the flattering advances she had made, Louisa's pity and complacency changed into indignation and the desire of revenge. She determined no longer to repress the assiduities of his Lordship; but, upon his solic[it]ing her hand for the two next dances,[2] she readily complied, and soon beheld anxiety and jealousy visible in every feature of Lady Jane.

Louisa perceived and pursued her advantage. —Her triumph was soon visible to every one, and she returned home with the consciousness of having wounded Lady Jane's heart more than her Ladyship's conduct had wounded her pride.

CHAPTER XX.
RESOLUTIONS.

It were unnecessary to follow Louisa through the different scenes of dissipation she engaged in, in all of which she was sure to be the object of Lord Ormington's adoration, till at

---

1 The pattern of the dance.

2 Confirming a partner for two consecutive dances was a gesture of marked preference. In Jane Austen's *Pride and Prejudice* Mr. Collins attempts to engage Elizabeth Bennett for the first two dances to show his interest, while Elizabeth had been planning to dance with Wickham, her main interest at that point in the novel.

length her Mortimer, out of compassion, for Lady Jane, and dread lest Louisa should incur the censure of the world, saw her triumph with pain, and resolved, if possible, to put a stop to it, and convince her, at the risk of giving her pain, of the impropriety of her conduct.

Mrs. Belmour, on the contrary, rejoiced in Louisa's conquest, and already looked upon the marriage of her rival and her faithless lover as entirely at an end.

No longer satisfied with secretly disapproving Louisa's conduct, Mortimer at length seriously resolved to avow his sentiments, and represent to her the cruelty she was guilty of, in endangering Lady Jane's happiness for life, by fixing on herself those attentions which her Ladyship only had a right to claim.

Full of this design, after giving Louisa a large supply of money to discharge some debts she had contracted, and to gratify some fresh wants, he handed her into her carriage, which she desired to stop at her jeweller's, and then proceed to the house of the Lady Beaufort's.

As he knew by these orders, she would be out all the morning, he took a solitary walk in the park, and giving himself up to reflection, he tried to fix on some gentle, delicate manner of reproving her indiscretion, intending to begin his task when she returned home; for to reprove, and give pain to Louisa, was indeed a task to the affectionate bosom of her husband.

Fear of weakening her regard for him, besides his natural want of firmness, made him almost incapable of fulfilling the task he had imposed on himself. Confidence in Louisa's affection was his chief, nay his only support against jealousy; and while convinced he alone was master of her heart, he saw without anxiety the admiration she excited in every one, and only from pity for Lady Jane, beheld with uneasiness the preference she gave to the attentions of Lord Ormington.

CHAPTER XXI.
UNEXPECTED VISITORS.

THOUGH surrounded by admirers, and charming all by the elegance of her manners, and the vivacity of her conversation, Louisa's eyes would frequently wander in search of her husband[']s, and having met them, would tell him by a glance of fondness, and an intelligent smile, that she enjoyed the admiration she excited, as much on his account as on her own, as it proved her worthy of being the object of his choice.

Accustomed to these proofs of regard from her, and building all his hopes of happiness on a continuance of them, how could Mortimer, without anxiety and hesitation, resolve to assume the office of a reprover, and run the risk of converting her smiles into gloom and discontent, and he went home with a beating heart, to wait for her return.

At the sound of a carriage he felt his courage fail, and he went to the door to meet her, in an agitation he could but ill conceal — when, instead of Louisa the Lady Beauforts entered, and before I proceed to account for their coming without her, and for the consequent surprize of her husband, it may be necessary to give a short account of the characters of these Ladies. — They were rather pretty than otherwise, and being daughters of a Duke, were stiled fashionable in manners and in person. — Nature had not been lavish in endowing their minds, nor had education improved the little abilities she had given them, but they were fully capable of envying the perfections they could not imitate, and as both of them had been desirous of being the choice of Mortimer, they looked upon Louisa with dislike, and would have rejoiced to have seen the harmony that subsisted between them, by some lucky accident destroyed; but it was the fashion to visit Mrs. Mortimer, and to be of her parties, therefore they veiled their dislike, and were always ready to receive her, and to go with her into public.

CHAPTER XXII.
PERPLEXITIES.

Upon the entrance of these ladies, Mortimer declared his surprize at seeing them, unaccompanied by Louisa, and asked the reason of it; expressing, at the same time, his apprehensions of some accident having happened to her.

"She was perfectly well, when we left her, (replied lady Anne,) but with respect to where she is now we are as ignorant as you. After exceeding the hour she had appointed to be with us, she came in visible discomposure, and begging us to give her all the money we had about us, she went with us to Dover-street;[1] there she alighted, saying, she would come home in a hack,[2] and desired us to wait for her here."

"Borrowed money of you ladies," cried Mortimer, "'tis very strange. I thought" — but recollecting himself, he checked his surprize, which was occasioned by his consciousness of the ample manner in which he had so lately supplied Louisa with money, and only dwelt upon the strangeness of her discomposure, and departure from her companions.

"'Tis very odd," he repeated, and from the fair sisters' looks, he saw they thought so too, and knowing the littleness of their minds, he determined to hide every emotion that should lead them to suppose Louisa's conduct had alarmed his suspicions.

The more he thought of it, the more he was perplexed, and whatever her motives were, he was angry with her for having put it in the power of two censorious women, to form a tale to her disadvantage.

Irritated and distressed by his own reflections, and by the malicious pleasure and curiosity the looks of the Lady Beaufort's expressed, he could scarcely behave to them with his usual politeness; but recollecting Louisa had borrowed money of them, he coolly asked the sum she owed them, and having money about him sufficient to repay it, he took notes to the

---

1 In the eighteenth century, part of a luxury shopping district near Bond St. and Albemarle St., and thus a fashionable promenade.

2 "A vehicle for hire; a hackney coach or carriage" (*OED*).

amount out of his pocket book, and was in the act of paying them, when Louisa entered the room.

"Oh! Ladies," she exclaimed, "have you then been telling tales of me!" while a deep blush overspread her cheek.

"Indeed they have," said Mortimer, coldly, "such tales as would alarm any husband's suspicions, and I beg, ma'am, you will favour me with an explanation of these mysteries. Lady Anne and Lady Mary wish it as much as I do, I imagine."

"Oh! Mr. Mortimer," cried both the ladies at once, "do not let any thing we have said discompose you, we meant nothing."

"Meant nothing!" cried Louisa, "what should you mean? I cannot suppose you capable of putting uncandid constructions upon my conduct, but still I must insist upon knowing what you have told Mr. Mortimer."

The sisters were confounded at her emotion, and Lady Mary at length undertook to inform her what they had told Mortimer.

Though conscious her conduct must appear mysterious, Louisa was too proud to enter into an explanation of it; but Mortimer insisted upon her explaining it, for though his heart and his reason had already acquitted her of any thing that required concealment, yet he knew the Lady Beaufort's would not be so easily satisfied, and he therefore seriously desired her to give some account of the events of the morning.

CHAPTER XXIII.
THE DISAPPOINTMENT.

LOUISA's cheeks glowed with indignation, and her emotions would not suffer her to speak, when the door was thrown open, and a young man rushed into the room, who, throwing himself at the feet of Louisa, faultered out a blessing on her, and burst into tears.

Mortimer stood motionless with surprise, the sisters looked at each other with evident marks of mortification in their countenances, while Louisa endeavoured to raise the stranger from his humble posture, and tears trickled down her cheeks.

"Compose yourself, Mr. Nelson," said she; "for, I suppose, you are he. Your visit is unexpected indeed.—I beg you will rise—Your behaviour distresses me."

"I will not rise," said the agitated man, "till I have implored Heaven to bless you and your's."—Then, rising, he staggered to a chair, and again burst into tears.

Mortimer was not an unmoved spectator of this scene; but, approaching Louisa, and tenderly taking her hand, "My dear Louisa," he exclaimed, "what does all this mean?"

"Are you Mr. Mortimer?" cried the stranger: "then you are a happy man indeed; for you are married to an angel! Oh, Sir, she has saved me and mine from misery!—She has paid the debt for which my merciless creditor confined me, and restored me, this blessed morning, to my dear wife and child!"

Mortimer pressed Louisa's hand to his lips, and, turning to the Lady Beaufort's, while his fine eyes glistened with tears, "I think the mystery is explained now," said he; "and, I hope, as much to your satisfaction, ladies, as to mine."

They blushed, and congratulated Louisa upon the opportunity she had met with of doing good, but reproached her for concealing her intention from them, as, they declared, they should have been happy to have contributed their share towards so meritorious an act.—They then curtsied and departed, little pleased to find an event, from which they had expected something detrimental to Louisa, turn out so much in favour of her.

As soon as they were gone, Mr. Nelson apologised for his intrusion—"But indeed, Ma'am," sobbed out the grateful man, "when I found myself restored to my child, and heard to whom I was obliged for my liberty, after thanking God for my deliverance, I thought my next duty was to thank you; and, indeed, had I been sure of dying at your feet, I must have acted as I did."

"Make no apologies," replied Louisa. "I forgive you, Mr. Nelson; but on condition that you go home to your good wife—she would not thank me for keeping you from her. Come to me to-morrow and let me know how your little girl does; and, if you want farther assistance, do not scruple to ask it."

Nelson repeated his thanks and blessings and departed, leaving Louisa to receive, the only reward for her goodness that she wished, the praises and tenderness of her husband. —But, as Mortimer wished to know how she became acquainted with the distresses of the Nelsons, Louisa began her narration in the following chapter.

CHAPTER XXIV.
HISTORY OF MR. NELSON.

"As I was looking over some trinkets at Grey's, my attention was attracted by the entrance of a young woman whose dress bespoke the extreme of poverty; yet an endeavour at neatness, visible amidst her rags, convinced me carelessness had no share in her tattered appearance. But, if her dress engaged my attention, her face and manner instantly interested my compassion. Her countenance was the image of despair, and the paleness of her cheeks seemed occasioned by disease as much as by sorrow.

"She took a ring from her pocket, and, with a voice scarcely audible, begged to know how much they would give her for the gold?

"The shopman told her they did not sell rings.

"'No!' faultered out the poor creature: 'pray then tell me who does.'

"'Such a person, in such a street,' mentioning names I have forgotten.

"'And what will they give for it, Sir?'

"'Oh, a mere trifle!' replied the man—'I don't exactly know; but it can't be much.'

"'Indeed, Sir,' was her reply, 'the value is great in my eyes, and nothing but absolute necessity should have forced me to part with it.'

"'That may be,' returned the unfeeling shopman; 'but you are no judge of the value of gold, good woman; it may get you a shilling or two.'

"'What, no more!' exclaimed the poor woman, 'Oh! my poor child!' and endeavouring to apologize for the trouble she had given, she hastily turned away.

"I was at some distance from her, but had heard all that passed; and I need not tell you, Mortimer, what I felt; I had already taken my resolution, and hastening after her, I stopped her at the door, and putting five guineas in her hand, I hoped it would enable her to keep her ring till another time.

"The poor woman gasped for breath, then grasping my hands, sobbed out her thanks.

"I was painfully affected, and desiring the footman to help her into the coach, 'This is no place to talk to you in,' said I, 'and as I want to know all your distresses, you shall get in with me.'

"The poor creature could not utter a word, and bidding James drive into the fields, I endeavoured to compose my agitated companion.

"An hysterical flood of tears relieved her, and as soon as her sobs and gratitude would suffer her to speak coherently, I learnt from her that her husband was a journeyman carpenter, that having got a hundred pounds with her, and another hundred by his industry, he had been bound for double that sum, for an imprudent friend; that his friend had absconded, and the creditor had come upon him for the full payment.[1] Two hundred pounds he had paid, but not being able to discharge the rest, he would have engaged to work it out, but the man, who owed him ill-will, refused his offer, and threw him into prison for the remainder, leaving her ready to lye-in, and obliged to sell their furniture to supply her wants.

"After she was delivered, she took in work for her bread, but anxiety and weakness brought on a fever, and had not a kind neighbour assisted her, she and her child must both have perished."

---

1 Copeland in *Women Writing About Money* estimates that an average salary for a common labourer at this time was about £25; thus the £200 the carpenter and his wife accumulated represents a substantial amount, and the £400 he stands bond for an extreme burden of debt (24).

CHAPTER XXV.
THE CONCLUSION OF THE HISTORY OF MR. NELSON.

"AFTER languishing two months, Mrs. Nelson was able to go on with her work, but what she earned was but just sufficient to keep them from starving; and, to compleat her distress, her child visibly declined, and apprehensions for her was added to sorrow for her husband.

"Her little girl seemed sinking daily before her eyes, and having no other resource, she determined to sell an old fashioned ring, given her by her mother, that she might procure advice and assistance for her, when chance led her into the shop in which I was so fortunate as to meet with her.

"The debt for which her husband was thrown into prison was a very large one, but what were two hundred pounds when put in competition with the happiness and lives of three innocent persons.

"I knew, Mortimer, you would not think the sum ill bestowed, and as her apparent distress made her tale but too authentic, I determined to appropriate the money you had given me to the relief of Mr. Nelson; but, as the sum wanted some pounds of being complete, after going with Mrs. Nelson to her husband's creditor, I determined to proceed to the Lady Beaufort's, as the nearest place to procure it, for the man refused to give Nelson his liberty, without an immediate discharge in full; and as the poor woman was impatient to go to the prison, and set her husband at liberty, I could not bear to keep her waiting till I returned home: therefore, after getting the money I wanted, I desired to be set down in Dover-street, where the creditor lived."

"Say no more Louisa," said Mortimer, tenderly, "I have heard enough to convince me still more what a treasure I possess in you; my whole fortune is yours; dispose of it as you please. Encrease the number of your pensioners, and believe I can never have an enjoyment equal to the pleasure I feel in gratifying your wishes!"

Louisa, already overcome with the events of the morning,

could not remain unmoved by the kindness of her husband, but leaning her head on his bosom, she only answered him by her tears.

Had Mortimer then had power to keep his resolution and tell Louisa of her faults, while her heart was softened, and exalted by the glow of self-approving virtue, he might have cured her of her indiscretions, perhaps for ever; but, delighted with her sensibility, and feeling his whole soul melted into tenderness, he could not bear the thoughts of giving her pain, when she had just been affording him such triumph and satisfaction.

CHAPTER XXVI.
PLEASING REFLECTIONS.

MORTIMER resolved now more than ever to leave Louisa to the reproofs of her own heart, and if they failed to amend her, he expected much from the example and advice of Caroline, who was expected in a few days. But the pleasure Louisa enjoyed from her generosity, to the Nelsons, seemed to promise that amendment in her which Mortimer so much wished for; it made the joys of dissipation, and the satisfaction of being admired, comparatively insipid in her eyes. But Louisa knew, from fatal experience, how unable she was to keep a good resolution, when the warm feelings that occasioned it were abated, to rely upon the determinations the events of the morning had produced.

That day, indeed, and the three following ones, were spent at home, and in the company of her husband only — but she looked forward to the fourth with pleasure, as the evening of it was to be spent at a foreign nobleman's, where most of her admirers were expected. Yet, to compound with her conscience for the pleasure she felt in the anticipation, and for which it secretly reproached her, she resolved to behave with the most becoming reserve, and to bestow no more upon Lord Ormington those seducing smiles which had made him forget the claims of Lady Jane, and draw upon Louisa, as well as upon himself, the indignant frowns of Lord Bertie.

Such was her determination, and, for once in her life, she

had resolution enough to act up to it. Mortimer beheld surprize and mortification on the face of Lord Ormington, and self-approbation on that of Louisa, while she received his marked attention with cold civility, and seemed to court the conversation of her own sex more than that of the other.

"Blessed change," said he to himself, "if it be a lasting one!" But, alas! he had not the satisfaction of reflecting that he had applied the severe remedy of reproof to the errors of Louisa—a remedy which could alone make her amendment lasting; therefore, his fears of her relapse were equal to his joy at the alteration visible in her, and a few days seemed to wear off so much the restraint Louisa had imposed upon herself, that she, insensibly, began to flirt with her old admirers, though to Lord Ormington she was still reserved; and that nobleman, piqued at the evident change in her manner, and rather alarmed at Lord Bertie's threatning to break off the marriage with his sister, if his Lordship continued to give her such cause for jealousy, resolved to return to his allegiance, and devote all his time to his intended bride.

CHAPTER XXVII.
DOMESTIC PLEASURES.

MAY was just begun, and Mortimer and Louisa, from different motives, were looking forward, with joyful expectation, to the arrival of Lord and Lady Fitzaubrey; when the former received letters from the country, requiring his immediate attendance there; and, though his absence was to be but for a week, Louisa thought of it with pain. It was the first time they had been separated since their marriage. "But it will give me an opportunity of convincing him of my affection," said Louisa mentally; "for I will not go to one public place while he is absent, to prove to him no company, and no pleasure, is welcome to me, that is not enjoyed with him."

Full of this sacrifice to affection, the greatness of which she could not help feeling, in spite of herself, Louisa told Mortimer her determination, and, though engaged to go with a party to Almack's, she sent word she should not be able to keep her engagement. Surprized, but delighted at these resolutions, Mortimer took an affectionate leave of Louisa; and, as she wiped away the tears the farewell occasioned, she secretly proferred a prayer, that heaven would enable her to become worthy of the affection of her husband.

The first days of his absence were spent in reading, in music, and in domestic concerns, which a long course of dissipation had made her neglect; and she retired to rest at an early hour, satisfied with herself, and grateful to the almighty hand that had showered down so many blessings upon her.

But where is the merit of being virtuous, while unassailed by temptations? Louisa had seen no one to tempt her to forsake her domestic scenes for the amusements of the world, and therefore she had little reason to glory in her newly acquired resolution.

The day before she expected her husband, was that on which the ball at Almack's was to be held; and, as the usual hour for going thither approached, she felt a sensation of regret and uneasiness which her reason disapproved. But summoning resolution to her aid, she sat down to write to her father; and, while she painted the scenes of amusement she had been engaged in, but, above all, while she expatiated upon the goodness and affection of her husband, she forgot the gaities she had so lately sighed for, and the only objects present to her mind, were Mortimer and Sir Charles.

CHAPTER XXVIII.
TEMPTATIONS.

LOUISA's pen did ample justice to the feelings of her heart, and she had just concluded her letter, and signed herself his happy daughter, when Mrs. Belmour entered, elegantly dressed, and on her way to the ball. Louisa started at the sight, while Mrs. Belmour expressed her surprize at Mrs. Mortimer's being the only distinguished belle of fashion that meant to be absent from Almack's that evening. — "Indeed," said Mrs. Belmour, "I heard you intended being absent, and could hardly believe what I heard; and I am come hither, resolved to break your resolution."

"My resolution is fixed," replied Louisa, "and not to be broken. I stay at home from choice, and my own fire-side is more pleasing to me, at this moment, than any other place."

"A new taste, I presume," returned Mrs. Belmour, "and, like all modern tastes, not likely to last long! Come, pray revoke your rash vow! The world will suppose Mortimer is jealous of you, and forbade you to go out, while he was not here to take care of you. Do, go and dress for the ball, and accompany me to it, or you will ruin your husband's reputation in the eyes of the ton!"

"I should be miserable," said Louisa gravely, "if I thought such a probability existed any where but in your lively imagination; but it cannot, I know it cannot! Therefore I beg you will go, and leave me."

"To your meditations, I suppose!" interrupted Mrs. Belmour. "No, indeed I will not! I am too much your friend, to suffer you to be absent from a scene more brilliant than any you have yet beheld. Several foreign noblemen are to be there, and the new ambassadors; and I cannot bear the idea of the finest woman in England being absent, when the beauty of English women will certainly be critically examined, and compared with that of other nations. Besides, I can't endure the thought of so many insignificant girls rejoicing at the idea of attracting attention, as you are not there to engross it, and pluming themselves upon conquests which one glance from you would deprive them of."

"I am not vain enough, my good friend, to believe my power so great," replied Louisa faintly, "but had I known the assembly would have been so brilliant, I would certainly have gone; it is too late now, besides, I told Mr. Mortimer I should not go, and he will think me weak and irresolute; no, indeed I cannot think of going."

Mrs. Belmour perceiving her irresolution, and in order to overcome her scruples entirely, "Your first objection is absurd, indeed," she exclaimed, "it is most fashionable in all, and certainly most polite in handsome women, to go late, as the last comer at any rate attracts attention, and if beautiful, is sure to fix it also; and your second objection is equally foolish; do you not think Mr. Mortimer enjoys your being admired as much as you do, and do you not suppose he will be as much mortified as you can be, when he hears every woman of fashion and beauty in England was at Almack's, except his wife? — If he were here, he would insist on your going."

"I know he would," replied Louisa, "but, as he is not — however — you have conquered — I will go."

CHAPTER XXIX.
THE BALL.

LOUISA had no sooner overcome her resolution, than ringing for her maid, she began to dress, talking incessantly all the time, lest silence should lead her to think, and thought prove an enemy to the pleasures she anticipated.

"Oh! had you seen Lady Jane Bertie, at Ranelagh, the other night," said Mrs. Belmour, interrupting her, "what airs of superiority she gave herself, how she prided herself on the recovered attentions of a lover, whom a smile from you would again render inconstant. Foolish girl! then the insolence of her address to me, asking the reason of your not being with me, and begging to know if you staid at home out of compassion to mankind."

Louisa's cheeks reddened with indignation, and the words of Mrs. Belmour sunk deep into her mind. As soon as she was ready to go, Mrs. Belmour led her to a long glass in the drawing room, bidding her survey her whole figure, and own it would have been a pity to have deprived the gay circle that evening of so bright an ornament.

Louisa smiled, and the consciousness of beauty, "glowed on her cheek, and sparkled in her eye,"[1] and never did a more lovely figure enter a ball room, or when there, attract more admiration.

Wherever she moved she heard a murmur of applause, except from a party of envious girls, amongst whom was Lady Jane Bertie, who said as Louisa passed, "I see nothing so extra-

---

1 Untraced.

ordinary in her, and I can never think those large staring eyes handsome."

Different, and more welcome observations reached her ears from the next party she passed, in which she saw Lord Ormington. — His constancy again vanished at sight of her, and sighing deeply, he enquired after the health of her happy husband.

Louisa received him with smiles, and transported at this change, the enamoured peer forgot Lady Jane, forgot the threats of Lord Bertie, and saw nothing but Louisa, and the hope of one day gaining her affection.

Elated by the admiration she excited, Louisa forgot reserve was more necessary in the absence of her husband, than when he was present, and that a beautiful married woman, left to her own guidance, was admirable food for observation, and a mark for calumny to point at.

Louisa, however, was too lively to think, and giving way to the natural gaiety of her disposition, she excited the envy and censure of her own sex, while she engrossed the attention of the other.

When the company began to disperse, Lord Ormington offered his service to find her coach, and eagerly ran to enquire for it, unmindful of Lady Jane, who stood almost alone, watching with anxiety every motion of her unworthy lover.

Lord Bertie seeing her distress, hastily approached her, and giving Louisa a look of scorn as he passed, took his sister's hand to lead her to her carriage, just as Lord Ormington had taken Louisa's, and as they passed, he rather loudly repeated the words, "infernal coquette," giving her, at the same time, a look more indignant than the former.

Lord Bertie's look and his words recalled Louisa to reflection, she saw the fault she had committed, and all her spirits and satisfaction vanished in a moment.

"Such, then," said she to herself, "are Lord Bertie's sentiments of me, and such may be the sentiments of all those who have flattered me to night. — Mean, despicable Louisa! to seduce a lover from his intended bride, and then glory in a conquest that disgraces me!"

Such were Louisa's reflections upon returning from an amusement so ardently wished for, and so highly enjoyed; such were the reflections that accompanied her to her pillow, and made all endeavours to slee[p vain.][1]

CHAPTER XXX.
THE AFFECTIONATE HUSBAND.

LOUISA arose at nine, though not in bed before seven in the morning, and, with the feelings of a culprit, awaiting the presence of his judge, she sat expecting the arrival of Mortimer. — At two he arrived. — As soon as he entered the room, Louisa's pale cheeks and sunk eyes engaged his attention and excited his fears.

"You are not well, and would not send to inform me of it, Louisa," cried he, in a tender but reproachful tone. "Had I known you were ill, not all the business in the world should have kept me from you."

Glad of an excuse for her visible dejection, as she could not summon up resolution enough to say she had been at Almack's the night before, from a painful consciousness of the impropriety of her conduct there, Louisa said, she had a cold and headach — and, overcome by want of rest, by the kindness of her husband, and her own self-reproaches, she fainted in his arms.

When she recovered, she found Mortimer supporting her, and expressing the utmost concern and apprehension. "This is too much," said she mentally — "I can't bear his kindness, while I feel I deserve his reproaches; but, from this moment, I will live for him alone, and renounce my follies for ever."

Having formed this resolution, her mind became more composed, and in a few minutes she fell into a sound sleep, which lasted some hours.

When she awoke, the first object she saw was Mortimer, who had not stirred from her bed-side; but, upon her declaring

---

1 The text of the British Library copy of the novel is defective at this point, as is the Harvard Library copy.

herself quite recovered, he left her, telling her, he had business to transact, and should not be home till the evening.

Louisa was loth to part with him — she did not like to be left to her own thoughts — and, when alone, they constantly dwelt upon her follies and indiscretions.

No sooner, therefore, was Mortimer gone, than she fell into a train of melancholy reflections — when a servant of Lord Fitzaubrey's arrived, bringing a letter from Caroline, informing her she and her Lord would be with her early the next morning.

The joy Louisa felt at the idea of seeing her friend was damped by the consciousness that she deserved her reproofs, and while she dwelt with pleasure upon the happiness Caroline's letter expressed, she reflected, with sorrow, that happiness equally unalloyed might be her own portion, were her resolution equal to her husband's indulgence.

Louisa, after the most mature deliberation, accompanied with some self-reproaches on a conduct which might, in the end, prove destructive to her happiness, wisely determined candidly to open her whole soul to Caroline, to own her errors, and ask her assistance to prevent a repetition of them.

CHAPTER XXXI.
DISTRESSING SENSATIONS.

FULL of schemes for the future, to avoid dwelling on the past, Louisa was unconscious how fast the moments flew, and the clock had struck ten, before she began to wonder at Mortimer's absence. At length he returned, and Louisa discovered on his brow unusual marks of care and uneasiness. He was visibly absent and dejected; spoke little, and that little in a broken faultering tone. But still his manner was affectionate, and to her enquiries, whether he was well, or if any thing disturbed him, he answered by a faint smile, and an assurance that nothing was the matter.

"So you were at Almack's last night!" said he, after a long silence. Louisa turned pale, and faintly answered, "Yes;" not daring to enquire who told him she was there, lest he should suppose she meant to keep her having been there secret from him. — Again they were silent; when Mortimer, starting up, said he had letters to write, and leaving her, went into his study.

As soon as he was gone, Louisa gave herself up to the most violent expressions of sorrow and apprehension. She feared she knew not what, and, convinced that something agitated Mortimer, she could not help thinking she was, in some measure, the cause of it.

In this wretched state of suspence she passed two hours, and she had but just wiped the tears from her eyes and taken a book to conceal her emotion, when her husband entered. She ventured to look up, and thought she perceived traces of tears upon his cheeks; and, when he begged her to sit up no longer, as he was sure she must want rest after the fatigue of the night before, she arose from her seat, and, throwing herself into his arms, declared, she must be a stranger to rest while he seemed uneasy, begging, in the most earnest manner, to know the source of his distress.

"I am no dissembler," replied Mortimer — "I own something distresses me. But tell me, Louisa, have you any doubts of my affection?"

"Oh no, no!" she answered, in a voice half suffocated with emotion.

"Then rest assured," replied he, "that what you wish me to impart would give you pain, and that affection only is the cause of my reserve. A few hours," he continued, struggling for composure, "will reveal, and, I hope, remove all my disquietudes."

"Oh, let me hear all now!" said Louisa, falling at his feet. "This suspense will kill me!"

Mortimer, instead of raising her, knelt by her, and, clasping his arms round her, raised his eyes to heaven, while tears streamed down his cheeks — then, tenderly embracing her, "Wait patiently till the morning," he exclaimed, and hurried out of the room, charging her, at the same time, to retire immediately to bed.

Louisa for some minutes was incapable of obeying him — at length, with tottering steps, she reached her apartment, and had been in bed half an hour when her husband entered the room.

He did not speak, and Louisa was incapable of beginning the conversation, but he sighed deeply, and she determined to counterfeit sleep, that she might watch him, and gain from his broken sentences some knowledge of the secret that laid heavy at his heart. —But her scheme was fruitless, for, fearful of disturbing her, Mortimer suppressed his agitation, and Louisa, pleased to think his uneasiness seemed abated, worn out with anxiety, soon gave herself up to real slumbers.

CHAPTER XXXII.
LETTER TO LOUISA.

At eight next morning Louisa awoke, and as she raised her head from the pillow, she saw with terror that Mortimer was gone; and what added to her distress, she felt her cheek wet with tears, which she was certain she had not shed.

The whole truth rushed upon her mind at once; "He is gone to fight," she wildly exclaimed, hurrying on her cloaths, "and he will be dead before I can overtake him." At the loudness of her exclamations, her maid ran into the room.

"Tell me where is my husband," cried the agitated Louisa, "when did he go out, and who went with him?"

"He went out half an hour ago, ma'am," replied the maid, frighted at the wildness of her looks.

"And which way did he go," rejoined Louisa, "but no matter, I shall find him, so let me pass," on saying this she endeavoured to reach the door, while her maid struggled to prevent her.

Louisa shrieked with impatience and rage, and the sound brought the rest of the servants up stairs, who all strove to prevent her executing her design, and exhausted with her efforts, she threw herself on the bed, more composed and tolerably rational, endeavouring to think her fears ill-grounded.

She continued some time in this dreadful uncertainty, when Mortimer's own servant knocked at her door, and asked admittance; he brought a letter for Louisa, which he informed her his master desired him to give her, when she awoke, but to take particular care she was not disturbed before her usual hour.

Louisa eagerly broke open the letter it was as follows:—

"How, best beloved of my heart, shall I summon up resolution enough to tell you the cause of the sorrow which your countenance convinces me you observe.—But you must know all—you must hear the motives of my conduct—that if the event be fatal, you may not think I wantonly sported with your happiness, or my own life. Besides I wish to prepare you for an event which, if it takes place, might otherwise be fatal, in your situation, and deprive you of a child and husband at once.

"Oh! Louisa, why did you not tell me you were at Almack's last night! But I will endeavour to proceed methodically.

"After I left you this afternoon, I went into the city to transact some business, and thence proceeded, on the same errand, to St. James's street. Being obliged to wait for the persons I wanted, I went into the St. James's coffee-house,[1] which I found entirely empty, and leaning my hand on a table in one of the boxes, began reading the papers. Soon after I heard two gentlemen enter the box behind me, and looking up, I saw they were Lord Bertie and a stranger.

"Concluding the former saw and knew me, I went on reading 'till I heard your name mentioned.

"'Pray, my Lord,' said the stranger, 'what do you mean by saying Lady Jane's marriage with Lord Ormington is not likely to take place?'

"'Why,' replied his Lordship, 'the fickle peer is caught in the toils of the most artful, despicable coquette in the world.'

"'What is her name?' asked the gentleman.

"'Your not knowing her by the description is a proof of your long absence from the fashionable world,' replied his Lordship. 'Her name is Mortimer, she is wife to the Mortimer I had once a quarrel with.'

"'Oh! I have heard of her,' replied the stranger, 'and is she capable of the coquetry you mention!'

"'Yes, indeed,' rejoined Lord Bertie, 'and even before her

---

1   Established in 1705 and a popular gathering place for both writers and members of the social elite. St. James's Street was noted for its coffee-houses, chocolate-houses, fine shops and gentlemen's clubs.

husband's face, who is so much a dupe to her arts, that he imagines her a prodigy of virtue, and thinks her forward advances proofs of the innocence of her intentions.'"

CHAPTER XXXIII.
CONTINUATION OF MORTIMER'S LETTER TO LOUISA.

"OH! Louisa, how my heart was torn by this discourse, but I was still silent; and the stranger addressing his Lordship, said, 'Surely, my Lord, you must judge harshly of Mrs. Mortimer. — I never heard her mentioned without respect, and her friend, Lady Fitzaubrey, is so amiable, that I must doubt the probability of her being as you describe her.'

"'Nay,' replied Lord Bertie, 'I do not say she is actually guilty, but the woman who is not startled at indulging the adultery of the mind, is not far removed from yielding to that of the body; and the former, I am sure, she is not free from. What looks she gave Lord Ormington last night she was at Almack's, and her flirtation with him was the wonder of every body.'

"I could restrain myself no longer, but starting from my seat, 'Villain you lie,' I exclaimed, and relying on your avowed resolution when I left London, I boldly asserted you were not at Almack's.

"Lord Bertie was at first speechless with rage and surprize, but recovering himself, he bestowed on me the names of dupe, listener, &c. &c.

"Such language was not to be borne, but having no weapon, and the noise bringing numbers into the room, we agreed to meet to-morrow morning behind Mountague house,[1] as, hurried away by the height of passion, and by old resentments, we had both gone too far to be satisfied without coming to extremities.

---

1 Probably Montagu House in Bloomsbury (later the British Museum), which appears to have been a popular site for duels. The *Spectator* No. 91, June 14, 1711, prints: "I shall meet you immediately in Hide-Park, or behind Montague House, or attend you to Barn Elmes, or any other fashionable Place that's fit for a Gentleman to dye in."

"I then proceeded to engage a second,[1] and returned home with feelings too wretched to be expressed.

"In spite of what had passed, I still thought you had not been at Almack's, as you had not mentioned being there, and I persisted in thinking Lord Bertie's speech the effect of malice, when your fatal *Yes*, upon my putting the question to you, convinced me his account was too authentic.

"Oh! Louisa, could you so soon forget—but I will not reproach you; if I survive the event of to-morrow, let a sense of the danger your imprudence has caused prevent you from erring again. If I fall—Oh! God—I cannot bear to think I may this evening behold you for the last time!—and perhaps to leave you for ever—a prey to the malice of a censorious world, which, unacquainted with your worth, and ignorant of your real goodness of heart, may extend their disapprobation of but one foible so far as to tarnish the lustre of all your other virtues and accomplishments.

"I can write no more—but you will wonder at my absence. I will go and persuade you to retire to bed. —"

CHAPTER XXXIV.
THE LETTER CONCLUDED.

"*Midnight.*

"THE greatest pang is over. —Perhaps I have heard you speak, and embraced you for the last time! Louisa, I have been praying Heaven to forgive me, if, in the anguish of my heart I arraign its providence. Yet only of myself ought I to complain: had I fulfilled, as I ought, the duties of a husband, my reproofs would have awakened you to reflection, and this cursed moment would have been spared us.

"I must conclude—the night is far advanced; yet I cannot bear to say farewell, lest it should be for ever!

"Oh, Louisa! a few months would have made me a father, and a few hours may —

1　According to duelling protocol, each combatant was accompanied by a second, a friend whose role was to observe that the appropriate codes were followed and that the matter of honour was dealt with fairly.

"The thought is madness — I will think only that Lord Bertie may fall by my hand (for too deadly is his resentment to me, to make it probable both of us should escape with life); but then, could I bear his blood upon my conscience! I must be wretched both ways.

"But I had forgotten — should you give birth to a living child, I leave it to the guardianship of your father and Lord Fitzaubrey. — And shall I not enjoy the delight of watching over it myself? — Sure Heaven will spare me for my child! But, oh, my soul! be resigned to its almighty will, and grateful for the happiness it allows thee, of meeting the approach of death while yet unconscious of an intentional crime.

"But the thought of leaving thee, Louisa, unmans me — the pen drops from my hand. I have scarce strength to say, Thou art at this moment dearer to me than ever!"

CHAPTER XXXV.
THE DUEL.

LOUISA read but little of Mortimer's letter. The first lines of it threw her into a state of insensibility, in which she continued a long time; and, when she recovered, she found herself in the arms of Lady Fitzaubrey.

Grief had made Louisa incapable of being overcome by joy, and she seemed to forget how long a time had elapsed since she had seen her friend — but at length she faintly cried, "Oh, Caroline! is it thus we meet?" and hid her face in her bosom.

Lady Fitzaubrey, upon her arrival, was informed of the probability of Mortimer's being gone to fight a duel, and of Louisa's distress in consequence of it, and sending her Lord to endeavour to find Mortimer, she ran up to the relief of her friend who was senseless, with the letter in her hand.

Wholly taken up with restoring Mrs. Mortimer to life, she had not seen the letter, but Louisa upon her recovery, gave it to her, telling her, to read that, and, if possible, not to hate her.

Caroline took it, and Louisa was waiting in breathless expectation to hear news of her husband, when they heard a noise at the street door, and soon after Lord Fitzaubrey, with a face full of horror, entered the apartment.

Louisa read her fate in his countenance, and bursting from his extended arms, ran along the gallery, and reached the bottom of the stairs, just as the bleeding body of her husband was brought into the hall.

Louisa uttered a cry of horror, and kneeling by him, grasped his hands with convulsive eagerness, beseeching him, in the most pathetic accents, not to curse her.

Mortimer, who was wounded past recovery, and unable to speak, could only press her hands to his lips, and gaze on her with the utmost fondness and compassion, but feeling death approaching, he raised his eyes to Heaven, as if imploring a blessing on her, and recommending to its protection her unborn infant, then laid his head on her bosom and expired.

CHAPTER XXXVI.
THE DESPAIRING WIFE.

LOUISA suffered herself without resistance to be taken from the body, she seemed insensible to all that passed, and remained for some time with her eyes fixed in one direction. At length she burst into a loud hysterical laugh, and fell into violent convulsions.

Louisa continued in strong convulsions some hours, and the next morning gave birth to a dead child. But though composed and quiet, after her delivery, nature had undergone such struggles, that she was pronounced incapable of surviving more than a few days. But affection will hope, though judgement despairs.

Caroline could not prevail on herself to think all chance of her life at an end, and could she but rouze her from her torpid state of grief, she hoped every thing from her youth and constitution.

Louisa, however, would listen to nothing but the tale of her distresses, would utter nothing but execrations on herself for having killed her husband and child, and having prevailed on Caroline to let her read the letter of Mortimer, she refused to return it, and indulged her despair by frequent perusals of it; while, forgetting the firm but humble hope which had till then distinguished her devotions, she persisted in thinking herself hateful in the sight of heaven.

In vain did Caroline represent to her the blameless tenor of her life, one foible excepted, in vain did she enumerate the benevolent acts she had performed, despair had possession of her soul, and her prayers ended in expressions of terror.

CHAPTER XXXVII.
THE CONCLUSION.

ONE day that Louisa had listened to the soothing discourse of her friend with more complacency than usual, Lady Fitzaubrey was surprised by hearing violent expressions of sorrow from the apartment adjoining, she enquired what they meant, and was told they proceeded from Mrs. Nelson, (whose story she had heard from the servants) who coming, as usual, to enquire about Louisa, and being told there were no hopes of her life, it had such an effect upon the spirits of this grateful creature, that she had fallen into violent hysterics.

Mrs. Nelson continued in these convulsive agitations a considerable time, but was at length brought a little to herself, by the kind assistance of the servants, who, fearful of disturbing their mistress, would have concealed the distressed state of Mrs. Nelson's mind, had not the heartfelt accents of grief which involuntarily escaped from her, been overheard by Caroline.

Full of anxiety and apprehension lest the seat of reason should be disturbed, from the unsettled state of mind under which her poor friend evidently laboured, and unable to admit any thought into her bosom which had not her for its object, Caroline determined to introduce Mrs. Nelson and her child into the presence of Louisa, hoping that the sight of these objects, who owed their bread, their happiness, and probably their existence to her, would do more towards re-establishing the serenity of her mind, than all her reasoning.

"See! my dear Louisa," exclaimed Caroline, leading in the still agitated woman and her child, "I bring you sweet comforters."

An expression of pleasure enlightened the changed countenance of Louisa, at sight of these objects of her benevolence —

"Comforters, indeed," she faintly said, "but, my good Mrs. Nelson, I shall soon need none."

"God forbid!" replied the poor woman, sobbing violently, "You are so good Heaven will spare you to administer comfort to the unfortunate."

Louisa answered only by a slight motion of the head, and looking earnestly at Mrs. Nelson, while that good woman continued:

"But see! Madam, how Providence has blessed your bounty towards us, in the thriving condition of my poor little girl; but for you she would not have been here now — indeed you have bestowed happiness on a wretched husband, and saved my child's life."

"And killed my own," said Louisa, shuddering.

"Dearest lady," said Mrs. Nelson, "Do not give way to this excess of sorrow which preys upon your spirits, but let the reflection springing from acts of virtue and beneficence, bring comfort to your troubled mind, and sustain it against your unhappy misfortune."

Louisa made no reply: when Caroline kissed her pale cheek in an agony of grief, and was about to offer her consolatory sentiments in addition to those of Mrs. Nelson and started to find the coldness of death on it.

Alarmed exceedingly, she rung for assistance, but it was too late. Louisa herself said her last agony was approaching, then supporting herself upon the arm of Caroline, and begging she would comfort her poor father, she raised herself up in an attitude of prayer, and extending her hand towards Mrs. Nelson and her child, while a gleam of satisfaction was visible in her countenance, "Father of Mercies, let *these* plead for me," she exclaimed, then sunk back exhausted on her pillow, and expired.

For the perusal of the thoughtless and the young, is this tale given to the world — it teaches that *indiscretions* may produce as fatal effects as ACTUAL GUILT, and that even the appearance of *impropriety* cannot be too carefully avoided.

FINIS.

Appendix A: Extracts from Amelia Opie's Letters

[Opie was an assiduous correspondent, and many of her letters are still extant. While there is no collected edition of these letters, a number were published in Cecilia Brightwell's 1854 biography, *Memorials of the Life of Amelia Opie*. Additional letters are scattered across archives in England and America. The selection here (including letters from Opie to Robert Garnham and from J. W. Grove) focusses on her letters pertaining to the *Dangers of Coquetry*, the first and second editions of *The Father and Daughter* in 1801 and her involvement in the final edition published in her lifetime by the publishers Grove and Sons in 1843.]

Amelia Opie to Robert Garnham (1801)

Indeed my husband is so fond of home, & I am so attached to his society, that the world has little to bestow capable of drawing me from my fireside without reluctance. My passion for musick would lead me to the Opera often, could I afford to go frequently—but I spend all my opera money in paying for lessons in singing from Viganoni the first Opera Singer—& if I can but hear him, I am contented. One song from Viganoni is to me worth all the musick in the world. You will, no doubt commend me for keeping up an accomplishment that gives pleasure to my friends, & husband—& I sing more than ever—& for thorough practice & English singing, my friend Mr. Biggs attends me—so I have two singing masters & I improve very much. You will suppose I have no[t] much time for dissipation, when I tell you of these musical engagements, & also of my constant application to writing, besides having to look after my family, & sit for hours & hours as a model to my husband—but methinks I hear you ask what is become of my epistle to Elizabeth—& my answer is, that I wished to give all the time, & consideration possible to a subject of such capability, & importance, & that I will be *years* about it, rather than publish it till I have done all I can do for it. But I have a volume now about to make its appearance consisting of a tale in prose, called the Father, & Daughter, an epistle from the Maid of Corinth to her lover, & some other poetical pieces. I expect to be out by [the] 1st of March—an anxious time this, but as I have felt the pulse of the public, & I find it beat kindly towards me, I am a little encouraged—my ["]Orphan Boy's Tale" was a good pioneer....

Amelia Opie to Mrs. Taylor (1801) [quoted in Brightwell 82–83]

I believe you were very right in what you said to me, about the good arising from my having delayed publishing my juvenile pieces; but some of those things which have now gained me reputation *are* juvenile pieces, written years ago; however, I am contented that I have, till now, lived unconscious of the anxieties of an author. I wish I was launched! As usual, all the *good* I saw in my work before it was printed, is now vanished from my sight, and I remember only its faults. All the authors of both sexes, and artists too, that are not too ignorant or full of conceit to be capable of alarm, tell me they have had the same feeling when about to receive judgement from the public. Besides, whatever I read appears to me so superior to my own productions, that I am in a state of most unenviable humility. Mr. Opie has no patience with me; but consoles me by averring that fear makes me overrate others, and underrate myself.

Amelia Opie to Mrs. Taylor (1801) [quoted in Brightwell 85]

I am glad on reperusing "The Dangers of Coquetry," that you think so highly of it. I read it at Seething soon after I married, and felt a great respect for it; and if I ever write a collection of tales, I shall correct and re-publish that, as *I originally wrote it*, not as it now is, in the shape of a novel with chapters. I believe I told you that Mr. Hoare was so struck with it, as to intend writing a play from it. I wish he would.

Amelia Opie to Mrs. Taylor (1801) [quoted in Brightwell 86–87]

Your question to me "what is this indescribable charm which attends the overflowings of one mind into another, when it finds itself understood?"—I can't answer; though, as you observe, the enjoyment is known to me. But this pleasure is not confined to the contemplation of well assorted minds; in everything we delight to see things *fit*, as we call it; even a scissars-sheath delights us when, on buying it, we find it sits *flush*—as the phrase is. No wonder then that, when mind fits mind, the pleasure should be so great. Yes!—as you say, July is coming; and I am coming, but late in July I doubt. I have not made out the author of the anonymous letter—I wish I had; yet, there I lie; mountains look largest and most sublime when they are shrouded partly in mist. The "British Critic" is something *awful*; but what is Parson Beloe? Pray tell my father that 750 are to be printed of the

Tale; it will be time enough to settle the number of the other volume when it is ready for the press. At present I am so incapable of writing!

Amelia Opie to Simon Wilkin, 18 January 1843

Josiah Fletcher & I have just had a long consultation together, & he has encouraged me to take the liberty of writing to thee to ask a great favour of thee, a *private* transaction it is to be a present at the least & *entre nous*. All my *egregiously sublime* & *delightful* works for such they *undoubtedly* are, are quite out of print in England & alas! I can't get a [cent] from America where there is a whole new [edition] published in 1838 (—but this is by the by—). About two months or more ago, I received a letter from Groves & Sons booksellers in Trinity Street ... asking my leave to reprint my works (no doubt Josiah says in the *small* edition now going) and offering to give me a certain number of copies for myself. I replied that I would consider the subject & on consulting Josiah, he said he would enquire the character of the Groves's — He learnt they were respectable people, & he agreed with me that it was a duty I owed myself to let [the] new edition be printed, as it would give me an opportunity of making corrections & leaving out what I *might wish* to leave out & so on—and as I had no scruple against doing this I resolved to *say yes*—Today the Groves have written requesting an answer as soon as is convenient & I therefore write to thee requesting thee to see them directly if possible, & negotiate for me—Josiah says copies are a poor remuneration, & I think so too.

Now d[ea]r friend, my case is before thee—& I anxiously await thy answer—

I was glad when J[osiah] said I might venture to write to thee & request thy aid but I never thought of such a daring proceeding till today when reminded that I *must* apply to *someone* by the receipt of Groves's letter....

Amelia Opie to Simon Wilkin, 3 February 1843

Having consulted with Josiah, I have at length come to the resolution to decline entirely friend Groves's proposal to part with my copyright *especially* as the rights of copy are now by law certified and established. But if he wishes to print an edition of my works, in small duo[deci]mo that is what I think he intended to do, I most thankfully accede to that—but as I have no means of selling the sets that he is inclined to give me, I had rather have two sets given me, & a *small* sum in money (I, being willing to *buy* of him whenever I want a *pre-sentation copy*) than accept a larger number of copies & *that all*—when I have ascertained *exactly* the new copyright law, & am *assured* of a *right* given me by that, which I am not now sure of, I shall know whether I can not reprint with my name, a tale published in 1821 *without* my name, being even *suspected* by [the] publisher—and I *think* it might be an advantage to friend Grove to *publish that*—But that is a *future consideration*—&c. May I trouble thee with this second commis-sion?....

Amelia Opie to Simon Wilkin, 24 May 1843

I return the paper & have scrawled in what I mean to insert in the document *to be signed*—But there is not one word of any *payment* to me—& I can't go about with a donkey to sell the copies he is willing to give me—This must not be—I *can't* think it right to give [?away?] my books.

To be sure I am getting & shall get nothing by the departed chil-dren of my brains, while I live. I am not unbenefiting myself. Should I not consult my lawyer? Thy beaufrere—The good man *runs a risk*, I *know*—but still my love of money makes me wish to have money, rather than books and in the end, he, by giving me so many copies diminishes his profits on [the] Edition.

Five guineas with a dozen copies would not be too *much*. Josiah says the volumes will be about 3/6 each he thinks—the price of all cheap editions or there abouts....

J. W. Grove to Amelia Opie, 26 August 1843

In answer to yours of the 23rd instant, I beg to acknowledge the receipt of the books you were kind enough to send, and must apolo-gize for not answering yours before, but had not quite determined what precise form and price they would best be published at. Shall take an early opportunity (most likely next week) of letting you know all the particulars and how we are proceeding. In the meanwhile should feel obliged by your writing an Advertisement to appear in the Public Papers....

Amelia Opie to Simon Wilkin, 27 August 1843

I must venture to burden thy kindness again. I sent up to W. Grove my Father and Daughter & Adeline Mowbray corrected by myself &,

in the last, two pages, as I think, crossed out—days passed, & I had no note to acknowledge the receipt. So I wrote again & yesterday received the enclosed—

Now dear friend I do not know how to draw up a proper advertisement—but I feel sure that thou dost & I should be obliged indeed if thou would do me this added kindness, & draw one up for us.

I should also be glad to ascertain whether he did receive ye books time enough to correct the faults. I corrected in pencil in The Father and Daughter & more especially in A Mowbray—the latter alterations I should be very unhappy not to have made—& would willingly pay for a cancel to have these made. Those in the 1st book are comparatively unimportant.

Amelia Opie to Joseph Gurney, 23 February 1844

Thy letter received this morning is worthy thee, and most kindly expressed—but it is a *true bill* that has been brought against me & I must abide the consequences—the most painful *far to me* whatever be the result is, that I have given pain to thee by permitting to be done what I felt was an act of *justice to myself.*

My tales were out of print ... and heartily glad was I when I found there was a desire for a reprint as it would give me an opportunity of correcting *whatever* I deemed amiss in the said publications.

I knew there was an entire new edition of them printed rather recently in America, & I was pleased to have an opportunity of doing in *England* what I wished I could have done in *America.*

I never thought, nor do I *now think* that in doing this I have *at all* violated my engagements as a Friend—I promised never to write things of the same sort again, nor have I done so—but though I freely admit that *novel-reading* as it is contemptuously called, (& with some justice) has a tendency to make young persons disinclined to serious, & more instructive reading, & is therefore pernicious I never said, because I never *thought* that *works of fiction* were *never to be read*—on the contrary, I believe simple moral tales the very best means of instructing the young & the *poor*—else *why* do the pious of all sects & beliefs, spread *tracts* in stories over the world. And why did the blessed Saviour teach in parables?

My own books (which Friends never read, & know nothing about) are in my belief moral tales—& many many proofs have the kind, & candid given me of the good they have occasionally done. These books, however full of errors, will survive me, and in many languages, (some of them at least) and when a few weeks (now *months*) ago, I thought my days were numbered, I remembered with comfort that I had nearly executed the task I had undertaken—& felt no *remorse of conscience* for having assisted the printer nor did I think myself *responsible* to any *human* being for having undertaken that task. I considered myself responsible to my God & my conscience. I had *prayed much* on the subject, when, near a year ago the application was made to me, & after some weeks consideration I agreed to the pro-posal. I got no *money* whatever by it only the pleasure of knowing that all mention of the great Name, & other blemishes are to be expunged in the new edition. I *never* thought & therefore never *said* that I *disapproved* "the genius" because if I had *I must have told an absolute falsehood*—& often have I *debated* this opinion with dearest Priscilla—on the contrary I have often felt gratitude to the Most High for having given me a talent by which as I have reason to believe, I have been permitted to do some good, to those who *seek* for amusements & *probably wish* for *instruction* in tales like mine.

"Tales" is the proper name for my little works. They are not (scarcely one of them) full of character & story enough for a novel.

It seems to me very strange that the advertizement should never have met thine eye sooner. But no—as it now is, I think it was not originally or certainly not so widely circulated nor even I assert that I knew my editorship or my aid as a corrector would have been so prominently brought forward *as it is now* is [sic].

Many of my religious friends & more than one *Friend* have said they thought I had *done right* & a pious lady whom I *never saw* & who is the editor of serious books has written to me expressing her plea-sure at this reprint—till thy note came, my mind was quite easy & satisfied & is now disturbed *only* by the consciousness that I have given pain to thee....

Appendix B: Reviews of Dangers of Coquetry *and* The Father and Daughter

1. Reviews of *Dangers of Coquetry*

i. *The European Magazine, and London Review* 17 (May 1790): 352.

THE Author of these volumes professes to have written them for the perusal of the thoughtless and the young, with a view to teach the unexperienced minds of females, that "*indiscretions* may produce as fatal effects as *actual guilt*, and that even the appearance of *impropriety* cannot be too carefully avoided." The Tale however by which these lessons are inculcated, possesses a double aspect; for while it attributes the most mischievous and dreadful consequences to a little innocent coquetry in the character of a *wife*, it shews them to have proceeded from an idle, ridiculous, and unfounded jealousy on the part of her husband. *Louisa Conolly* marries *Mr. Mortimer*, and, contrary to her promise, attends a *partie* to *Almack's*, without the permission of her husband; where, to match the pride and arrogance of a rival beauty, she permits *Lord Ormington* to whisper soft nonsense in her ear. Vanity and female revenge blow, through the trumpet of Fame "*the horrid deed to every eye;*" and it at length reaches the knowledge of her husband in the shape of *conjugal infidelity*. The jealous feelings of his heart represent the picture of *injured honour* to his mind. He challenges the supposed seducer, and falls a victim to his own credulity, in having too rashly given credit to a report derogatory to the virtue of his innocent wife. [Note that the reviewer confuses Lord Ormington and Lord Bertie here.] The style in which this Novel is written, is simple and unadorned, and the language in general very correct; but it does not possess sufficient *interest* to move the heart, nor a sufficient *probability* to convince the understanding. There are, however, many virtuous sentiments and moral reflections interspersed throughout the work.

ii. *Critical Review* 70 (September 1790): 339.

The moral to be drawn from this work is so good, that we are blind to the dulness, the insipidity, and improbability of the narrative. "It teaches that indiscretion may produce as fatal effects as actual guilt; and that even the appearance of impropriety (especially in women) cannot be too carefully avoided."

iii. *The English Review* 17 (March 1791): 234.

"For the perusal of the thoughtless and the young is this tale given to the world ... it teaches that *indiscretion* may produce as fatal effects as ACTUAL GUILT, and that even the appearance of impropriety cannot be too carefully avoided." Such is the object of this sensible and moral novel. The characters are well drawn; the incidents rising naturally from each other exhibit in their fatal catastrophe a solemn warning to the fair sex to avoid the dangers of coquetry. The following portrait of a coquette is sketched with truth and good sense:

"A coquette in your sex is, in my opinion, as detestable as a libertine in ours, and has certainly less excuse for her fault than the latter can boast. The libertine has passion for his excuse; and those who know the force of it in the bosom of youth, should make some allowances for its effects; but in cold blood to take pains to destroy the happiness of others, to wound an inexperienced heart, for the sake of wounding it, as an un-whip'd urchin torments a worm for the pleasure of seeing it writhe about in torture; to seduce lovers from their affianced brides, husbands from their wives, and all to gratify a thirst of admiration, and a despicable vanity, with but a grain of passion to plead her excuse; this is the conduct of a finished coquette; and this is the character, though gilded over by beauty and accomplishments, which will ever deserve and ever meet my abhorrence."

2. Reviews of *The Father and Daughter*

[Opie's volume was reviewed in a variety of periodicals: the notice in *The European Magazine* mentions only the tale, while *The Monthly Review* devotes most of its attention to the poems. The notice in *The Critical Review* appeared well after the second edition had been printed and responds not only to the tale but to its already established popularity. Even the newly initiated *Edinburgh Review*, while ostensibly evaluating Opie's *Poems* (1802), looks back in its inaugural issue to pen critical judgments on *The Father and Daughter*.]

i. *The Critical Review, or Annals of Literature* 35 (May 1802): 114-117.

We are by no means surprised that this work should have passed through the first edition before we had an opportunity of stating our opinion of its merits. The public have, by the extensiveness of its circulation, given a decisive verdict in its favour; and though we would not lay it down as a universal rule that the public voice is the voice of just taste, yet we must observe, that the general approbation bestowed upon a story like that under our consideration, "simple in its construction and humble in its pretensions," affords strong presumptive evidence that it is calculated strongly to arrest the attention and to interest the feelings. This conclusion, which we drew from the circumstances in which it was submitted to our notice, was amply confirmed by its perusal. Seldom have we met with any combination of incidents, real or imaginary, which possessed more of the deeply pathetic. The moral inculcated by this tale is seriously impressive. It exhibits in the most affecting point of view the misery consequent upon the illicit indulgence of the passions; and the effect of the awful lesson which it teaches is not impaired by any intermixture of levity of dialogue or pruriency of description. The style of the authoress is elegant and correct, free from ambitious ornament, and never degenerating into colloquial negligence. We will not, by analyzing the story of the Father and Daughter, diminish the pleasure of such of our readers as may be induced to read the work itself; but, as a specimen of Mrs. Opie's skill in composition, we shall make an interesting extract, only premising that the heroine, Agnes Fitzhenry, after having been tempted by the wiles of Clifford to quit her indulgent father, and, after the lapse of a considerable space of time, being convinced of the villany of her seducer, is represented as returning in the dreariness of a winter's night to the house of her parent.

[Quotes the scene in which Agnes meets the mad Fitzhenry, from "Agnes was now arrived at the beginning of a forest" to "Agnes beheld her father!!!"]

ii. *The Monthly Review; or Literary Journal* 35 (May 1801): 163-166.

THE pleasures of melancholy are suited only to minds of uncommon susceptibility,—to those persons who may be said to have a sympathetic *taste* for *distress*; and from readers of this class, the tale of woe now before us will meet with peculiar acceptance. For ourselves, we own that we have been truly affected by the perusal of it, since it is replete with interest, and possesses pathos enough to affect the heart of the most callous of *critical* readers. Our only consolation, under the first impression on our feelings, arose from the hope and persuasion that the story is *not* founded on *Fact*, though the tragic part and the catastrophe may be too often exemplified in the consequences attending the profligacy of our young men of fortune and fashion.

Mrs. Opie speaks thus modestly of her production ... [quotes preface].

As this narrative is not well adapted for either abridgment or detail, we shall only add our brief commendation of its moral tendency, and proceed to take some notice of the poetical pieces which the ingenious authoress has added to the prose part of this publication. The first and most considerable of these small but pleasing productions is "An Epistle supposed to be addressed by Eudora, the Maid of Corinth, to her Lover, Philemon, informing him of her having traced his shadow on the wall, while he was sleeping, the night before his departure to a foreign country; together with the joyful consequences of this action." The Argument is thus given:...[quotes from the Pliny Epigraph].

This accidental discovery, according to the Epistle, brought Dibutades into great fame and fortune. We shall copy a part of Eudora's address, as a sufficient specimen of Mrs. Opie's poetical compositions: [quotes ll. 1-96: "Yes, I must write ... the grandeur of his swelling brow."]

This is not the first time that we have introduced the Muse of Mrs. Opie to the approbation of our readers....

iii. *The European Magazine* 40 (September 1801):194.

A very affecting moral story. The incidents, which are of a domestic nature (as, indeed, the title imports), occur naturally, and "come home to the business and bosoms" of every class of readers. The scenes of distress in which Agnes and Fitzhenry are involved, Mrs. Opie has depicted with great force and effect; and the lessons that she inculcates do credit to her head and heart.

Of the general tendency of the work, we cannot convey a more clear idea, perhaps, than may be formed from a perusal of the following lines, with which the fair Author has concluded it. [Quotes from "Peace to the memory of Agnes Fitzhenry" to the end of novel.]

iv. *The Edinburgh Review* 1 (October 1802): 113-22. [Review of the *Poems*, including the following commentary on *The Father and Daughter*.]

THE anxiety of a young writer, who yields, with trembling hands, the first production of his genius, to the survey of a world, unknown to him in all but this one fearful circumstance, that the praise, of which he is ambitious, and the neglect or scorn which he dreads, are dependent on its voice, whether of judgment or caprice, is a feeling that requires, for compensation, a large share of the fame, which it is probably never to receive; as, however great the multitude who have shared alike the misery of expectation, the happy recompense must belong only to a few. Yet, there is a feeling, perhaps more painful than this first anxiety, when the young writer of a work which has raised him to popularity, submits his powers a second time to criticism, of which he has already exhausted the indulgence, and which now expects to applaud, rather than to forgive. The favour excited by past excellence, is a favour which requires progression in its object; and though, in some, it may be the heedless partiality of friendship, is, in those higher minds that may be considered as representing posterity, more like the interest felt by an upright judge, which, though it allow him to delight in merited acquittal, never induces him to palliate guilt, but rather to consider delinquency as aggravated by the previous character of the culprit. There is, besides, an innocent selfishness, which modifies our opinions by an influence unperceived, and persuades us, that success is more difficult of attainment, because we have ourselves succeeded. It is not so much, however, in this imagined increase of difficulty, as in the actual increase of penalty, that the evil of reputation is felt by the fortunate. It is now no longer a simple, and almost unknown failure, which he has to dread. He has brought a multitude around him by his triumph; and a failure would now have all the disgrace of degradation. There has not been a single voice of applause, that would not add to his remembrance its whole weight of ignominy; and amid the variety of possible sentences, there is thus only one to which he can look with desire, because all those less degrees of praise, which would have satisfied his humbler ambition, must now be accompanied with the mortifying ideas, of disappointment in his readers, and of inferiority in himself.

It was probably with feelings similar to those we have described, that Mrs Opie committed to the world her volume of poems. To a very large number of readers, "The Father and Daughter" had already made its appearance a promise of much delight. That it has completely satisfied the expectations which her novel had excited *in us*, we will not say. It would be, at best, an ambiguous compliment; and preferring therefore an opinion, which has no reference to the past, we are ready to admit, that her volume of poems has afforded us much pleasure, and that it would have obtained for its author a very considerable reputation, though her former work had been wholly unknown.

But, while we thus express our praise of Mrs Opie's miscellany, we do not wish it to be considered as applicable to the whole, or even to the greater number, of the pieces of which it consists. These are of very various species of composition, and are perhaps still more different, in merit, than in subject. In the tender song of sentiment and pathos, there is uncommon elegance; but, in pieces of greater length, which require dignity, or even terseness of expression, and an easy development of thoughts, which rise complicated in the moment of fancy, there is a dissimilarity of character, in every respect, which contrasts, without relieving, the sweetness of the simpler pictures. Mrs Opie's mind is evidently more adapted to seize situation, than to combine incidents. It can represent, with powerful expression, the solitary portrait, in every attitude of gentler grief; but it cannot bring together a connected assemblage of figures, and represent each in its most striking situation, so as to give, as it were, to the glance of a moment, the events and the feelings of many years. When a series of reflections is to be brought by her to our view, they must all be of that immediate relation, which allows them to be introduced at any part of the poem, or we shall probably see before us a multitude, rather than a group. She is therefore wholly unfit for that poetry, which endeavours to reason, while it pleases; and, powerful as she is in solitary pathos, we do not think that she is well fitted for bringing before us the connected griefs and characters of the drama. She has, indeed, written a novel; and it is one which excites a very high interest: But the merit of that novel does not consist in its action, nor in any varied exhibition of character. Agnes, in all the sad changes of her fortune, is still the same: and the action, if we except a very few *situations* of the highest excitement, is the common history of every seduction in romance. Indeed, we are almost tempted to believe, that the scene in the wood occurred first to the casual conception of the author, and that, in the design of fully displaying it, all the other events of the novel were afterwards imagined....

We remember, that, in "The Father and Daughter," we frequently regretted the intrusion of the writer of the tale, when we were wholly occupied with the misfortunes of her heroine. Reflections of anticipation are always injurious to the interest excited, as they diminish curiosity; and reflections on the past are superfluous, and offensive to the reader's vanity, if they state what may naturally be inferred from the circumstances of the tale, and call us away too coldly to reason, when the inference is forced. But, above all, reflection is unnatural, when introduced by a sufferer in the midst of distress. Dear thought! Blest thought! Sad thought! &c. are parentheses which we wish to see banished from poetry. Who pauses, in impassioned soliloquy, to determine the classification of his own feelings?....

Appendix C: Contemporary Responses to The Father and Daughter

1. Thomas Robinson to Henry Crabb Robinson, 31 July 1801

As the production of an acquaintance you will probably likewise be interested to hear that Mrs. Opie has lately sent forth a Tale, and which as it was contained in a slender vol[ume] I had the patience to read. It is intitled The Father and Daughter. It is quite enough for me to say of it, that it interested me, and I was pleased to find that I have a few strings about my heart, which are capable of receiving a vibration of sympathy. I was convinced that for once in my life, I had something within me more than a clod of the valley. The story is very simple, and the distress of it arises from seduction. Many modern Novels seem to be written with a view to inculcate or censure some fashionable moral or political opinion. And I have imagined that Mrs. O. in her production intended to support a middle opinion betwixt the free notion of Godwin, on female chastity on the one hand, and the puritanical prudish doctrine of Miss Hannah More on the other....

2. Mrs. Thomas Clarkson to R. E. Garnham, 20 May 1802

I have lately had a very long letter from Mrs. Opie. By wh[ich] I learn that she is amazingly noticed & courted by titled folk & learned folk & rich folk & all sorts of folk. I do not envy her. Her book has been amazingly successful wh[ich] I consider as rather a misfortune than otherwise—it will encourage her to scribble on & I am almost certain that she will never produce any thing better.

3. From "Mrs. Opie," *The European Magazine, and London Review* (May 1803)

To speak of living merit is often a difficult, and always a delicate, task: whether we censure or commend, there are readers who will be ready to impute to us illiberal or unworthy motives: happy, however, is it for our present purpose, that we possess, in the writings of Mrs. Opie, ample and undoubted testimonies of the strength of her judgment, and of the goodness of her heart. "The Father and the Daughter," in opposition to the fantastic fictions which have disgraced the regions of romance, this amiable writer professes to be—a tale, founded in simple nature; as such, perhaps, there never was a composition so admirably calculated to rouse the passions in the cause of virtue, and to correct that false sensibility, that degenerating excess of sentiment, which have been proved to be incompatible with the real interests of humanity. The concluding sentences of this pathetic and deeply-affecting story cannot be too often impressed upon young minds: they breathe the purest spirit of philanthropy and good sense. As a proof of the high esteem in which "The Father and the Daughter" is held, it has not only had a very extensive circulation in this country, but has been twice translated into the French language....

4. From *The Gentleman's Magazine* 76.2 (August 1806): 752

LINES

Occasioned by reading Mrs. OPIE's *affecting Tale of "The Father and Daughter."*

NOT for the joys which wealth can bring,
    Or Fancy picture to the eye,
Would I exchange the crystal spring
    Which flows to Sensibility.

More hallow'd than the shrine, where oft
    The pilgrim bends the votive knee,
The eye which beams benignly soft
    With tributary tears to thee.

For well the soft tear can impart,
    With eloquence too all its own,
How sweetly throbs the owner's heart,
    To every finer feeling prone.

For he who never kindly strove
    To chase away the tear of woe,
Nor e'er from friendship or from love
    Experienc'd the sweets that flow,

May haply glide through life, unknown
    To ills which like the tempest lower;
But never will his bosom own
    Thy sacred glow — thy soothing power.

In vain would Opie's tender tale
    Of woe, so fraught with luxury,
Upon his stubborn soul prevail
    To shed a tear—to heave a sigh.

And yet, what bosom would not melt,
    Or trembling pearl what eye not shed,
At all the wretched Father felt
    When Agnes was for ever fled.

Hark! he exclaims, in accents wild,
    In infamy oh! let her live!
And yet, she is my child! my child,
    Return, and I will yet forgive!

Thou didst return, ill-fated fair,
    Regardless of the pelting storm,
To view with bitterest despair
    A maniac father's shatter'd form;

To tremble at the look of fire
    Which darts beneath his clouded brow,
Which says—Didst thou too leave a sire
    To heave the sigh of endless woe?

As round the cheerful fire we sit,
    To Fanny I the tale impart,
Who mean-time weaves the silken net,
    Or busy plies the needle's art.

But ever does the rising sigh
    The progress of the tale impede,
And ever does my Fanny's eye,
    O'erpower'd with strong emotions plead.

True as the needle to the North,
    Maternal feelings swell her breast,
Whilst in the pride of conscious worth,
    She rocks the fancied babe to rest.

But still resound its plaintive cries,
    Chill'd by the blast and wet with rain;

In vain she lulls it with her sighs,
    For still is heard Fitz-Henry's chain.

Sweet babe, that chain which makes thee start,
    Which only makes thy tears to flow,
Tells to thy mother's throbbing heart,
    A tale of unimagin'd woe.

Oh! may'st thou, Fanny, never feel
    Such woes, if haply such there be!
And if along thy cheek should steal
    The tear of sensibility;

Oh! may'st thou ever in my arms
    Learn to forget each rising care;
And ever from the world's alarms,
    Oh! may'st thou seek protection there!

Then shall the tale contrasted prove
    To thee, my partner and my pride!
And then, too, shall the sweets of love
    Endear to us our own fire-side.

5. From "Mrs. Opie," *The Ladies' Monthly Museum* (February 1817)

Mrs. Opie's first publication, The Father and Daughter, a tale, with other pieces, 8vo. 1801, is generally read and admired. This tale shows the dire consequences of seduction in a stronger light than any publication we know of. The amiable writer professes that this tale is founded in simple nature; as such, perhaps, there never was a composition so well calculated to rouse the passions in the cause of virtue; and as a proof of the high esteem in which it is held, it has not only had a very extensive circulation in this country, but has been translated into the French language. Indeed all her productions are written with the laudable view, and none in the English language are better, or so well calculated, for the improvement of her own sex in morals and virtue, in all their respective relations of daughter, wife, and mother. Her forte is evidently in plaintive description, and horror-struck scenes of woe, which she marks with great feeling, and a strong and bold hand; her delineations are so forcible as to arrest the attention, and leave never-to-be-forgotten traces in the mind.

Appendix D: L'Agnese

[The most substantial adaptation of *The Father and Daughter* for the stage was Paër's opera *Agnese di Fitz-Henry*. The libretto for the work was written by Luigi Buonavoglio, based on an Italian translation of the tale by Filipo Casari. First produced in Italy at the Teatro Ponte d'Altera, near Parma, in 1809, the opera later premiered in London at the King's Theatre on 15 May 1817.]

1. From *Agnes; A Serio-Comic Opera, in Two Acts*

[The scenes below are taken from *L'Agnese; Dramma—Semiserio in Due Atti*, an edition of the libretto featuring facing page translations in Italian and English, published in 1817 and sold at the Opera House in Haymarket. In this adaptation of Opie's tale, Fitzhenry becomes Conte Uberto di Fizendry (Hubert in the English translation), and Clifford becomes Ernesto, who is designated as husband of Agnes in the Dramatis Personae. Caroline Seymour and her father become Carlotta and Don Pasquale.]

i.

ADVERTISEMENT

THE deeply-interesting tale by Mrs. Opie, *The Father and Daughter*, soon proved too powerful to be confined within the limits of one country and one language;—it forced its way, shortly after publication, into various parts of Europe, and in Italy was converted into a Serio-Comic Drama in prose, by Filippo Casari, under the title of *Agnese di Fizendry*. This, becoming extremely popular, was adapted for the Lyric Stage by Luigi Buonavoglia, who, omitting some Characters and Scenes, in order to facilitate the musical performance and shorten the representation, delivered it into the hands of Paër, the celebrated Composer; and this joint production, which has met with the most distinguished success abroad, is now performed for the first time in this country.

Many pieces of Music in this Opera have been published in London, and are well known to all Amateurs of Music. The unqualified approbation which they have received operated as a strong motive for giving the Work to the Public in an entire state. It may not be improper to observe, that the Poem follows the original as closely as possible; except in the termination,—Mrs. Opie's Novel concluding with the death of Hubert immediately after the recovery of his reason.

ACT I.

SCENE II.

Night begins to disappear, and the Scene is gradually made lighter by the approach of Morning.
Agnes without either hat or veil, leading her little Daughter by the hand.
Cavatina.

Agnes. All is silent around me; the voices have ceased; the day begins to dawn; I have no longer cause for terror.

I thought I heard among them the voice of my betrayer: what does the author of my misfortunes now require? Why does he follow me?

My child, you have no longer a father! — You were born, alas! to misfortune.

————

Heaven justly punishes me: in an evil hour I fled from a father, who adored me; I yielded to the dictates of an imprudent passion. For seven years I have concealed myself from his researches, and perhaps, dreadful thought, have hastened his death. — Father, dear father, if you still live, to your arms will I return;—at your feet will I pour out my sorrows;—let my contrition, my sincere repentance—(*A distant rattling of chains is heard.*) Gracious heaven! what sound is this?—(*The sound approaches nearer.*)—Chains! It is certainly so; my ear does not deceive me. — My daughter, for what are we reserved? —(*The sound continues to approach.*)—Let us save ourselves; but where, oh where, shall we find a place of concealment? —(*She hurries across the stage; at length places her daughter in a recess, and hides herself behind a tree.*)—Heaven be our friend— for you alone, my child, I tremble.

SCENE III.

(*Hubert appears dressed in a dark surtout, his head and neck bare, his beard neglected, his hair matted and dirty. One stocking has fallen down, and exposes his naked leg. From his waist hangs a chain, which drags on the ground.*

He enters, looking attentively round him on all sides. His look is unsettled.)

Duet.

Hub. Oh, Yes! yes! — I shall find it.

Agnes. What terror I feel.

Hub. They tell me I shall not — but, yes, I shall certainly find it.

Agnes. Just Heaven! What shall I do?

(Hubert in traversing the stage, still with his eyes fixed on the ground, approaches Agnes, who shews the greatest agitation, and at length seeing him get near to her, utters a cry.)

Agnes. Oh God!

Hub. *(Starts, looks up—at sight of her utters a loud cry, and flies with precipitation)*—Ah! —

Agnes. My spirits fail me, — I am sinking with alarm.—*(Long pause.)*—Who can this unhappy man be? — Perhaps some malefactor escaped — No — if it were so, why should he fly from me? — What can he fear from a wretched woman.

Hub. *(Returning to the bottom of the stage)*—I shall find it.

Agnes. From his actions and his gestures I now discover the truth. — It is some poor creature bereft of reason, who has eloped from the adjoining hospital.

Hub. I shall find it.

Agnes. Let me observe him — I may remain here unnoticed.

Duet.

Hub. Yes, I shall assuredly find the tomb which encloses the remains of my beloved daughter.

(Looking about.)

Agnes. It is a daughter's death then that has deprived him of reason.

Hub. It is not true that she eloped — No, she is dead.

Agnes. Heavens! What does he say?

Hub. It was false.

Agnes. What a thought assails me! — It is — it is himself — it is my father!

Hub. Father! Who? No, I am not a father. — I have no children.

Agnes. *(Having just recognised him, falls at his feet. Hubert, at sight of her, removes so suddenly as to throw her to the ground—he then retires to the back Scene, his eyes, as before, fixed on the earth—Agnes remains kneeling.)*

Behold the dreadful consequence of my transgression. — Take my life, O Heaven! but restore my father to reason.

Hub. (Approaching her with emotion.) Lady, do you weep? Rise; your grief affects me.

Agnes. (Rising, and with difficulty restraining herself.) Well, I will not weep.

Hub. And will you stay with me?

Agnes. I will stay with you, for ever.

Hub. After so many years of grief and anguish, I feel at sight of you, returning tranquillity.

Agnes. He has passed years in complaint and sorrow,—of that sorrow I am the fatal cause.

Hub. Approach me, dear lady, —you give me comfort.

Agnes. Oh God!

Hub. What are you seeking, what are you doing here? Do not remain in this place. — Yes I shall find it—let them say what they will. Dogs, rascals, I have escaped them. —Oh, yes—what joy, what delight, when I find it. —But no, no,—if she is dead, a stone only, a cold stone, and a little dust. —Tell me lady, what is your name?

Agnes. My name?

Hub. Yes.

Agnes. My name is—

Hub. Dear lady, will you help me to look for it?

Agnes. Any request of yours. —Fa—Sir, I will comply with.

Hub. Sir? Oh, no. That name does not become your lips. I do not like it. I will not—

Agnes. And what must I call you *(aside.)* I cannot contain myself.

Hub. I shall find it, I shall certainly find it. —Come, follow me.

(Taking her hastily by the hand.)

Agnes. (alarmed.) Whither?

Hub. (with much seriousness.) Do you ask? Are we not to search?

Agnes. Yes, I attend you—but first let me take my daughter.

Hub. (with fury) How? What? Daughter?

Agnes. Yes, father.

Hub. (horror-struck and in the greatest rage.) Father! daughter! Oh names of horror—you tear my heart. —Where is she—let her die.

(Runs to a tree, and breaks off a large bough.)

Agnes. Oh Heaven! Charlotte, my daughter! Help.

SCENE IV.

The Keeper of the Hospital, with followers—the same.

Keep. There he is, seize him.

(The followers run behind Hubert and bind him to drag him away.)

Hub. Cruel, inhuman men.
Agnes. (interposing.) Stay, he is my father.
Keep. Go—take him away.
Agnes. Ah no! Let him stay.
Hub. Dogs, dogs. *(He is dragged off by force while the keeper holds back Agnes.)*
Agnes. Ah, my father!
Keep. Your father? Are you then the daughter whose conduct has driven him mad? Very good! Oh yes, pray weep: but your tears come a little too late, my pretty lady.

[*Exit.*

Agnes. Heaven, how low am I sunk! Too well have I deserved this treatment! But come, my daughter, let us follow. The powers above, that see my remorse,—that look down upon my sincere penitence,—will, I hope, restrain their just anger.

[*Exeunt.*

iii.

ACT II.

SCENE XII.

Hubert descends, singing in an under voice.

Cavatina.

The life of man is a stormy and troubled sea,—in the tomb alone he finds repose.

————

D[on]. Pas[quale]. Do you call this a cure?

D[on]. Gir[olamo]. Be silent.

D. Pas. I attend.

Hub. (looking about here and there in the garden, plucks up some grass rather impatiently.) How every thing has fallen into disorder! This girl does not take the pains she used to do formerly. *(Pause.)* Well, there is still something I cannot comprehend.

D. Pas. I believe you.

Hub. I wish, but am unable, to recollect some circumstances of the past. I seem to have a void in my head.

D. Pas. That is the case! I have no doubt that his brains are evaporated.

Hub. I am confused, disordered, bereft of sense. I appear to be alone in the universe.

D. Pas. Oh Lord! to my sorrow there is also myself.

Hub. To have had a long sleep, and to persuade myself that those sorrows of which such indistinct traces remain were only a dream.

D. Pas. Oh yes! a dream.

D. Gir. (Having spoken in the back scene to Agnes, she goes into the house; then turns to D. Pasquale.)
For you then —

D. Pas. What for me?

D. Gir. This is the time.

D. Pas. And must I — ?

D. Gir. (pushing him) I beseech you, go.

D. Pas. (trembling) What an alarming situation! *(At a distance)* Good day, friend!

Hub. (turning with vehemence) Ah!

D. Pas. (alarmed and retreating) Ah!

Hub. (addressing him with cheerfulness) Pasquale, my friend, why do you keep back? Come, I was wishing for you.

D. Pas. (aside) This is a favourable omen, certainly — Here I am.

Hub. But what is the matter? you tremble.

D. Pas. Tremble? You are mistaken. It is true that I feel cold.

Hub. (vehemently) Cold? And I am hot, I burn —
                    (Taking him by the hand.)

D. Pas. (aside) It is so indeed — what a situation is mine!

Finale.

Hub. Could you but feel this devouring flame which fires my breast — scorches, annihilates me!

D. Pas. Could you but feel this biting cold which makes me shiver—
  makes my teeth chatter!

Hub. (with vehemence) I assure you—

D. Pas. (alarmed) And I certify to you.

Hub. (breaks into laughter) Ha—ha—ha!—

*(Takes Don Pasquale by the hand, and looks him in the face laughing. The
other does the same, but in a constrained manner. Hubert returns to a very
serious mood, and Don Pasquale is disturbed.)*

D. Pas. (aside) He becomes serious; what will he do?

(D. Pasquale removes to a distance, but is held by Girolamo.)

D. Gir. Where are you retreating? Do not go away.

D. Pas. Ah! I will not stay.

D. Gir. But hear me.

D. Pas. I will remain, but I will keep at a distance. I am weary of this.

*(D. Girolamo advances, holding Charlotte by the hand. Agnes is on the ter-
race, the others looking on.)*

D. Gir. Dear friend.

Hub. (Seeing Charlotte, utters a cry and runs to her, but stops suddenly.) Ah
  Agnes—no—
  (Remains a moment in meditation, looks again at Charlotte, and sighs.)
  My Agnes expired in these arms.

D. Gir. My dear friend, why are you so confused, so pensive?

Hub. (with the utmost sadness, and almost weeping) She—you—I dare
  not explain what passes in my breast.

Char. But where is your daughter?

Hub. (vehemently) Who?

D. Pas. (aside) Ah! there we are again.

D. Gir. Oh, charming Agnes!

Hub. (with fury) What do you seek?—what do you ask? Ah! you kill
  me—She is dead.

*(D. Girolamo makes a sign to Agnes, who runs to the table,
and takes the harp.)*

Char. What do you say?

(Agnes plays a prelude on the harp.)

Hub. What sound is that?
Char. Do you not hear?
Char./D. Gir. There she is—amusing herself by playing on the harp.

(Hubert turns, sees her, utters a piercing cry, and falls into the arms of Don Girolamo. Agnes shews the utmost agitation; the rest stand attentively observing. Don Pasquale is still unable to conceal his terror.)

Hub. Oh heaven, how my heart beats! Do I dream, or am I awake? Agnes! Oh joy! What happiness is this! I cannot support myself; my limbs fail me.
Agnes./Vesp[ina]./Ern[esto]. Oh heaven, what emotion!
    What a moment is this!
    Support me/her—Oh joy!
    Let me/Do you cheer him with my/your voice.
    Heaven assist me/her. Give me/her strength.
D. Gir./Char. Why this emotion? Why so sad? It is Agnes. Hear her. Go, make haste. *(To D. Pasquale.)* It is she—look at her. What are you afraid of?
D. Pas. Alas, what emotion! What a moment is this!—Joy—delight!—I go instantly. *(To D. Gir.)* My legs tremble—my heart beats.

(Agnes sings, and accompanies herself on the harp. Hubert is moved alternately by joy and grief; looks towards the window; embraces D. Girolamo and D. Pasquale with transport; lifts his eyes to heaven to return thanks, and finally makes an effort to run towards Agnes; but sinks exhausted into the arms of Don Pasquale and Don Girolamo, who conduct him to a seat under the arbour.)

Agnes. If the good shepherd finds his lost lamb, his grief quickly changes to joy; with his melodious pipe he makes the hills resound, nor does his countenance shew that he was ever unhappy. So if Agnes returns to her father—
Hub. Ah friends!—let her come—let her come to me—I faint—I die! *(Faints.)*
D. Gir. Agnes, hasten hither; you alone can now restore your father to the use of reason.
Agnes. I come; assist me, oh Heaven, and hear my prayer. Oh, if you feel compassion for the unhappy, restore to me my father.

(Descends.)

D. Pas. For my part I want no more disasters. I have been sufficiently ill-treated already, and am resolved to follow the example of Cato.

All. Rejoice — Heaven restores to us our good master!

Agnes. Friends — Oh God! Speak, may I hope?

D. Gir. You may hope.

Agnes. Ah! flattering hope, what joy it brings!

Chorus.

Flattering hope already makes her joyful.

Char./Vesp. See, he recovers.

Agnes. (Throwing herself on her knees, and taking his hand with transport.) Oh, my father!

Hub. (With extreme vehemence.) Father! Who? — Great God! — *(seeing her.)*— Agnes!

Agnes. Oh, my father!

All. Happy moment!

Hub. How can it be? *(Raises Agnes, holds her in his arms, and looks at them all with uncertainty.)*— You — you! — Great God! speak to me.

All. Friend,/Sir,/Father,/ be tranquil.

Hub. Agnes! Are you Agnes?

All. Pitying heaven has brought her back to her affectionate father.

Hub. (Embracing Agnes with the greatest joy and transport.) My daughter!

Agnes. My father! Oh, what happiness! — That I at length hold you in my arms puts an end to my grief, to my sighs.

Hub. Never more shall you be separated from me.

Agnes. I will stay with you for ever.

D. Pas./D. Gir./Carl./Vesp. But we, Sir —

Hub. My friends, I owe you thanks. I would say how much — but my head is confused — I cannot express them.

D. Pas. Oh joy — delight — transport — *(Aside.)*— nevertheless it is advisable to keep in the rear a little longer.

Ern. Sir,— at your feet I venture to kneel for pardon.

Hub. What do you want? Who are you?

Ern. I am —

Agnes. (Suddenly taking her daughter, and kneeling on the other side of him.) He is my husband, the father of this —

Hub. Oh God!

Agnes. Look at her; she holds out her little arms, and longs to —

Hub. (Embracing the child.) Enough, my dear daughter! — No more — rise; — let me, oh let me breathe — The knot which Heaven has tied I will not unloose.

All. Heaven at last pities you, and rewards your virtue.

Agnes. Thanks to kind Heaven, that terminates my sufferings.

(Hubert remains sitting under the arbour, and embracing the child; Agnes and Ernesto on each side of him.)

All. The clouds are dispersed, the day is again serene! After a storm of trouble and misfortune tranquility returns; our souls again know happiness.

End of the Opera.

2. Reviews of *L'Agnese*

i. *The Times,* 16 May 1817.

KING'S THEATRE

The celebrated opera of *Agnese,* by PAËR, was performed last night at this theatre, for the benefit of Madame CAMPORESE, and for the first time in this country. This work originally appeared at Milan, eight or nine years ago, where it was received with so much enthusiasm that it had a run of more than 50 nights. Mrs. OPIE's interesting tale of *The Father and Daughter,* from which the drama is taken, was translated soon after its first publication into most of the European languages; and it is a proof of the fidelity to general nature with which her portraits are drawn, that her writings have become almost universally popular. In Italy the subject was soon adapted for the theatre, having been converted into a serio-comic drama, in prose, by FILIPO CASARI, under the title of *Agnese di Fizendry.* This proving extremely attractive, was adapted for the lyric stage, by LUIGI BUONAVOGLIA ; who, omitting some characters and scenes, in order to facilitate the musical performance, and to shorten the representation, delivered it into the hands of Paër, the celebrated composer.

The late hour at which the opera concluded renders it impossible to do adequate justice to this production; we therefore decline making any observations at present, proposing on some future occasion to bestow on it the full consideration which it deserves.

ii. *The Times*, 19 May 1817.

KING'S THEATRE

PAËR'S Opera of *Agnese*, which was brought out at this Theatre on Thursday, was repeated on Saturday evening. The following is a sketch of the story, which, though of very simple structure and few incidents, possesses uncommon interest: —

Agnes (Madame CAMPORESE), the daughter of *Count Hubert* (AMBROGETTI), a Neapolitan nobleman, has eloped from his paternal care with *Ernesto* (BEGREZ). The unfortunate father is in consequence seized with insanity, and is placed in confinement. *Agnes*, after an interval of seven years, offended at the duplicity of her lover, is returning home. The drama opens with *Ernesto* (who had discovered her flight) and some followers in search of her. *Agnes* herself next appears, without hat or veil, leading her little daughter; she soon after encounters her unhappy parent, who has escaped from his keepers, and discovers that he has lost his reason; from some emotions awakened in him at the sight of her, the hope is suggested to her, that he might be restored by her personal attendance on him; she obtains permission for this purpose, through the means of *Don Pasquale* (NALDI), a humane governor of the hospital in which *Hubert* is confined. The most impressive scene in the whole piece is that which follows her introduction to her father's apartment. In one part of it, *Hubert*, unconscious of the presence of *Agnes*, is endeavouring, but in vain, to recollect the words of a song which in happier days his daughter used to sing to him. *Agnes*, observing his distress, supplies them—the strongest emotion is excited—he appears to recognize her for a moment, but relapses into distraction; a mental conflict ensues, which his frame can no longer support—he faints—*Agnes* kneels at this feet kissing his hand, and the act closes. The second act is employed in developing the mode of cure projected by *D. Girolamo*, the chief physician (RIGHI), which consists in bringing the patient to his own house, and restoring all about it to the state existing before the elopement of *Agnes*, to produce the impression that all his sufferings were no more than a dream. The idea of *Agnes* being first excited by placing her portrait in his chamber; *Vespina* (Madame PASTA), the servant, brings in his coffee, as if made as usual by his daughter. He afterwards descends into the garden, where he is saluted by *Girolamo* and *Pasquale* as old friends; he recognizes them, but with some signs of distraction; he is still mentally brooding over the recollection of *Agnes*, and at the sight of *Charlotte* (Signora MORI), the daughter of *Pasquale,* whom he takes for her, is on the point of relapsing: at that moment *Girolamo* makes a sign to *Agnes,* who preludes on her harp; he turns, sees, and recognizes her, and falls quite overcome into the arms of his friends. While in this situation, *Agnes* sings a song, accompanied on the harp; his cure is here completed, his reason is restored—he makes an effort to run towards her, but his strength again fails him. *Agnes* hastens to him, they embrace with transport; when he recovers, *Ernesto* is introduced and reconciled. While *Hubert* remains supported by them, the chorus of peasants and domestics expressing their joy at his recovery, the curtain falls.

PAËR's music is not of the highest order; it is perhaps neither very original, nor very profound; its character is sweetness, pathos, and a peculiar felicity of adaptation to scenic representation; more attractive qualities, at least, than the elaborate productions of the art when not seconded by high imagination and genius. PAËR is remarkable, too, for his great judgment: he understands perfectly what we may call the modelling of an opera; he knows where to employ the *recitativo parlanti,* or speaking recitative; where an increased interest requires the recitative accompanied; and where the subject should rise into the full melody, into regular r[h]ythm and movement. These circumstances, by the way, if properly considered, constitute the true attraction of the opera itself. Once allow for the elevation of the recitative above ordinary dialogue, and we obtain a natural gradation of sentiment and passion, without that abruptness which attends the transition from speaking to singing; there is then a certain congruity between the parts and the whole, without which no production will bear the scrutiny of taste. We particularly impress this remark, because it is the clue to the knowledge of the true merits of an entertainment which deserves to be held in general estimation.

The music of *Agnese,* however excellent, is subordinate in point of interest to the drama, which is one of the most pathetic we have ever seen represented: for this effect, however, it is chiefly indebted to the extraordinary acting of Mesdames [sic] CAMPORESE and AMBROGETTI, which produced such an impression on us, that we find it difficult to convey a just idea of it without going more into detail than we generally allow ourselves to do on the performances at this theatre. Nothing can exceed the purity of tone and truth of feeling which pervades this vocal performance of Madame CAMPORESE, of which, the Cavatina "tutto è silenzio intorno," the air she repeats to assist the recollection of the unfortunate *Hubert,* and her prayer in the second act, "Il Padre, o ciel, mi rendi," are striking examples. It is difficult to say whether her singing or her acting were most successful. The manner in which she checks herself in the third scene, when about to call *Hubert* by the name of father—her application to *Pasquale* to be admitted to attend on him in the hospital—the whole scene in the apartment where *Hubert* is confined—and, above all, the last, where he is restored to reason, and she rushes into his embrace, produced the greatest effect. Ambrogetti seemed to have abandoned for the occasion all idea of fine singing; it was throughout a voice choaked with emotion, distorted with frenzy, or sinking under insupportable anguish. We shall not soon forget the fixed look with which, at his first appearance, he advanced to the front of the stage—his eye intensely marked the brooding of a distempered mind: subsequently, after the interview with *Agnes*, when they are about to retire, and he is roused to madness at the word "daughter," his utterance of the words, "oh nome orribile," was inimitably fine: his endeavour to recollect the words of a song above alluded to, and his final recovery of reason, were no less admirable; in short, in point of action, his *Hubert* is, throughout, a most striking performance. Those who have seen the celebrated singers PELLEGRINE and TANCHIARDINI, in this character, allow that in this last particular they have been exceeded.

CAMPORESE and AMBROGETTI are so exclusively the chief attraction of this opera, that the other performers require only a brief notice. NALDI gave *Don Pasquale* with some humour, but we thought him occasionally a little inattentive to the musical effect. His trio in the first act with *Charlotte* and *Vespina* was encored. BEGREZ sustained the part of *Ernesto* with skill and judgment; his voice is of very good compass, but wants power. Signora MORI, from the nature of her part, was almost a cipher. Madame PASTA, in the character of *Vespina*, had very little to do, and that little she entirely spoiled; her performance was without meaning and without effect.

We object in this drama to the frequent use of the snuff-box in the most pathetic scenes, and particularly to the pipe with which *Hubert* enters in the second act; both which, however conformable to foreign manners, should be omitted in deference to those of this country. We also wish left out the joke practised by *Hubert* on *Pasquale*, towards the conclusion, in catching his fingers in his snuff-box; it is quite out of character, and violates the decorum of the scene.

Upon the whole, this opera possesses great merit; and has been brought out in a manner that reflects credit on the taste and exertions of Mr. AYRTON, the present manager, who proves himself well qualified for the arduous office he has undertaken....

iii. "Chronicles of the Italian Opera in England," *The Harmonicon, a Journal of Music* 1 (1830): 247.

Ambrogetti: — Genius and enthusiasm, combined with a versatility of histrionic talent seldom equalled on any stage, elevated to the first rank of his profession a man whose voice was neither distinguished for compass, tone, execution, nor any one of the qualities usually looked for in a first singer. In don Giovanni he was the veritable reckless profligate.... The next night you might see him embodying the sorrows and insanity of Mrs. Opie's distracted father. But here the *vraisemblance* was too harrowing: Ambrogetti had studied the last degrading woe of humanity in the hospitals, where all its afflicting varieties were exemplified, and had studied it too well. Females turned their backs to the stage to avoid the sight; but a change of posture could not shut their ears to the dreadful scream of partial recognition with which the first entrance of his daughter was marked. Kemble, Young, and Siddons, combined in the confession that madness had never found such a representative; and the very perfection of the picture shortened its exhibition. The scene was too true to Nature for Nature to endure it....

Appendix E: Smiles and Tears

1. From Mrs. C. Kemble, *Smiles and Tears; or, The Widow's Stratagem* (1815)

[Mrs. Charles Kemble's *Smiles and Tears; or, The Widow's Stratagem: A Comedy, in Five Acts* debuted at the Theatre Royal, Covent Garden, on 12 December 1815. As the Advertisement points out, this play attempts to blend the melodrama of *The Father and Daughter* with French farce, with interesting results: Fitzhenry becomes Fitzharding, Agnes becomes Cecil, and Clifford/Mountcarrel becomes Delaval/ Glenthorne.]

i.

ADVERTISEMENT.

I AM too proud of public approbation, not to put my name to a production so highly honoured by the applause which it has received; but I should be wanting in candour as well as gratitude, were I not fairly to acknowledge the sources from which that applause has chiefly been derived. To Mrs. Opie's beautiful Tale of *Father and Daughter*, I am indebted for the serious interest of the Play; upon a French Piece in one Act, entitled *La Suite d'un Bal Masqué, some* of the lighter scenes were founded — to the exertions of the Manager, and the talents of the Performers also, I unquestionably owe much; and it is no small addition to the pleasure which I feel in the success of the Piece, that I have an opportunity of subscribing myself, their much obliged,

And truly humble Servant,

MARIE THERESE KEMBLE.

Craven-Hill,

Tuesday, Dec. 19, 1815.

ii.

ACT III.

SCENE II.

A gloomy part of Richmond Park — several Trunks of Trees lying here and there — Twilight.

Enter CECIL, *with an Infant wrapped in a Shawl.*

Cecil. Your cries, at length, are hush'd in sleep, my precious infant! and cold and hunger are, for awhile, forgotten! How awful is this silence! no sound falls on my ear, but the tumultuous beating of my frightened heart—lie still, lie still; your throbbings will awake my babe—how comes this mist before my eyes? I'm very faint—My child, my child! I can no longer bear your weight; *(she sinks, placing the Infant upon the trunk of one of the trees.)*— What agony is this? numbed as my limbs are by the stiffening blast, a scorching fire consumes my brain!—Can this be fear? It is, the terror of a guilty conscience: there was a time, when neither solitude nor night had power to terrify me—but I was innocent then; then I had not offended Heaven, whose protection I dare not now implore.—Ha! I hear a voice—Oh! welcome, welcome sound!—Yet, should it be any one whom I have known in other days—an idle fear; for if it should, night's friendly shadows will conceal the features of the guilty Cecil.—I'll follow his footsteps—in common charity, he'll not deny that comfort to a wretched, houseless wanderer!

Fitz. (Without.) Ha, ha! have I escaped you, ruffians? here I shall be safe from their pursuit.

(He is seen climbing the wall, and with the assistance of the arm of a tree, lets himself down upon the Stage; in this effort he breaks one of the smaller branches, and uses it as a weapon of defence.)

—Here will I lie concealed—they shall not again imprison me!

Cecil. Some miscreant escaped from justice! What will become of us?

Fitz. There, there they go!—One, two, three, four!—So, so; lie close; they are gone, they are gone, and now I breathe again.

Cecil. Alas! a maniac! what's to be done? shall I conceal myself? No; I'll make for the gate, and endeavour to regain the public road. *(FITZHARDING turns suddenly round)*

Fitz. What are you? one lying in ambush to entrap me? Wretch! advance one hair's breadth, and I fell you to the ground! *(Raising the broken branch)*—Ah! a woman!

Cecil. Yes; one without the power or wish to harm you.

Fitz. That's false—you are a woman, born only to betray—I know you are leagued against me—but thus—*(Threateningly.)*

Cecil. O! for my child's sake, do not harm me.

Fitz. A child!—have you a child? give it me—let me strangle it, before the little serpent turns to sting the breast that nourished it—pity is folly—if she live, she lives to blast your comfort. I had a child, a child more precious to me than my own heart's blood—but she betrayed me—made a gay festival to welcome me upon my return from a long, tedious journey—invited guests too—three hideous guests! Seduction, Penury, and Despair—With the first she fled, and left me victim to the other two.

Cecil. What do I hear? what horrid vision darts across my brain! Can it be? No, no! and yet, altho' destruction follow, I must, I will be satisfied. *(She throws off* FITZHARDING'*s Hat, recognizes, and falls at his feet.)*—Great God! my father!

Fitz. (*Raising her, looks wistfully in her face, and laughs wildly—pause.)* They are coming—you will not give me up to my pursuers— you will have more compassion than my unnatural daughter.

Cecil. Can I hear this, and yet not curse thee, Delaval?

Fitz. Ha! does that damn'd name again assail my ears? Does *he* pursue me still? what new torment can he inflict upon me? Yes, yes, I see him now—where is my daughter, villain? Give her back— restore her to me, polluted as she is, and I will bless you—but you have murdered her—your barbarous hand has nipped my pretty rose-bud ere it was blown, and now she lies, scorn'd, pale, and lifeless—monster! no longer shall your poisonous breath infect the air—an injured father strikes this poniard to your faithless heart—no struggling—down—down—Oh, oh! *(*CECIL *supports him.)*

Cecil. (*Weeping)* O, sight of horror! will all the agony I feel restore your peace, belov'd, much injured father!

Fitz. (*Recovering—feels her cheeks.)* How! weeping! tears, real tears! poor thing, poor thing! don't cry—I cannot be a partner in your grief—since my poor Cecil died (for she is dead, is she not?) I have not shed a tear.

Cecil. Oh, Heaven! too much, too much to bear!

Fitz. Poor thing! poor thing! *(Pause.)* You will not leave me, will you? *(Draws her close to his bosom.)*

Cecil. Leave you! O never, never; I will serve you, live for you, die for you.

Fitz. Come then, come with me; and I will shew you Cecil's grave; and we will strew fresh yew and cypress over it—Come, come!

(As he is leading her away, voices of the Keepers are heard without—1st
Keeper. "This way, this way; I'll follow him over the Wall—do you secure the
Gate."—He leaps from the Wall, two more come on at the Gate.)

Fitz. I hear them, they are coming—don't let them tear me from
   you—save, O, save me!
Cecil. Kind people, hear me! he is my father—leave him to my tender
   care!
1st Keep. O yes, you'll do much good; I wish we had more hands with
   us—step across to the cottage, and see if you can get any body to
   assist.

                                                          [Exit 2nd Keeper.

Cecil. You call in vain for assistance—no power on earth shall part
   us—once again, I tell you he is my father.
1st Keep. That may be—but what can you do for him? you had better
   stand aside, young woman; you'll only get yourself hurt.
Cecil. You shall tear me limb from limb, rather than separate me from
   him.

              Re-enter 2nd Keeper, with Cottager.

1st Keep. (To Cottager.) There, do you take charge of the young woman
   and keep her off—Now, now!—*(They rush forward to seize him.)*
Fitz. The first who approaches, I will lay dead at my foot—folded in
   your arms I fear them not.

   *(A scuffle ensues, on which they are separated—*FITZHARDING *disarmed,*
                  and dragg'd away.)

—Save me from these butchers! O save me, save me!
                          [Exeunt FITZHARDING *and Keepers.*

Cecil. O, for the love of mercy! let me follow him.
1st Keep. (Without.) Bind his hands!
Cecil. No, no; for the love of Heaven, no! Inhuman men! I must, I will
   go to him. O cruel! cruel! O my poor deceived, unhappy father!
   (She breaks from the Cottager, and endeavours to follow her Father, but her
strength fails her, and she sinks upon her knees; the Cottager supports her, and
the Curtain falls.)

ACT V.

SCENE III.

An Apartment in the Asylum.

Enter Lord GLENTHORN.

Lord G. What have I heard! am I myself infected, or have I really beheld my Cecil, and her frantic father? and could I view the frightful spectacle occasioned by my crime, and not expire upon the spot! Inhuman Stanly! were not the agonies of remorse sufficiently acute, but you must superadd this scene of horror? should Cecil scorn my unfeigned repentance, I have no remedy, no hope for this world or the next.

Enter STANLY *and* CECIL.

Stan. Grieve not, that you must leave him now — the impression given to his mind, will be a powerful auxiliary in Lady Emily's plan; while you remain here, I will give orders for his immediate conveyance to my house, and trust to Providence, to crown our efforts with success.

[Exit STANLY.

Cecil. Success! alas! I have not deserved it — but, my Father, whose life has been one scene of pure unsullied goodness, for his sake, Heaven may extend its mercy, and change our present misery, to joy unutterable — *(Lord* GLENTHORN *timidly advances.)* — What do I see? Delaval, here! this shock at least might have been spared me.

Lord G. Cecil!

Cecil. Ah! leave me — 'tis not my wish to upbraid you, Delaval, therefore leave me — lest suffering under anguish, great, sure, as ever human breast endured, I vent my feelings in reproach and bitterness.

Lord G. Spare me not, Cecil; pour deepest curses on my head — I have deserved them all.

Cecil. No, Delaval; in my acutest moments of affliction, when scarcely mistress of my desperate thoughts, I have recollected that you were the father of my infant, and all my maledictions have been changed to fervent prayers for your repentance.

Lord G. Those prayers were heard, my Cecil: truer contrition never touched a sinner's heart, tha[n] that which Heaven has awakened here—by that remorse, and for our tender infant's sake, let me conjure you—

Cecil. Delaval, desist! nor, by appealing to a mother's weakness, strive to shake a resolution which is now irrevocable.

Lord G. At your suspicions of my sincerity, Cecil, I have no right to feel offended—your worst reproaches cannot wound more keenly than those of my own self-accusing conscience! but by my regenerated heart I swear, that every future hour of my life shall prove my truth, every faculty of my soul be bent to repair the wrongs that I have done you, and bring back peace and comfort to your heart.

Cecil. Peace! O, cast a look within yon cell, behold my father, driven to madness by my guilt, then tell me where a wretch like me should look for peace! That your sentiments have undergone a change so conducive to your future welfare, Heaven knows how truly I rejoice!—for me, I have imposed a sacred duty upon myself, to which every instant, every thought, must be assiduously dedicated—to your protection I dare now assign our child; it would have eased my afflicted heart to have wept over him sometimes; but to comfort I have no claim, and even that sorrowful consolation I will forego for his advantage—receive him, Delaval! teach him to shun the vices which have destroyed our happiness, and never, Oh! never let him know the wretched being to whom he owes existence!

Lord G. (*Striking his forehead.*) Fool! Fool! what a treasure hast thou cast away!

[*Exeunt severally.*

iv.

ACT V.

SCENE V.

A Room in Stanly's House, hung with Pictures; a full length of Cecil, playing upon the Harp occupies the centre: it is covered by a green Curtain.

FITZHARDING, STANLY, *Lady* EMILY, *Sir* H. CHOMLEY,
Mrs. BELMORE, *and* O'DONOLAN *discovered.*

Fitz. Yes, I remember now, 'twas there, on summer evenings I used to
sit with one, too dearly loved, and watch the sun-beams sparkling
in the stream.

Sir Hen. And shall again, I hope, Sir.

Fitz. Never, never; she was snatched from me by the damned artifices
of a human fiend—Oh! never, never!

Stan. Stung by remorse, and eager to repair the wrongs that he has
done you—he comes to give her to your arms again, and crave
your blessing on their union.

Fitz. For shame, for shame! falsehood but ill becomes that silvered
head.

Stan. By Heaven—

Fitz. You mock me, Sir; I tell you she is dead—Poor Cecil! Cold!
cold! cold!

Lady E. (Drawing back the curtain.) Has not this portrait some resemblance to her?

Fitz. Ha! hide her, hide her! she has shot lightning thro' my veins!—
and see, see, see, at her command, the spirits of departed joys flit
quickly by, pointing and grinning at me as they pass—Oh! let
me fly—*(as he is rushing off, she plays and sings "Tears such as,"
&c.)*—Why, yes, that voice! and yet, O, tell me, art thou real, or
sent by Hell to tantalize and torture me?

Cecil. (Rising in the frame.)—Oh! my beloved father!

Fitz. (In extacy.)—Ha! 't is not illusion—for by the thick pulsation of
my heart, I feel 't is she, my long-lost child, my much-loved,
erring, and forgiven Cecil! *(They rush into each other's arms, then
Cecil falls at his feet, and embraces his knees.)*

Lady E. This is a spectacle, on which even Heaven smiles—Repentance, kneeling at the feet of Mercy! *(The Curtain falls, and the
Play concludes.)*

THE END

2. Reviews of *Smiles and Tears*

i. *The Times*, 13 December 1815.
[The names of the characters given by *The Times* do not correspond exactly with those in the published play. In particular, the reviewer apparently believes that a female character cannot be named Cecil, so she becomes Cecily in the review.]

COVENT GARDEN THEATRE.

We were prevented, by want of room, from giving, in our paper of yesterday, an account of the Comedy which was brought out on Tuesday night at Covent-garden Theatre. It is entitled "*Smiles and Tears, or, The Widow's Stratagem*," and the following are the Dramatis Personae: —

Sir Henry Cholmondoley	Mr. C. KEMBLE.
Colonel O'Donnellan	JONES.
Stanley	FAWCETT.
Delaval	ABBOTT.
Fitzharding	YOUNG.
Lady Emily	Mrs. C. KEMBLE.
The Widow Belmour	FAUCIT.
Cecily	Miss FOOTE.
Mrs. Jeffreys	Mrs. GIBBS.

Delaval, a broken libertine, pays his addresses to *Lady Emily*, a rich widow, who detests him, and favours *Colonel O'Donnellan*. A letter, which betrays this matrimonial design of *Delaval*, is found by *Cecily*, the daughter of *Fitzharding*, who has eloped with him from her father, under assurances of marriage, and lived for some time as his mistress. The detection of *Delaval's* treachery drives her from his roof, and in her wanderings through a forest, she meets a maniac, who threatens her with destruction for being a woman, and her infant, lest it may grow up in vice and ingratitude. The wretched maniac is her own father, who believes her dead, yet feels an undefinable attachment to the female who kneels to him for mercy. The keepers discover and seize him; his daughter appeals to *Old Stanley*, a person of fortune, who inhabits the house, once *Fitzharding's* property, to intercede with her father's keepers that she may be permitted to attend and soothe him under his affliction. In the mean time *Delaval*, who, on his father's death, has succeeded to a peerage, becomes a sincere penitent for the miseries he has brought upon *Fitzharding* and his daughter; and finding that she is protected by *Stanley*, commissions that gentleman to offer her his heart and hand: by the joint attentions of *Cecily*, *Stanley*, and his niece *Lady Emily*, the unfortunate father is recovered. He is introduced to an apartment in his own former mansion, where a scene is prepared that strikes at once upon his imagination, and restores his memory to its wonted power. After he has been suffered to gaze for some moments upon many well-known objects, a curtain is drawn aside, where, within the frame of a large picture, stands his daughter, leaning on her harp, in the white robes, and dark tresses, which he had so often contemplated with a parent's fondness. He acknowledges the likeness, but bewails her death; when suddenly her harp sounds—she sings an air to which he had been accustomed—and rushes into his arms now opened to receive her. Such is the story, with which, under a different form, our readers are probably well acquainted, but which, though it constitutes the principal subject, occupies but little of the action of this play. The Comedy consists of the adventures and manœuvres of four personages, to three of whom we have not yet adverted. *Lady Emily* has conversed at a masquerade with a certain *Sir H. Cholmondeley*, whom she has smitten, albeit under a masque, with a grievous affection for her person. The Baronet having hunted out her Ladyship's abode, indites a love letter, begging permission to visit her. Now there is domiciliated, under the same roof, the *Widow Belmour*, between whom and the aforesaid *Sir H. Cholmondeley*, there is carried on a law suit, which has descended to them from their parents, and brought with it no small share of mutual animosity, though it is of importance to remember, that they have never seen each other. *Lady Emily* having secured a gay Colonel for herself, can do no less than plot a little on behalf of her friend, the widow. She therefore speculates on bringing about a match between her and the masquerading Baronet; thus reversing the usual course of things, and *finishing* their disputes by marriage. But as they are known to boast of hating each other, they must be brought into contact with some address. *Lady Emily*, therefore, desires *Sir Henry* to assume, when he visits her, the name of *Grenville*,—while, under some plea of caprice or amusement, she prevails on *Mrs. Belmour* to personate herself. Here are certainly some good comic materials; but we cannot say much of the ability with which they have been wrought. The whole plot is developed in the first act, and little therefore left to expectation. The first and second, and half of the third, are insupportably tedious and unprofitable. The first scene of serious interest is the meeting between *Fitzharding* and his daughter, where YOUNG's performance was in the highest degree original and affecting. The first approach to genuine comedy was the interview (we think in the 4th act) between *O'Donnellan*, and *Sir Henry*, when the former is persuaded that the Baronet is his rival. This play has the good fortune to improve as it advances: the fourth and fifth acts make some amends for the tedium of the first and second; but we would repeat our recommendation, that the whole should be compressed into three. As for the characters,—they are all, but one, extremely common; and that one is so far from common as to be now a-days absolutely unnatural. The *Colonel O'Donnellan*, intended by the author, is a being of the last century—just as much as *Squire Western* would be called so, if thrust into a modern play.... *Colonel O'Donnellan*, however, such as he has been designed, is very fairly represented by Mr. JONES. The other characters were extremely well performed. Mrs. C. KEMBLE is an acquisition to any theatre; her dexterous and friendly widow, *Lady Emily*, is a genuine specimen of spirited and easy acting. Mr. C. KEMBLE is always seen to most advantage in comedy. His manner is gay and gentlemanly; and he is necessarily divested of those exaggerations of voice and action, into which his tragic efforts have so frequently betrayed him. YOUNG had little to do, but quite enough to make us lament how little. FAWCETT's character was equally below his level. Miss FOOTE played with much sweetness and feeling; but we think she might be exempted from the awkward addition which the netitious baby seemed to make to her wanderings in the wood. The play was full as well received as it deserved to be; but will never attain a lasting rank in the records of the English drama.

ii. *Theatrical Inquisitor, and Monthly Mirror* (1815): 478–80.

Tuesday, Dec. 12. —Mrs. Charles Kemble has this evening re-entered the list of candidates for dramatic fame in a double capacity, and certainly claims our warmest thanks for her endeavours to rescue the stage from that odium which has of late been cast upon it, owing to the miserable productions which have been brought forward by the managers, and encouraged by the ignorant mass of the public; she has presented us with a new comedy in five acts, called "Smiles and Tears["]; a piece of the *seconde ordre*, which deserves some commendation although possessing no very great powers of attraction. We feel ourselves called upon in this instance to bestow praise upon the intention, rather than upon the production of the Author; to see talent endeavouring to make its way through the host of buffooneries, which beset the stage on every side, and which has hitherto had such firm possession of our national theatre, is to us a most pleasing object.

We know not how far in the present instance we are justified in considering man and wife as one, but we presume this comedy to be the joint effort of Mr. and Mrs. C. Kemble; we entertain a very high respect for the abilities of the former, and shall ever be happy to see him meet with the encouragement he deserves: he possesses an education which cannot fail to prevent his committing any very gross error, but men of the first talents sometimes err; such appears to us the case respecting this comedy; from his superior knowledge of the French language, we confess we feel a little surprised that his own good sense should not have suggested to him the propriety of selecting some more imposing production, or rather, that he should not have pointed out to his cara sposa many pieces more calculated for the English stage than the one she has chosen.

Notwithstanding the plays of the French are, generally speaking, of a very light and flimsy description, yet some may be found of intrinsic merit. This production is what they term *Comédie larmoyante*; it has been rendered such by the union of one of Mrs. Opie's most affecting tales, with a frivolous little piece called *La suite d'un bal masqué*; the latter is the very epitome of French manners. A fashionable beau falling over head and ears in love with a lady of *ton* before he has ever seen her face; addressing *couplets* to the tip of her little finger, or the peculiar turn of her nose, and various other frivolities, are calculated to please at the *Français*, but something more is required on the boards of an English Theatre; that something Mrs. Charles Kemble has not exhibited in her new comedy. The incidents in "Smiles and Tears" are injudiciously blended together; they are by far too numerous; we are able to discover the drift of the *denouement* from the commencement, the performance thereby loses half the interest it would otherwise excite, and is consequently rendered heavy and insipid, the mind becomes fatigued, and we are induced to wish for the conclusion long before it actually takes place. Some pleasure may be derived from perusing a piece of this description, it is then at the option of the reader to pass over those parts where the dialogue is introduced for no other purpose than that of lengthening the scene; in representation it is quite the reverse; the observer is there compelled to endure a prolixity which has no other effect upon the mind than that of rendering the play extremely tedious.

iii. *British Lady's Magazine* 13 (1 January 1816): 58.

On the 12th December, a new comedy, under the title of "Smiles and Tears," was announced at this theatre. With eager curiosity, and we hope with candid expectations, we waited for the drawing up of the curtain to a *new comedy!* — Alas! alas! What shall we say? There is a line of the Prologue to Goldsmith's play of "She Stoops to Conquer," which we quote from memory:

> *"The Comic Muse, long sick, is now a-dying!"*

Verily, verily, we believe she is now, in real right earnest, *dead!* — A comedy! — Why, who was the wag that could have started the suggestion of writing a comedy upon the subject of Mrs. Opie's exquisitely pathetic tale of the "Father and Daughter?" One of the finest pictures of imagined woe that ever was drawn, to form the chief scene in a comedy! — Shall we proceed? Yes; — we must add, that, as a contrast to this tale of *tears*, the author has introduced a love-story. There is a certain Lady Emily, a lady of fashion, (or, as the phrase was in former times, a *fine lady*,) who is in love with an Irish officer, very jealous and very vain. A stratagem is contrived by Lady Emily, to introduce her friend, Mrs. Belmour, to Sir Henry Chumleigh, between whom and her ladyship there is a pending law-suit. The parties, thus brought togther under feigned names, are inspired with mutual affection; and the development of their real characters tends only to strengthen their attachment. This part of the comedy might possibly have been rendered productive of *smiles*, but there was little proof of that capability afforded. To be plain — the borrowed serious part of this drama was spoiled by distortion; and the comic part elicited no sparks of wit or humour.

"Maniac Father" (a melodrama based on Moncrieff's *The Lear of Private Life*) at the Bower Saloon in London, 5 August, 1850. By kind permission of the Michael R. Booth Theatre Collection, University of Newcastle, Australia.

Appendix F: The Lear of Private Life

[On 27 April 1820, W.T. Moncrieff's *The Lear of Private Life! or, Father and Daughter, a Domestic Drama* appeared at the Royal Coburg Theatre, London. Only a week earlier, the great Edmund Kean had triumphed as the mad King Lear, and London audiences still vividly remembered Ambrogetti's moving performance of the mad father in Paër's opera *Agnese*. Moncrieff's play marries the two earlier works, and Junius Brutus Booth "played the hero with liveliest success for fifty three nights" (see "Moncrieff" entry in the *Dictionary of National Biography*). The excerpts below show both the close adaptation of parts of Opie's text as well as the radical changes to other aspects of the tale that Moncrieff believed stage presentation required. Some minor name changes were also made: Fitzhenry becomes Fitzarden and Clifford becomes Alvanley; Agnes remains Agnes.]

I.

REMARKS,
TO THE SECOND EDITION.

WHO has not wept over MRS. OPIE's popular and pathetic story "Father and Daughter," upon which this piece is founded? It has been translated into almost every modern language, and dramatized at various Foreign Theatres, and has ever proved a fruitful source of interest and tears. The Italians have a Prose Drama on the subject, by Philippo Cæsari, and an Opera, "Agnese," by Luige Bonavoglio, composed by the celebrated Paer; the French have a Melo-Drama founded on it, and the powerful pathos of the story, has not been overlooked by the sensitive Germans: with the exception of its forming an Episode, in Mrs. C. Kemble's Comedy "Smiles and Tears," the present piece is the only English Drama to which it has given birth. In the leading incidents of this piece, no material deviations have been made from the original story, but such as were absolutely necessary for unity of action and dramatic effect. Ten months are supposed to have elapsed between the first and second acts, but that is a stretch of imagination, which, from the nature of the story, could not be avoided. The comic portions of the piece are not remarkable for strength or breadth, but they do not ill assort with the more serious part of it: they sufficiently relieve, without breaking in upon the sacred sorrow of the story, which would have rendered rude mirth out of place; they are simple, but natural. Ambrogetti, in the Father of the Italian Piece, had just been harrowing the town with a delineation of the distressful malady of the character so painfully true to nature, as to be almost too much for human feeling to witness; and Kean had sounded a mighty note of preparation for his appearance in the distracted Lear of Shakespeare. To take advantage of the interest excited by these circumstances, and adequately display the talents of Booth, then engaged at the Coburg, was the object of the Author in producing the Lear of Private Life, and as far as theatrical effect upon an audience went, his utmost expectations were fully satisfied. The piece had the advantage of being extremely well acted on its first representation. That highly talented, and very amiable woman, Mrs. W. Barrymore, sustained the character of Agnes; Miss Love, was the Emily; and Miss Watson, the Meriel: Roxby Beverley performed the simple hearted Gilbert; Coveney the Rattleton; and manager Davidge the old steward, Michaelmas, while the little great Booth, was himself the Fitzarden: had the eccentric Junius Brutus always acted as he did then, praise would have been superfluous, and censure fruitless: it must still be in the memory of the many who flocked to witness its representation, that neither the revolting fidelity of Ambrogetti's aberrations in Ubaldo, nor the terrific truth of Kean's ravings in Lear, drew down more tears, or awakened deeper sympathy, than did Booth's efforts in Fitzarden; the effect of his acting was as powerful and universal, as the pathetic eloquence of Corporal Trim on the death of young Master Bobby the fat Scene-Shifter was melted into sympathy; the burley Door-Keeper blubbered, while sobs in the pit and gallery, and hysterics in the boxes, sufficiently proved, that nature has an echo in the human heart to which she never speaks unanswered. Mrs. Opie well knew this fact when composing the tale that forms the ground work of this Drama, and did not act unwisely in discarding the adventitious and artificial woes of love, in all her stories, for the more genuine and stronger emotions, produced by the kindred feelings of relationship, and the sacred sympathies of nature's dearest ties: it was well said of her, that if we could convert the tears of pity into pearls, she would deserve the richest coronet of them that was ever bestowed by the hand of sympathy to grace the brows of genius. It is to be hoped her new connexion with the FRIENDS, will not stand in the way of her literary persuits, we shall account them any thing but *friends* if it does.

May, 1828.

2.

ACT II.

SCENE III.

—A Forest.—Lights down, and snow.—Evening.

Enter AGNES *and* CHILD, L. H.

Agnes. Darkness is gathering around me, and I have still four dreary miles of toil and wretchedness to travel before I reach my father's—how awful is this silence! A human voice would sound like rapture, and yet what voice is there I should not shrink to hear? In my happiest days I never entered this lone wood without a fearful awe, but, now, a wandering wretched outcast—a mother, without the sacred name of wife! Oh, it strikes tenfold terror to my soul! What's that? Fool, fool, it was but fancy! Alas! I was not always timid and irritable as now, but then I was not always guilty! My child, dear witness of my love and shame—I can no longer bear thee, no! no!—I sink! Ha! *(Sinks on the ground, placing her child on the trunk of a tree.—Storm rises.)* Where am I? *(recovering after pause.)* Ha, here still! a fearful storm too, gathering in the sky! *(It begins to snow.)* What will become of me? Thou sleep'st in peace, my child, nor heed'st the bitter blast— would I could sleep like thee: the storm increases, I must proceed before this falling snow conceals my track: protect me, Heaven! *(noise without.)* Ha! what noise is that? a man advancing? oh, let me fly! Yet, wherefore, it may be some poor wanderer like myself, desirous of companions. If so, I shall rejoice in the encounter.

Enter FITZARDEN, *from back, dressed in a dark rude suit, his head and neck bare, his beard neglected, his hair matted and dirty, one stocking fallen, exposing his naked leg; from his waist hangs a chain, which drags upon the ground.*

Agnes. Chains, gracious Heaven! surely it is some felon, and we may both be murdered! My boy, my boy, for what art thou reserved? *(aside.)*
Fitz. *(Looking round.)* I do not see them—rascals, cowards, I have escaped them, I have escaped them! ha! ha! ha!
Agnes. Some wretch escaped from justice; save me, Heaven! *(aside.)*
Fitz. Ha, I see them, they are there! But they do not see me. Softly,

softly, they pass me, they thread the thicket! Six sturdy rogues; I'll hide me in yon cowslip. Ha! they are gone. I'm free, I'm safe again! Where is my horse, I'll live no more in England!

Agnes. Some wretched maniac! how can I safely pass him? *(aside.)*

Fitz. No, no, I'll to Siberia: its snows less chaste than she,— will better shroud my child than these false flakes which melt as they surround me, like the world, and leave me cold and naked! Ha, a spy! *(Seeing Agnes, and tearing off a branch of a tree.)* Wretch, thou shalt perish: thus, thus, I strike!

Agnes. Oh, spare me! spare me! *(Sinks on her knee.)*

Fitz. A woman! and in my power! *(Lets the branch fall.)* 'tis well, or I would crush thee! now answer, hast thou seen them? I cannot see them; no, I have escaped them—rascals, cowards, I have escaped them. Ha! ha! ha! what have you got there?

Agnes. My child! Oh, do not harm my child!

Fitz. A child! strangle it, kill it, if thou'rt wise; I like not children—If we love them, do they not flee from us? if we trust them, do they not betray us? I had a child myself, but she is dead—they said she fled from me—fled from me with a lover—'twas false, she died; she was too good to leave the poor fond father who adored her. Besides, I saw her funeral. Dogs, liars as they are! Do not tell any one, I got away from them last night! and now am wandering here to seek her grave!

Agnes. Gracious God, what is it I forebode? It is, it must be he! I cannot bear this torture, this suspense: let me look closer—yes it is my father! *(Gives a wild scream and falls senseless at his feet—Fitzarden plays with the straw he has twined round his girdle, and laughs idiotically—the storm growing more violent—after a short pause, Agnes revives.)* Yes, 'tis too surely he—father! dear father!

Fitz. Ha, father, I am no father, the name is mockery! I was a father once, but she I loved fled from me—yes, deserted me, went off with the rank fiend, Seduction; would'st thou think it, and I loved her so tenderly, I held my heart's blood cheap to her—but still she left two precious comforters behind! Poverty and Despair, and I have banquetted with both.

Agnes. Oh, could'st thou see this sight, Alvanley! thou'dst—

Fitz. What, Alvanley! Monster! Robber! Murderer! where is he? give him to my eyes; I have two daggers, there shall drink his blood! Revenge hath been with me, and she hath promised to turn my grasp to iron when I meet him! Give me my daughter, monster! I will have no struggling, slave! My knee is on thy breast. Down,

down, and let me tread thy life out. There wretch, there! below
the surface of the earth I've crushed thee; and I can smile again!
ha! ha! ha!

Agnes. Horrible sight! can a whole life of tears wash out the deep
remembrance of this hour?   *[weeps bitterly.*

Fitz. Tears! in tears poor thing, poor thing—don't cry, don't cry! I
cannot cry, I have not cried for years! Not since my poor child
died—for she is dead, is she not? Come, come, come, you will
not leave me, will you?

Agnes. Leave you! Oh, never, never! I'll live, I'll die with you!

Fitz. True, true, yes she is dead, and we'll go seek her grave; the snow
has hidden it, but we shall find it soon. I say that snow's less fair,
less pure, less cold than her dear bosom; 'tis a brave winding
sheet—cold! cold! cold! We shall find it soon: a plain stone only,
and a little dust; Ha! those snow flakes, see, they mock at these
grey hairs—they say my child deserted me, and every other for
her sake must die. Prepare!

Agnes. Oh, father, spare me! Help, for mercy's sake.

A wild struggle, just as Fitzarden is overpowering Agnes.

Enter KEEPERS, *from* B. S. L. H.

Keep. Ha! have we caught you? Seize him!

Fitz. They are coming, they are coming; hide me, hide me! *(to Agnes.)*

Agnes. Oh, hear me, hear me! Leave him, I conjure you, to my care: he
is my father; you may safely trust him. Thus on my knee—
(kneels.)

Keep. Your father, young woman—and what then? you can do nothing with him! you should be thankful to us for taking him off
your hands.

Fitz. Don't let them tear me from you! *(aside to Agnes.)*

Keep. Your father; you are the daughter I suppose then, that brought
him to this pass.—Aye, aye, you may well weep, but your tears
come a little too late, my fine lady; come, boys, bring him along.

Agnes. You shall not tear him from me! I have deserted, left him once;
but now I'll die ere I resign him!

Fitz. Stand off—the first who stirs, my bolts shall lay him lifeless! Oh,
villains! murderers!

Agnes. Spare him for mercy's love, he is my father, I alone can cure
him. Leave him with me; and I will ever bless you!

Keep. A pretty joke indeed, we shall have the daughter as well as the father soon: I don't think there's a pin to choose between them. Come, lads, bring him along, we can bind his hands in the village.

Fitz. You shall have racks for this, when I am free.

Exit Fitzarden, borne off by Keepers, B. S. R. H.

Agnes. Inhuman men! I'll take my child, and follow at all hazards. *(Goes to the bank and finds her child insensible with the cold.)* Ha! cold and sleeping—it is the sleep of death! Monster, that I am! destroyer of my child, as well as father! But it perhaps is not too late. My curse may not be yet completed. My child may yet recover! Oh, let me fly to gain him warmth and succour. Unhappy Agnes! when will thy cup of misery be filled?

[Staggers off with child. R. H.

3.

ACT III.

SCENE IV.

A Landscape.

Enter ALVANLEY, R. H. *and* ADDER. L. H.

Alvan. It is but too clear, Agnes and her child have perished; and I, wretch, am her murderer!

Adder. This scarf and veil I found in a neighbouring forest, on the banks of a river, in whose cold bosom she has doubtless sought repose.

Alvan. No doubt, no doubt, she but visited the scene of her crime, to expiate it: her father mad and impoverished herself scorned and deserted by her seducer! What firmness could survive it? What now remains for me, but to search for her poor remains, and in a splendid monument perpetuate her virtues, and my villany—her repentance, and my despair.

Adder. Seek some relief—

Alvan. Aye, rush from folly to folly: mix with the heartless world, the pale cold form of Agnes for ever at my side—hear her accusing voice in every breeze, see her reproachful look at every board—poisoning my pleasures—shutting out my peace—drag through a lingering round of weary, hopeless, years, and die the execrable victim of my vices, with the cor[r]oding consciousness that Agnes' parting breath breathed curses on me. Oh, 'tis too much, my soul shrinks from the prospect! One bold step ends this anguish: she has but gone before, and I will follow. Agnes, I come! *(Raises a pistol to his head.)*

Enter RATTLETON and EMILY. L. H.

Rat. Hold, madman! what is it you would do? Ha, Alvanley! the seducer of Miss Agnes— *(Recognizing him.)*
Alvan. Who now would die for her, as she has died for him.
Emily. Agnes dead! forbid it, Heaven! she lives to bless us all.
Alvan. What! Agnes living? then I'm not a murderer: thank God, thank God for that. *(Drops pistol.)* Oh, my friends, speak for me, plead for me, I implore; I am a penitent, heart-broken man! Every bar to our union is removed. Let me make every reparation in my power, and restore her to that rank in society from which my guilt seduced her.
Emily. This looks like penitence: she comes! Let her not see you yet!
Alvan. But will you promise?—
Emily. I will, I will; you must assist me, Rattleton.
Rat. Assist you, dearest Emily—aye, that I will. I am a thoughtless volatile fellow, ready to laugh at every folly as it rises: but though many may say that I have very little head, I trust no one can deny I have a heart. She comes, and with our father. This way, leave all to Emily; we'll wait your signal.

[Exit Rattleton and Alvanley. R. H.

Emily. Blessed sight! he once again her friend, the world will quickly follow!

Enter AGNES and GOODALL. L. H.

My dear, dear, Agnes! *(Embracing her.)* I cannot wait your sanction to embrace her, Sir. *(to Goodall.)*
Good. No, no, affection will not be schooled; one warm greeting of the heart is worth fifty hollow ones of the hand; but you have my full permission. We have seen Fitzarden, he has been moved to tears.
Agnes. But he did not recollect me:—
Good. He will in time; some gleams of recollection often broke upon him; so long accustomed to regard you dead, he cannot all at once resign the thought; besides, his present habitation, your sad

appearance, altered by grief and suffering; this menial dress — all, all forbad his perfect recognition. A scheme has flashed upon me: I will have his favorite room in my house altered to represent his cell, will change his dress while sleeping and convey him thither unknowing: have you attired as you were wont to be — take his senses by surprise: thoughts of past times will all recur again, he'll know you, bless you, and make all of us happy.

Agnes. Goodness and virtue meed you.

Good. I'll about the preparations immediately; walk you slowly down to my house with Emily, and by that time every thing shall be completed.

[Exit Goodall. L. H.

Agnes. With what a beating heart I wait the event; could I but once more hear him call me by my name, and bless me with his forgiveness, I should die in peace; and something tells me my hopes will not be vain. We yet may pass our days in peace together, estimable Emily.

Emily. Should your father recover, my dear Agnes, but one thing will be wanting to complete your happiness! — Alvanley's repentance and reparation.

Agnes. Oh, name him not — he is a villain!

Emily. Yes, but a repentant one.

Agnes. He is the murderer of my peace and honor!

Emily. But still he is the father of your child.

Agnes. He is my seducer!

Emily. He will be — your husband.

Agnes. My husband! is he not bound unto another?

Emily. No, every obstacle to your union is removed: his father dead: his heart alive to virtue.

Agnes. Is he not in London, brooding o'er fresh villany?

Emily. No, he is here.

Agnes. Here!

Enter RATTLETON *and* ALVANLEY, *rushing out.* R. H.

Alvan. Yes, at your feet, *(Kneels.)* Agnes, my adored, my injured Agnes! can you forgive a wretch like me — the source of all your errors, all your woes?

Agnes. Alvanley, cruel, guilty, wretched, penitent, Alvanley! partner of my crimes! — my heart —

Rat. I'll not have another word said, your hearts are agreed on the subject, and whatever you may say doesn't signify a button. Alvanley, I wish you joy in this double accession to your honors, and your honor; Agnes, I shall soon wish you joy on your nuptials, for you shall be married directly. Emily and I have been foolish enough to commit matrimony, and we must positively have somebody to keep us in countenance. But we must off to old dad in law's, he will be waiting for us. No words; this way, this way. Come, Emily.

[*Exeunt Rat. & Em. L. H.*

Alvan. My heart's too full for thanks — Agnes.
Agnes. Truant! Alvanley! Husband!

[*Exeunt Alvanley and Agnes L.H.*

4.

ACT III.

SCENE V.

The favorite apartment of Fitzarden decorated with Pictures—a frame in centre, with steps leading up to it, a green baize before it—Fitzarden discovered asleep on a sofa—Goodall, Rattleton, and Emily, behind the sofa watching him—the Keeper standing on the opposite side.

Good. There, that will do, that will do; have you every thing ready?
Rat. Yes — do you think he will be waking soon?
Keep. 'Tis near his time, sleep is mechanical with him: it has been rather a habit than otherwise, of late.
Good. Away, away, then; *(Exit Keeper. L. H.)* if I don't prove a good doctor in this case, I'll never take out a diploma for insanity, but confess myself more mad than my patient. We will commence operations directly: see, he arouses himself.

[*Fitzarden awakes.*

Fitz. Sleeping! would I could sleep like her! in her lone cell, she sleeps the sleep of death; how long will this continue? I had a dream of days long past, bright days! would it would come again. Great Heaven! what change, what place is this? Oh, I should know this spot: is reason dawning, or is madness coming? No cell, no chains, no straw? no, no, I am not mad! Who's that, who's that?
Rat. A friend!

Fitz. Have I a friend? No, no! She was snatched from me by the damned artifices of a human fiend! who called himself my friend. No, no! 'tis false, I have no friend!

Good. Alvanley, stung by remorse, and eager to repay the wrongs he's wrought you, now comes to give her to your arms again, and crave your blessing on her union.

Fitz. For shame, for shame! old man! falsehood but ill becomes that hoary head: age should be mate to truth!

Good. By heaven, I——

Fitz. You mock me, Sir. I tell you she is dead, poor Agnes. Yes, cold! cold! cold! Oh! that I could again behold her!

Emily. (Drawing back the curtain, and discovering Agnes behind seated at harp.) Has not this portrait some resemblance to her?

Fitz. Ha, what do I see, the shade of Agnes? Father of mercies, do not thus deceive me!—In pity mock not thus a wretched father—cheat not my eyes with phantasies of her I ne'er shall see again.—Bring not thus back bright memories of past joys, gone, lost for ever!—shut not out returning reason.—Still there, then I must fly—I feel despair! rage! madness! agony! all, all, returning: they rise, they rave within me! One last, *last,* look—and thus I tear myself away from this bright mockery! proof to the sorceries that would ensnare my soul! Yes, yes there is no tarrying here. Away! away!

> [*As he is rushing off,* R.H. *Agnes plays and sings,*
> *"Tears such as tender fathers shed, &c"*

That voice! that song! and yet, no, no! but still that form! oh, tell me art thou real or sent by hell to tantalize my soul!

Agnes. (Rising in the frame.) Father! beloved father!

Fitz. Ha, 'tis no illusion! each sense assures me.—My heart's throbs confirmation of their truth.—Oh, bliss beyond mortality! all, all proclaim thee living! I know, I feel 'tis thou; my long-lost child, my much-loved, erring and forgiven Agnes!

They rush into each others arms, she falls then at his feet, and embraces his knees—Alvanley, followed by Gilbert and Meriel, enters with the child, and kneels by Agnes.—Picture.—The Curtain falls to music.

Appendix G: Songs and Airs

In the first edition of *The Father and Daughter* Opie included as poems a number of works which had already been printed and circulating as song lyrics for melodies composed or arranged by Edward Biggs. He, along with the opera singer Viganoni, acted as a voice coach for Opie, who by this time was establishing a reputation as a performer. In 1807 a biography in *The Cabinet; or, Monthly Report of Polite Literature* noted that Opie "may be said to have been unrivalled in that kind of singing in which she more particularly delighted. Those only who have heard her, can conceive the effect which she produced, in the performance of her own ballads.... Mrs. Opie ... created a style of singing of her own, which though polished and improved by art and cultivation, was founded on that power which she appears pre-eminently to possess, of awakening the tender sympathies and pathetic feelings of the mind" ("Mrs. Opie," *The Cabinet* 217). Most of her songs were published by Robert Birchall, who also ran a "Musical Circulating Library": in an age when women were expected to both play and sing, Amelia Opie's songs, with their emphasis on the performance of affective pathos, were undoubtedly popular items in the repertoire of many young ladies.

1. "A Hindustàni Girl's Song," Air III of *A Second Set of Hindoo Airs*, reproduced by permission of the British Library.

2. "A Mad Song," Song VI of *Six Songs ... Dedicated to the Right Honorable Lady Willoughby De Eresby*, reproduced by permission of the Syndics of Cambridge University Library.

3. "The Orphan Boy's Tale" reproduced by permission of the British Library.

A HINDUSTÀNI GIRL'S SONG,

'Tis thy will, and I must leave thee.

ADAPTED by MR. BIGGS.

Air III.

Ent.d at Stat.rs Hall.   Printed for R.t Birchall 133 New Bond Street.   Price 1.s

'Tis thy will, and I must leave thee, O then best belov'd farewell!

I forbear lest I should grieve thee, half my heart felt pangs to tell.

N.B. The Melody of this plaintive Air, is but little known, among the Hindoos, and is said to have originated very lately from the following circumstance:

An European, previous to his departure for England, being desirous of restoring to her Parents, an Hindoo Girl, who had lived for some years in his family; sent her to them, in a Palanquin, some days journey up the Country. The Girl, was extremely attached to her Master, and was so affected at parting with him, that, according to the relation of the bearers of the Palanquin, she could not be prevailed on, to receive any sustenance during the journey, and was incessantly singing this melody, (which they were able to retain) to words expressive of her attachment; which are here, so well imitated by M.rs OPIE.

Soon a british fair will charm thee, thou, alas! her smiles must woo,

but tho' she to rapture warm thee, don't forget thy poor HINDOO.

2

Well I know this happy beauty,
Soon thy envied bride will shine;
But will she by anxious duty,
Prove a passion warm as mine.
If to rule be her ambition,
And her own desires pursue;
Thou'lt recall my fond submission,
And regret thy poor HINDOO!

3

Born perhaps to rank and splendour,
Will she deign to wait on thee;
And those soft attentions render,
Thou so oft hast prais'd in me.
Yet, why doubt her care to please thee.
Thou must every heart subdue;
I am sure each nymph that sees thee,
Loves thee, like thy poor HINDOO!

4

No — ah! — no! — tho' from thee parted,
Other nymphs would peace obtain;
But thy LOLA, broken hearted,
Ne'er, O ne'er will smile again:
O! how fast, from thee they bear me,
Faster still, shall death pursue;
But 'tis well — death will endear me,
And thou'lt mourn thy poor HINDOO!

SONG. VI.
A Mad Song.
COMPOSED by MR BIGGS.

Price 1. 6

RECIT.vo

Ha! what is this that on my brow presses with such a weight of power, HENRY they say was forc'd to go to Heaven to fix our bridal hour; Then on his Tomb why should I sorrow. He's gone but he'll return to-morrow but he'll return to-morrow.

20

Recᵛᵒ Pia:
But all's not right in this poor heart, yet why should
Recᵛᵒ Arpeggio

a tempo
I his loss de _ _ plore! it was in _ _ deed a pang to
a tempo e senz' arpeggio

più moto
part, But when he, comes he'll rove no more and

all and all to-day can laugh can laugh at sorrow, when

sure of being blest to-morrow, of being blest to-morrow.

Poor foo - lish Child! How pleas'd was I, when News of Nelson's Vic'try came, along the crowded Streets to fly, And see the light.ed windows flame? To force me home my Mo _ ther sought __ She could not bear to see my Joy; for with my Fa_ther's life 'twas bought, And made me a poor ORPHAN BOY! The Peoples shouts were long and loud; My Mother, shud'ring, clos'd her ears: "Re _ joice, re _ joice," still

cry'd the croud—My Mother answer'd with her tears. "Oh why do

tears steal down your cheek", cry'd I, "whilst o___thers

shout with joy?" She kiss'd me; and in ac__cents weak, She

call'd me her Poor ORPHAN BOY! What is an ORPHAN BOY?" I

said; When sudden___ly she gasp'd for breath, And her eyes

clos'd! I shriek'd for aid; But, ah! her eyes were clos'd in Death!

Appendix H: Chastity

1. From Hannah More, "On the Danger of Sentimental or Romantic Connexions," *Essays on Various Subjects, Principally Designed for Young Ladies* (1777)

THE present age may be termed, by way of distinction, the age of sentiment, a word which, in the implication it now bears, was unknown to our plain ancestors. Sentiment is the varnish of virtue to conceal the deformity of vice; and it is not uncommon for the same persons to make a jest of religion, to break through the most solemn ties and engagements, to practise every art of latent fraud and open seduction, and yet to value themselves on speaking and writing *sentimentally*....

ERROR is never likely to do so much mischief as when it disguises its real tendency, and puts on an engaging and attractive appearance. Many a young woman, who would be shocked at the imputation of an intrigue, is extremely flattered at the idea of a sentimental connexion, though perhaps with a dangerous and designing man, who, by putting on this mask of plausibility and virtue, disarms her of her prudence, lays her apprehensions asleep, and involves her in misery; misery the more inevitable because unsuspected. For she who apprehends no danger, will not think it necessary to be always upon her guard; but will rather invite than avoid the ruin which comes under so specious and so fair a form.

SUCH an engagement will be infinitely dearer to her vanity than an avowed and authorized attachment; for one of these sentimental lovers will not scruple very seriously to assure a credulous girl, that her unparalleled merit entitles her to the adoration of the whole world, and that the universal homage of mankind is nothing more than the unavoidable tribute extorted by her charms. No wonder then she should be easily prevailed on to believe, that an individual is captivated by perfections which might enslave a million. But she should remember, that he who endeavours to intoxicate her with adulation, intends one day most effectually to humble her. For an artful man has always a secret design to pay himself in future for every present sacrifice. And this prodigality of praise, which he now appears to lavish with such thoughtless profusion, is, in fact, a sum œconomically laid out to supply his future necessities: of this sum he keeps an exact estimate, and at some distant day promises himself the most exorbitant interest for it. If he has address and conduct, and the object of his pursuit much vanity, and some sensibility, he seldom fails of success; for so powerful will be his ascendency over her mind, that she will soon adopt his notions and opinions. Indeed, it is more than probable she possessed most of them before, having gradually acquired them in her initiation into the sentimental character. To maintain that character with dignity and propriety, it is necessary she should entertain the most elevated ideas of disproportionate alliances, and disinterested love; and consider fortune, rank, and reputation, as mere chimerical distinctions and vulgar prejudices.

THE lover, deeply versed in all the obliquities of fraud, and skilled to wind himself into every avenue of the heart which indiscretion has left unguarded, soon discovers on which side it is most accessible. He avails himself of this weakness by addressing her in a language exactly consonant to her own ideas. He attacks her with her own weapons, and opposes rhapsody to sentiment. — He professes so sovereign a contempt for the paltry concerns of money, that she thinks it her duty to reward him for so generous a renunciation. Every plea he artfully advances of his own unworthiness, is considered by her as a fresh demand which her gratitude must answer. And she makes it a point of honour to sacrifice to him that fortune which he is too noble to regard. These professions of humility are the common artifice of the vain, and these protestations of generosity the refuge of the rapacious. And among its many smooth mischiefs, it is one of the sure and successful frauds of sentiment, to affect the most frigid indifference to those external and pecuniary advantages, which it is its great and real object to obtain.... (78-83)

FATHERS *have flinty hearts*, is an expression worth an empire, and is always used with peculiar emphasis and enthusiasm.... (90)

BUT young people never shew their folly and ignorance more conspicuously, than by this over-confidence in their own judgment, and this haughty disdain of the opinion of those who have known more days. Youth has a quickness of apprehension, which it is very apt to mistake for an acuteness of penetration. But youth, like cunning, though very conceited, is very short-sighted, and never more so than when it disregards the instructions of the wise, and the admonitions of the aged. The same vices and follies influenced the human heart in their day, which influence it now, and nearly in the same manner.... (93-94)

2. Catharine Macaulay, from LETTER XXIV, *Flattery—Chastity—Male Rakes* in Part I, *Letters on Education* (1790)

But the most difficult part of female education, is to give girls such an idea of chastity, as shall arm their reason and their sentiments on the side of this useful virtue. For I believe there are more women of understanding led into acts of imprudence by the ignorance, the prejudices, and the false craft of those by whom they are educated, than from any other cause founded either in nature or in chance. You may train up a docile idiot to any mode of thinking or acting, as may best suit the intended purpose; but a reasoning being will scan over your propositions, and if they find them grounded in falsehood, they will reject them with disdain. When you tell a girl of spirit and reflection that chastity is a sexual virtue, and the want of it a sexual vice, she will be apt to examine into the principles of religion, morals, and the reason of things, in order to satisfy herself on the truth of your proposition. And when, after the strictest enquiries, she finds nothing that will warrant the confining the proposition to a particular sense, she will entertain doubts either of your wisdom or your sincerity; and regarding you either as a deceiver or a fool, she will transfer her confidence to the companion of the easy vacant hour, whose compliance with her opinions can flatter her vanity. Thus left to Nature, with an unfortunate biass on her mind, she will fall a victim to the first plausible being who has formed a design on her person. Rousseau is so sensible of this truth, that he quarrels with human reason, and would put her out of the question in all considerations of duty. But this is being as great a fanatic in morals, as some are in religion; and I should much doubt the reality of that duty which would not stand the test of fair enquiry; beside, as I intend to breed my pupils up to act a rational part in the world, and not to fill up a niche in the seraglio of a sultan, I shall certainly give them leave to use their reason in all matters which concern their duty and happiness, and shall spare no pains in the cultivation of this only sure guide to virtue. I shall inform them of the great utility of chastity and continence; that the one preserves the body in health and vigor, and the other, the purity and independence of the mind, without which it is impossible to possess virtue or happiness. I shall intimate, that the great difference now beheld in the external consequences which follow the deviations from chastity in the two sexes, did in all probability arise from women having been considered as the mere property of men; and, on this account had no right to dispose of their own persons: that policy adopted this difference, when the plea of property had been given up; and it was still preserved in society from the unruly licentiousness of the men, who, finding no obstacles in the delicacy of the other sex, continue to set at defiance both divine and moral law, and by mutual support and general opinion to use their natural freedom with impunity. I shall observe, that this state of things renders the situation of females, in their individual capacity very precarious; for the strength which Nature has given to the passion of love, in order to serve her purposes, has made it the most ungovernable propensity of any which attends us. The snares therefore, that are continually laid for women, by persons who run no risk in compassing their seduction, exposes them to continual danger; whilst the implacability of their own sex, who fear to give up any advantages which a superior prudence, or even its appearances, give them, renders one false step an irretrievable misfortune. That, for these reasons, coquettry in women is as dangerous as it is dishonorable. That a coquet commonly finds her own perdition, in the very flames which she raises to consume others; and that if any thing can excuse the baseness of female seduction, it is the baits which are flung out by women to entangle the affections, and excite the passions of men.

I know not what you may think of my method, Hortensia, which I must acknowledge to carry the stamp of singularity; but for my part, I am sanguine enough to expect to turn out of my hands a careless, modest beauty, grave, manly, noble, full of strength and majesty; and carrying about her an ægis sufficiently powerful to defend her against the sharpest arrow that ever was shot from Cupid's bow. A woman, whose virtue will not be of the kind to wrankle into an inveterate malignity against her own sex for faults which she even encourages in the men, but who, understanding the principles of true religion and morality, will regard chastity and truth as indispensible qualities in virtuous characters of either sex; whose justice will incline her to extend her benevolence to the frailties of the fair as circumstances invite, and to manifest her resentment against the underminers of female happiness; in short, a woman who will not take a male rake either for a husband or a friend. And let me tell you, Hortensia, if women had as much regard for the virtue of chastity as in some cases they pretend to have, a reformation would long since have taken place in the world; but whilst they continue to cherish immodesty in the men, their bitter persecution of their own sex will not save them from the imputation of those concealed propensities with which they are accused by Pope, and other severe satirists on the sex. (218-22)

3. From William Godwin, Chapter IX, *Memoirs of the Author of A Vindication of the Rights of Woman* (1798)

I am now led, by the progress of the story, to the last branch of her history, the connection between Mary and myself. And this I shall relate with the same simplicity that has pervaded every other part of my narrative. If there ever were any motives of prudence or delicacy, that could impose a qualification upon the story, they are now over. They could have no relation but to factitious rules of decorum. There are no circumstances of her life, that, in the judgement of honour and reason, could brand her with disgrace. Never did there exist a human being, that needed, with less fear, expose all their actions, and call upon the universe to judge them....

The partiality we conceived for each other, was in that mode, which I have always regarded as the purest and most refined style of love. It grew with equal advances in the mind of each.... There was, as I have already said, no period of throes and resolute explanation attendant on the tale. It was friendship melting into love. Previously to our mutual declaration, each felt half-assured, yet each felt a certain trembling anxiety to have assurance complete.

Mary rested her head upon the shoulder of her lover, hoping to find a heart with which she might safely treasure her world of affection; fearing to commit a mistake, yet, in spite of her melancholy experience, fraught with that generous confidence, which, in a great soul, is never extinguished. I had never loved till now; or, at least, had never nourished a passion to the same growth, or met with an object so consummately worthy.

We did not marry. It is difficult to recommend any thing to indiscriminate adoption, contrary to the established rules and prejudices of mankind; but certainly nothing can be so ridiculous upon the face of it, or so contrary to the genuine march of sentiment, as to require the overflowing of the soul to wait upon a ceremony, and that which, wherever delicacy and imagination exist, is of all things most sacredly private, to blow a trumpet before it, and to record the moment when it has arrived at its climax.

There were however other reasons why we did not immediately marry. Mary felt an entire conviction of the propriety of her conduct. It would be absurd to suppose that, with a heart withered by desertion, she was not right to give way to the emotions of kindness which our intimacy produced, and to seek for that support in friendship and affection, which could alone give pleasure to her heart, and peace to her meditations. It was only about six months since she had resolutely banished every thought of Mr Imlay; but it was at least eighteen that he ought to have been banished, and would have been banished, had it not been for her scrupulous pertinacity in determining to leave no measure untried to regain him. Add to this, that the laws of etiquette ordinarily laid down in these cases, are essentially absurd, and that the sentiments of the heart cannot submit to be directed by the rule and the square. But Mary had an extreme aversion to be made the topic of vulgar discussion; and, if there be any weakness in this, the dreadful trials through which she had recently passed, may well plead in its excuse. She felt she had been too much, and too rudely spoken of, in the former instance; and she could not resolve to do any thing that should immediately revive that painful topic.

For myself, it is certain that I had for many years regarded marriage with so well-grounded an apprehension, that, notwithstanding the partiality for Mary that had taken possession of my soul, I should have felt it very difficult, at least in the present stage of our intercourse, to have resolved on such a measure. Thus, partly from similar, and partly from different motives, we felt alike in this, as we did perhaps in every other circumstance that related to our intercourse. (148-57)

4. From Hannah More, "On the Effects of Influence," *Strictures on the Modern System of Female Education* (1799)

Novels, which chiefly used to be dangerous in one respect, are now become mischievous in a thousand. They are continually shifting their ground, and enlarging their sphere, and are daily becoming vehicles of wider mischief. Sometimes they concentrate their force, and are at once employed to diffuse destructive politics, deplorable profligacy, and impudent infidelity. Rousseau was the first popular dispenser of this complicated drug, in which the deleterious infusion was strong, and the effect proportionably fatal. For he does not attempt to seduce the affections but through the medium of principles. He does not paint an innocent woman, ruined, repenting, and restored; but with a far more mischievous refinement, he annihilates the value of chastity, and with pernicious subtlety attempts to make his heroine appear almost more amiable without it. He exhibits a virtuous woman, the victim not of temptation but of reason, not of vice but of sentiment, not of passion but of conviction; and strikes at the very root of honour by elevating a crime into a principle. With a metaphysical sophistry the most plausible, he debauches the heart of woman, by cherishing her vanity in the erection of a system of male virtues, to which, with a lofty dereliction of those that are her more peculiar and characteristic praise, he tempts her to aspire; powerfully insinuating, that to this splendid system chastity does not necessarily belong: thus corrupting the judgement and bewildering the understanding, as the most effectual way to inflame the imagination and deprave the heart.

The rare mischief of this author consists in his power of seducing by falsehood those who love truth, but whose minds are still wavering, and whose principles are not yet formed. He allures the warmhearted to embrace vice, not because they prefer vice, but because he gives to vice so natural an air of virtue: and ardent and enthusiastic youth, too confidently trusting in their integrity and in their teacher, will be undone, while they fancy they are indulging in the noblest feelings of their nature.... (33-34)

Some of our recent popular publications have adopted and enlarged all the mischiefs of this school, and the principal evil arising from them is, that the virtues they exhibit are almost more dangerous than the vices. The chief materials out of which these delusive systems are framed, are characters who practise superfluous acts of generosity, while they are trampling on obvious and commanded duties; who combine inflated sentiments of honour with actions the most flagitious; a high tone of self-confidence, with a perpetual breach of self-denial: pathetic apostrophes to the passions, but no attempt to resist them. They teach, that chastity is only individual attachment; that no duty exists which is not prompted by feeling; that impulse is the main spring of virtuous actions, while laws and religion are only unjust restraints; the former imposed by arbitrary men, the latter by the absurd prejudices of the timorous and unenlightened conscience.... (35)

But the most fatal part of the system to that class whom I am addressing is, that even in those works which do not go all the lengths of treating marriage as an unjust infringement on liberty, and a tyrannical deduction from general happiness; yet it commonly happens that the hero or heroine, who has practically violated the letter of the seventh commandment, and continues to live in the allowed violation of its spirit, is painted as so amiable and so benevolent, so tender or so brave; and the temptation is represented as so *irresistible*, (for all these philosophers are fatalists,) the predominant and cherished sin is so filtered and purged of its pollutions, and is so sheltered and surrounded, and relieved with shining qualities, that the innocent and impressible young reader is brought to lose all horror of the awful crime in question, in the complacency she feels for the engaging virtues of the criminal.... (38)

About the same time that this first attempt at representing an adulress in an exemplary light was made by a German dramatist, which forms an æra in manners; a direct vindication of adultery was for the first time attempted by a *woman*, a professed admirer and imitator of the German suicide Werter. *The female Werter*, as she is styled by her biographer, asserts, in a work intitled "The Wrongs of Women," that adultery is justifiable, and that the restrictions placed on it by the laws of England constitute one of the *Wrongs of Women....* (48)

But let us take comfort. These projects are not yet generally realised. These atrocious principles are not yet adopted into common practice. Though corruptions seem with a confluent tide to be pouring in upon us from every quarter, yet there is still left among us a discriminating judgement. Clear and strongly marked distinctions between right and wrong still subsist. While we continue to cherish this sanity of mind, the case is not desperate. Though that crime, the growth of which always exhibits the most irrefragable proof of the dissoluteness of public manners; though that crime, which cuts up order and virtue by the roots, and violates the sanctity of vows, is awfully increasing,

> 'Till senates seem,
> For purpose of empire less conven'd
> Than to release the adult'ress from her bonds;

yet, thanks to the surviving efficacy of a holy religion, to the operation of virtuous laws, and the energy and unshaken integrity with which these laws are *now* administered; and still more perhaps to a standard of morals which continues in force, when the principles which sanctioned it are no more; this crime, in the female sex at least, is still held in just abhorrence: if it be practiced, it is not honourable; if it be committed, it is not justified; we do not yet affect to palliate its turpitude; as yet it hides its abhorred head in lurking privacy; and reprobation *hitherto* follows its publicity.

But on YOUR exerting your influence, with just application and increasing energy, it may in no small degree depend whether this corruption shall still continue to be resisted. For, from admiring to adopting, the step is short, and the progress rapid; and it is in the moral as in the natural world, the motion, in the case of minds as well as of bodies, is accelerated on a nearer approach to the centre to which they are tending.

O ye to whom this address is particularly directed! an awful charge is, in this instance, committed to your hands; as you shrink from it or discharge it, you promote or injure the honour of your daughters and the happiness of your sons, of both which you are the depositaries. And, while you resolutely persevere in making a stand against the encroachments of this crime, suffer not your firmness to be shaken by that affectation of charity, which is growing into a general substitute for principle. Abuse not so noble a quality as Christian candour, by misemploying it in instances to which it does not apply. Pity the wretched woman you dare not countenance; and bless HIM who has "made you to differ." If unhappily she be your relation or friend, anxiously watch for the period when she shall be deserted by her betrayer; and see if, by your Christian offices, she can be snatched from a perpetuity of vice. But if, through the Divine blessing on your patient endeavours, she should ever be awakened to remorse, be not anxious to restore the forlorn penitent to that society against whose laws she has so grievously offended; and remember, that her soliciting such a restoration, furnishes but too plain a proof that she is not the penitent your partiality would believe; since penitence is more anxious to make its peace with Heaven than with the world. Joyfully would a truly contrite spirit commute an earthly for an everlasting reprobation! To restore a criminal to public society, is perhaps to tempt her to repeat her crime, or to deaden her repentance for having committed it; while to restore a strayed soul to God will add lustre to your Christian character, and brighten your eternal crown. (51-55)

Appendix I: Coquetry

1. Joseph Addison, *The Spectator* No. 281, Tuesday, 22 January 1712

Pectoribus inhians spirantia consulit exta. — Virg.
[Virgil, *Aeneid*, iv.64: "And anxiously the panting Entrails views."
Dryden]

HAVING already given an Account of the Dissection of a *Beau's Head*, with the several Discoveries made on that Occasion; I shall here, according to my Promise, enter upon the Dissection of a *Coquet's Heart*, and communicate to the Publick such Particularities as we observed in that curious Piece of Anatomy.

I should perhaps have waved this Undertaking, had not I been put in mind of my Promise by several of my unknown Correspondents, who are very importunate with me to make an Example of the Coquet, as I have already done of the Beau. It is therefore in Compliance with the Request of Friends, that I have looked over the Minutes of my former Dream, in order to give the Publick an exact Relation of it, which I shall enter upon without further Preface.

OUR Operator, before he engaged in this visionary Dissection, told us, that there was Nothing in his Art more difficult, than to lay open the Heart of a Coquet, by reason of the many Labyrinths and Recesses which are to be found in it, and which do not appear in the Heart of any other Animal.

HE desired us first of all to observe the *Pericardium*, or outward Case of the Heart, which we did very attentively; and by the Help of our Glasses discerned in it Millions of little Scars, which seem'd to have been occasioned by the Points of innumerable Darts and Arrows, that from Time to Time had glanced upon the outward Coat; though we could not discover the smallest Orifice, by which any of them had entered and pierced the inward Substance.

EVERY Smatterer in Anatomy knows, that this *Pericardium*, or Case of the Heart, contains in it a thin reddish Liquor, supposed to be bred from the Vapours which exhale out of the Heart, and being stopt here, are condensed into this watry Substance. Upon examining this Liquor, we found that it had in it all the Qualities of that Spirit which is made Use of in the Thermometer, to shew the Change of Weather.

NOR must I here omit an Experiment one of the Company assured us he himself had made with this Liquor, which he found in great Quantity about the Heart of a Coquet whom he had formerly dissected. He affirmed to us, that he had actually enclosed it in a small Tube made after the manner of a Weather-Glass; but that instead of acquainting him with the Variations of the Atmosphere, it showed him the Qualities of those Persons who entered the Room where it stood. He affirmed also, that it rose at the Approach of a Plume of Feathers, an embroidered Coat, or a Pair of fringed Gloves; and that it fell as soon as an ill-shaped Perriwig, a clumsy pair of Shooes, or an unfashionable Coat came into his House: Nay, he proceeded so far as to assure us, that upon his Laughing aloud when he stood by it, the Liquor mounted very sensibly, and immediately sunk again upon his looking serious. In short, he told us, that he knew very well by this Invention whenever he had a Man of Sense or a Coxcomb in his Room.

HAVING cleared away the *Pericardium*, or the Case and Liquor above-mentioned, we came to the Heart itself. The outward Surface of it was extremely slippery, and the *Mucro*, or Point, so very cold withal, that upon endeavouring to take hold of it, it glided through the Fingers like a smooth Piece of Ice.

THE Fibres were turned and twisted in a more intricate and perplexed Manner than they are usually found in other Hearts; insomuch, that the whole Heart was wound up together like a Gordian Knot, and must have had very irregular and unequal Motions, whilst it was employed in its Vital Function.

ONE Thing we thought very observable, namely, that upon examining all the Vessels which came into it or issued out of it, we could not discover any Communication that it had with the Tongue.

WE could not but take Notice likewise, that several of those little Nerves in the Heart which are affected by the Sentiments of Love, Hatred, and other Passions, did not descend to this before us from the Brain, but from the Muscles which lie about the Eye.

UPON weighing the Heart in my Hand, I found it to be extreamly light, and consequently very hollow; which I did not wonder at when upon looking into the Inside of it, I saw Multitudes of Cells and Cavities running one within another, as our Historians describe the Appartments of *Rosamond's* Bower. Several of these little Hollows were stuffed with innumerable Sorts of Trifles, which I shall forbear giving any particular Account of, and shall therefore only take Notice of what lay first and uppermost, which upon our unfolding it and applying our Microscope to it appeared to be a Flame-coloured Hood. [In #265, 3 January 1712, Addison comments on the fashion of wearing hoods of various colours: "When *Melesinda* wraps her Head in Flame Colour, her Heart is set upon Execution."]

WE were informed that the Lady of this Heart, when living, received the Addresses of several who made Love to her, and did not only give each of them Encouragement, but made every one she conversed with believe that she regarded him with an Eye of Kindness; for which Reason we expected to have seen the Impression of Multitudes of Faces among the several Plaites and Foldings of the Heart, but to our great Surpize not a single Print of this Nature discovered it self till we came into the very Core and Center of it. We there observed a little Figure, which, upon applying our Glasses to it, appeared dressed in a very Fantastick Manner. The more I looked upon it, the more I thought I had seen the Face before, but could not possibly recollect either the Place or Time; when at length one of the Company, who had examined this Figure more nicely than the rest, shew'd us plainly by the Make of its Face, and the several Turns of its Features, that the little Idol that was thus lodged in the very Middle of the Heart was the deceased Beau, whose Head I gave some Account of in my last *Tuesday's* Paper.

As soon as we had finished our Dissection, we resolved to make an Experiment of the Heart, not being able to determine among our selves the Nature of its Substance, which differed in so many Particulars from that of the Heart in other Females. Accordingly we laid it into a Pan of burning Coals, when we observed in it a certain Salmandrine Quality, that made it capable of living in the Midst of Fire and Flame, without being consum'd, or so much as sindged.

As we were admiring this strange *Phænomenon,* and standing round the Heart in a Circle, it gave a most prodigious Sigh or rather Crack, and dispersed all at once in Smoke and Vapour. This imaginary Noise, which methought was louder than the Burst of a Cannon, produced such a violent Shake in my Brain, that it dissipated the Fumes of Sleep, and left me in an instant broad awake. (167-172)

2. Catherine Jemmat, "The Lady's Resolve" (1762)

> Whilst thirst of praise, and vain desire of fame,
> In ev'ry age is ev'ry woman's aim;
> With courtship pleas'd, of silly toasters proud,
> Fond of a train, and happy in a crowd;
> On each poor fool bestowing some kind glance,
> Each conquest owing to some loose advance;
> While vain coquets affect to be pursu'd,
> And think they're virtuous, if not grossly lewd;
> Let this great maxim be my virtue's guide;

In part she is to blame that has been try'd;
He comes too near, that comes to be deny'd.

3. From *Memoirs of a Coquet; or the History of Miss Harriot Airy* (1765)

i. [Introduction]

To three parts of the fair sex, the love of admiration has been a fatal passion: it is a frivolous one at best: — it always throws a woman into trifling, and very often into trying situations, from which, if she escapes with her virtue, she has better luck than she ought to expect: but when she goes so far as to endanger her virtue, she hardly ever escapes with that purity of character on which every woman should set the highest value. If she is satisfied with her own prudence, she will not find the world so well convinced of it: and the censures of the world every woman should endeavour to avoid by the integrity of her conduct, and the consistency of her behaviour. She who, by her indiscretions, though without any criminal designs, affords the world hints for suspicion, should not be surprised, if those hints are improved to her disadvantage.

> —back-wounding calumny
> The *whitest* virtue strikes;

and if *that* cannot escape, how doubly cautious ought a woman to be of her reputation!

Harriot Airy, the heroine of the following sheets, at the age when girls are generally taken up with their dolls, discovered a stronger propensity to amuse herself with *living*, than with *inanimate play-things*. She had several intrigues before she was out of her hanging-sleeves, and was thoroughly versed in all the mysteries of *jiltism*, if I may venture to use the word, before she entered into her teens. ...

As she was smart and sensible, a lively and good-humoured companion, she was the darling of her parents, who ruined her, by letting her constantly have her own way on every occasion, and never attempting to cross her wildest whims and most fanciful freaks. Blind to her bad qualities, because too fond of her good ones, they suffered her mind to be, like a neglected garden, disfigured with the most noxious weeds. All the education she had was of a trifling kind. It was the *shell* only they studied, with diligence, to polish: the inward *gem* they totally disregarded. They made her conceited and fantastical, by the injudicious praises bestowed on her to her face, and spoilt her for a woman, by making her believe she was a Goddess. They kept a great deal of polite company, to which *Harriot* was always exhibited to the best advantage, in order to entertain them—she pleased every body; for there was something in her address irresistibly attracting.

And here I cannot help reflecting a little on the absurd behaviour of parents in the education of their children—of their daughters in particular. To make them agreeable in their persons, and showy figures in the eye of the world, is their principal purpose. — The accomplishments they bestow on them tend to make them coquets— for, with such accomplishments, they are naturally filled with a strong desire to display them; and the flattering speeches which they receive on a public display of them, before they are out of their teens, are sufficient to spoil them for wives and mothers. — To a frivolous education, and to boarding-school accomplishments and connections, the present numerous race of coquets are owing. — And till parents study more to embellish the minds, than to adorn the persons of their daughters, they cannot wonder that so few are fit for a domestic life. — If a girl has beauty, she is in a very fair way to have her head turned; for no care, no cost is spared, to set that beauty in the most flattering light: and those who have made any observations on the girls of the age, will confess with me, that the admiration of their persons is the surest key to their bosoms. — For this kind of adulation the oldest, and the most deformed, have as strong a relish as the young and the charming. — But these are remarks too trite, and therefore I will trouble the reader with no more of them. (1-6)

ii. [Conclusion]

From year to year, however, she went on in pursuit of what she could never obtain—a husband—for who would think of *settling* with her who behaved with equal freedom to every man she met with, and discovered, by every turn of her eyes, and every movement she made, that the love of admiration was her ruling passion?—Whenever that is the passion, no man can be sure of a domestic companion—For where it is strongly predominant before marriage, it is rarely weakened afterwards: and who would chuse to be tied to a wife, for the entertainment of the public?—He who could love such a woman, is, I own, of a more liberal way of thinking; for I am so narrow as to suppose, that there can be no felicity in the marriage state, where the parties contracted are not wholly attached to each other—and strike out all their happiness at home.

That there are many *Harriots* in this gay metropolis, (and where, indeed, is the city without them?) nobody, who reads these memoirs, will deny — that all girls, who behave like her, should meet with disappointments, disquietudes, and vexations, peculiar to her sex, nobody will wonder. — Disappointment is always the consequence of indiscretion; and they who lead a life of folly, must expect to finish that life with disquietude. — A youth of vanity is ever an introduction to an age of vexation. — These are disagreeable truths to those for whom they are here written; but they are, nevertheless, truths which might be, if attended to, useful to those who despise them. —

She who, when she comes to the last pages of this volume, throws it away with contempt, and wonders what the author means by the solemnity of his conclusion, is a *Harriot* in her heart — Of *her* approbation I can have no hopes; but in order to convince her of the justness of my assertions, as examples are always more efficacious than precepts, I only wish she would let me introduce her to the heroine of these sheets, in her retirement from the world. — An old coquet in retirement is, perhaps, the most unhappy being to be imagined. — She cannot review her past life with any satisfaction; she envies every girl she sees too much to enjoy the present, and the natural levity of her disposition prevents her from receiving any comfort from future, expectations. — In this miserable state *Harriot* languishes out the winter of life in obscurity, for she cannot bear those scenes in which she can no longer excite the least attention; and the recollection of the ill use she made of her vernal years, is a perpetual torment. — By indulging the most mortifying ideas, and dwelling on the most gloomy reflections, her mind and her body are both impaired: and she who was only the object of ridicule and contempt, now deserves the highest compassion;—for, with a good heart, and a cultivated understanding, superior to thousands of her sex, she, though guilty of a thousand follies, committed no crimes; and tho' she was often indiscreet, abhorred vice. — She lost her character, but she preserved her virtue.

How much happier would the gay females of this age be, and to how much more advantage would they appear in the eyes of those whom they wish to attract, if, when they are dressing for a rout, they would sometimes condescend to think on their reputation! (192-95)

4. Catharine Macaulay, LETTER XXIII, *Coquettry* in Part I, *Letters on Education* (1790)

THOUGH the situation of women in modern Europe, Hortensia, when compared with that condition of abject slavery in which they have always been held in the east, may be considered as brilliant; yet if we withhold comparison, and take the matter in a positive sense, we shall have no great reason to boast of our privileges, or of the candour and indulgence of the men towards us. For with a total and absolute exclusion of every political right to the sex in general, married women, whose situation demand a particular indulgence, have hardly a civil right to save them from the grossest injuries; and though the gallantry of some of the European societies have necessarily produced indulgence, yet in others the faults of women are treated with a severity and rancour which militates against every principle of religion and common sense. Faults, my friend, I hear you say; you take the matter in too general a sense; you know there is but one fault which a woman of honour may not commit with impunity; let her only take care that she is not caught in a love intrigue, and she may lie, she may deceive, she may defame, she may ruin her own family with gaming, and the peace of twenty others with her coquettry, and yet preserve both her reputation and her peace. These are glorious privileges indeed, Hortensia; but whilst plays and novels are the favourite study of the fair, whilst the admiration of men continues to be set forth as the chief honour of woman, whilst power is only acquired by personal charms, whilst continual dissipation banishes the hour of reflection, Nature and flattery will too often prevail; and when this is the case, self preservation will suggest to conscious weakness those methods which are most likely to conceal the ruinous trespass, however base and criminal they may be in their nature. The crimes that women have committed, both to conceal and to indulge their natural failings, shock the feelings of moral sense; but indeed every love intrigue, though it does not terminate in such horrid catastrophes, must naturally tend to debase the female mind, from its violence to educational impressions, from the secrecy with which it must be conducted, and the debasing dependancy to which the intriguer, if she is a woman of reputation, is subjected. Lying, flattery, hypocrisy, bribery, and a long catalogue of the meanest of the human vices, must all be employed to preserve necessary appearances. Hence delicacy of sentiment gradually decreases; the warnings of virtue are no longer felt; the mind becomes corrupted, and lies open to every solicitation which appetite or passion presents. This must be the natural course of things in every being formed after the human plan; but it gives rise to the trite and foolish observation, that the first fault against chastity in woman has a radical power to deprave the character. But no such frail beings come out of the hands of Nature. The human mind is built of nobler materials than to be so easily corrupted; and with all the disadvantages of situation and education, women seldom become entirely abandoned till they are thrown into a state of desperation by the venomous rancour of their own sex.

The superiority of address peculiar to the female sex, says Rousseau, is a very equitable indemnification for their inferiority in point of strength. Without this, woman would not be the companion of man, but his slave; it is by her superior art and ingenuity that she preserves her equality, and governs him, whilst she affects to obey. Woman has every thing against her; as well our faults, as her own timidity and weakness. She has nothing in her favor but her subtlety and her beauty; is it not very reasonable therefore that she should cultivate both?

I am persuaded that Rousseau's understanding was too good to have led him into this error, had he not been blinded by his pride and his sensuality. The first was soothed by the opinion of superiority, lulled into acquiescence by cajolement; and the second was attracted by the idea of women playing off all the arts of coquettry to raise the passions of the sex. Indeed the author fully avows his sentiments, by acknowledging that he would have a young French woman cultivate her agreeable talents, in order to please her future husband, as with as much care and assiduity as a young Circassian cultivates her's to fit her for the harem of an eastern bashaw.

These agreeable talents, as the author expresses it, are played off to great advantage by women in all the courts of Europe; who, for the arts of female allurement, do not give place to the Circassian. But it is the practice of these very arts, directed to enthral the men, which act in a peculiar manner to corrupting the female mind. Envy, malice, jealousy, a cruel delight in inspiring sentiments which at first perhaps were never intended to be reciprocal, are leading features in the character of the coquet, whose aim is to subject the whole world to her own humour; but in this vain attempt she commonly sacrifices both her decency and her virtue.

By the intrigues of women, and their rage for personal power and importance, the whole world has been filled with violence and injury; and their levity and influence have proved so hostile to the existence or permanence of rational manners, that it fully justifies the keeness of Mr. Pope's satire on the sex.

But I hear my Hortensia say, whither will this fit of moral anger carry you? I expected an apology, instead of a libel, on women; according to your description of the sex, the philosopher has more reason to regret the indulgence, than what you have sometimes termed the injustice of the men; and to look with greater complacency on the surly manners of the ancient Greeks, and the selfishness of Asiatic luxury, than on the gallantry of modern Europe.

Though you have often heard me express myself with warmth in the vindication of female nature, Hortensia, yet I never was an apologist for the conduct of women. But I cannot think the surliness of the Greek manners, or the selfishness of Asiatic luxury, a proper remedy to apply to the evil. If we could inspect narrowly into the domestic concerns of ancient and modern Asia, I dare say we should perceive that the first springs of the vast machine of society were set a going by women; and as to the Greeks, though it might be supposed that the peculiarity of their manners would have rendered them indifferent to the sex, yet they were avowedly governed by them. They only transferred that confidence which they ought to have given their wives, to their courtezans, in the same manner as our English husbands do their tenderness and their complaisance. They will sacrifice a wife of fortune and family to resentment, or the love of change, provided she give them opportunity, and bear with much Christian patience to be supplanted by their footman in the person of their mistress.

No; as Rousseau observes, it was ordained by Providence that women should govern some way or another; and all that reformation can do, is to take power out of the hands of vice and folly, and place it where it will not be liable to be abused.

To do the sex justice, it must be confessed that history does not set forth more instances of positive power abused by women, than by men; and when the sex have been taught wisdom by education, they will be glad to give up indirect influence for rational privileges; and the precarious sovereignty of an hour enjoyed with the meanest and most infamous of the species, for those established rights which, independent of accidental circumstances, may afford protection to the whole sex.

5. *Lady's Monthly Museum* (June 1799): 467–70

"*ON COQUETRY*, IN A LETTER TO A FRIEND."

My dear Matilda,

You ask the occurrences of my past life, and are surprised at the events that could occasion a young and beautiful woman to seclude herself from the world. Alas! my friend, that beauty was the cause of all my misfortunes. — Often have I said, nothing should make me recal those events — but you have children; and may they, warned by my life, never give way to that worst of passions — Coquetry!

My father died ere I had attained my fourth year. He was the younger brother of a good family, but marrying an amiable woman possessed of no fortune, without their consent, they ever after refused to see him. My father's little property dying with him, my mother was left destitute. She applied to his family — they refused to see her, and laughed at her distress. Fortunately, at this time, my mother's brother arrived in England from India, where he had acquired a considerable fortune. Young as I then was, I still remember his tenderness to my mother — with what affection he embraced me; and, as the tear (which he in vain endeavoured to suppress) dropped on my cheek, vowed never to forsake me. — My mother survived my father only two years, and I lost, as I then thought, my only friend. In my grief for her loss I had forgot my uncle. His fondness increased daily, and I soon ceased to remember a mother had ever existed. I was naturally of a good disposition, but, never being contradicted, was become a little tyrant: my uncle saw it, and resolved on sending me to school. I entreated to remain where I was, and promised amendment: it availed little — he was determined, and, for the first time in my life, I experienced a refusal. My anger knew no bounds — I threatened I know not what — passion threw me into fits, which obliged me to keep my bed several weeks. He now saw the necessity of my going from home; but, as he could not behold my tears unmoved, left the house a few days before I went to school.

The time I passed there I have since found to have been the happiest of my life; though I then impatiently looked forward to that time, when, leaving school, I hoped to become my own mistress. The day so long wished for arrived, when, at the age of sixteen, I bade adieu to my school-fellows, and returned to my uncle. He received me with the affection of a father. Alas! I did not long enjoy it — a violent fever terminated his existence in six short months after my return from school. He left me his whole fortune, and appointed a guardian, with whom I was to reside till I had attained my twentieth year.

Mr. Monson was a worthy man. He had one daughter, about my own age. As she is no way connected with my life, I shall only tell you she was a studied Coquet. As soon as my fortune was known, I was surrounded by admirers: — Lord Lawson and the Honourable Edward De Gray were among the first who contended for my hand. De Gray's fortune was not so considerable as the former's, but in every thing else he was his superior, and not few were the women who envied my conquest.

It was now two years since he offered me his hand, which I did not refuse; yet still I coquetted with Lord Lawson. — Mr. Monson saw the pain I inflicted on a worthy heart with anger, and insisted on my either marrying or dismissing De Gray. My choice was already made — I loved De Gray, and gave him my hand. For several years we lived happily. My husband's only pleasure was in contributing to my felicity; till, at an assembly, for the first time since my marriage, I met Lord Lawson. He was the same chattering, affected fop as ever; lamented his having buried himself in the country, since it had deprived him of seeing me; with a great deal more nonsense; and before we parted we were as friendly as ever. He was my constant visitor at home, and *chaperone* abroad. His frequent visits displeased De Gray — "The world, my dear Julia," said he, "is censorious; it already talks of Lord Lawson's visits here; oblige me, therefore, the next time he calls, by not being at home."

His language I thought betrayed want of confidence in me, and, conscious I did not deserve it, I refused. It was the only time I saw him angry —

— "If you, Madam, are insensible of the impropriety of your conduct, I am not; therefore, the next time Lord Lawson calls, I shall give orders for him not to be admitted."

He kept his word, and I thought him a tyrant! Instead of concealing our disagreement, I mentioned it every where. Lord Lawson heard it, and in a few days I received the following note:

"Why will my dear Mrs. De Gray remain longer with a tyrant, insensible of her value, and not fly to a man who adores, and will protect her from insult? — I remain your devoted admirer,

LAWSON."

I now saw the imprudence of my conduct. I had forfeited the esteem of the man I loved, and rendered myself insulted by one I despised; and had the world been in my possession, I would have given it to recover the good opinion of my husband. I knew not how to act:—if I shewed the letter to De Gray, a duel must have been the consequence. I resolved, therefore, to express my abhorrence of his proposal in a letter. I had scarcely began writing, when I was interrupted by the arrival of visitors. I snatched up the letter I was writing, but, in my hurry, forgot the one I had received, which lay open on the table. I recollected it too late—it was gone—my fears told me De Gray had it. Alas! they were too soon realized—He was brought home apparently lifeless!—Half distracted, I flew to him. He was still sensible, though weak from loss of blood, and, in a voice hardly articulate, he uttered—

"My dear Julia, I die assured of your love!—Imprudence was your only foible—I used you too harshly—Can you forgive me?"

"It is I who ought to ask forgiveness!" said I.—His soul was fled!—Nearly frantic, they dragged me from his bed. For a long time my life was in danger. Youth and a good constitution enabled me to recover. Lord Lawson lived only a few months.

As soon as my health was restored, at the age of twenty-six, I retired to this cottage—never to revisit that world which has caused my misfortune! Yourself and your charming daughters are my only acquaintance. In Arabella I discover a disposition to Coquetry: to her, therefore, I recommend my Life as a lesson, which I hope she will avoid, and never, by sad experience, prove the misery which, soon or late, attends Coquetry!

I remain, my dear Mathilda, your sincere friend,

JULIA DE GRAY.

Appendix J: Madness

1. From Cecilia Lucy Brightwell, *Memorials of the Life of Amelia Opie* (1854)

[Brightwell's *Memorials of the Life of Amelia Opie* records the following account taken from Opie's own unfinished "record of the most interesting events of her life" (12-17). Visiting madhouses or "bedlams" was a common pastime in the eighteenth century, often as a lesson in the horrors of the failure of reason. Opie's parents were relatively enlightened in their efforts to diminish fear and arouse compassion in their daughter.]

I believe I was naturally a fearful child, perhaps more so than other children; but I was not allowed to remain so. Well do I remember the fears, which I used to indulge and prove by tears and screams, whenever I saw the objects that called forth my alarm. The first was terror of black beetles, the second of frogs, the third of skeletons, the fourth of a black man, and the fifth of madmen.

[Opie then details the process of familiarization used by her parents to cure her of the first four fears.]

The fifth terror was excited by two poor women who lived near us, and were both deranged though *in different degree*. The one was called Cousin Betty, a common name for female lunatics; the other, who had been dismissed from bedlam as incurable, called herself "old happiness," and went by that name. These poor women lived near us and passed by our door every day; consequently I often saw them when I went out with my nurse, and whether it was that I had been told by her, when naughty, that the mad woman should get me, I know not, but certain it is, that these poor visited creatures were to me objects of such terror, that when I saw them coming (followed usually by hooting boys) I used to run away to hide myself. But as soon as my mother was aware of this terror she resolved to conquer it, and I was led by her to the door the next time one of these women was in sight; nor was I allowed to stir till I had heard her kindly converse with the poor afflicted one, and then I was commissioned to put a piece of money into her hand. I had to undergo the same process with the other woman; but she tried my nerves more than the preceding one, for she insisted on shaking hands with me, a contact not very pleasing to me: however, the fear was in a measure conquered, and a feeling of deep interest, not unmixed with awe, was excited in my mind, not only towards these women, but towards insane persons in general: a feeling that has never left me, and which, in very early life, I gratified in the following manner: —

When able to walk in the street with my beloved parents, they sometimes passed the city asylum for lunatics, called the bedlam, and we used to stop before the iron gates, and see the inmates very often at the windows, who would occasionally ask us to throw halfpence over the wall to buy snuff. Not long after I had discovered the existence of this interesting receptacle, I found my way to it alone, and took care to shew a penny in my fingers, that I might be asked for it, and told where to throw it. A customer soon appeared at one of the windows, in the person of a man named Goodings, and he begged me to throw it over the door of the wall of the ground in which they walked, and he would come to catch it. Eagerly did I run to that door, but never can I forget the terror and trembling which seized my whole frame, when, as I stood listening for my mad friend at the door, I heard the clanking of his chain! nay, such was my alarm, that, though a strong door was between us, I felt inclined to run away; but better feelings got the mastery, and I threw the money over the door, scarcely staying to hear him say he had found the penny, and that he blessed the giver. I fully believe that I felt myself raised in the scale of existence by this action, and some of my happiest moments were those when I visited the gates of bedlam; and so often did I go, that I became well known to its inmates, and I have heard them say "Oh! there is the little girl from St. George's" (the parish in which I then lived.) At this time my mother used to send me to shops to purchase trifling articles, and chiefly at a shop at some distance from the bedlam, which was as far again from my home. But, when my mother used to ask me where I had been, that I had been gone so long, the reply was, "I only went round by bedlam, mamma."

But I did not confine my gifts to pence. Much of my weekly allowance was spent in buying pinks and other flowers for my friend Goodings, who happened to admire a nosegay which he saw me wear; and as my parents were not inclined to rebuke me for spending my money on others, rather than on myself, I was allowed for some time to indulge in this way the interest which early circumstances, those circumstances which always give bias to character through life, had led me to feel in beings whom it had pleased the Almighty to deprive of their reason. At this period, and when my attachment to this species of human woe was at its height, a friend of ours hired a house which looked into the ground named before, and my father asked the gentleman to allow me to stand at one of the windows, and see the lunatics walk. Leave was granted and I hastened to my post, and as the window was open I could talk with Goodings and the others; but my feelings were soon more forcibly interested by an unseen lunatic, who had, they told me, been crossed in love, and who, in the cell opposite my window, sang song after song in a voice which I thought very charming.

But I do not remember to have been allowed the indulgence of standing at this window more than twice. I believe my parents thought the excitement was an unsafe one, as I was constantly talking of what I had said to the mad folks, and they to me; and it was so evident that I was proud of their acquaintance, and of my own attachment to them, that I was admonished not to go so often to the gates of the bedlam; and dancing and French school soon gave another turn to my thoughts, and excited in me other views and feelings. Still, the sight of a lunatic gave me a fearful pleasure, which nothing else excited; and when, as youth advanced, I knew that loss of reason accompanied distressed circumstances, I know that I was doubly eager to administer to the pecuniary wants of those who were awaiting their appointed time in madness as well as poverty. Yet, notwithstanding, I could not divest myself entirely of fear of these objects of my pity; and it was with a beating heart that, after some hesitation, I consented to accompany two gentlemen, dear friends of mine, on a visit to the *interior* of the bedlam. One of my companions was a man of warm feelings and lively fancy, and he had pictured to himself the unfortunate beings, whom we were going to visit, as victims of their sensibility, and as likely to express by their countenances and words the fatal sorrows of their hearts; and I was young enough to share in his anticipations, having, as yet, considered madness not as the result of some physical derangement, but as the result, in most cases, of moral causes. But our romance was sadly disappointed, for we beheld no "eye in a fine phrensy rolling," no interesting expression of sentimental woe, sufficient to raise its victims above the lowly walk of life in which they had always moved; and I, though I knew that the servant of a friend of mine was in the bedlam who had been "crazed by hopeless love," yet could not find out, amongst the many figures that glided by me, or bent over the winter fire, a single woman who looked like the victim of the tender passion.

The only woman who had ought interesting about her, was a poor girl, just arrived, whose hair was not yet cut off, and who, seated on the bed in her new cell, had torn off her cap, and had let the dark tresses fall over her shoulders in picturesque confusion! This pleased me, and I was still more convinced I had found what I sought, when, on being told to lie down and sleep, she put her hand to her evidently aching head, as she exclaimed, in a mournful voice, "Sleep! oh, I cannot sleep!" The wish to question this poor sufferer being repressed by respectful pity, we hastened away to other cells, in which were patients confined in their beds; with one of these women I conversed a little while, and then continued our mournful visits. "But where (said I to the keeper) is the servant of a friend of mine (naming the patient) who is here because she was deserted by her lover?" "You have just left her," said the man. "Indeed," replied I, and hastened eagerly back to the cell I had quitted. I immediately began to talk to her of her mistress and the children, and called her by her name, but she would not reply. I then asked her if she would like money to buy snuff? "Thank you," she replied. "Then give me your hand." "No, you must lay the money on my pillow." Accordingly I drew near, when, just as I reached her, she uttered a screaming laugh, so loud, so horrible, so unearthly, that I dropped the pence, and rushing from the cell, never stopped till I found myself with my friends, who had themselves been startled by the noise, and were coming in search of me. I was now eager to leave the place; but I had seen, and lingered behind still, to gaze upon a man whom I had observed from the open door at which I stood, pacing up and down the wintry walk, but who at length saw me earnestly beholding him! He started, fixed his eyes on me with a look full of mournful expression, and never removed them till I, reluctantly I own, had followed my companions. What a world of woe was, as I fancied, in that look! Perhaps I resembled some one dear to him! Perhaps—but it were idle to give all the perhapses of romantic sixteen—resolved to find in bedlam what she thought *ought* to be there of the sentimental, if it were not. However, that poor man and his expression never left my memory; and I thought of him when, at a later period, I attempted to paint the feelings I imputed to him in the "Father and Daughter."

On the whole, we came away disappointed, from having formed false ideas of the nature of the infliction which we had gone to contemplate. I have since then seen madness in many different asylums, but I was *never disappointed* again.

2. "Proposals for the establishment of a Lunatic Asylum under the Care of Friends, to be called The Southern Retreat" with Amelia Opie's letter to Joseph John Gurney, 8 August 1839.

[By the 1830s the model for the humane treatment of the insane was an institution named The Retreat, founded in York in the North of England by the Quaker Samuel Tuke in 1796. Distressed by the death of a Quaker girl soon after her admission to the York Asylum, Tuke proposed the establishment of an institution for the care of Friends, conducted in a more domestic manner, without visible bars or manacles. By the time the first account was published in English in 1813, it had become recognized as a progressive step in the "moral" treatment of madness.

In 1839 an attempt was made to establish a similar institution in the south of England, to be called the Southern Retreat. A printed prospectus was circulated, and Opie brought it to the attention of her friend Joseph John Gurney. Unfortunately, the Southern Retreat was never established. The letter she wrote on a blank page of the document follows this transcription of the "Proposals."]

PROPOSALS FOR THE ESTABLISHMENT OF A LUNATIC ASYLUM UNDER THE CARE OF FRIENDS, TO BE CALLED THE SOUTHERN RETREAT.

To those who are acquainted with the merits of the Lunatic Asylum, under the care of the Society of Friends near York, called the Retreat, it is presumed that little need be said, either to set forth the benefits which that Institution has conferred, and still continues to confer, or to produce conviction as to the further benefits which might yet be obtained, by the establishment of a similar Institution within a moderate distance from London.

Although there are already numerous Lunatic Asylums in the neighbourhood of the Metropolis, which enjoy a well merited reputation, in consequence of the general care and management of their Directors, yet it is certain that a strong preference exists in the minds of Friends, in favour of sending such members of the Society as may be affected with mental alienation to York, where their religious peculiarities are not likely to subject them to any annoyance or inconvenience, rather than to allow them to be exposed to some trials, which in their peculiar state, would not be unlikely to occasion an increase of moral and physical suffering. In the case of persons in low circumstances, these difficulties would probably be felt in the greatest degree — but those in affluence cannot be always exempt from them.

An Institution such as is here suggested, would therefore not merely be a saving of much expensive, painful, and fatiguing travelling, but would enable many, to whom the advantages of the Retreat are necessarily denied, to enjoy precisely similar advantages, with, very probably, the addition of some others which will be presently noticed.

It has been the practice at the Retreat not merely to receive on higher terms Patients from the wealthier class of Friends, but also Patients belonging to other Religious Professions, whose relatives repose confidence in the management of the Institution, and who are willing to pay on such liberal terms as contribute greatly to benefit the funds of the establishment. A similar course might doubtless be adopted by the Managers of a Lunatic Asylum under the care of the Society of Friends, situated in the vicinity of London. The advantage would be reciprocal, for the higher class of Patients, whilst aiding the funds of the Establishment, might be so distinct from the poorer class as to be subject to no degree of annoyance from them, but they would derive great benefit from the superior medical and other treatment which the Superintendant and Medical Director would, as experienced practical men, be ever ready to suggest.

The feasibility of this project is almost demonstrated by the fact that the Managers of the Retreat at York, have within a comparatively short time contemplated the establishment of such an Institution by the employment of their own accumulated funds. Local changes which have induced the Directors to abandon the plan, have not, however, materially diminished the expediency of the measure, which has been approved by competent judges in the Medical Profession, and is called for by the fact that it has repeatedly been found necessary to send Insane Friends to Asylums in no way connected with the Society.

Should the foregoing proposal obtain the concurrence of a sufficient number of supporters, the present time would be peculiarly favourable to its adoption, since there is an opportunity of obtaining for the medical direction of the proposed institution, the services of Dr. FOVILLE, whose intimate theoretical and practical acquaintance with this branch of medicine, justly entitles him to the very highest place in this department.

The advantages of treatment under his direction would doubtless not be confined to the inmates of the Institution, but a most important reform in the medical and physical treatment of the Insane might reasonably be expected to spread from this Institution to most of the considerable Lunatic Asylums in this country.

As the Northern Retreat has had the merit of contributing materially to improve the moral management and personal condition of British Lunatics, so its Southern counterpart might be equally happy in effecting a similar amelioration in the very important but too much neglected branch, to which belongs the medical treatment of mental and cerebral disease....

[Opie's letter follows.]

My dearest friend,

In spite of thy kind assurances that my letters are welcome to thee, I am glad of an opportunity to send thee with a page & a half from myself something more important and interesting than a whole sheet from me. Perhaps this prospectus has been already sent to thee, but, probably, not. However, I feel such a strong wish that thou shouldst patronize the intended institution, that I will do what others may not have done. I highly admire the benevolent views which principled the scheme—viz. the device of lightening the expence of maintaining *in asylums insane relations to persons of small incomes*—and honestly own that I often believe *I* may one day or other need to be so helped *myself.*

Not in my *own person*, but I do positively expect that my poor dear cousin Tom's strange career will end in decided madness. Perhaps, incipient hereditary insanity may have been the origin of his follies; & that love of speculation, that utter callousness to advice, & entreaty, & that high opinion of his own superior cunning ... which seem to me wholly inconsistent with a sane mind. I expect every day to hear he is in a prison, whence no one can deliver him—no one belonging to him *would* deliver him save myself, & I am pretty sure my whole remaining property would not. Thou seest therefore, that I, *selfishly,* wish this new asylum to succeed, that, one time or other, I may profit by the facilities it holds out to persons of my class....

3. From William Battie M.D., *A Treatise on Madness* (1758)

[William Battie (1706-76) served as governor of Bethlem Hospital in 1742 and then went on to be a leading figure in the founding of St. Luke's Hospital for Lunaticks in 1750-51, an institution offering an alternative approach to and care for madness. He wrote *A Treatise on Madness* in 1758 as an attack on conventional forms of treatment that included "bleeding, blisters, caustics, rough cathartics, the gumms and fætid antihysterics, opium, mineral waters, cold bathing, and vomits."

In arguing *"that management did much more than medicine,"* he shifted attention from administering medicines which generally failed to techniques of management that attempted to direct and recondition the mind, turning it away from deluded associations. Moreover, by stating that "Madness ... rejects all general methods," he sought to individualize the treatment of the insane. Finally, by considering "madness as a disease of the imagination," Battie initiated an approach that led to modern psychiatric method.]

i. From SECT. I. *The Definition of Madness.*

[N]o one ever doubt[s] whether the perception of objects not really existing or not really corresponding to the senses be a certain sign of Madness. Therefore *deluded imagination*, which is not only an indisputable but an essential character of Madness, ... precisely discriminates this from all other animal disorders: or that man and that man alone is properly mad, who is fully and unalterably persuaded of the Existence or of the appearance of any thing, which either does not exist or does not actually appear to him, and who behaves according to such erroneous persuasion... (5-6).

ii. From SECT. X. *The Regimen and Cure of Madness.*

THE Regimen in this is perhaps of more importance than in any distemper. It was the saying of a very eminent practitioner in such cases *that management did much more than medicine*; and repeated experience has convinced me that confinement alone is oftentimes sufficient, but always so necessary, that without it every method hitherto devised for the cure of Madness would be ineffectual.

Madness then, considered as delusive Sensation unconnected with any other symptom, requires the patient's being removed from all objects that act forcibly upon the nerves, and excite too lively a perception of things, more especially from such objects as are the known causes of his disorder; for the same reason as rest is recommended to bodies fatigued, and the not attempting to walk when the ancles are strained.

The visits therefore of affecting friends as well as enemies, and the impertinent curiosity of those, who think it pastime to converse with Madmen and to play upon their passions, ought strictly to be forbidden.

On the same account the place of confinement should be at some distance from home: and, let him be where he will, none of his own servants should be suffered to wait upon him. For all persons, whom he may think he hath his accustomed right to command, if they disobey his extravagant orders will probably ruffle him to the highest pitch of fury, or if they comply will suffer him to continue in a distracted and irresolute state of mind, and will leave him to the mercy of various passions, any one of which when unrestrained is oftentimes more than sufficient to hurry a sober man out of his senses.

Every unruly appetite must be checked, every fixed imagination must if possible be diverted. The patient's body and place of residence is carefully to be kept clean: the air he breaths should be dry and free from noisom steams: his food easy of digestion and simple, neither spiritous, nor high seasoned and full of poignancy: his amusements not too engaging nor too long continued, but rendered more agreeable by a well timed variety. Lastly his employment should be about such things as are rather indifferent, and which approach the nearest to an intermediate state (if such there be) between pleasure and anxiety.

As to the cure of Madness, this like the cure of any other disease consists, 1. In removing or correcting its causes: 2. In removing or correcting its symptoms: 3. In preventing, removing, or correcting its ill effects (68-70).

iii. From SECT. XI. *The Cure of Madness.*

As to the seventh class of remoter causes, *viz. tumultuous and spasmodic passions, such as joy and anger,* in case the patient is not in immediate danger of his life, nothing of any great consequence is to be done at first; in hopes that these passions and their muscular effects will, as they are frequently known to do, subside of themselves. But, whenever *anceps remedium* is the indication, after sufficient depletion and diminution of maniacal pressure thereby occasioned, we must have recourse to the specific, that is to the unaccountably narcotic virtues of the Poppy. And, if notwithstanding this temporary relief any one particular passion seems to engross the man or continues beyond its usual period, in such case the discretion of the Physician must determine how far it may be adviseable or safe to stifle it by a contrary passion. I say *safe,* because it is almost impossible by general reasoning to foretell what will be the effect of fear substituted in the room of anger, or of sorrow immediately succeeding to joy... (83-84).

When the ninth class of remoter causes demands our care, *viz. unwearied attention to any one object,* as also *love, grief, and despair,* any of these affections will sometimes be annihilated by the tumultuous but less dangerous and sooner subsiding passions of anger or joy. But, if such instantaneous alteration from one extreme to the other appears either not feasible or too shocking to be attempted with safety; bodily pain may be excited to as good a purpose and without any the least danger. It being a known observation, though as much out of the reach of human reason as are most others which occur in the animal œconomy, that no two different perceptions can subsist at the same time any more than the two different species of morbid muscular action, *viz. the convulsive and the constrictive.* Therefore vesicatories, caustics, vomits, rough cathartics, and errhines, may be and in fact often are as serviceable in this case of fixed nervous Sensation as in obstinate muscular constriction, inasmuch as they all relieve and divert the mind from its delirious attention, or from the bewitching passions of love, grief, and despair... (85).

iv. From SECT. XII. *The cure of the symptoms and consequences of Madness. And some observations upon the whole.*

And thus ends our inquiry into the causes effects and cure of Madness. But, before we quit this subject, it may not be improper to subjoin a few remarks, which will readily occur to every one who recollects the premises, and is moreover satisfied of their reasonableness.

We have therefore, as Men, the pleasure to find that Madness is, contrary to the opinion of some unthinking persons, as manageable as many other distempers, which are equally dreadful and obstinate, and yet are not looked upon as incurable: and that such unhappy objects ought by no means to be abandoned, much less shut up in loathsome prisons as criminals or nusances to the society.

We are likewise, as Physicians, taught a very useful lesson, *viz.* That, altho' Madness is frequently taken for one species of disorder, nevertheless, when thoroughly examined, it discovers as much variety with respect to its causes and circumstances as any distemper whatever: Madness therefore, like most other morbid cases, rejects all general methods, *v.g.* bleeding, blisters, caustics, rough cathartics, the gumms and fætid antihysterics, opium, mineral waters, cold bathing, and vomits.

For bleeding, tho' apparently serviceable and necessary in inflammation of the brain, in rarefaction of the fluids, or a plethoric habit of body, is however no more the adequate and constant cure of Madness, than it is of fever. Nor is the lancet, when applied to a feeble and convulsed Lunatic, less destructive than a sword.

And, altho' blisters, caustics, and sharp purges quickned with white Hellebore, and indeed all painful applications, not only evacuate and thereby relieve delirious pressure, but also rouse and exercise the body, and seem more peculiarly adapted to Insensibility when it is a symptom or consequence of Madness; nevertheless these and all pungent substances are to be tried with great caution, or rather are not to be tried at all in fits of fury. Nor does even defect of sensation allow their use, whenever such defect is occasioned by the preceding excess of the nervous energy, or when it is accompanied with spasm....

As to Opium, notwithstanding what hath been before said concerning the great relief obtained by this powerful drug in some particular circumstances, it is no more a specific in Madness than it is in the Small Pox. For no good whatever can be expected but from its narcotic virtue, and much harm may arise therefrom when improperly administered....

Lastly with respect to Vomits, tho' it may seem almost hæretical to impeach their antimaniacal virtues; yet, when we reflect that the good effects which can be rationally proposed from such shocking operations are all nevertheless the consequences of a morbid convulsion, these active medicines are apparently contraindicated, whenever there is reason to suspect that the vessels of the brain or nervous integuments are so much clogged or strained as to endanger a rupture or further disunion, instead of a deliverance from their oppressive loads....

To which remarks arising as just conclusions from reasoning upon the unavoidable action of vomits and rougher purges, I shall beg leave to add some cautions, which experience has suggested as necessary to be communicated to the young practitioner, even when such active medicines are proper. *viz.* 1. If the season of the year is in the choice of the Physician, to prefer the Spring or Autumn, as being in neither extream of cold or heat: 2. Not to persist in their use at any one time for a longer term than six or eight weeks: 3. Even during that term to give a respite every other or at least every third week from all drugs except the gumms, neutral salts, or gentle solutives: 4. As soon as the patient visibly approaches to a state of sanity, entirely to discontinue these and all other violent methods; that the animal fibres, which have been strained either by the causes of Madness or perhaps by the means of removing them, may be at liberty to recover their natural firmness and just approximation of particles, which a repeated concussion will certainly prevent (93-99).

4. From John Monro M.D., *Remarks on Dr. Battie's Treatise on Madness* **(1758)**

[The Monro family ran Bethlem Hospital for 128 years. John Monro (1715-91) took over control of the institution from his father in 1751 and continued its supervision until his death in 1791. Although the Monros had published nothing on madness prior to 1758, John Monro responded sharply to the criticism implied in Battie's *Treatise* of that year. In *Remarks on Dr. Battie's Treatise on Madness*, Monro defends the traditional treatments practiced in Bethlem. Considering madness as "a vitiated judgement," Monro advocates purges, vomits, and bleedings as well as restraint and isolation.]

i. ADVERTISEMENT.

MADNESS is a distemper of such a nature, that very little of real use can be said concerning it; the immediate causes will for ever disappoint our search, and the cure of that disorder depends on *management* as much as *medicine*. My own inclination would never have led me to appear in print; but it was thought necessary for me, in my situation, to say something in answer to the undeserved censures, which Dr. Battie has thrown upon my predecessors. (n.p.)

ii. From SECTION I. *Of the definition of Madness.*

The author's definition of madness, as well as I can collect it, is this; *the perception of objects not really existing, or not really corresponding to the senses,* is a *certain sign of madness; therefore* DELUDED IMAGINATION *precisely discriminates this, from all other animal disorders.*

    Definitions are of no use, unless they convey precise and determinate ideas; and if this be one of the right kind, I am very unfortunate in not being able to comprehend it. It is certain the *imagination* may be *deluded* where there is not the least suspicion of madness, as by drunkenness, or by hypochondriacal and hysterical affections; there may be real madness where the *imagination* is not affected; so that a *deluded imagination* is not in my opinion the true criterion of madness. The *judgment* is as much or more concerned than the imagination, and I should rather define madness to be a *vitiated judgment*, though I cannot take upon me to say that even this definition is absolute and perfect.

    Aretæus in his description of madness has the following remarkable sentence; .... *These men* (the *melancholy*) *are mistaken in their perception, they see objects that are not present, as if they were present, and they fancy they see what appears to no other person: whereas, those who are furious, see exactly as they ought, but do not judge of objects as they ought to judge.* That is, they see right, but judge wrong. This observation, though not universally true, may very properly be applied to the manner in which madmen are frequently affected; and is so far of use, as to shew, that even the antients observed more faculties of the mind to be vitiated than one.... from whence we may fairly conclude, that the above-mentioned *definition*, which attributes the whole of this disease to any one faculty of the mind, taking no notice of the rest, is by no means a true *definition*. (3-5)

iii. From SECTION V. *Of the regimen and cure of madness.*

Notwithstanding we are told in this *treatise*, that madness rejects all general methods, I will venture to say, that the most adequate and constant cure of it is by evacuation; which can alone be determined by the constitution of the patient and the judgment of the physician.

The evacuation by *vomiting* is infinitely preferable to any other, if repeated experience is to be depended on; and I should be very sorry to find any one frightened from the use of such an efficacious remedy by it's being called a *shocking operation, the consequence of a morbid convulsion.* I never saw or heard of the bad effect of *vomits*, in my practice; nor can I suppose any mischief to happen, but from their being injudiciously administered; or when they are given too strong, or the person who orders them is too much *afraid of the lancet.*

The prodigious quantity of phlegm, with which those abound who are troubled with this complaint, is not to be got the better of but by repeated *vomits*; and we very often find, that *purges* have not their right effect, or do not operate to so good purpose, until the phlegm is broken and attenuated by frequent *emeticks.*

Why should we endeavour to give the world a shocking opinion of a remedy, that is not only safe, but greatly useful both in this and many other distempers? however, to obviate the apprehensions, that may be conceived from such an account, it would be worth while to peruse some cases related by Dr. *Bryan Robinson*, who does not seem to have been at all alarmed at this *shocking operation*, which, he tells us, he has prescribed for a whole year together, sometimes once a day, sometimes twice, and that with the greatest success....

Bleeding and *purging* are both requisite in the cure of madness; but *rough catharticks* are no otherwise particularly necessary in this distemper than on account of the phlegm, and to conquer the obstinacy of the patients, who will sometimes frustrate the operation of more gentle medicines. (50-52)

5. From William Cullen, *First Lines of the Practice of Physic* (1788)

[Like Monro, William Cullen (1710-1790) is a staunch advocate of medicine over psychology. Cullen's approach to insanity is based on his belief in its physiological rather than psychological source. Attributing its cause to lesions in our judging faculty, he recommended treatment designed to coerce patients into more rational behavior. Thus his treatise advocates restraints, instilling fear of the attendant in patients, and isolation from friends and family. At a time when more and more practitioners were moving to the psychological understanding of insanity, Cullen's influential treatise reinforces older methods of dealing with the mad.]

i. From Chapter II, OF MANIA, OR MADNESS. [Definition and Symptoms]

From Section MDLVIII

THE circumstances which I have mentioned ... as constituting delerium in general, do more especially belong to that kind of it which I shall treat of here under the title of MANIA.

There is sometimes a false perception or imagination of things present that are not; but this is not a constant, nor even a frequent, attendant of the disease. The false judgment, is of relations long before laid up in the memory. It very often turns upon one single subject: but more commonly the mind rambles from one subject to another, with an equally false judgment concerning the most part of them; and as at the same time there is commonly a false association, this increases the confusion of ideas, and therefore the false judgments.... Maniacal persons are in general very irascible; but what more particularly produces their angry emotions is, that their false judgments lead to some action which is always pushed with impetuosity and violence; when this is interrupted or restrained, they break out into violent anger and furious violence against every person near them, and upon every thing that stands in the way of their impetuous will. The false judgement often turns upon a mistaken opinion of some injury supposed to have been formerly received, or now supposed to be intended; and it is remarkable, that such an opinion is often with respect to their former dearest friends and relations; and therefore their resentment and anger are particularly directed towards these....With all these circumstances, it will be readily perceived, that the disease must be attended very constantly with that incoherent and absurd speech we call raving. Further, with the circumstances mentioned, there is commonly joined an unusual force in all the voluntary motions; and an insensibility or resistance of the force of all impressions, and particularly a resistance of the powers of sleep, of cold, and even of hunger; though indeed in many instances a voracious appetite takes place. (144-47)

ii. From OF MANIA, OR MADNESS. [Treatment]

Section MDLXII.

Restraining the anger and violence of madmen is always necessary for preventing their hurting themselves or others: but this restraint is also to be considered as a remedy. Angry passions are always rendered more violent by the indulgence of the impetuous motions they produce; and even in madmen the feeling of restraint will sometimes prevent the efforts which their passion would otherwise occasion. Restraint, therefore, is useful, and ought to be complete; but it should be executed in the easiest manner possible for the patient, and the strait waistcoat answers every purpose better than any other that has yet been thought of. The restraining madmen by the force of other men, as occasioning a constant struggle and violent agitation, is often hurtful. Although, on many occasions, it may not be safe to allow maniacs to be upon their legs or to walk about, it is never desirable to confine them to a horizontal situation; and whenever it can be admitted, they should be more or less in an erect posture....

From Section MDLXIII.

The restraint mentioned requires confinement within doors, and it should be in a place which presents as few objects of sight and hearing as possible; and particularly, it should be removed from the objects that the patient was formerly acquainted with, as these would more readily call up ideas and their various associations. It is for this reason that the confinement of madmen should hardly ever be in their usual habitation; or if they are, that their apartment should be stripped of all its former furniture. It is also for the most part proper, that maniacs should be without the company of any of their former acquaintance; the appearance of whom commonly excites emotions that increase the disease. Strangers may at first be offensive; but in a little time they come to be objects either of indifference or of fear, and they should not be frequently changed.

From Section MDLXIV.

Fear[,] being a passion that diminishes excitement, may therefore be opposed to the excess of it; and particularly to the angry and irascible excitement of maniacs. These being more susceptible of fear than might be expected, it appears to me to have been commonly useful. In most cases it has appeared to be necessary to employ a very constant impression of fear; and therefore to inspire them with the awe and dread of some particular persons, especially of those who are to be constantly near them. This awe and dread is therefore, by one means or other, to be acquired; in the first place, by their being the authors of all the restraints that may be occasionally proper; but sometimes it may be necessary to acquire it even by stripes and blows. The former, although having the appearance of more severity, are much safer than strokes or blows about the head. Neither of them, however, should be employed further than seems very necessary, and should be trusted only to those whose discretion can be depended upon. There is one case in which they are superfluous; that is, when the maniacal rage is either not susceptible of fear, or incapable of remembering the objects of it; for in such instances, stripes and blows would be wanton barbarity. In many cases of a moderate disease, it is of advantage that the persons who are the authors of restraint and punishment should be upon other occasions the bestowers of every indulgence and gratification that is admissible; never, however, neglecting to employ their awe when their indulgence shall have led to any abuse. (151-55)

6. From Andrew Harper, *A Treatise on the Real Cause and Cure of Insanity* (1789)

[The most radical of the writers on madness represented here, Andrew Harper (?-1790) wrote *A Treatise on the Real Cause and Cure of Insanity* as a more humane approach to treating the insane. His approach is representative of the growing emphasis on psychiatric management that became known as the "moral cure." Unlike Cullen, he was not entrenched in the academic medical establishment; unlike Monro and Battie, he was not associated with a specific madhouse. Careful to isolate that insanity which arises from psychological sources from that attendant upon specific physiological disorders,

Harper advocated a more sympathetic treatment which saw excessive restraint and violent purges as more harmful than therapeutic.]

i. [Definition of Madness]

Here it may be necessary to remark that by the word Insanity I mean a real unequivocal mania or madness, such a mania as characterizes itself by an alienation of reason, a depravation of the intellectual powers, and an ungovernable impetuosity of disconnected ideas and irrational conduct. This is that kind of madness and that alone which deserves the name of Insanity. (19)

ii. [Symptoms]

The symptoms of Insanity are all clearly marked .... The clamorous ravings, the furious gusts of outrageous action, the amazing exertion of muscular force, the proud and fanciful sallies of imagination, and the excessive propensity to venereal intercourse, are striking testimonies of redundant energy in the nervous system.... (25-26)

iii. [Causes]

Although some one fixed impression, or train of similar impressions, be manifestly the sole, general cause of mania, I will not contend but that Insanity may sometimes result from the sudden invasion of some deep, intense idea, or the rapid succession of several exorbitant ideas, or affections, whether elevant or depressive. I never knew but one instance of this nature, where a person in consequence of alarming news, was seized during the night with a violent, settled mania: and yet it deserves to be remembered that this person's mind had dwelt intensely for a long time before, on the same object. It is also true that long continued exertions of the mind, even upon various and promiscuous objects, if not relieved by frequent relaxations, by holding the mental faculty in a state of too quick and acute modulation, or irritation, will undoubtedly give the mind some degree of predisposition to the attack of Insanity.

In every individual case of mania, without perhaps a single instance to the contrary, the torrent of the passions always flows in some particular channel, and the powers of the mind are chiefly spent upon one principal, over-ruling object. This characteristic circumstance ever inseparable from mania, I know, has generally been considered as the effect of some distinct species of the malady. But this supposition certainly has no good foundation, therefore the symptom in question is a strong proof of the authenticity of my arguments, and justifies the assertion that it is always some particular impression rivetted in the mind, that generates Insanity. (41-43)

iv. [Treatment]

I shall now proceed without delay, and with as much brevity as possible, to establish a plan of treatment, and determine the method of cure, and for the sake of perspicuity shall consider this part of the subject under the two distinct heads of corporal, and mental indications.

The influence of the mind upon the body can only produce general limited effects, and operate to a certain degree, while the influence of the body on the mind may be increased, diminished, modified and varied, a thousand different ways.

In the first stage of real Insanity, there are three positive, corporal indications, and a negative one.

The first is to bring the tones of the nervous system, into such a state of temperature as to render it insusceptible of high, sthenic excitability.

The second is to open all the channels of excretion, secretion and circulation, by way of regulation or balance to the nervous motions.

The third is to procure such sedative effects or an attempering crises as tend to abate the acuteness of sensorial modulation, by giving a free progression and transmission to the nervous power.

The negative indication is the avoidance of all causes which produce direct excitement or irritation, without pervious impulse.

In order to answer the first indication, the patient must lose blood, at proper intervals, and in small quantities, till the pulse be less full and less frequent during the paroxysms, according to the degree of vital force, and habit of body, in general. I am fully satisfied of the expediency of this preliminary step, being confident that there never was nor ever will be a mania, in which venæsection, less or more, would be improper in the beginning.

The second indication, with regard to excretion, must be effectuated by administering gentle aperients, to diminish the elasticity of the tones, so far as coincides with the former indication, and in such a manner as to remove abdominal obstructions, if any be....

The third indication, which is to diminish the acuteness of the sensorial modulation and nervous motion, by procuring sedative effects, or attempering crises, is obtained by means of exercise, change of air, *licentia veneris*, the warm bath, music, and sleep. All these have a powerful tendency to take off mental irritation, and consequently to remove, or lessen the aptitude to paroxysms.

The degree of exercise should be very considerable, and ought to be continued regularly till it occasions lassitude and hunger.

Change of air is highly requisite, because it promotes the circulation, and increases the secretions, in general, and the diaphoresis of the skin and lungs, in particular. A dry and temperate air is most beneficial, while the extremes of heat and cold are equally unfavourable.

Moderate *licentia veneris* is particularly calculated to compose the mental faculty, and its propriety is obvious in different points of view.

The warm bath, or semicupium, as a gentle relaxant, may be used now and then, especially if the skin be dry, and the habit tense.

The aid of music, particularly that kind which is most agreeable to the patient, should be employed, as it opens the secretions, and by harmonizing the movements of the mind, gives the nervous power a gentle, pervious impulse. Yet if the patient has been excessively fond of music, it might, in that case, possibly be hurtful, by reason of its being too consonant to the morbid train of ideas, or the prevailing mental note.

Sleep being the grand *quietus* of the mind, is a most desirable state, both with regard to its duration, because the longer it continues, the more is the mental tranquility established, as well as with respect to its effects, because the incongruous tumult of ideas being calmed, a more settled, natural connexion is likely to succeed, and also on account of the promotion of corporal health throughout the system. When sleep is perfectly natural, which it is when proceeding from any common cause of temporary debility, or when induced by any of the sedative effects just described, the patient fully reaps all its valuable advantages; but when sleep is procured by opiates, it is then artificial, and not being the effect of debility, but the spurious cause of a transitory debility....

Of the truth of this assertion I am well convinced both from reason and experience, and must therefore condemn the use of opium in mania, as being exceedingly improper and pernicious, notwithstanding I know it to be the common practice to administer it very liberally in this disease.

The negative indication, being the avoidance of all causes which produce excitement or irritation without pervious impulse, comprehends in its views, acrid, heating and astringent medicines, improper regimen, and unnecessary coercion....

The custom of immediately consigning the unfortunate victims of

Insanity to the cells of Bedlam, or the dreary mansions of some private confinement, is certainly big with ignorance and absurdity. This practice, 'tis true, may answer the purpose of private interest, and domestic conveniency, but at the same time it destroys all the obligations of humanity, robs the sufferer of every advantage, and deprives him of all the favourable circumstances which might tend to his recovery. I am very positive that Insanity may be cured with great certainty and expedition, in the beginning, and I am equally convinced that confinement never fails to aggravate the disease. A state of coercion is a state of torture from which the mind, under any circumstances, revolts. In the worst cases, where some sort of restraint is indispensibly necessary, the patients hands should only be muffled or manacled, and the whole range of an undarkened room should be assigned for his use. Confinement thwarts every salutary purpose, and defeats every effort which nature makes. If it were possible to give full scope to the extravagant humours and excentric vagaries of incipient Insanity, I can conceive it very probable that the mind would pursue the fantastic delusion, through the path of distracted ideas, till the powers of mental action being spent, and the corporal system materially changed, the tumultuary motions would consequently cease, and the calm serenity of established reason resume its natural influence.

The mental indications are as follows.

To endeavour to discover and disannul the particular cause that affects the mind.

To indulge every rational or even whimsical notion.

To obviate all active, fatiguing exertions of the mental faculty.

To remove, as much as possible, all unpleasing ideas, and all intense impressions whether pleasing or painful, if the mind be too ardently disposed to continue under them.

On the first appearance of Insanity it is generally practicable enough to trace the particular cause that affects the mind; and this cause will always be found to be either some object of desire, or else of habit. In both cases the impulse of the mind must be either gratified, by the possession of the real object, or of some other as nearly resembling it as possible, or it must be repressed, by withdrawing the mind in a gradual insensible manner, or by sudden and effectual means, from its fixed object, to some new and opposite engagement.

When the disease has been of some duration, it is then requisite that every notion, whether whimsical or rational, should meet with some degree of indulgence, although at first the prevalent notions ought to have been completely satisfied, or totally suppressed. If the mind should adopt some particular amusement, be partial to any favourite study or employment, or imbibe some new fancy, it would be very improper to restrain these sallies, or to force the mind suddenly from its choice. But still the mental faculty must not be permitted to dwell long on any of these predilections. (46-64)

Appendix K: Substantive Variants in The Father and Daughter

[Changes to *The Father and Daughter* were relatively minor over the many editions published by Longman from 1801 through 1819 and the final 1843 edition produced by Grove and Son. The largest number of changes occurred between the first and second editions, although Opie took pains to make a few minor changes for the 1843 edition. Unless otherwise noted, changes are as they appear in the second edition.]

65   to God!] *omitted* [1843]
66   But short was thy triumph, sweet Agnes, and long was thy affliction] *omitted*
69   dearest] nearest [1843]
      he does] he do
70   and then having] . Having then
      not to be complied with] to be frustrated
71   him once, flatter him with the hope she would do it again, till by this means] his unreasonable wishes on this subject once, to make him expect she would do so again, and continue to lead a single life;–because in that case
      horrors] agony [1843]
      caresses] *omitted* [1843]
      every day saw] saw every day [1843]
      had been, till now] ,till now, had been
72   to Scotland] for Scotland [1843]
      upon her knees] with tears of contrition [1843]
74   temptations, and struggles] and contending feelings
75   that Agnes] when she
      she rolled herself on the floor] *omitted*
      and implored] she implored
76   sufferings] suffering [1843]
      that his reason for not marrying again was, the fear of a second family's diminishing the strong affection he bore to her] that the fear of a second family's diminishing the strong affection which he bore to her was his reason for not marrying again
      child she] child with which she
      as well as its mother] perhaps

degree of] *omitted* [1843]

77 gloom she] gloom under which she
   under] *omitted*
   almost] also [1843]
   almost forgot she] forgot for a moment that she
   again was Agnes] Agnes was once more
   O God!] *omitted* [1843]

78 "At these times lead me to him," she would say] At these
   times she would say, "Lead me to him;
   lay] laid [1843]

79 urging] alleging [1843]
   the kind] her kind

80 For it is a common remark, that if his heart were not as
   bad as his head is good, he would be an honour to
   human nature; but] *omitted* [1843]
   (which is only four-and-thirty)] *omitted* [1843]

81 his lordship] the speaker [1843]
   support] bear
   his lordship] the gentleman [1843]
   his lordship] his companion [1843]
   his lordship] his companion [1843]

82 his lordship] the speaker [1843]
   his lordship] her unknown friend

83 to have been] that he had been
   of his astonished lordship] of the astonished narrator
   house] theatre
   from his lordship's supporting hand, who with the other
   was collaring the intoxicated brute that had insulted
   her–] up with the look and tone of phrensy–
   O! God!] Heavens![1843]

84 for the love of God!] for mercy's sake [1843]
   What the consequence of his lordship's addressing Agnes
   might have been, cannot be known: whether he would
   have afforded her the protection of a friend, if she
   wished to leave Clifford, or whether she would have
   accepted it, must remain uncertain; but before he could
   overtake her,] But before Agnes had proceeded many
   steps down the street
   lordship] accuser [1843]

85 the at last awakened] the awakened
   occasioned her to feel] which she felt while contemplating
   lordship!] lord!

part as good friends as ever] part good friends
"is it for a wretch like *this* I have forsaken the best of
    parents!] "and have I then forsaken the best of parents
    for a wretch like this!
this 'bitter] the 'bitter
in better] in a better
86 And indeed, they met no more.] *omitted*
    And hastily wrapping up] She hastily therefor wrapped
    up
of which ... want] which in ... of
she took] and took
from the White Horse in Picadilly] from Picadilly
she immediately] she therefore immediately
or the outside] or on the outside
87 unnoticed] undisturbed
    and fortify] and to fortify [1843]
88 trackless] lonely
    then, in] So saying, in
    infamy] disgrace [1843]
90 wretch's] creature's [1843]
91 soothe] sooth
    with the rapidity of lightning] with his former rapidity
    returning] coming back
92 endeavoured] tried
    but in vain] the features of which the darkness had hith-
    erto prevented her from distinguishing; she however
    tried in vain
    They had] But as they had [1801, 2nd]] But they had
    [1843]
    and irretrievable] *omitted* [1843]
93 O God!] *omitted* [1843]
    tearful] tearless
95 How long she remained so is uncertain, but when]
    When
    –starting up,] Then hastily rising,
98 milk and bread] bread and milk [1843]
    and leave a fork and spoon only for her to eat with] *omit-*
    ted
    attention] intention [1843]
    kind friends] good friends [1843]
    rich again] rich you shall
103 heaven] Heaven [1843]

O God!] Oh dear! [1843]

104 you were spirited] you was spirited [1843]

105 she gave way to] to which she gave way

106 in a place that used to echo with her praises] *omitted* [1843]

109 then staying] then on a visit

111 of my troubling you] why I have troubled you with this narration

my guilt ... of] of which ... deprived him

smile on] bless [1843]

113 pathetic] affecting

the song] the air

bade her to do so] bade her

114 he ran] he walked

for the love of God] for pity's sake [1843]

and the clanking of irons] *omitted* [1843]

recollection] idea

117 sense she entertains of it] sense of it which she entertains

120 gladdened the heart of the] gratified

122 it is indeed] so it is

madam, I believe] madam," replied Mr. Seymour, "I believe

I believe there is little chance] perhaps [1843]

But, fallen as she is, she is still Agnes Fitzhenry," resounded through the room.] *omitted* [1843]

bear this] bear to hear this [1843]

123 crime] guilt [1843]

124 shrinking, like a sensitive plant, from the touch or censure] shrinking from censure like a sensitive plant from the touch

125 Thank God!] I am so glad! [1843]

126 who was about eight years old] who was saying her lesson

128 the lover consented] he consented

129 and more heartfelt respect] *omitted* [1843]

Thank God!] Thank Heaven! [1843]

ragged] humble

her duty to the poor] that which she owed the indigent

130 in a consciousness of present usefulness the bitter sensations of past neglect] the consciousness of past neglect in that of present usefulness

impassioned] impassionate [1843]

132 tail] skirt
133 without a great coat and] *omitted*
     state he was in] state in which he was
134 When, therefore, a proper occasion offered] And taking
     advantage of a proper opportunity
135 offered him so much a year, on condition he suffered]
     offered so much a year, on condition of his suffering
136 which human nature shudders at] at which human
     nature shudders
     parsimonious] frugal [1843]
137 the first time] *omitted*
     store] first cargo
     cakes, &c.] cakes
     chicken, &c.] chicken, and other things
138 had then] had then and always would have]
     always] *omitted*
     remain] continue
139 purpose] purport [1843]
142 would to God] that [1843]
     for the love of God] pray [1843]
     had great pleasure in paying] generously presented to
146 caresses and joy her child] caresses of her child, and the
     joy which he
     to her father] to Fitzhenry
147 evening, he, though ... was disturbed] evening, though ...
     he was disturbed [1843]
150 Gracious God!] Merciful God! [1843]
152 all the while] *omitted*
153 and she was going] but before she could proceed
     had fainted] had nearly fainted [1843]
     follow his lordship] follow him
     replied he] *omitted* [1843]
     child] boy
154 so noble-minded] such [1843]
155 cried his lordship] he replied [1843]
     rolled] cast himself
156 For, though the victim of seduction may in time recover
     the approbation of others, she must always despair of
     recovering her own.] *omitted*
     The image] lest the image
     will probably] should

Select Bibliography

Selected Works by Amelia Opie

[The most complete bibliography of Opie works to date can be found in Macgregor. The following list contains the volumes produced during Opie's lifetime in Britain and with her consent. Individually published poems and tales, including the late 1840s reprints, are not included here. Almost all of her works went through multiple editions, making a complete and accurate listing of each volume precarious at best. We have attempted whereever possible to build on Macgregor by checking her bibliography against existing copies of Opie's works and against the records for the Longman publishing house; however, the following list should be considered as largely provisional and gives a general sense of the regular availability of her works in the first half of the nineteenth century.]

Primary Texts by Opie

Adeline Mowbray, or The Mother and Daughter; A Tale, in Three Volumes. 3 vols. London: Longman, Hurst, Rees, and Orme; Edinburgh: A. Constable and Co., 1805.

———. 2nd ed. 3 vols. London: Longman, Hurst, Rees and Orme; Edinburgh: A. Constable and Co., 1805.

———. 3rd ed. 3 vols. London: Longman, Hurst, Rees, Orme, and Brown, 1810.

Adeline Mowbray; or, the Mother and Daughter, A Tale. [1 vol.] New and Illustrated Edition. London: Longman, Brown, Green, and Longmans; London: Grove and Sons, 1844.

The Black Man's Lament; or How to Make Sugar. London: Harvey and Darton, 1826.

Dangers of Coquetry. 2 vols. London: W. Lane, 1790.

Detraction Displayed. London: Longman, Rees, Orme, Brown, and Green; Norwich: S. Wilkin, 1828.

An Elegy to the Memory of the Duke of Bedford: Written on the Evening of His Interment. London: T.N. Longman and O. Rees, 1802.

The Father and Daughter, A Tale, In Prose: With An Epistle From The Maid of Corinth to Her Lover; And Other Poetical Pieces. London: Longman and Rees, 1801.

The Father and Daughter, A Tale, In Prose. 2nd ed. London: Longman and Rees, 1801.

———. 3rd ed. London: Longman and Rees, 1802.

———. 4th ed. London: Longman and Rees, 1804.

———. 5th ed. London: Longman, Hurst, Rees, and Orme, 1806.

———. 6th ed. London: Longman, Hurst, Rees, and Orme, 1809.

———. 7th ed. London: Longman, Hurst, Rees, Orme, and Brown, 1813.

———. 8th ed. London: Longman, Hurst, Rees, Orme, and Brown, 1819.

———. 9th ed. London: Longman, Hurst, Rees, Orme, Brown and Green, 1825.

———. A New and Illustrated Edition. London: Longman, Brown, Green, and Longman; London: Grove and Sons, 1843.

Illustrations of Lying, in All its Branches. 2 vols. London: Longman, Hurst, Rees, Orme, Brown and Green; Norwich: S. Wilkin, 1825.

———. 2nd ed. London: Longman, Hurst, Rees, Orme, Brown, and Green, 1825.

———. 3rd ed. London: Longman, Hurst, Rees, Orme, Brown, and Green, 1827.

Lays for the Dead. London: Longman, Rees, Orme, Brown, Green and Longman, 1834.

———. 2nd ed. London: Longman, Rees, Orme, Brown, Green, and Longman, 1840.

Madeline. A Tale. 2 vols. London: Longman, Hurst, Rees, Orme, and Brown, 1822.

The Negro Boy's Tale, A Poem, Addressed to Children. London: Harvey and Darton; Norwich: S. Wilkin, 1824.

New Tales. 4 vols. London: Longman, Hurst, Rees, Orme, and Brown, 1818.

———. 3rd ed. 4 vols. London: Longman, Hurst, Rees, Orme, and Brown, 1819.

Poems. London: T.N. Longman and O. Rees, 1802.

———. 2nd ed. London: T.N. Longman and O. Rees, 1803.

———. 3rd ed. London: Longman, Hurst, Rees, and Orme, 1804.

———. 4th ed. London: Longman, Hurst, Rees, and Orme, 1806.

———. 5th ed. London: Longman, Hurst, Rees, and Orme, 1808.

———. 6th ed. London: Longman, Hurst, Rees, Orme, and Brown, 1811.

Simple Tales. 4 vols. London: Longman, Hurst, Rees, and Orme, 1806.

———. 2nd ed. 4 vols. London: Longman, Hurst, Rees, and Orme, 1806.

———. 3rd ed. 4 vols. London: Longman, Hurst, Rees, and Orme, 1809.

———. 4th ed. 4 vols. London, Longman, Hurst, Rees, Orme, and Brown, 1815.

Tales of Real Life. 3 vols. London: Longman, Hurst, Rees, Orme, and Brown, 1813.

———. 3rd ed. 3 vols. London: Longman, Hurst, Rees, Orme, and Brown, 1816.

Tales of the Heart. 4 vols. London: Longman, Hurst, Rees, Orme, and Brown, 1820.

Tales of the Pemberton Family; For the Use of Children. London: Harvey & Darton; Norwich: S. Wilkin, 1825.

———. 2nd ed. London: Harvey and Darton; Norwich: S. Wilkin, 1826.

Temper, or Domestic Scenes; A Tale In 3 Volumes. 3 vols. London: Longman, Hurst, Rees, Orme, and Brown, 1812.

———. 2nd ed. 3 vols. London: Longman, Hurst, Rees, Orme, and Brown, 1812.

———. 3rd ed. 3 vols. London: Longman, Hurst, Rees, Orme, and Brown, 1813.

Valentine's Eve. 3 vols. London: Longman, Hurst, Rees, Orme, and Brown, 1816.

———. 2nd ed. 3 vols. London: Longman, Hurst, Rees, Orme, and Brown, 1816.

The Warrior's Return and Other Poems. London: Longman, Hurst, Rees, and Orme, 1808.

———. 2nd ed. London: Longman, Hurst, Rees, and Orme, 1808.

Song Lyrics by Opie

Opie, Amelia. "The Orphan Boy's Tale." Music by Thomas Wright. London: Goulding & Co., n.d.

———. *A Second Set of Hindoo Airs with English Words Adapted to them by Mrs. Opie and Harmonized, for One, Two, Three, and Four Voices, (or for a Single Voice) with an Accompaniment for the Piano Forte or Harp by Mr. Biggs*. London: Rt. Birchall, n.d.

———. *A Second Sett of Welsh Airs, with English Words, written to them by Mrs. Opie. Harmonized & Arranged for One, Two, Three, & Four Voices, with an Accompaniment for the Harp or Piano Forte, by Mr. Biggs*. London: Rt. Birchall, n.d.

———. *Six Songs Written by Mrs. Opie, Set to Music with an Accompaniment for the Harp, or Piano Forte, and Dedicated to the Right Honorable, Lady Willoughby, De Eresby; by E. S. Biggs*. London: Rt. Birchall, n.d.

———. *Twelve Hindoo Airs with English Words Adapted to them by Mrs. Opie, and Harmonized for One, Two, Three, and Four Voices, with an Accompaniment for the Piano Forte or Harp, by Mr. Biggs*. London: Rt. Birchall, n.d.

Modern Editions of Opie's Works

Adeline Mowbray; Or, The Mother and Daughter. Intro. Gina Luria. 3 vols. 1805. New York: Garland, 1974.

Adeline Mowbray or The Mother and Daughter. Intro. Jeanette Winterson. 1844. London: Pandora, 1986.

Adeline Mowbray. Intro. Jonathan Wordsworth. 1805. New York: Woodstock, 1995.

Adeline Mowbray. Eds. Shelley King and John B. Pierce. 1805. London: Oxford UP, 1999.

Elegy to the Memory of the Late Duke of Bedford. Intro. Donald H. Reiman. 1802. New York: Garland, 1978.

The Father and Daughter, A Tale, in Prose. Ed. with intro. Peter Garside. 1801. London: Routledge/Thoemmes, 1994.

Poems. Intro. Donald H. Reiman. 1802. New York: Garland, 1978.

The Warrior's Return / The Black Man's Lament. Intro. Donald H. Reiman. 1808 / 1826. New York: Garland, 1978.

Selected Biographical Studies

"Amelia Opie." *The Athenaeum*, no. 1363 (10 December 1853): 1483.

Brightwell, Cecilia Lucy. *Memorials of the Life of Amelia Opie Selected and Arranged From Her Letters*. London: Longman, Brown, & Co., 1854.

Howard, Susan K. "Amelia Opie." In *British Romantic Novelists, 1789-1832*. Ed. Bradford K. Mudge. Detroit: Gale Research, 1992. 116: 228-33.

Macgregor, Margaret E. "Amelia Alderson Opie: Worldling and Friend." *Smith College Studies in Modern Languages* 14, no. 1-2 (1932-1933): i-xi, 1-145.

Menzies-Wilson, Jacobine, and Helen Lloyd. *Amelia: The Tale of a Plain Friend*. London: Oxford UP, 1937.

Monkhouse, William Cosmo. "Mrs. Amelia Opie." *The Dictionary of National Biography*. Eds. Sir Leslie Stephen and Sir Sidney Lee. 22 vols. Oxford: Oxford UP, 1921-1922. 14: 1120-4.

"Mrs. Opie." *The European Magazine and London Review* (May 1803): 323-4.

"Mrs. Opie." *The Ladies' Monthly Magazine* 5 (February 1817): 61-4.

"Mrs. Opie." *The Leisure Hour* 3 (1854): 633-8.

Ritchie, Anne Thackeray. *A Book of Sibyls*. London: Smith, Elder, & Co., 1883.

Simmons, Jr., James R. "Amelia Opie." In *British Short-Fiction Writers, 1800-1880*. Ed. John R. Greenfield. Detroit: Gale Research, 1996. 159: 261-4.

St. Clair, William. *The Godwins and Shelleys: The Biography of a Family*. London: Faber and Faber, 1989.

Taylor, Mrs. John. "Mrs. Opie." *The Cabinet; or, Monthly Report of Polite Literature* 1 (1807): 217-9.

Works Cited/Recommended Reading

Addison, Joseph. "No. 281, Tuesday, January 22, 1712." In *The Spectator*. 8 vols. London: S. Buckley and J. Tonson, 1712-1715. 4:167.

Andrews, Jonathan, Asa Briggs, Roy Porter, Penny Tucker, and Keir Waddington, eds. *The History of Bethlem*. New York: Routledge, 1997.

Baillie, Joanna. "De Monfort: A Tragedy." *A Series of Plays*. Ed. Donald Reiman. 3 vols. Romantic Context: Poetry; Significant Minor Poetry 1789-1830. New York: Garland, 1977. 1:301-411.

Barbauld, Anna Letitia. *The Poems of Anna Letitia Barbauld*. Eds. William McCarthy and Elizabeth Kraft. Athens: U of Georgia P, 1994.

Battie, William. *A Treatise on Madness*. London: J. Whiston and B. White, 1758.

Boase, George Clement. "William Thomas Moncrieff." *The Dictionary of National Biography*. Eds. Sir Leslie Stephen and Sir Sidney Lee. 22 vols. Oxford: Oxford UP, 1921-2022. 13: 618-20.

Brissenden, R. F. *Virtue in Distress: Studies in the Novel of Sentiment From Richardson to Sade*. London: Macmillan, 1974.

Buck, Anne. *Dress in Eighteenth-Century England*. London: B. T. Batsford, 1979.

Burgoyne, John. *The Heiress. A Comedy in Five Acts.* London: J. Debrett, 1786.

"Chronicles of the Italian Opera in England." *The Harmonicon* 1 (1830): 246-8.

Churchill, Charles. "The Rosciad." *The Poetical Works of Charles Churchill.* Ed. with Intro. Douglas Grant. Oxford: Oxford UP, 1956. 1-34.

Clarkson, Mrs. Thomas. Letter to Robert E. Garnham. 20 May 1802. *Crabb Robinson MSS.*, Vol. 1800-1803, f. 40. Dr. Williams's Library, London.

Copeland, Edward. *Women Writing about Money: Women's Fiction in England, 1790-1820.* Cambridge Studies in Romanticism, no. 9. Cambridge: Cambridge UP, 1995.

Cullen, William, M.D. *First Lines of the Practice of Physic.* A new edition, corrected and enlarged. 4 vols. Edinburgh: C. Elliot; London: C. Elliot, T. Kay and Co., 1788.

Cunnington, Phillis, and Catherine Lucas. *Costume for Births, Marriages, and Deaths.* London: Adam and Charles Black, 1972.

Eberle, Roxanne. "Amelia Opie's *Adeline Mowbray*: Diverting the Libertine Gaze; Or, The Vindication of a Fallen Woman." *Studies in the Novel* 26: 2 (1994): 121-52.

Ellis, Markman. *The Politics of Sensibility: Race, Gender and Commerce in the Sentimental Novel.* Cambridge Studies in Romanticism, no. 18. Eds. Marilyn Butler and James Chandler. Cambridge: Cambridge UP, 1996.

Fergus, Jan, and Janice Farrar Thaddeus. "Women, Publishers, and Money, 1790-1820." *Studies in Eighteenth Century Culture* 12 (1987): 191-207.

Godwin, William. *Enquiry Concerning Political Justice and Its Influence on Modern Morals and Happiness.* Ed. Isaac Kramnick. 1793. New York: Penguin, 1985.

——. *Memoirs of Wollstonecraft.* Intro. Jonathan Wordsworth. London: J. Johnson and G.G. and J. Robinson, 1798. New York: Woodstock Books, 1993.

Goldsmith, Oliver. "The Deserted Village." *Collected Works of Oliver Goldsmith.* Ed. Arthur Friedman. 7 vols. Oxford: Oxford UP, 1966. 4: 285-304.

Gonda, Caroline. *Reading Daughters' Fictions, 1709-1834.* Cambridge Studies in Romanticism, no. 19. Cambridge: Cambridge UP, 1996.

Harper, Andrew. *A Treatise on the Real Cause and Cure of Insanity.* London: Stalker and Waltes, 1789.

Hill, Bridget, ed. *Eighteenth-Century Women: An Anthology.* London: Unwin Hyman, 1984.

Howard, Carol. "'The Story of the Pineapple': Sentimental Abolitionism and Moral Motherhood in Amelia Opie's *Adeline Mowbray.*" *Studies in the Novel* 30 (1998): 355-76.

Howells, W. D. *Heroines of Fiction.* 2 vols. New York: Harper and Brothers, 1901.

Hunter, Richard, and Ida Macalpine, eds. *Three Hundred Years of Psychiatry 1535-1860: A History Presented in Selected English Texts.* New York: Oxford UP, 1963.

Inchbald, Elizabeth, *Nature and Art.* 2 vols. London: G.G. and J. Robinson, 1796.

Ingram, Allan, ed. *Patterns of Madness in the Eighteenth Century.* Liverpool: Liverpool UP, 1998.

Jemmat, Catherine. "The Lady's Resolve." *The Memoirs of Mrs. Catherine Jemmat, Daughter of the late Admiral Yeo, of Plymouth, Written by Herself.* 2 vols. London: Mr Walker's, 1762. 2: 125-6.

Kean, Raymund. *Edmund Kean: Fire From Heaven.* London: Hamish Hamilton, 1976.

Kelly, Gary. "Amelia Opie, Lady Caroline Lamb, and Maria Edgeworth: Official and Unofficial Ideology." *Ariel: A Review of International English Literature* 12: 4 (1981): 3-24.

——. "Discharging Debts: The Moral Economy of Amelia Opie's Fiction." *The Wordsworth Circle* 11 (1980): 198-203.

——. *English Fiction of the Romantic Period, 1789-1830.* Longman Literature in English Series. London: Longman, 1989.

Knight, Joseph. "Edmund Kean." *The Dictionary of National Biography.* Eds. Sir Leslie Stephen and Sir Sidney Lee. 22 vols. Oxford: Oxford UP, 1921-1922. 10: 1146-53.

"Lines Occasioned by Reading Mrs. Opie's Affecting Tale of 'The Father and Daughter'." *The Gentlemen's Magazine* 76: 2 (August 1806): 752.

Macaulay, Catharine. *Letters on Education.* Revolution and Romanticism, 1789-1834. London: C. Dilly, 1790. New York: Woodstock, 1994.

Mackenzie, Henry, *Julia de Roubigne, A Tale, In a Series of Letters.* 4th ed. 2 vols. London: A. Strahan and T. Cadell, 1787.

Memoirs of a Coquet. The Flowering of the Novel: Representative Mid-Eighteenth Century Fiction 1740-1775. London: W. Hoggard, 1765. New York: Garland, 1974.

Moncrieff, W.T. *The Lear of Private Life! or, Father and Daughter, a Domestic Drama in Three Acts.* 2nd ed. London: Thomas Richardson, 1828.

Monro, John, M.D. "Remarks on Dr. Battie's Treatise on Madness." In *A Treatise on Madness and Remarks on Dr Battie's Treatise on Madness.* Intro. and anno. Richard Hunter and Ida Macalpine. London: Dawsons, 1962.

Moore, Hannah. *Essays on Various Subjects, Principally Designed for Young Ladies.* London: J. Wilkie and T. Cadell, 1777.

Nicholl, Allardyce. *A History of Early Nineteenth-Century Drama, 1800-1850.* 2 vols. Cambridge: Cambridge UP, 1930.

Ogden, James. "Introduction." *Lear From Study to Stage: Essays in Criticism.* Eds. James Ogden and Arthur H. Scouten. Madison: Fairleigh Dickinson UP, 1997. 11-30.

Opie, Amelia. Letter to Robert E. Garnham. 20 May 1802. *Crabb Robinson MSS.*, Vol. 1800-1803, f. 40. Dr. Williams's Library, London.

——. Letter to Joseph John Gurney. 23 February 1844. Gurney Papers, Temp. MSS 434.1/380. Friends' Library, London.

——. Letter to Simon Wilkin. 3 February 1843. M4281 f.140. Norfolk Record Office, Norwich.

——. Letter to Simon Wilkin. 24 May 1843. M4281 f.141. Norfolk Record Office, Norwich.

——. Letter to Simon Wilkin. 26 August 1843. M4281 f.142. Norfolk Record Office, Norwich.

——. Letter to Simon Wilkin. 27 August 1843. M4281 f.143. Norfolk Record Office, Norwich.

——. Letter to William Hayley. 27 November 1815. Hayley XXVII 13. Fitzwilliam Museum, Cambridge.

Hartnoll, Phyllis, ed. *The Oxford Companion to the Theatre.* 4th ed. Oxford: Oxford UP, 1983.

Paër. *L'Agnese; Dramma Semiserio, Per Musica, In Due Atti / Agnes; A Serio-Comic Opera, in Two Acts.* London: W. Winchester and Son, 1817.

Parry-Jones, William. *The Trade in Lunacy: A Study of Private Madhouses in England in the Eighteenth and Nineteenth Centuries.* London: Routledge & Kegan Paul; Toronto: U of Toronto P, 1972.

Porter, Roy. *Mind Forg'd Manacles: A History of Madness in England From the Restoration to the Regency*. Cambridge, Mass.: Harvard UP, 1987.

Rev. of *Agnese di Fitz-Henry*, by Paër. In *London Times* (16 May 1817).

Rev. of *Agnese Di Fitz-Henry*, by Paër. In *London Times* (19 May 1817).

Rev. of *Dangers of Coquetry*, by Amelia Opie. In *European Magazine and London Review* 17 (May 1790): 352.

Rev. of *Dangers of Coquetry*, by Amelia Opie. In *Critical Review* 70 (September 1790): 339.

Rev. of *Dangers of Coquetry*, by Amelia Opie. In *The English Review* 17 (March 1791): 234.

Rev. of *Poems*, by Amelia Opie. In *The Edinburgh Review* 1 (October 1802): 113-22.

Rev. of *Smiles and Tears*, by Mrs. Charles Kemble. In *London Times* (13 December 1815).

Rev. of *Smiles and Tears*, by Mrs. Charles Kemble. In *Theatrical Inquisitor, and Monthly Mirror* (1815): 478-80.

Rev. of *Smiles and Tears*, by Mrs. Charles Kemble. In *British Lady's Magazine* 13 (1816): 58.

Rev. of *Tales of the Heart*, by Amelia Opie. In *The Monthly Review* 92 (1820): 375-87.

Rev. of *The Father and Daughter*, by Amelia Opie. In *The Monthly Review: or Literary Journal* 35 (1801): 163-66.

Rev. of *The Father and Daughter*, by Amelia Opie. In *The European Magazine* 40 (1801): 194.

Rev. of *The Father and Daughter*, by Amelia Opie. In *The Critical Review, or Annals of Literature* 35 (1802): 114-17.

Robinson, Thomas. Letter to Henry Crabb Robinson. 31 July 1801. *Crabb Robinson MSS.*, Vol. 1800-1803, f. 40. Dr. Williams's Library, London.

Rochefoucauld, Duke de la. *Maxims and Moral Reflections by the Duke De La Rochefoucauld*. London: Minerva, n.d.

Schama, Simon. *Citizens: A Chronicle of the French Revolution*. London: Viking, 1989.

Scull, Andrew. *The Most Solitary of Afflictions: Madness and Society in Britain 1700-1900*. New Haven: Yale UP, 1993.

Sheridan, Richard Brinsley. "Epilogue." *The Dramatic Works of Richard Brinsley Sheridan*. Ed. Cecil Price. 2 vols. Oxford: Oxford UP, 1973. 2: 823-4.

Spender, Dale. *Mothers of the Novel: 100 Good Women Writers Before Jane Austen.* London: Pandora, 1986.

Staves, Susan. "British Seduced Maidens." *Eighteenth-Century Studies* 12 (1980-81): 109-34.

Stone, Lawrence. *The Family, Sex and Marriage in England, 1500-1800.* New York: Harper and Row, 1977.

Todd, Janet. *Sensibility: An Introduction.* London: Methuen, 1986.

Tout, Thomas Frederick. "Junius Brutus Booth." *The Dictionary of National Biography.* Eds. Sir Leslie Stephen and Sir Sidney Lee. 22 vols. Oxford: Oxford UP, 1921-1922. 2: 848-9.

Ty, Eleanor. *Empowering the Feminine: The Narratives of Mary Robinson, Jane West, and Amelia Opie, 1796-1812.* Toronto: U of Toronto P, 1998.

Weinreb, Ben, and Christopher Hibbert, eds. *The London Encyclopaedia.* London: Macmillan, 1984.

Wollstonecraft, Mary. *A Vindication of the Rights of Woman.* Ed. Carol H. Poston. 2nd ed. New York: Norton, 1988.